TESANIA
Trannyth's
Keep

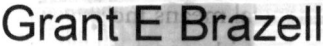

Grant E Brazell

National Library of Australia Catalogue-in-Publication entry:

Copyright © 2009 by Grant E Brazell

Tesania : Trannyth's keep / written by Grant E Brazell.

ISBN 978-0-9871115-0-0

Fiction / Fantasy

Cover artwork © by Soojin Mitton

Map artwork © by Jessica Tanaka

A823.4

Published by Lyshan Press

Printed in the United States of America

First Printing: April 2011

DEDICATION

To my father
My dad, my teacher, my guide, my friend

ACKNOWLEDGMENTS

I would like to acknowledge and thank all those people who helped this story become what it could be.

To my wife, Kim, for patiently reading and editing each chapter and rewrite along the way. To my son, Matthew, for his inspiration and ideas. To Vicky Gardner, you were the first to embrace my work and your encouragement and advice helped me to the end.

Thank you to my beta readers; Kim Brazell, Vicki Gardner, Guy Brazell, Shere Kahn, Jessica Tanaka, Eric Johnson, Elizabeth Harris, Arthur Wallis, Casey Hoffman and Taryn Knuth. To all of you I owe a debt of gratitude. Your feedback and support of TESANIA and the characters was a great help and motivation.

Edna Tancred, Debbie Sutherland and Sean Mitton, your support was uplifting.

Thanks to Jessica Tanaka for the wonderful artwork on the map of Eldanal and Soojin Mitton for the fantastic cover art.

And finally to my friends at Forward Motion for Writers. Just having somewhere to ask questions and chat amongst other writers was a truly fun, enlightening and wonderful experience.

Grant E Brazell

1 INNOCENCE LOST

Tesania drew short, sharp breaths as she lay beneath the cavernous roots of the trees outside her village. Her trembling hands clutched at the little girl in her arms, she tried to calm them; they defied her and continued to shake. She knew their pursuer was out there somewhere, tracking them, hunting them. Her eyes darted between the gnarled old trunks, desperate to see where it might be. "We need to move," she whispered.

The girl's tear-streaked face peered up, her voice quivering as she spoke, "What is it? Why is it chasing us?"

"I have no idea, Liale." Tesania's gaze returned to the forest as she struggled to stand. "We need to get back to the village." Reaching down, she pulled the girl up onto her back. "Father will know what to do."

"But it will catch us," Liale sobbed. "It will hurt us."

"Quiet, Liale. It will hear yo…" Tesania froze as the crack of a dry branch echoed through the trees. Fear shot through her as she turned and glimpsed the black haired arm of the beast through the bare branches. "It found us!" Stumbling backwards, she struggled to turn in the drifts of autumn leaves. "No!" she cried as the beast turned, screeching as it rushed through the forest toward them. The leaves entangled Tesania's legs as she strained to climb the slippery incline. Snatching at some exposed roots and rocks she dragged herself onto a narrow, well worn path and fled.

The beast crashed through the forest behind them, tearing through the low hanging branches.

Tesania felt Liale's grip loosening as she ducked under a branch. "Hold on," she gasped as she reached back and jerked the little girl higher, feeling small satisfaction as Liale's arms clamped around her neck, almost choking her. Breathing heavily, she searched the forest ahead. The path meandered through the trees, offering little chance of escape. Sweat stung her eyes as she darted her head around. The beast careened through the forest, its effortless gait easily overcoming them. Tesania surged forward, her throat burning; the muscles in her legs thundering with pain. Feeling Liale's arms again slipping from her neck, she clung tightly to the little girl's legs, desperate to hold her in place. Tears began to run freely down her face as she pushed past her exhaustion and drove onward.

A thicket of brush seemed their only hope. Veering off the track, Tesania stumbled and slid down a small embankment and sank up to her knees, the litter of the forest once more dragging at her legs as she pushed forward. The beast leapt into the leaves close behind, its ragged breaths thundered in Tesania's ears while Liale sobbed into the nape of her neck.

Gaining, the beast was almost upon them as it screeched a guttural cry of triumph. Visions of Liale being torn apart drove Tesania on. Lunging forward, she winced as a jagged branch ripped at her cheek. Ducking under the limbs she struggled to push through the thick growth. The beast smashed into the trees behind them. Tesania lost her footing and stumbled, Liale rolling off her back as she sprawled on the ground. "Go!" Tesania screamed at the little girl, ignoring her tears as she pushed her forward.

The beast cried out in frustration as the twisted branches slowed its momentum. Unable to tear its way through, it shot out its long arm, clawing at Tesania's ankle, ripping her skin.

Pain shot along Tesania's leg. She tried to pull free, the beast's grip tightening as she struggled, its eyes ablaze with hatred. Desperate to get her friend to safety, she jerked her leg. "Get off me!" She kicked at its hand and jerked again and again. Sensing the beast's grip slipping, Tesania threw her weight backwards, its claws tearing at her skin as her leg wrenched free. Spinning onto her knees, she scrambled after Liale, the beast screeching as she escaped.

The little girl lay curled in a ball among the twisted roots of a tree. Tesania gripped her shoulder. "Are you ok?"

"No!" Liale's voice was muffled.

Tesania pulled Liale onto her knees as she snatched a glanced back at the beast tearing at the branches. She glimpsed what she thought was a sword protruding from a belt strapped around its body. Confused, she turned back to Liale. "We have to move. Come on!" Struggling through the brush, they clambered over roots and ducked under branches. Eventually the trees thinned and gave way to lush, green fields. Tesania looked gratefully over the grass to the thatched roofs of their village in the distance. Groaning as she bent and picked Liale up, she straightened and helped the little girl onto her back. "We have to let father know about the beast," she said as she started toward their homes. Her ankle throbbed as she walked, her legs ached, her whole body felt bruised. Glancing back at the trees, she quickened her pace as she thought of the beast behind them.

Liale's trembling face peered around at Tesania. "Where did it come from?"

"I've no idea," Tesania shrugged. "Hopefully father will know."

"I thought it was going to kill us!"

Tesania sighed as she remembered the beast's eyes. Shivering, she said, "We were very lucky."

"You ran very fast."

"I didn't have much choice," Tesania laughed. She was pleased to hear her friend laugh along with her. They grew silent as they walked to the village, Tesania turning regularly check that the beast wasn't following. "Hang on," she called to Liale when they reached the main street and stepped over the sludge-filled gutter dug into the side of the dusty road.

"There's your mommy." Liale pointed toward Tesania's whitewashed home.

"Mother!" Tesania called.

"Hello, Tes." Her mother's eyes narrowed as the two girls reached her. "What happened to you two!?"

"I have to see Father. There's a beast in the forest. It tried to kill us."

"A beast?" her mother frowned as she reached out and took Liale from Tesania's back. "What kind of beast?" she asked while lowering the little girl on the dusty ground.

"I've never seen anything like it." Tesania dragged her hands through her tangled hair, wincing as a trickle of salty sweat ran down her face and bit at the raw welt on her cheek. "I'm hoping father might know."

Taking a piece of cloth from her pocket, her mother gently wiped at Tesania's face. "He's in his smithy."

Frowning, she took Tesania's hand. "Oh, Tes. Come into the house. We need to clean this up."

Tesania stepped back, wincing as her ankle throbbed with pain. Shaking her head, she said, "No. I need to talk to father now! He needs to call a meeting straight away." Squatting, she reached out and grasped Liale's shoulders. "Go straight home. Tell your mother what happened."

"I will." Liale waved as she turned toward her house.

"I'll come by later and explain it to her," Tesania called as Liale ran off. "And stay inside!" Standing, she shook her head as they watched the little girl go. "I thought I was going to lose her."

"You're both home safe," her mother said as she slipped her arm through Tesania's. "We'd better go and tell your father about this beast."

"He'll have to gather the council," Tesania said as they started toward her father's blacksmith shop. "They need to know what's out there."

Dark smoke rose from the crude brick chimney at the back of the blacksmith building, scenting the air with the familiar smells of charcoal and heated metals. Tesania peered into the smithy. "I can't see him. He's not..." Her head whipped around as she felt her mother stiffen. "What's wrong?"

Her mother's face creased in confusion. Tesania followed her gaze along the street to a cloud of dust. Chaos was erupting, villagers screaming and shoving through one another as they ran.

Tesania cringed as she saw Liale trip and fall; the villagers trampling over her as if she wasn't there. "Liale!" Tes cried as she started toward the little girl, her eyes growing wide with terror as a horde of the hideous black beasts emerged from the clouds of dust. Thin and sinewy with matted black hair covering their bodies, their lustful cries reverberated along the street; the swords clutched in their clawed hands hacking and stabbing as they chased down the villagers.

Tesania's mother snatched at her arm. "Tes. Run!"

"No!" Tesania screamed as a beast rushed toward Liale, raising its sword above its head. Struggling to break her mother's grasp Tesania watched in horror as the sword arced down and sliced through the little girl's body.

"Liale... No!" Tesania jerked against her mother's grip. "Let me go!" she wailed as she dug her fingers into her mother's hand, struggling to free herself.

"You can't help her, Tes. It's too late," her mother yelled.

Tesania's head snapped back to her friend, tears welling in her eyes. "No!" she moaned as Liale's life ebbed in rivulets of red from her shattered body.

"Liena, Tesania!" Tesania's father shouted as he ran from his smithy, darting through the frantic villagers as he tried to reach them. "Run! Get out of here!"

Not comprehending, Tesania stared at him in a daze; lost in the bloodshed quickly approaching them. A beast ran at her, snarling, saliva flying from its jagged jaws. Her father sprinted toward it. The beast stepped sideways, meeting him with its curved sword as it drove the point deep into his chest.

"Father!" Tesania shrieked as her father stood pinned on the beast's sword. His dying eyes turned to her. "Tesania, ru..."

Wrenching its sword free of her father's now lifeless body, the beast turned slowly toward her, its breath ragged, the blood dripping from the cold metal in its hand splashing onto the dusty ground.

"Run Tesania!" her mother yelled as she lunged between Tesania and the beast. The beast's hand hammered against her chest as he shoved her backward. The sun reflected brightly off the blood stained sword as the beast raised it and stepped quickly toward her.

"No!" Tesania wailed. The beast's cold eyes leered at her, its lips drawing back into a hideous grin as the razor sharp blade ran across her mother's throat. Blood burst from the ruptured arteries, splattering the beast's face. Licking the warm, sticky fluid from its lips, the beast's eyes never left Tesania. She stood, frozen in horror, as her mother collapsed to her knees, her blood running freely, soaking her once white dress. "Mother!"

Bellowing an exultant cry as it shot out its sinuous arm, the beast entwined its calloused fingers in Tesania's long, dark hair and dragged her closer. Grasping at the beast's fingers, she fought to break its grip, her nails ripping into the flesh of its hand. "Let me go!" She kicked at its legs. The beast laughed as she threw herself off balance.

Staring at the brutal face only inches from her own, she cringed. Fetid yellow tusks curved upward past a large flat nose. Small fierce eyes set back under heavy brows burned hatred back at her, its putrid breath engulfing her, choking her as she tried to scream.

The beast raised its sword slowly toward her throat. Desperately she threw her hand to her chest, whimpering as the sword drew closer. Her hand searched, scrambling over her skin until her fingers touched the cross that hung around her neck, a present from her father. Grasping it, she wrenched it free.

The beast's brow creased in confusion as it saw hope flicker across Tesania's eyes. Too late it realized the danger.

Tesania whipped her arm into the air and thrust the cross toward the beast, driving it with all her strength and desperation into its eye, bursting it like a ripe grape.

Screeching with pain, the beast dropped its sword, throwing Tesania to the ground. Stumbling and clutching at its face, it ripped at the cross, clawing to get it out.

Tesania scrambled toward the discarded weapon; her hands shaking as she clutched the hilt.

The beast turned toward her, glaring at her as it tossed the cross and its shattered eye aside. Teeth bared, fury contorting its face; it rushed her.

Tesania strained to lift the heavy sword, struggling under the weight of the blade. She managed to raise the point off the ground as the beast slid to a halt in front of her. "No!" Tesania uttered, shaking her head as she stepped backwards, struggling to keep the sword in the air.

The beast jerked forward, smashing its hand against her wrist. The sword flew free of her grip, clattering onto the ground as the beast swiped at her head. Tesania flinched. The fist caught her on the cheek, knocking her off her feet. Pushing herself up on her arms she coughed as the choking dust billowed around her head.

The beast reached down. Twisting its fingers through her hair once more, it pulled her to her feet. Pain tore through Tesania's scalp as she clawed at its hand.

"Leave her alone!" A defiant scream ripped through the air.

Tesania's eyes flew up. "Ardon!"

Blood cascaded from the beast's ruined eye socket as it spun around. Crouching, it snarled as her father's apprentice heaved its heavy sword from the ground.

"Run, Tesania!" Ardon cried as he took advantage of the weapon-less beast and drove the sword at its tough hide. "There's nothing you can do here!" he grunted as he wrenched the sword back.

Tesania scrambled to her feet and started toward the beast's back. "It will kill you too!"

"No! Get out of here!" Ardon yelled frantically. The beast flashed out a hand, catching Ardon around his throat as it knocked the sword aside. "Go!" he managed to croak, his eyes bulging from the pressure on his windpipe.

Tesania looked desperately at her parents and then to Liale. With fear gripping her heart, she turned and fled.

All she could think of was the forest. Certain the beast's sword would pierce her back as she stumbled across the grass, she ran on. Plunging into the trees, she slithered down an embankment, crashing against the roots of an old tree. Shivering with fear, her breath came short and ragged. "I can't help them!" she cried out as the sounds of the continuing massacre carried through the gently swaying trees. Rolling onto her knees she crawled deeper into the safety of the forest.

2 SADNESS

Tesania's swollen eyes filled with tears as she relived the horrifying attack. "No!" she wept as the memories came flooding back, the tears streaming down her face stinging the graze on her cheek. Curling into a ball, she gripped the sides of her head, squeezing, straining to drive the images out. She sobbed as her mind's eye forced her to endure the nightmare of her parents' death once more.

Mist seeped into the hollows where she sat shaking, curling around the twisted roots. The sound of birds singing their evening songs echoed through the trees as a butterfly flitted past her face. Cocking her head to the side, Tesania listened for any sounds from the village; wondering at the silence and if the beasts were still there. She knew she would need to move indoors before dusk brought on the bitter cold. The villagers' doors were usually closed by now with the gently warming fires flaming and crackling in the fireplaces.

Her ankle throbbed as she crawled to the top of the roots and stumbled upright onto a worn old track. Shivering as the coldness pricked at her skin, she crept through the woods; moving from trunk to trunk until the village appeared through the foliage. The rough bark of an ancient oak scratched at her cheek as she peered out from behind the giant tree. Eerie quietness greeted her; even the birds had fallen silent.

Dead villagers littered the main street, their blood marking almost every building. There was no sign of the beasts, no sounds, no fires or even smoke from the chimneys. It was as if they had disappeared.

Not caring anymore, Tesania stumbled across the grass clearing toward her parents. They lay a few feet apart. "Mother..." she sobbed, sinking to her knees beside them. Cringing at the gash across her throat, she quickly looked away.

"Father..." she groaned at the blood congealing around the jagged hole in his chest. Reaching out, she gently closed the lids over his sightless eyes.

Trembling, she stood and walked toward their home. Her pace quickening as she neared the door that hung ajar, blocking the way. "Murderers!" she screamed, kicking the door off its twisted hinges. Stumbling inside, she stood and looked at the wreckage. The attackers had smashed their way through; chairs lay on their sides, shattered crockery strewn across the floor.

Tesania wandered numbly to her parents' bedroom and snatched up a blanket before turning and walking back to where they lay. Dropping to her knees she dragged at the shoulders of her mother's dress, falling as she strained to move her side-by-side with her father. Tenderly, she placed her father's hand over her mother's, tears spilling down her cheeks as she pulled the blanket over their faces. "I love you," she whispered as she slowly stood.

Hollowness filled her as she walked along the street. "Liale," she groaned, collapsing to the ground and letting her tears run free, her body racking and heaving as she mourned beside her little friend.

Dragging herself to her knees, she reached out and touched Liale's cheek. "So cute."

As darkness chased the last light of the day from the once peaceful village, Tesania shook her head. Heartbroken, in shock, not knowing what to do, she walked in a daze to her shattered home.

Absentmindedly, she picked up an old iron stoker and prodded at the coals of the fireplace, adding logs from the neatly stacked pile beside the hearth. Flames slowly licked at the wood as she dropped the stoker on the floor and stood in a daze.

The firelight played along the rough whitewashed walls as she stood among the wreckage of her home. As thoughts of the beasts and her parents lying slain in the street swept through her mind a soft noise, almost imperceptible vibration, drew her attention to the dark hallway leading to her parents' bedroom. "Why!" she cried out. As her anger rose the vibrations grew more insistent.

With her nerves tingling, she reached for an old candle, not much more than a stub, and walked to the bedroom. The flame quivered as she inched through the door and stood peering into the gloom filled room, her knuckles turning white as she reached out and gripped her mother's shredded pillow. The vibrations tugged at her overwrought senses, calling her, demanding her attention. Placing the candle on the bedside stand, she turned toward the noise. Gripping the handle of her father's closest, she breathed deeply and threw it open.

The dim light of the candle barely drove the darkness from the corners of the closet as Tesania stood staring at the bundle of old oilcloth bouncing and chattering against the worn wooden shelf. Reaching in, she grasped the cloth, drawing it out as she turned toward the bed.

She knew what the cloth contained. Her father's prized family heirloom, passed from generations ago. He swore that he could feel power in it, maybe even magic. To

Tesania's touch though, it had always seemed cold and lifeless.

Yet today it hummed in her hands, vibrating excitedly as she sat on the bed and slowly peeled the oilcloth away. The metal came into view, glinting as it caught the candles wavering light. It felt alive as she reached out and touched it.

She paused, with her palm hovering on the worn leather grip. Gently closing her hand around the hilt she drew the blade from its sheath. It flashed brightly, making her blink. The grip felt like shifting sand as it rushed to form to the creases in her hand. A warm sensation shot along her arm, racing through her body and tingling at her nerves as she moved the sword in front of her eyes.

Mesmerized, she ran her fingers along the polished blade; wondered at the sword's lightness as she twisted her wrist and moved it about. The guard was a simple bar, the grip bound in leather with thin bronze wire holding it tightly in place. The pommel, a plain orb fashioned from polished silver. The ornate scabbard molded in the same silver with intricate scroll designs inlaid with bronze.

The sword hummed softly in her hands. As ideas of revenge swept through her tortured mind it blazed brightly, hues of orange running excitedly along its length. "Where did you come from?" she whispered.

Standing, she strode from the room. "You murdered my parents... Liale... Ardon... All of my friends!" Slamming the sword back into its sheath, she uttered, "I will find you! And then it will be your turn to die!"

3 THE UNKNOWN

Sunshine flickered playfully through the window of Tesania's small bedroom as a bird sang its morning song. Slowly she came out of her slumber, her eyes flashing open as the crushing reality of the previous day set in.

Swinging her feet onto the cold dirt floor, she sat digging her knuckles into her temples while trying to decide what to do. Steeling herself, she numbly dressed before walking out the bedroom door. Having no desire to eat she ignored the shattered kitchen and made her way into the blood stained street.

Blinking as the early morning sun invaded her eyes, she walked slowly toward her father's smithy. The fires had grown cold overnight, but the smells she had known all her life still lingered in the crisp air. Heaving a heavy tool from the wall she headed toward the river.

The sharp pick dug easily into the grassy winter earth overlooking the gently flowing water of the Lyiera River. Tesania had chosen her mother's favorite picnic place on the banks; where they had often sat and played during her childhood. Time and again she raised the pick above her head; working to dig a shallow hole big enough to lay her parents and Liale to rest.

Straining, she used every ounce of strength she possessed to drag them from the dusty street where they had been slain. Tears flowed down her reddened cheeks as she threw the last of the dirt on their grave and collapsed to the ground, exhausted and filthy.

Staring up at the swaying trees, her thoughts raced. *I have to leave. I can't stay here. Not anymore.* Clumsily climbing to her feet, tears glistening in the sunshine, she said, "I love you. Goodbye Mother, goodbye Father. Rest in peace little one." Turning slowly she left her parents' side for the last time.

~

After bathing, Tesania pulled her father's old traveling bag from the top of his closet. Placing it on the kitchen table she packed it with hard matured cheese, a crusty loaf of bread and some dried fruit from the pantry, her father's best knife, some coins from the earthen jar behind her parents' nightstand, a worn old water skin, and a well used tinder box, her mother's heavy cloak and her warmest clothes. Lastly she lowered the strap for the ornate sword and scabbard over her head, it settled on her shoulder, the weight surprisingly small.

Her thoughts raced as she walked from the village. *Where will I go?* North was all she could think of, north, where she might find answers in the Royal City.

Tesania's feet felt leaden as she crossed the grassy clearing and moved toward the forest. Stopping where she had taken refuge during the massacre, she reached out and gently ran her hands over the familiar knotted trunks of the trees. Their rough, furrowed bark was alive with insects while soft pillows of moss crowded the hollows in and around the roots. Birds and insects chirped and chattered while the wind whispered in the high overhead branches.

The woods stood as a barrier. She felt fear; knowing that if she proceeded she was entering an unknown land and future. Moving on would break the bond with the pretty little village she had lived in all her life. Yet, knowing there was nothing here for her now she steeled herself and stepped tentatively into the forest. A small animal watched her, twitching it whiskers before scampering away. Step by step her pace quickened as her conviction grew.

A path wandered through the myriad of trees, sometimes seeming to head in completely the wrong direction. She stopped only occasionally to eat some dried fruit and sip water, knowing, from stories told in the village long house, that the far edge of the forest was a day and a half continuous walking with the town of Lyiera just to the north from there.

As the day wore on, Tesania searched the skies. The sun was now well to the west, its soft light still managing to find its way through the sparse leaves on the branches that stood out like crooked old fingers in the canopy of trees. As the coolness of evening pricking at her skin, she searched for a suitable place to spend the night. A twisted oak presented a little alcove where she could sleep, secure in the old tree's protective embrace while a small brook babbled past on its way to an unknown destination. Stones from the edge of the brook made a cozy little fireplace. Collecting small branches and twigs, Tesania opened her tinderbox and removed the well-used flint and steel. Well practiced; it was only a short time before a small flame took to the kindling.

Sitting with her back to the tree, she picked up her father's sword. "What am I doing?" she asked aloud as she gazed at the water through the flickering fire, her fingers tracing the intricate designs of the scabbard. "Where am I going?" All she could think to do was approach the town of Lyiera, talk to the authorities and find her way from there.

Wrapping herself in heavy clothing and a cloak, the coals of the fire tended and glowing, she lay down. Years of fallen foliage created a firm but comfortable bed while the soft burble of the brook helped her slowly drift off to sleep.

~

Rustling leaves startled Tesania awake. A small, mole like creature inched toward its burrow with her bag in tow. "Oh no you don't!" cried Tesania. The creature jumped, releasing the bag as it hissed and backed against the tree with its hackles raised.

Caught up in her robes, Tesania struggled to stand. The creature seized the bag again and scrambled toward its burrow. The air split as an arrow passed within inches of Tesania. A sickening thud tumbled the creature over; it lay motionless in the soft morning light.

Tesania instinctively rolled toward the old oak, her hand brushing the sword that she had leant against the tree the night before. It vibrated, demanding her attention. Instinct drew her hand to the hilt and with a hiss of metal the blade slid clear of its sheath.

The crack of a tinder dry twig made her start. Certain it must be the beasts, she waited, her breath ragged as she pressed against the tree, its rough bark digging painfully into her back. Hearing nothing, she slowly peered from behind the old oak's trunk. A man stood some twenty paces away, an arrow nocked to his bow.

Relief flooded through Tesania as she saw it wasn't the beasts, quickly turning to suspicion when the man stepped lightly toward her. "I'm armed," she warned.

The stranger smiled. "I'm not in the habit of harming young ladies."

Tesania studied him closely. His green eyes appeared to laugh at her while white teeth flashed from behind his wide smile. A longbow nestled snugly in his left hand; his right held the string of the bow. Around his waist was a simple belt holding a dagger and sword, sheathed in polished silver and black scabbards.

The stranger stood comfortably; watching her. "Tell me. What brings a lady such as you to these woods alone?" he asked.

"I'm no lady," Tesania snapped.

"Very well," he continued, renewing his smile. "Young girl; if I may."

"I don't know you, sir!" Tesania replied. "My business is my own."

"Come now," he stepped a few paces closer. "A lady... err.., young girl, doesn't travel these woods alone. Unless she is troubled."

"Who sir, may I ask, are you?"

"I am called Deavon, and I am a King's Ranger." He again moved forward, ten paces now from the old tree.

"Come no closer, please!" Tesania implored.

"Very well," he said as he stopped. "At least let me prepare the creature for the fire."

Tesania didn't know what to do. She wanted to trust this ranger, craving company, desperate to tell of her ordeal, her parents and the beasts. Lowering her guard slightly, she picked up the animal and tossed it a few yards from where he stood. In the few seconds she had looked away he had replaced his arrow to its quiver and laid his bow aside.

Tesania studied him again as he prepared the carcass by the brook. She knew that trusting him would be a risk, but also realized that her life would now require her to rely on her instincts. Her gut told her this man might be an ally worth having.

"May I use your fire?" he asked as he stepped closer.

"You may," she replied warily. "But; come near me at your folly!"

His disarming smile flashed once more across his face. "I serve the King and protect his subjects," he replied. "It is my intent to help, not harm."

The fire hissed and flared as the meat dripped its juices. Tantalizing aromas drifted through the morning air as he looked at her through the smoke that rose up and tangled itself among the old oak's branches. "Where have you come from?" he asked.

Tesania hesitated as tears welled in her eyes. Looking quickly away, she paused before answering in a quivering voice, "I'm from Aryd villa..." her voice caught as a sob wracked her body. After a few quiet moments she lifted her eyes to the fire and whispered softly, "My parents; are dead."

Deavon watched her as she stared into the flames. Gently he asked, "Both your parents? How did this come to pass?"

Tears rolled down Tesania's cheeks as she whispered, "They came out of nowhere.., killed..." Her eyes flashed up to meet his. "Everyone!"

"Who?" Deavon asked as he sat up. "Who came out of nowhere?"

"Bea..,sts!" she exclaimed, the word catching in her throat.

"Beasts!" he hissed. "They've come this far already! The King didn't think they'd reach this far for many months."

"The King knows of them!" Tesania snapped, anger instantly rising above her tears. "Why doesn't he stop them?"

Deavon measured his answer as he removed the meat from the fire. Drawing his dagger, he cut it in two, offering half to Tesania. She accepted it gingerly, but declined to eat and lay it down on an exposed root beside her.

Deavon pulled strips of meat away from the carcass in his hand and chewed slowly as he watched her. "I suppose I should start at the beginning," he said as he adjusted his position. "Many years ago a novice by the of

Trannyth trained at the Mages Guild in Carella. He was gifted and quickly learned the ways."

"What are the ways?" Tesania interrupted.

"The ways is the term used by the Mages Guild to describe their magic, and the formulas that derive them," he advised as he tore off another piece of meat. "Trannyth soon grew seditious and eventually started to cast forbidden magic. The teachers admonished him, but the power had already seduced him. The Archmage intervened, stripping him of his rank and banning him from using magic, his staff to be broken." Licking juice of his fingers, he continued. "Unfortunately they underestimated him. He was far more powerful than they imagined him to be, killing a teacher as he fled the guild. No one knew where he went. They searched, but to no avail. Many years passed with no sighting of him, not even a whisper and he was all but forgotten."

"What does that have to do with the King stopping the beasts?" Tesania asked in confusion.

"I'm getting to that," he smiled. "If you'll let me."

"Sorry," Tesania mumbled as she picked a few shreds of meat from her portion of the meal.

Throwing his stripped carcass away as he stood, Deavon walked to the brook. Crouching, he turned his head back to her as he washed his hands. "A short while ago rumors of a large camp in the wastelands surfaced. Trannyth had reappeared, bent on revenge. He's using forbidden magic to create the beasts."

Returning to the fire he squatted to warm his hands by the heat of the coals. "The King doesn't have an army large enough to send against him. Besides, the mountain passes make any large scale attack impossible."

"How is it they attacked my village then?" Tesania asked.

"Trannyth has sent forth raiding parties of beasts. Their attacks have been limited to the north and along the west-coast. Until now." He paused. "I must report to the King. You can travel with me as far as Rilmir, if you wish."

"I want to speak to the King!"

"It's doubtful you would be granted an audience," Deavon laughed as he stood. "As I said, I'll take you as far as the city of Rilmir; there you can talk to the Authorities." As an afterthought, he added, "And since we'll be traveling together, it may make our life easier if you told me your name?"

Tesania frowned. Rilmir was not at all where she wanted to go. "My name's Tesania, but people call me Tes," she said, deciding that Rilmir, at the very least, was a start.

4 LYIERA TOWNSHIP

The Mid afternoon sun cast dappled light through the thinning trees as Tesania and Deavon drew closer to the northern edge of the forest. They had made good headway during the cool morning as they walked along the well worn track winding its way through the giant old trunks, having stopped only for a small meal at midday.

"What does a King's Ranger do?" Tes asked.

"We're the King's guard."

"Where are you from?"

"Wyvern City, the King's city," he replied.

"You're on an errand for the King?"

"I am. Or should I say, I was," Deavon replied carefully. "The King tasked the rangers to warn the outlying villages of the beasts' activities and to help with their defenses. I was dispatched to Aryd. He bowed his head. "Unfortunately; too late."

"What defense could my village have mounted against them?" Tesania asked as she stared at the ground. "My father was the only one who knew how to wield a sword."

Deavon looked at her. "Was your father a soldier?" he asked gently.

"No. He was the Blacksmith," she replied.

"Your father was the smithy? Was it he who made your sword?" he asked, nodding toward her shoulder.

"No," Tes replied, shaking her head. "It's been passed through our family for generations. My father knew little of it." Not sure if he would believe her, she decided not to tell of the power that flowed through her when she had drawn the sword in her parents' bedroom.

"It looks expensive," he said as he looked closely at the scabbard strung across her shoulders. "When we get to Lyiera, put it under your cloak," he advised as the grand old trees of the forest gave way to a field of ankle high grass.

Tesania stood on her toes in an effort to see what might be on the far side of the field, shaking her head when grass was all she could see.

"Lyiera is north-east from here; by the river." Deavon pointed. "Not too far now."

Tes watched him adjust his bow as they walked. About twenty-five years of age, he looked every bit the part of an experienced traveler. "Could you teach me to use a bow?" she asked.

"I can," he replied. "But it's not an easy thing to master."

They fell quiet as a well-worn road appeared in the grass. Smoke curled lazily from a farmer's cottage. A wagon, drawn by four oxen trundled across a field of Lucerne littered with huge bundles of hay. Turning onto the road as the sun turned its attention toward the horizon, they proceeded toward the town. The farms grew more frequent, grains overflowing from dozens of silos while fields of fruits and vegetables stretched into the distance. The people were friendly and happy, waving as they passed.

"There're lodgings to be had in the center of town," Deavon said as they reached the outskirts of the town. "Try to keep a low profile."

"Why?" Tesania asked while moving the sword under her cloak as best she could. It stuck awkwardly into her neck.

"There're undesirable people here that might wish to cause you harm," he warned.

The main street of Lyiera was of compacted dirt, furrowed and worn by countless cartwheels. People bustled in and out of the whitewashed shops while the sounds of steel against anvil emanated from the smithy and music and raucous yells came from several of the inns.

"Stay close," Deavon warned as he pointed up the road. "The Boar's Head's the quietest place to stay."

Keeping to the right side of the street, they stepped on crudely cobbled stones as passing horses strained at the creaking yokes of carts and wagons, throwing choking dust into the air. Tes couldn't help thinking it would be a quagmire if it rained. Looking back in wonder at the busy town she hurried to catch Deavon as he led the way through the plain wooden door of the inn.

~

Greedy eyes watched the sword hilt protruding from the young girl's cloak. *An easy target,* the greasy little man thought. *Except for the ranger.* Quickly he walked down a shadow filled side alley and disappeared.

~

"You wish to take a room?" asked the eager innkeeper, his chubby hands rubbing together.

Deavon nodded. "And we would partake of one of your fine meals as well."

The innkeeper's eyes took Tesania in, a smile growing on his face.

Deavon leaned forward onto the counter, looking directly into the innkeeper's eyes. "Separate rooms if you will," he growled. "But make sure they're adjoining."

"Of course sir," the innkeeper mumbled nervously while holding his hands up in placation.

Tes wandered into the main room of the inn as Deavon made the arrangements for their rooms. A crackling fire warmed the room from one corner. A bar running along the west wall held dozens of earthenware mugs stacked on its surface while large barrels of ale sat against the back whitewashed wall. Neat rows of wooden tables filled the area, several of them taken by travelers quietly talking amongst themselves. Tesania's stomach growled in anticipation of the appetizing aromas wafting toward her from the open door leading to the kitchen.

"Please follow to your rooms," suggested the innkeeper as he swept past her and headed for the worn old stairs on the far side of the inn.

Tesania walked a few paces behind, continuing to take in the ambience of the room as they ascended the stairs.

"Room six," said the innkeeper as he opened the door and ushered Tes in. A soft looking bed filled half of the room. A bowl and pitcher on a nightstand stood in one corner. Thin dusty curtains covered a small window overlooking the noisy street.

The innkeeper groaned as he straightened after lighting the small fire. Rubbing his lower back, he smiled at Tes. "The old back isn't what it used to be," he said as he arched backwards and then started for the door. "I trust you'll be comfortable. Please call me if you should require anything. Dinner is available in the dining room after dusk. Enjoy your stay."

"Thank you," replied Tesania as the door creaked closed. Sinking gratefully onto the bed, she quickly lost interest in food as weariness overtook her and she succumbed to sleep.

~

As darkness crept over the Township, a soft knock roused Tes from her slumber. "Yes?" she mumbled sleepily as she struggled to move to a sitting position in the soft folds of the bed.

"The evening meal is being served downstairs. Would you like to accompany me?" Deavon asked through the door.

"Can you give me a minute?"

"I shall knock again shortly."

Tesania climbed out of the bed and quickly bathed with a small piece of cloth which she dipped into the cool water from the pitcher. Selecting a dress from her pack which was made of simple homespun material cut in a peasant's style, she slipped it over her head. A floral belt that her mother had embroidered fitted snugly around her waist. Finally, she tied her hair with a ribbon.

A short time later, Deavon knocked again. When Tesania came to the door he stood staring. As if sensing her discomfort; he smiled. "Forgive me."

Tes blushed and pushed quickly past him before heading for the stairs. The main room hummed with voices and activity while two waitresses navigated the room, delivering ales and food. A bard sang in one corner, strumming his mandolin. Weaving toward the bar, Tes excused herself as she squeezed between tables and chairs, Deavon following close behind..

The innkeeper sang out as they approached, "I see you've joined us for dinner! Bessy! Show them to a table!"

Bessy threaded her way towards them. A buxom lady wearing a flowing light brown skirt with a white frilled apron, her white shirt tied above her elbow, brown vest laced at the front with a matching mop cap trying unsuccessfully to hold back her flowing red hair. "We kept a nice table in the corner for you to sit," she said happily as she led the way across the room brushing away the few stray hands that snaked out to stop her. "Don't worry about them," she smiled at Tes. "They're harmless."

The table she seated them at was cut from a slab of redwood, about three-foot wide. Plates and crude cutlery were set, a bowl of herbs standing in the center. "What can I get you?" Bessy asked as she wiped a few stray crumbs off the table. "We have fresh fish from the river or beef stew."

Tesania thought for a moment. She loved fish, but had never tried beef stew in her life. Looking up at Bessy, she smiled. "I'd like to try the beef stew, please," she said hesitantly. "No. Maybe the fish. Oh, I don't know. I can't decide."

Deavon laughed. "I'll have the stew, thank you, Bessy."

"The same for me," Tes added as she felt a blush breaking over her face.

Bessy smiled. "Can I bring you both a tankard of ale?"

As Deavon nodded, Tesania quickly replied, "No thank you."

"An Apple cider then?" Bessy asked.

"Please; that would be nice." As she watched the waitress run the gauntlet of hands toward the bar, Tes said, "I've never been to a place like this. In my village we only had the long house. It was more of a meeting place than an inn."

"This is one of the more favorable ones," Deavon replied gravely. "There're many that are very dangerous places. You should avoid them when you can."

They sat in silence for some time. Tes watched the other patrons in the room. There was such a diversity of people. Many wore clothes and spoke in ways she had never seen or heard.

Deavon watched her closely; eventually asking, "What are your plans? What will you do once we reach Rilmir City?"

Tesania sat up quickly, looking directly into his eyes. "My plan!" she stated. "Is to find this Trannyth and make him pay!" Pausing, she looked down at the table before quietly whispering, "He owes me a debt."

Deavon watched her as she stared at the table. After a few moments, he gently said, "Trannyth's a very strong mage, skilled in the ways, with an army around him. The King himself hasn't found a way to rid Eldanal of him. I'd put your ideas of revenge aside if I were you."

"I'm not some cowardly maiden!" Tesania flared. "I won't forget my family and friends and the way they died, nor will I rebuild my life wondering if the beasts will attack and take it from me again!" She paused, glaring at the table before uttering between clenched teeth. "If the King can't find a way to kill him and the beasts, I will! This I promise!" She looked up at him. "If I die trying; then so be it!"

"You may very well die.., in that endeavor," he replied as he watched her.

Tesania frowned at him before turning away and studying the inn. Forty odd people filled the tables. Crude candelabras hanging from the ceiling dimly lit the room while a few tendrils of smoke escaped being drawn up the chimney and drifted lazily through the air. The room buzzed with conversations, a few early starters already singing along with the bard. She watched as the waitress returned with their drinks.

~

Across the room the greasy little man leant against the bar.

"What do you want Burrit?" asked the innkeeper sourly.

"Just looking to have some ale and watch the show," he replied as he threw a few coins on the bar. "A tankard of your finest ale please innkeeper," he said with a smirk as he settled himself where he could keep a watchful eye on the girl and her companion.

~

"There you go," Bessy smiled as she returned to Tes and Deavon. "A farmer just outside town makes the cider; it's absolutely delicious. Your meals should be along shortly."

"Thank you," replied Tes. "Are you usually this busy?"

"The Boar's Head's very popular. Most nights we're quite full," she smiled. "It's still early." she winked at Tesania. "Trust me. It'll get rowdier as the night wears on."

Deavon raised his tankard to Tesania. "To the journey ahead."

Tesania didn't return the toast; her thoughts had drifted back to her village. Sitting in silence, she wished she was at home washing the evening dishes with her mother.

Their meal, when it arrived, looked delicious. The spicy aromas caused Tesania's mouth to water, drawing her mind back to the present. A freshly baked loaf of bread, with a large pat of butter was also served with the stew. They ate in silence. Realizing that she hadn't eaten much in the last few days Tes cleared her plate in short order, sopping up the last of the gravy with a piece of the bread before pushing it aside. "That was perfect," she sighed.

"Yes," Deavon agreed. "It was a fine stew. Would you like another cider?" he asked as he pointed to her empty tankard.

Tes nodded. Deavon caught Bessy's attention. As they waited for their drinks they sat back and enjoyed the evening. The Bard sang many popular songs, men stood on tables dancing and singing loudly, and later in the night Bessy performed a memorable song.

"Time to retire," Deavon suggested, clapping Bessy as he rose.

Tesania followed, yawning as she climbed the stairs. She looked forward to a good night's sleep in the comfortable bed.

"Goodnight," she said to Deavon as she pushed her door shut. After changing she slipped tiredly between the rough sheets, the feather stuffed pillow cushioning her head perfectly as she drifted quietly into sleep.

5 A THIEF IN THE NIGHT

Burrit made his way across the dark street. Earlier he had cautiously followed the girl as she left the dining room and climbed the stairs toward her room. A smile crept across his face as he realized the ranger had taken a separate room. Noting the door the girl entered, he descended the stairs and left the Inn.

Two hours had slowly passed as he waited. The inn was now empty, the lights extinguished for the night. An experienced thief, the tumblers of the inn's front door lock swiftly fell into place. He crept up the stairs, careful of his footfalls to avoid any betraying noise. Finding her door, he quickly picked the lock.

The old iron hinges groaned in protest as he pushed the door open. Pausing, he listened, hardly daring to breath. Relieved that the girl had not stirred or called out, he entered. The moon dimly lit the room, enabling him to make out the bed and the nightstand. Stepping slowly, he reached out and closed his grip around the sword that leant against the wall, his heart racing as he turned back toward the door.

~

Tes rose from the depths of sleep. Laying half awake; she foggily attempting to decide if the noise had been in a dream. Movement alerted her senses, her eyes flashing open as she came fully awake and watched a shadow move across the dark room. Realizing it was not a dream she sat upright, yelling, "Who're you? What're you doing in my room?"

The intruder fled at the sound of the Tesania's voice, careening out of the door and down the stairs.

By the time Tesania reached the hall Deavon had rushed from his room. "What is it?" he demanded as he rubbed at his sleep filled eyes.

"A man was in my room!" Tes cried, gesticulating down the stairs. "He took my sword!"

Deavon took the stairs two at a time. Bursting out of the front door of the inn he caught the fleeing thief in the corner of his eye as he turned into an alley. "Stop thief!" he shouted.

~

Burrit struggled. His aged and mistreated body no match for the ranger. Realizing that his knowledge of the town was his only means of escape, he ducked around a building and swerved to the right, crashing through the door of the smithy's barn. Climbing an old ladder to the loft he ran to the window. *Let's see if he can find me now?* he thought as he jumped to the roof of a neighboring building.

~

Deavon slid to a halt as he rounded the corner near the smithy's barn. The thief was nowhere to be seen. He peered behind a broken-down wagon and some old barrels standing against the wall. "Where are you?" he called out. "You can't hide forever."

Cautiously he stepped through the door behind the wagon. The barn was quiet with no sign of his quarry. Climbing the ladder he checked the loft, soon realizing the thief had slipped away.

~

Tesania quickly threw on some clothes and a cloak before dashing out the door. Darkness filled the empty street as she rushed from the front entrance of the inn. Deavon and the thief had disappeared. Peering one way, then the other, she eventually turned to her right. Running swiftly along the street, she stopped abruptly as Deavon materialized from the darkness.

"Where is he?" Tes asked as she looked into the blackness behind him.

"I followed him down the alley." Deavon motioned, shaking his head. "But he disappeared."

"My sword. Is it lost?" Tesania groaned.

"Not yet," he replied. A confused frown creased his forehead as he wondered where the thief may have gone. "Let's walk along the street. We may yet catch him."

Tesania walked down the left side of the street, looking into the alleys and doorways. Tears welled in her eyes as she realized her father's precious sword was lost. *What was I thinking? Only two days from home and already I'm at the mercy of a simple thief. How can I possibly take on a whole army?*

Despairing as the last house in the street came into view in the murky darkness, Tes looked across to Deavon. A shingle slipped and tumbled from a roof above her, startling her as it shattered on a wagon a few feet from where she stood. "On the roof!" she screamed to Deavon, pointing at the building in front of her.

Deavon sprinted to the wagon, vaulting onto the seat before leaping onto a large woodpile stacked against the house. With a short jump, he gripped the edge of the roof and pulled himself up.

The thief panicked at the ranger's quick ascent. Turning, he ran. Deavon followed, jumping from roof to roof in hot pursuit. Shingles dislodged and slipped from under their feet, making headway precarious. "Stop!" yelled Deavon.

~

Burrit had no intention of stopping, fearing what this ranger would do to him. Slipping as he launched for the next building, he came up short, his body crashed into the edge of the roof. Crying out in pain, he tried to hold on. Anxious to gain some purchase on the roof, he threw the sword from his grasp; it bounced across the shingles before slithering off the roof and thudding to the grass below.

~

Deavon made the jump easily. Crouching carefully on the treacherous shingles he reached for the other man's hand. The thief refused to take it, shaking his head as another shingle slipped from its position.

A crowd of townsfolk had gathered, woken by the thunderous noise of running footsteps on their roofs. They stood with Tesania, watching the two men outlined against the moon.

"Take it!" implored Deavon as he offered his hand once more.

"You'll kill me anyway!" the thief growled.

"That, I won't do," said Deavon. "I will however, hand you to the sheriff. Take my hand! If you don't, you'll fall!"

The thief released his grip on the roof and snatched Deavon's hand, pulling with all his strength. Deavon, realizing his danger, quickly twisted his wrist, releasing the little man's grip as the last shingles holding him slipped over the edge. He watched the horror on his face as he disappeared into the darkness of the night.

Slowly retracing his steps across the roofs, Deavon finally climbed down the woodpile near the wagon. Tes patiently waited for him with her recovered sword in her hand.

"What of the thief?" Deavon asked hesitantly.

"One of the townsfolk said he's dead," Tes replied, her voice trembling. "They've sent for the sheriff."

Deavon shook his head. "I tried to save the man," he said bitterly. "Such a needless death."

"We saw that you tried. There was nothing else you could do," Tesania replied in a quiet voice, almost a whisper. "He even tried to pull you over the edge with him." After a few thoughtful moments, she looked up at his face with sadness in her eyes. "I'm sick of death! First my family! Now this stranger! When will it end?"

"The road you've chosen is littered with death, Tes," he said as he wiped a tear from her cheek. "I'm afraid you may have to get used to it." Gently, he placed his arm around her shoulder and led her toward the inn. "The sheriff will want to talk to us but he'll have to wait until morning. Let's try to get some sleep."

~

The sheriff called early, asking them to accompany him to the site of the previous night's activities. The thief was indeed dead. Witnesses had confirmed that Deavon was not at fault. The sheriff said, "He'll be no loss to this town. I can assure you."

Turning back to the inn, Deavon said, "Let's get some breakfast. I'd like to reach the hills today."

The smell of fried ham and eggs assaulted Tesania's senses as they walked back into the inn. She sat gratefully at a table in the main room and snatched up a knife. A short time later she pushed her plate aside. "I'm so full," she said, cradling her stomach.

Deavon laughed as he stood. "I'm glad to hear that. We have a long day of walking ahead of us."

Tesania climbed the stairs after Deavon and collected her belongings from her room. Deavon met her on the landing and walked with her to the innkeeper. Placing a few coins on the bar, he said, "I would certainly recommend your inn to anybody needing lodgings in these parts."

Tes nodded in agreement.

"Thank you, sir," the innkeeper replied as he performed a small bow. "That is a pleasure to hear. Please allow me to apologize again for the events of last night."

Tes reached into her bag as Deavon walked to the door and pulled out a small coin. "Can you please give this to Bessy? I so enjoyed her performance last night."

"Of course. Consider it done," the innkeeper said as he held out his chubby little hand.

"Thank you." Tesania waved as she walked to the door.

"A very nice gesture," Deavon remarked as they walked onto the dusty street. "Though I doubt she'll ever see it."

"Why?" Tesania questioned, surprised at his remark.

"The innkeeper, whilst not a thief like our friend last night, is a businessman. He would consider her paid with her wages. In his eyes, any extra would be rightfully his." He looked at her seriously. "You have to understand. You're in a different world now. A village where everybody knows their neighbors and respects their property and rights is a far cry from the towns you'll encounter. The cities are far worse, attracting all sorts of people; many the dregs of society. You'll learn. Just be on your guard."

Tes half turned back to the inn, wanting to go straight back and demand that the coin be passed on but thought better of it. Looking up at the roofs, she saw a man was already repairing the missing shingles. "Where to now?" she asked.

"First we must visit the grocery. My supplies are running short," he said as he led the way across the street.

Tesania rushed to dodge an oncoming horseman who made no attempt to avoid her before galloping on down the street. *He's right,* she thought sadly. *That would never happen in Aryd.*

The grocery presented an array of goods that bewildered Tesania. Vegetables of types her village had never seen. Bottles of boiled candies stood in colorful lines, loaves of bread filled the shelves while sacks of grains and seeds spilled out onto the floor. Shelf after shelf was crammed with wondrous goods for sale. She wandered about the store in amazement while Deavon made his purchases. He laughed in her direction. "You look like you want to buy the whole shop."

"It's amazing," she replied. "But no, not the whole shop. I'd like to buy some cheese and bread though." There were such a number of choices that it took some time for her to choose. "And some sweets," she added while guiltily looking sideways at Deavon. He tried, unsuccessfully, to suppress a grin whilst pretending he hadn't heard.

Dust billowed from a passing cart as they left the shop, causing Tesania to cover her face as they made their way along the road to the north-east and started on the long walk toward the hills and Rilmir.

6 TRANNYTH'S DESIRE

Trannyth stood at the window of his Tower Keep, dressed in a midnight black robe with brilliant silver adorning the hem, the oversized hood casting his face in shadow. A gem of the deepest purple, set in a silver amulet, sat against his chest. In his left hand nestled a staff of simple notched wood topped by a stone of the same deep purple. Plains of barren stone and rocks filled his view to the mountains.

His Keep sat some three days walk north of the Britath Mountains. A fortress; magically raised from the surrounding stone. Towering cliffs on three sides overlooked the battlements adorning the buttressed, batter style wall. Arrow loops pierced the parapet at regular intervals. A gatehouse protected the road leading to the heavy iron gates which in turn protected the ward of smooth rock fronting the entrance to the great hall. Barracks nestled on either side of the hall, an eighty-foot tower rising from the centre, dominating the sky.

"What news of the raiding parties?" he snapped at the group of mages gathered in the turret room of the tower.

"They wreak havoc, My Lord. A few troops of soldiers have been dispatched to intercept our beasts. They have not yet been successful."

"And the King?"

"The King has called the Council to Wyvern City, while a call to arms has been issued to the Militia."

"Production of the beasts has been stepped up as I ordered?" Trannyth asked coldly.

"My Lord," said another of the mages. "The Ogre grows weak. His life force is nearly spent. If we drain much more he will surely die."

"Find another, you fool!" Trannyth sneered as he spun around, malice emanating from the cowl covering his face. Each mage dropped their eyes to the floor as Trannyth's gaze passed over them. Turning back to the window he dismissed them with a gesture. "Leave me!" The mages quickly backed from the room, no one wishing to further ignite his wrath.

Trannyth turned as the mages exited and walked to an ornately carved podium in the middle of the room. Constructed of plain stone, it stood three feet tall. He placed his hand on the orb that sat atop it, translucent, about eight inches in diameter with blue mist swirling inside like clouds on a windswept day. It held the power of his beasts. From each one transformed in his hideous workshops; a part of its life force entered the orb, binding it to him. Through it, he forced them to his will.

~

Many years had passed since those fools in Carella had tried to suppress him. From the start of his schooling the magic had coursed through his veins. A natural, the ways had come to him easily while others around him struggled with the simplest of spells.

The teachers were at first excited, then fearful as the power he could wield became apparent. Many counseled him, attempting to channel him onto the right path. With a life of servitude to the King not to his liking, he gradually started invoking forbidden magic. Fellow students suddenly found their books turned to stone, walls blocking hallways leading to the dorms. Items he coveted began to disappear magically from their belongings.

The teachers admonished him. He scorned them and continued to experiment. Deformed animals, many with their appendages in unnatural places, started appearing throughout the school. He took great delight in the girls' screams.

One overcast morning he watched from the dorm window as the Archmage stepped from his elaborately decorated carriage. Golden threads sewn into his flowing, ocean blue robes chased one another to form intricate designs. An elaborate staff of polished mahogany topped by a gleaming silver orb in the grip of an eagle's claw finished the pompous air of the high level mage.

Summonsed to the Headmaster's rooms, Trannyth sat as the Archmage read from a prepared scroll. "The laws cannot be tampered with. You have performed forbidden magic, against the advice and wishes of your teachers. You will, on this day, be stripped of your rank and your staff shall be broken. You are forbidden to practice magic ever again. Any attempt to do so will result in your arrest and execution." He paused, looking directly at Trannyth from below his bushy grey eyebrows. "Do you understand!?" he barked.

Trannyth sat impassively, refusing to respond. Slowly rising, he looked from the Headmaster to the Archmage. His voice dripping contempt, he said, "You are fools! The magic chose me, not I it!" Turning toward the door, he said brashly, "You are correct. From today I am not a mere mage of the King and in the future he will call me My Lord as he grovels at my feet!" Storming out the door, he snarled, "Try to stop me. If you dare!"

Returning to his room, he threw his belongings into a pack and grasped his staff before striding purposefully out the elegantly hand carved front doors.

A cry stopped him as he reached the bottom of the wide stone stairs that opened onto the manicured grounds of the school. The Headmaster and three teachers burst from the building. "Stop!"

Trannyth slowly turned. "Do not try to stop me. You know my power. Stand in my way and you will perish!"

One teacher raised his staff, throwing a spell at Trannyth. Easily he blocked it with his own staff. "I warned you!" he growled as he sent a fatal spell, at frightening speed, directly at the teacher's chest. The teacher, with no time to parry, flew backward, landing against the sculpted stone doorframe as the life ebbed from his body. The other teachers had no time to react as a maelstrom of air engulfed Trannyth. Realizing the strength of the spell he was about to cast, they fled. The magic crackled as it hit the front of the school, stones crumbling as the archways gave way, dust filling the air. By the time the air cleared and the coughing headmaster peered from behind the rubble, Trannyth was gone.

Travelling for many months, Trannyth found lodgings in the seedy side of Rilmir. Working laboriously at the ways he developed new spells to manipulate nature; experimenting on rats and roaches, even travelling to manipulate the gnarled old trees growing in the nearby forest.

Frequenting a tavern where the lower echelon of the mage society spent their free hours, he slowly built a secret society. Many years passed as he trained them in the forbidden ways. Recruiting well; they brought higher ranked mages to the fold, using these contacts to have some of their number assigned to the King's Court while others were attached to the councils of the other major cities of Eldanal.

With his network in place, Trannyth turned his attention to finding a suitable fortress from which to mount his campaign of revenge. Travelling for almost a year, he finally crossed the mountains and found, what was in his eyes, the perfect place on the stony plains of the wastelands. The mountains stood as a natural barrier to any army the King could muster, the passes easily blocked and protected while the open plains allowed any approaching foe to be seen for many miles. A promontory commanded a plain riddled with underground caves. The perfect place to build his Keep.

On returning to Rilmir, he spent many months preparing, organizing the society, and procuring stocks of food and equipment. Slowly his mages left the city over the period of a month, aware that movement en-mass would arouse suspicion. They met, finally, in the foothills of the Britath Mountains above Orash; their meager camp sitting on the banks of the Wyvern River. A week passed as they planned the trip over the mountains. Much of the pass they would take sat on precarious ledges, other sections threaded through tight canyons where two men could not walk abreast. On a brisk spring morning, thirty-two mages started the trek. Days of blistering, hazardous walking saw them enter the foothills overlooking the Wastelands, two of their number short.

Again they set camp. Being city dwellers, the hard mountainous pass had fatigued them beyond their belief. Five days they spent in the encampment, ranging out to hunt fresh food. The returning hunters reported to Trannyth the sighting of an ogre inhabiting the hills.

Watching as they butchered a black, bear like beast, known as a banmora, Trannyth, always looking for a new experiment, turned to the others. "I want that ogre. Alive!"

They stared at him for a long while, recalling the ogre. It was huge, with gnarled limbs that could tear them apart as they would tear a piece of bread.

"Now!" he bellowed.

Quickly deciding that capturing the ogre presented far less danger than defying their new Lord, they set forth. Five of them left the camp, none of them confident that they would return.

~

Raug was the only ogre for miles around. He sat quietly by the little creek that ran past his cave, the meat held in his giant fist almost completely gnawed off the bone. The man-things worried him. Yet, so far, they had left him well enough alone.

Hearing them well before they came into sight, he turned to watch as they passed. Usually they kept a good distance as they skirted his pile of bones. That they feared him amused his simple mind. This time however they fanned out and walked slowly up the small hill, directly toward him.

Rising, he let out a warning bellow that reverberated through the trees; birds took to flight as small animals scampered for their burrows.

Pausing, the mages looked to one another for courage. Raug, sensing that they meant to harm him, careened down the slope. With the impetus of a rampaging boulder he smashed into the mage in the centre with such force that he died instantly, his body crushed.

Flailing his arm to the right, he caught another man-thing on the side of the head. With a war like cry he bent his scarred, wart covered knee, bringing his huge foot into the air before cannoning it down. The mage had no chance, the weight and strength of the ogre crushing his chest, snuffing his life out in a heartbeat.

The others, having had time to scramble out of range of his deadly arms, fired spells at him. They stung as they bounced off his thick hide; enraging him further. He lunged toward the closest man-thing intent on crushing his bones to dust.

A powerful binding spell penetrated his skin. With his feet now immobile, he crashed to the ground. Snorting and bellowing he tried desperately to free himself of the spell. The mages worked quickly to bind his body with spells of constriction.

~

Casting a spell that freed the ogre's legs, the mages herded him towards their camp. Many hours after the five of them had left camp, three returned, the subdued ogre roaring as sparks of magic drove him along.

Trannyth walked to the ogre where it sat against a tree, its body bound in renewed spells of constriction. The ogre watched him with loathing smoldering in its eyes.

"The ogre's hatred will serve us well," he said as he returned to the central fire. "Tomorrow." he looked around the gathered mages. "You will capture several of the banmora. I will use this ogre's life force to make my army."

Capturing twenty banmora proved a simple task. The animals, while large and strong, lacked intelligence. Trannyth stood watching them, his cruel mind quickly calculating the results of the experiments he would perform upon them.

The two-day journey to the promontory was smooth and without incident. The banmora herded together and were easily directed with only the odd spark from a following mage. The ogre however, continued to vociferate, his red-hot angry glare wilting all but Trannyth. Five mages were forced to follow behind and on either side of him, constantly prodding him in the right direction.

Continuously he fought to free himself from the constriction spells, making it necessary to stop every hour to renew them.

The caves near the promontory, formed eons ago by forgotten rivers, provided areas where Trannyth and his people could set up storerooms and create the unsavory workshops where the animals would be painfully transformed to make their army.

The ogre was placed in a small cave adjoining the main workshop. Strong ropes bound him to the wall, arms and legs outspread. He bellowed continually, eventually degenerating to low, sad moans. "Raug, kill man-things, gnaw their bones," he muttered to himself. The fire never left his eyes, hatred and malice burning out whenever a mage came into his view.

Trannyth set twenty of his mages to working on his Keep before starting his experiments with the beasts. Magically extracting a small part of the ogre's life force, he cast one of the spells he had so carefully studied and perfected during his self-imposed exile in Rilmir. The banmora, bound on a slab of rock, writhed and shrieked as the pain of being transformed triggered every nerve in its body.

The resulting beast was impressive in size. Its ogre head fearsome with sharp teeth and vicious curved tusks on either side of its jaws. However it was a stupid beast, when released it sat docile in the corner. When a mage attempted to approach it screamed before throwing him across the stony floor. Trannyth, in a fit of rage, threw a spell that killed it instantly.

Many days passed as he pondered the docile beast. The problem was obvious to him now. The ogre, while aggressive when attacked, was simple minded. The banmora, no more than a herding animal with no appreciable pattern of thought. The only way that he would be able to make an army of them was by imbuing some kind of mental ability.

As he watched his mages create the domed roof of the great hall of the Keep, he seized upon an idea. An orb infused with his own life force and will could, with a small adjustment to the transformation spell, tie a part of the beasts' life force into a vessel, giving them purpose, and he total control.

Carefully he melted some of the discarded bottles they had brought along, casting a spell at the glowing, molten mass of glass oozing from the pot. As the liquid cooled he gently grasped it and held it on his palm. His black heart sang as he looked at the perfect glass sphere. After searching his mind for days on end for a way he could use to infuse the orb, he ultimately cast a spell that instantaneously turned it translucent with blue mist curling lazily inside.

Gripping the orb, he strode into the workshop. "Prepare a banmora!" he commanded as he approached the ogre. The ogre bellowed at him, spittle flying from its gnashing teeth as it strained at its bonds. Trannyth laughed. "You had better get used to it my friend," he said as he pointed his staff at the ogre's chest and once more drew from its life force as it thrashed in pain.

Thoughtfully walking back into the workshop, Trannyth stood in front of the banmora, its hide flickering as its muscles twitched with fear. Raising his staff, he cast the spell. A spark jumped to the animal, it writhed in agony as the mist inside the orb swirled with excitement.

When the beast had settled, Trannyth commanded, "Release it." As a mage untied the restricting ropes the beast rose to its feet and stood calmly before him. He studied it for a short while. Standing seven feet tall, its thin and sinewy body half-ogre, half-animal. It showed obvious agility and strength. Pleased, he asked, "Do you understand me?"

The beast lowered its eyes to his and replied in a deep guttural voice, "Yes, My Lord."

Trannyth exulted, issuing instructions as he left the workshop, "Send for instructors to train them in battle. I want smiths here immediately. Set their shops up in the caves."

7 ONWARD

Tesania and Deavon walked at a steady pace along the road leading out of Lyiera Village. A farmer, seeing them coming, came to his gate and offered them some refreshments. "The wife makes the cider," he said. "This year's harvest was a good one."

"Mm," Tes delighted. "This is the same cider I had at the inn last night."

"So you stayed at the Boar's Head did you?" the farmer asked.

"Indeed," replied Deavon. "A very nice establishment."

"Aye, one of the better ones; in these parts anyway," replied the farmer. "Where're you folks headed?"

"We plan to make the hills today," answered Deavon. "Then on to Rilmir."

"I'd be on my guard if I were you," the farmer warned. "A traveler came through earlier this morning and said there was funny goings on in the hills. Said he came over them, the day before last. Said he'd travelled with a troop of soldiers looking for some kind of beasts," he informed.

Deavon inquired quickly, "Were the soldiers still with him?"

"No, just him. Said they stayed on at the foot of the hills to track those beasts of theirs." answered the farmer. "Well, I had better get back to it, before the wife sees me standing around gabbing and takes the broom to me," he chuckled to himself as he walked up the hill toward his worn old barn.

"Thank you for the cider," Tes called cheerfully after him.

"We'd better go," said Deavon worriedly. "I'd like to reach the hills well before sunset."

The road degraded to a track as they walked farther from the town and turned toward the Lyiera River. The river flowed slowly between the wide set banks. Winter flowers adorned the edges; white petals covering the land like snow. Tesania enjoyed watching the geese and ducks and counted the fish as they leapt from the water; the sun glistening brilliantly off their silver-scaled bellies before they flopped back in the river with a splash. Deavon, striding ahead, constantly had to call her to catch up.

"I'm not as travel hardened as you," she complained when he called her for the eighth time.

"That I can see," he laughed. "Or maybe you're too distracted?"

As the sun reached for its zenith, Deavon said, "Let's stop and have a little to eat."

Tesania gratefully agreed as she sank to the ground on a carpet of thick green grass at the very edge of the river. Shadows from an overhanging willow danced and played in the light breeze as its branches wistfully reached for the running water below.

Deavon tore some bread from a new loaf and then cut some cheese and a few portions of cured sausage. Handing some to Tes, he asked gently, "Did you see the beasts when they attacked your village? And how is it you alone survived?"

"Yes," Tes replied calmly as she rolled the piece of bread between her fingers. "Mother and I were on our way to see father in his smithy. A commotion broke out at the end of the street, people were running and screaming. About twenty beasts burst from the dust. I've never seen anything so ugly, they were hideous. People ran." She looked into his eyes. "My father rushed from his smithy, to see what the commotion was about, a beast charged toward us, he jumped in front of it." She shivered, turning her head to the river. "He wasn't a warrior, what could he do?" she looked back to Deavon, anger, tinged by sadness in her eyes. "It stabbed him! Right there! In the middle of the street! Then it slashed my mother across the throat!" As her anger subsided, she sat quietly looking down at her feet.

Deavon slowly tossed twigs from the willow into the water. Tesania eventually came back from her thoughts. "I screamed, the beast grabbed me by my hair. I managed to stab it in the eye with my cross," she said as she subconsciously brought her hand to her neck. "My father's apprentice tried to help me. The beast attacked him. I was going to help him." Her eyes searched Deavon's, pleading for him to understand. "He begged me to run," she said, gently feeling her cheek as she relived the beasts attack. "The beast had him by the throat. I didn't know what to do. So I ran! I couldn't face them!" Guilt played in her eyes, "I hid in the woods." Her head dropped now in shame. "Under some roots. They must have forgotten me, or didn't care. I lay there until dusk, too scared to move. When I returned to the village all the people were dead, the women, the children, they hadn't spared anyone. Except me."

Deavon gently placed his hand under her chin, slowly raising her face until her eyes meet his. "You too would be dead, if you hadn't run." He paused, looking for the right words to say. "Your parents had already fallen; the beasts would still have completed their mission. The only difference is you would now be dead too. There's no reason for you to be ashamed; you did as anyone in your position would do. Even I may have run in the same situation."

Tesania looked at the river again. She knew that he spoke the truth. Reaching for her sword, she looked back to him. Full of conviction, she said, "After you teach me the bow, I also wish to learn to use my sword." She ran her hand along the molding on the scabbard. "It has some kind of power," she said, looking up at him. "When I first drew the sword, it was like..," she paused, thinking as she looked away, "like, it was made for me. I could feel its energy running through my whole body. I want to be able to wield it, to harness its power!" Her eyes flicked back to his. "I must be prepared for when I hunt this Trannyth down."

Deavon had hoped she would forget her desire for revenge. He saw now a clarity and determination in her eyes that wouldn't be easily swayed from the obligation she had assumed. "May I?" he asked as he reached for her sword. "Trannyth will not be an easy target for you to reach. Do you realize the enormity of the task you have set yourself?" he gently asked.

"I do! My conviction hasn't changed from last night! If I don't avenge my parents, who will?" she questioned intensely.

Deavon studied the sword, drawing it a few inches to inspect the blade. He looked into the distance, in deep thought. Coming to a decision, he said, "You can accompany me to the King's City, if you so wish? There, I'll talk to my superiors and ask for their advice." As he passed her sword back, he said, "Hopefully the scholars may have some knowledge of this sword of yours."

Tes beamed at him. "I do wish to go to the King's City!" she said gratefully.

Deavon rose and walked to the water's edge to fill their water skins. "Finish your meal. We'd better move on."

Tesania watched him as she ate the last of her bread. She was glad that she'd decided to trust this man and was quickly growing to enjoy his company.

~

The remainder of the day passed slowly. They talked of Tesania's village and friends as they walked. The hills became visible as the afternoon wore on. "Are those the hills we're heading for?" Tes asked hopefully.

"They are," replied Deavon as he looked ahead. "We should be at a well used campsite in about an hour."

"Oh.., I shall be glad to rest; my feet are killing me," Tesania sighed thankfully. She looked at him sideways. "What about you? All we've talked about is me and my village. Where were you born? What made you decide to be a King's Ranger?"

Deavon smiled as he replied, "My Parents live just outside the town of Orash, on the fork of the Wyvern and Tarmikos Rivers. I was born the fourth of four brothers, with one sister born after me. We grew up on our family estate, doing our chores and gallivanting around the fields."

"Why didn't you stay there? It sounds lovely," Tes wondered.

"When I turned eighteen it was obvious that my older brothers would take over the farm when my father grew too old." He paused, remembering. "While I love my family, a life of farming under my brothers was not what I had in mind. One day, when I was in town picking up some supplies, a party of rangers recruiting for the King demonstrated their skills with the bow." He looked embarrassedly at her. "I guess their imposing presence impressed me. I was always keen to use my bow, hunting creatures in the woods. But the bows they carried.., I'd seen nothing like them before. They had a range of over six hundred feet." His fingers worked along his own rangers bow as he spoke. "A few months later I decided to leave the farm and head to Wyvern City where I joined the rangers." He looked at her as he continued, "I spent three years training in archery and combat before graduating. With honors, may I say," he added, winking at her. "Because my father's a lord, I was attached to the Elite King's Guard."

"You're a lord?" Tesania asked quickly, her eyes growing wide with disbelief.

"Is that so hard to believe?" he asked, feigning hurt. "Truth be told, I'm not. The title passes down through succession, so my older brother will become the lord of my father's estate when that time comes." He laughed as he saw disappointment flash across her face. "It has its advantages. I hold privileges in the Royal City that others do not."

"Like?" Tes asked.

"Like," he answered as a grin grew across his face. "As I've already said. I'm a member of the Elite King's Guard. I could only join them because I'm the son of a lord. Also, I can attend functions in the palace and it gives me an acceptance with the lords and ladies that grace the King's Court."

"Are you betrothed?" Tesania asked, a little too quickly.

Deavon laughed again. "No, I'm not betrothed. Some of the ladies have tried, but so far I've managed to avoid that situation."

Tes thought silently for a while. That word, ladies, scared her a little. "What are the ladies like in the King's Court?" she nervously asked. "I've heard they're beautiful. Are their dresses truly made from silk and other fine fabrics? Do they really wear lavish amounts of jewelry? Will I be allowed to talk with them? Would they even want to talk to a village girl like me?" Realizing she was gushing like a little girl, she stopped abruptly. Blushing, she looked away from him so he couldn't see her face.

Deavon thought for a few moments before answering her. Smiling at her, he said, "Yes, there are many beautiful ladies. Many though are wisps of things. They spend their days preening themselves, picking out dresses and gossiping with the other so called, ladies. Many have no real substance; they're only interested in their station. They'd betray their so-called friends in a second to gain a higher station in the court. You're right though," he said as he looked at Tes. "Their dresses and jewelry are exquisite. The unmarried ones float around the court trying to attract the attention of every available man. The higher his rank the more he's pursued."

He paused, thinking how to best continue. "They'll talk to you, if only to discover their new opposition. They despise competition, so you'll need to be on your guard. Don't get me wrong. There are many that are very nice and will befriend you given the chance. But I say again; be on your guard, always.

"And the Queen? Is she beautiful?"

"The Queen is an elegant beauty. Her dresses are made from the finest materials and she commands any room she enters." Again he paused, looking ahead. "I see smoke from a campfire up ahead. Don't worry about the ladies of the court. I have a friend who'll help you with dresses and such. For now, be quiet," he said, holding his finger to his lips.

The woods thickened as they neared the hills; Deavon motioned for Tes to follow him off the track and into the trees. "I'd rather see who our friends ahead are before we approach them. Follow me, quietly," he instructed as he pushed on into the woods, picking his way through the old trees.

Tesania carefully followed, mindful of her footfalls while trying to avoid making any noise. They could soon hear voices in the distance. Deavon whispered, "They sound human at least. Let's move on. Slowly." They crept onward as Deavon's eyes scanned the woods ahead.

"For a ranger you sure do make some noise, don't you?" questioned a sneering voice from behind them. Tes whirled around; Deavon followed, drawing his sword in the blink of eye. A woman leant against a tree some twenty feet from where they stood. She held a long sword in her right hand, the blade resting on her shoulder. Standing about five-foot-nine, she was muscled and lithe. Light brown hair flowed freely over her bare shoulders. A brown leather bodice topped her brown leather pants with calf high boots. Tes noticed a hunting knife and the sword's scabbard on a wide leather belt around her waist while a cape flowed down her back.

"What brings you to these woods?" Deavon asked, relaxing and sheathing his sword as he spoke. "Her captain must have posted her here as a sentry," he whispered to Tesania.

"You can ask the boss," the soldier said, pointing toward the smoke. Placing two fingers to her mouth, she gave a shrill whistle. "I wouldn't try to sneak up on them though, if I were you," she laughed.

They walked toward the fire. With no need to be quiet, Tes asked curiously, "Who was she?"

"She's a soldier of the King. An outer sentry I gather; for the troop that the farmer mentioned this morning," he replied. Looking at her sideways, he laughed. "I guess we'll have to work on our stealth."

The trees thinned at the edge of the clearing. Deavon called, "Well met!" A few of the soldiers in the encampment came toward them, hands on hilts; most ignored them.

"Well Met," one of them replied, holding his hand out to Deavon. "I'm Theris, captain of this sorry bunch," he smiled as he gave an expansive wave with his arm.

"I'm Deavon, and this is Tesania." Deavon motioned. "We wish to share your camp tonight, if that is all right by you?" he asked politely whilst looking around.

"A pleasure," replied Theris. "I'll be glad of some fresh company." He started to walk toward the centre of the camp, Tes and Deavon followed. "Grub will be on in a few minutes. Just stew I'm afraid."

"Stew sounds wonderful," Tesania hungrily replied. "I'm famished."

Theris laughed heartily. "The cook will be glad to hear that."

Deavon and Tesania were directed to where the sleeping area was arranged. Tes happily took the pack from her back, dropping it on the ground. Taking the sword from her shoulder, she placed it under the pack. Deavon watched her. "We'll have to ask Theris if he has a spare utility belt for you to attach that to. It'll be much easier for you to carry, and importantly, draw if required."

Tesania nodded as she walked to a water skin tied to a tree. Gratefully she washed her face, neck and arms. Feeling refreshed, she turned to Deavon. "Let's see about some food."

They each took a beaten metal plate from a log near the fire, filling it from the large pot of stew beside the embers. A man approached, Tes assumed him to be the cook, and handed them some dry, hard bread. "Thank you," said Deavon. Tesania nodded with a smile.

Deavon rose after finishing his meal and excused himself. "I'd like a word with the captain. I'll be back shortly."

Tes nodded as he left and then scanned the encampment. She counted twenty eight soldiers. Some played dice, others sat in small groups talking quietly whilst they cleaned and polished their weapons. She watched as a woman walked toward her. Recognizing her as the one who had stopped them earlier in the woods, she groaned. The woman sat down, right next to her. Reaching over to the pot she filled her plate with stew.

"Giddy's my name," she said, rubbing her hand on her trousers before holding it out to Tesania.

"Tesania," Tes replied, a little peevishly as she reluctantly took it.

Giddy's grip was less than gentle as they shook hands. "That your boyfriend?" she asked, gesturing toward Deavon with her chin.

"No! We're just travelling together," Tesania replied defensively, feeling the blush beginning to rise up her face.

Giddy attacked her stew as if it were an opponent in a duel. Tes looked away. Her gaze fell on Deavon as he continued to talk to the captain. *I wonder what they're talking about?* she thought.

Giddy, watching Tesania closely, asked, "So if you're not with him, do you think I have a chance?"

"No! I do not!" Tes flared as she stood. Turning, she stormed toward the sleeping area. Giddy roared with laughter as she fell backwards off the log.

~

Deavon talked with Theris for many hours about the happenings in Eldanal. Finally, he asked about the troop and their mission.

"We were dispatched from Rilmir Barracks to investigate rumors of attacks by beasts." Theris said. "We found some bodies, but no sign of the beasts. We crossed to this side of the hills hoping to find them here, to no avail. The hills are thickly wooded so we assume they're either a small band that hid away as we passed through, or a large band that's moved on."

"So you feel they may still be in the hills?" Deavon asked worriedly; thinking that he and Tes would have to pass over them the next day.

"Don't know," Theris shrugged. "They could be. If they're a small band they wouldn't attack a troop this size anyway."

"No, but they may attack Tes and I! We'll need to be on our guard," said Deavon earnestly.

"We'll be returning to Rilmir in a week. You could wait and cross with us?" offered Theris.

"Too long I'm afraid," replied Deavon. "I need to get to the King as quickly as possible." Yawning, he said, "I might turn in now. Thank you for your hospitality."

"A pleasure," replied Theris. "Good night." He sat thinking as he watched Deavon disappear into the night.

8 TAKEN BY STEALTH

The ranger, Aldan, sat among the thick tendrils of a massive choker vine; his view of the mountain path uninterrupted. Turning his head he looked down the track. Satisfied that his two partners were well hidden from sight he returned his gaze to the path.

Three days had passed while they waited; hoping one of Trannyth's mages would attempt to cross back to the Orash side of the mountains. Arriving at dawn, they waited till dusk, withdrawing each evening to their horses and camp some three miles back.

Pain shot through his leg as a cramp contracted his muscles. Conscious of not betraying their trap, he pulled silently at the top of his foot until the discomfort eased.

His thoughts turned to the previous day when seven beasts had rumbled past their positions; their leader driving them on with guttural curses. He shuddered as he remembered the size of them and the vicious looking swords they carried.

Ignoring the beasts, they had maintained their cover. The task set him was to capture at least one mage and return them to Wyvern City without delay; not to take on an army of the beasts. His mind wandered, dreaming of a tankard of ale in one hand with a busty wench in the other. Lost in his own thoughts, he almost missed the first sounds of approach on the track.

Whipping his hand up in signal to the other two, his attention snapped back to the task at hand. Watching as two mages wandered lethargically toward him, he adjusted his position, nerves jangling as he prepared to take them. They had planned an ambush, mindful of not doing battle with mages that may be stronger than they could handle.

Aldan sat quietly, watching as they passed. Satisfied that they suspected nothing and were paying little attention to their surroundings he gave a signal that sprung the trap. Two burly rangers hurtled from their positions close to the track, tackling the two mages to the ground before they had a chance to react.

Aldan sprung from his hiding place, arrow nocked and drawn. He relaxed. The mages, taken completely by surprise, lay flat on their faces; struggling in vain as their hands were being securely trussed.

"What do we have here?" he asked as he kicked the closest mage onto her back. "A brace of pigeons?"

The mage sneered at him and spat before hurling abuse at all three of her captors.

Aldan laughed. "Gag them," he said. "I don't want to listen to that all the way home."

When the mages refused to rise to their feet, Aldan seized the girl's hair and lifted her bodily off the ground. Screaming, she struggled indignantly to free herself as he drew her face close to his. "Do as you are told," he growled as he pulled her head back and dug the point of his knife into her throat, "and you won't get hurt." He laughed as he looked into her fear filled eyes and thrust her forward, down the track. "I hope we'll have no problems from you?" he asked ominously to the other mage as he rose from the ground.

Yelping through his gag, the mage rushed past him. "Get their staffs and make sure they're always securely bound," he ordered as he sheathed his knife. "I don't want any nasty little surprises in the middle of the night."

People stared when they marched the two captive mages into the town of Orash. Re-provisioned, they rode continuously for days. Aldan was keen to rid himself of his captives, the girl especially as she streamed abuse and expletives every time her gag was removed.

The Wyvern City gates came into view at dusk on the fourth day. Aldan gratefully handed his prisoners to the guards. "I'm sure you'll enjoy your stay," he cruelly laughed, patting the girl's head as she passed.

9 INTO THE HILLS

Tesania awoke in the early morning sunshine. Dreams of beasts charging toward her with swords raised had ensured a restless night's sleep. Rolling over, she saw that Deavon's things had already been bundled into his pack; she wondered where he could be.

Rising, she washed her face and arms thoroughly before pulling a comb through her hair. With everything carefully packed away, she headed to the fire.

Gratefully she accepted a plate of gruel as she sat down. She thought it plain, but slowly ate it with a rough wooden spoon. The campsite was a hive of activity. It appeared the soldiers were preparing to leave.

Deavon walked toward her, Theris by his side. The horrible woman from the night before followed closely behind them. *What's she doing with them?* Tes thought sourly.

"Good morning, Tes," called Theris as they approached. "I trust you had a good night's sleep?"

"Yes, thank you," replied Tes with a tired smile. "Although I was a bit restless." She looked at Deavon before saying, "Bad dreams." Giddy stood to the left of them; Tes made a point of looking the other way.

"We'll be leaving shortly, as soon as you've finished your breakfast," Deavon advised her. "The Captain has asked Giddy here," he said pointing, "to report the troop's movements to the generals. She'll be accompanying us across the hills and onto Rilmir City."

"No!" groaned Tes. "Why her?"

Giddy smiled. Deavon stared at her, shocked. Theris abruptly said, "Take care! Giddy's a fine soldier. In fact, if I had to choose one of these people to go into battle with it would be her!"

"Oh," said Tes as she looked down to her feet. "Sorry. I didn't mean to be rude."

Giddy laughed. "Yes you did," she provoked as she held out a spare utility belt. "But that's ok, kid. I don't mind."

Tesania's head jerked up as she glared into Giddy's eyes. "I am not a kid!" Snatching the belt she turned and stalked away.

Theris turned to Giddy. "Settle it down. She's just a girl."

"Just having fun, boss," she replied with a twinkle in her eye.

Deavon shook his head, wondering as he walked to his pack if Tes was right about the soldier.

The soldiers gathered around, wishing them a brief farewell as the group of three moved into the hills. Giddy took the lead, Tes following with Deavon at the rear.

The path into the hills snaked its way between boulders and trees. The well travelled ground allowed an easy ascent; still the uphill climb soon took a toll on Tes' untrained legs. Giddy eventually started to outpace them, leaving Tes and Deavon languishing behind.

"Giddy, stay together! We don't know what's in these hills," Deavon called. "Tes, let's have a small rest."

"The girl's too slow," Giddy complained as she slowly retraced her steps.

"I'm not a mountain goat like you!" Tes shot back at her.

"All the same, let's stay together," Deavon interrupted.

He shared out some dried fruit as they sat. Tes sipped some water, groaning when Deavon suggested they move on.

Glaring at Giddy's back, Tes was not at all happy. She could see that the soldier was well trained and fit, just by looking at her. That didn't stop her wishing that any other member of the troop was with them instead.

Giddy slowed and kept to Tes' pace as the climb became steeper. Tes labored on, breathing hard and wishing she was somewhere else. The path came to a dead end at the foot of a boulder. Giddy clambered up with ease. Turning, she knelt and reached her hand down to help Tesania.

Tes stared at it, refusing to take it. Confused by the offer from the otherwise unpleasant woman, she looked to Deavon.

He nodded his head toward Giddy's hand. "Take it," he gently said.

Reaching out slowly, as if she were about to touch a snake, Tes took the offered hand. Giddy pulled her up effortlessly, Deavon scrambling up behind. Tes smiled half-heartedly at Giddy, still wary. "Thank you," she said quietly.

"We'd be here all day otherwise," Giddy replied with a crooked smile as she turned and continued up the path.

Tes looked sideways at Deavon. He returned a half smile. "Let's go," he said.

The hours passed slowly; Tes grew wearier and slowed considerably more. Giddy, surprisingly, slowed her pace to stay with her. Tes waited for the remarks, but they never came.

"Let's stop here for a while," Deavon suggested as they came to a small clearing at the crest of the hills. A break in the trees offered a spectacular view of the plains on the Rilmir side, with the Lyiera River winding its way into the distance. Tes felt a hollow feeling in her stomach as she imagined how far they still had to go.

Giddy lay on the ground, propped on one elbow, seemingly without a care. Tes took some bread and cheese from her pack, using her father's knife to cut a few slices from each.

Giddy watched her. "Here, try some of this," she said tossing Tes a small piece of dried meat. "It's beef jerky, favored by all discerning soldiers of the king," she laughed as she ripped a piece in two with her teeth.

Tes smelt the offering dubiously; surprised that it wasn't unpleasant she took a small bite. Tangy flavor assaulted her tongue. Swallowing, she quickly ate the remaining piece.

"Apparently they marinate it first and then smoke it with hickory bark. Not bad is it?" asked Giddy.

"It was nice," Tes replied guardedly. She looked away, not wanting to engage her in conversation.

Giddy turned her attention to Deavon. "What're your plans for today?" she asked.

"I want to clear these hills. If we can make the camp on the Rilmir side I'll be happy," he replied.

"You'll have to pick your pace up, won't you, sweetheart?" Giddy suggested as she turned to Tes once more. Smiling, she said, "Don't worry, it's all downhill from here."

Tes didn't answer, rolling her eyes as she looked toward Deavon. "Can we make it today?" she asked.

"I can't see why not. As Giddy says, the going is easier on the Rilmir side," he answered. "Rest a little while longer." Turning back to Giddy, he asked, "Where are you from?"

"I grew up in the village of Estom," Giddy replied.

"A nice little village," Deavon smiled. "What made you become a soldier?" he asked curiously.

"A small village and I don't mix too well, so I left and joined the Army," she shrugged. "Don't regret it either, not for one minute. Fresh air, travel and all the jerky I can eat," she laughed as she tossed the last piece into her mouth.

Deavon laughed, Tes could only raise a weak smile. "Come on," he said. "Let's get out of these hills."

The path down the hills was far less steep than the other side. It wound lazily through the growth and Tes found the walking much easier. Finding she could easily keep up with Giddy, she started to enjoy the day. The sun shone brightly, birds chattered in the trees, an eagle voicing an occasional call to its mate as it soared in the blue sky above them. She hummed a tune, a song her father used to sing to her, stopping abruptly when Giddy began to hum along.

Hours passed by; the path leveled slightly, making their headway easier still. The woods seemed to draw in on them. It was only a matter of a few hundred yards before it opened out again. Tes turned a worried look at Deavon. "The birds have gone quiet," she said. "And my sword is vibrating."

Deavon looked around the woods. "Giddy, keep…" He didn't get a chance to finish the sentence as Giddy froze in mid stride. Her hand flew to the hilt of her sword, her other snapping up over her shoulder, warning them to wait. Slowly she drew her sword and made her way back to them, moving backward, step by step.

Looking from Tes to Deavon, she emphatically motioning them to keep their voices down, whispering, "I think there's something up ahead, hidden in the woods." she pointed. "It could be an animal. Best we be sure."

"It could also be beasts!" whispered Deavon urgently.

Tes swung her head to look at him, shock written distinctly on her face. "Beasts? Here? How do you know?"

Deavon smiled weakly. "It stood to reason that the beasts Giddy and her friends were hunting may still be in these hills. That's the main reason Theris sent her with us; to help me protect you." He looked into her eyes guiltily. "Forgive me for not telling you earlier. I had hoped this situation wouldn't come to pass and I didn't want you to worry."

"You didn't want me to worry!" Tes gasped. "There may be beasts ahead of us.., and you!" She looked him up and down, hurt in her eyes. "you think it best not to tell me! When would have been best? Hmm? When they had a blade to my throat!"

"It wasn't like that," he whispered back.

"Can you two have your little tiff later? I think we have more pressing problems at hand," Giddy whispered urgently as she kept a watch down the path.

Deavon shook his head. "I'm sorry, Tes," he said as he took charge once more. "Draw your sword," he instructed. As she started to protest, he said, "I know you have no training, but an untrained sword can still be of use. Giddy, we have to go through, or return to the Lyiera side. Either way, if those are the beasts they'll attack us." He freed his sword, checking that it was ready to draw before positioning his quiver and nocking an arrow to his bow.

Giddy stood comfortably; a gleam in her eyes. Deavon stood deep in thought. Tes shook; she'd faced these beasts and knew what they could do. Drawing her sword, it hummed as before, glowing as she held it in her hand. Lifting it into the air, she gasped. Fire flickered excitedly inside the sword, like a reflection in a mirror, along the length of its polished silver blade. Tes stood mesmerized; the familiar feeling of power coursing through her as it had in her father's bedroom only a few short days ago.

"That's some sword, sweetheart." Giddy whispered as she turned her own in her hand. "Mine feels like a piece of tin now." She winked as she looked up at Tes who returned a worried smile.

Deavon interrupted them. "Stay together and move slowly. Giddy, you're still in the lead. Tes, this time I want you at the rear." He looked seriously at both of them. "It's more than likely there are beasts on the path ahead; are you ready?"

Giddy adjusted her grip on her sword before replying nonchalantly, "Always ready."

Tes swallowed deeply, she wasn't at all ready to face the beasts again. She looked from Giddy to Deavon, fear radiating in her eyes.

"We don't have a real choice," Deavon said to her quietly. "You want to avenge your parents. This is the path we must follow to achieve it."

Tes stared at him. "You haven't seen what they can do. I have, remember!"

"Your parents were killed by beasts?" Giddy asked, appalled.

"Her whole village, a few days ago," replied Deavon. "Now isn't the time. We can discuss it once we clear these hills."

"If we clear them," Tes said gravely.

Giddy placed a hand gently on Tes' shoulder. "Deavon and I will make sure you get to Wyvern City. A few beasts won't stop us, will they?" she asked as she looked at Deavon.

Deavon shook his head. "No; no they won't."

Tesania knew it was all bravado. Giddy had no idea of what they were about to face. She tried to smile as she looked up at her. "I'm sure the beasts will panic and run when they see a big goat like you coming down the hill at them."

"That's the spirit!" Giddy grinned. Looking to Deavon, she said, "No use hanging around here, we've got beasts to kill. Let's go!"

Moving off slowly, Giddy's eyes took in every part of the woods. Deavon followed, his bow at the ready, his eyes also scanning ahead.

Tes took up the rear, her attention taken by her sword. She carried it out in front of her, the fire flickering in the blade. She thought it curious that the flames slowly grew brighter and more agitated whilst its hum grew more distinct. The flames grew to a crescendo as they crept down the path; she wondered what it could mean.

The track opened out into a small clearing as she continued to ponder the sword; the hum lessening as the flames slowly diminished. In a flash it came to her; the sword is warning of danger, the closer the danger the more agitated the sword. If it's fading then that means. "They're behind us!" she called urgently as she spun around.

Four beasts exploded from the foliage of the trees, not ten feet from where Tes stood. Deavon's arrow passed her ear by a matter of inches, a beast fell, dead, the arrow protruding from its eye. The three remaining beasts bellowed as they plunged down the hill.

Giddy charged past Tes, sword raised, meeting the blow of the first beast and turning it aside. The beast adjusted quickly and slashed at her, she ducked, just in time as the sword whistled harmlessly over her head. Upright again in an instant she lunged at its chest; the beast easily blocked her. The second beast was upon her as she pulled her hunting knife whilst fending away another blow.

Deavon grabbed Tes by the shoulder. "Run!" he yelled as he surged past her, sword in hand. He parried a blow from the third beast as it attacked Giddy's back. Tes stood frozen, in shock she just stared. "Go!" roared Deavon. "You can't help us here!"

Tes turned and fled, running as fast as she could. Tears came to her eyes as she left her new friends to be slain by the beasts. As thoughts of her village raced through her head, her parents, little Liale, dead in the street, she slid to a stop. "I ran from them at the village! I won't run from them again!" she uttered through clenched teeth as she turned, her sword flaring as she charged back to the fight.

Deavon and Giddy were pitched in battle with the beasts. Giddy had a gash across her right arm, blood oozing from a wound on her side. She fought like a demon; her sword and knife meeting blow after blow from the beasts. Deavon, with blood running from numerous wounds on his arms and body, had moved to her back, he fought with speed and accuracy, the beast though was an even match. They fought bravely, but the beasts, with their superior number and strength were slowly gaining the upper hand.

"You killed my mother!" Tes screamed with fury as she slashed the nearest beast across the back of its knees. With severed tendons it crashed to the ground, its high pitched shriek reverberating through the woods. Tes, with the ease of an experienced warrior twirled the sword in her hand and with the blade pointing toward the beast's throat she drove it down with all her weight and anger. The beast's blood gushed as the sword tore through its arteries, soaking the grassy ground. Tes looked into its eyes as it gave a last guttural moan. "And my father," she said in a scarcely audible whisper.

Adrenaline pumping, she turned her attention to the beast on Deavon. The beast, sensing its danger, changed its focus to her. She parried and feinted, sidestepping nimbly, their blades flashing and ringing as they met, time and again. The beast, on the defensive, backed away. Finally it could go no farther, its back against a giant oak tree.

Giddy's beast was struggling. With only one opponent she started to slip through its defenses. Blood ran down its chest from multiple wounds. The beast spun in an instant and hurtled down the track. Giddy flew after it in hot pursuit.

"No!" yelled Deavon. "Giddy! Stay together!"

Giddy paid no attention as she disappeared around a bend in the track, issuing an exultant cry as she ran.

Deavon turned back to the beast. Taking his chance as it raised its arm to parry a blow from Tes, he slid his sword between two ribs. The beast roared with pain, its heart pierced, it quickly died as it slumped to the ground. Tesania sucked in deep breaths as she stood staring at the beast, her body now tired and shaking. She looked at Deavon. "We killed them," she said in a quivering voice.

"Yes! But we still have Giddy to worry about, come on!" Deavon urgently grabbed her arm and started down the track.

They moved quickly but there was no sign of Giddy. Against Deavon's advice Tes yelled Giddy's name. As she became increasingly upset she called more often with her voice rising to a scream. They saw no signs that the beast and Giddy may have stopped and once again battled. Eventually, they came out of the hills. Tesania turned, saying, "We have to go back and find her."

Deavon held out his arm, restraining her. "There's nothing we can do for her now She would have answered if she could. It's nearly dark and we don't want to be in the hills overnight, especially if that beast is still alive."

"You think she's dead?" Tes asked, looking at him in shock and disbelief.

"I didn't say that. Giddy's an experienced warrior; she may still be alive," he replied calmly.

"Then I'm going to look for her! She could be injured!" Tes said fretfully, renewing her efforts to climb back into the hills.

"Tesania!" Deavon said in a commanding voice. "You will not go back into those hills tonight! Do you understand me?"

Tes' shoulders slumped. "We can't just leave her up there!" she said sadly, a tear running down her cheek.

"Giddy made her decision when she charged after that beast. She should have stayed with us," he insisted. "If I could help her I would. Right now I have to ensure our safety. So tonight we camp in the campsite near the river. One of us will have to be on guard throughout the night." He looked at the hills over his shoulder. "That beast may wish to avenge its brethren."

"So you do think she's dead!" Tes said weakly, Giddy's loss and her own tiredness starting to overtake her.

"Come on, the cold will be in soon. Let's get to the campsite, light a warm fire and have something to eat," he said as he guided her by the elbow.

Tes walked limply, lost in thought as they travelled the short distance to the campsite. The day's events were crashing in on her; visions of the beast's dying eyes, blood spurting from ruptured arteries, her sword humming gleefully as it guided her hand in battle. It was all too much for her tired mind. She wanted to forget, to sleep and never wake up. Walking numbly into the campsite she sat on a log. Deavon started a fire and soon had some water from the river boiling. He made herb tea, passing a mug to Tes as he gently said, "It's not your fault."

"It's funny," Tes whispered sadly. "This morning I couldn't have cared what happened to Giddy." She looked into Deavon's eyes. "And now that I do care." tears started to roll once more down her cheeks. "She's gone!"

Deavon sat quietly, not really knowing what to say. Turning his head to Tes, he said quietly, "Many more good people will be lost before Trannyth and his beasts are halted."

They sat in long silence as they drank their tea. Deavon eventually rose and fried some slices of sausage in a pan taken from his pack. Tes declined to eat any, preferring to suck on one of her sweets. "What now?" she asked as she stared hollowly into the flickering fire.

Deavon watched her face in the firelight. "Why don't you have a wash and get changed," he said as he stood and picked up her discarded sword. "I'll clean the weapons whilst you do."

Tes rose, her aching muscles protesting as she retrieved her pack and removed a fresh dress, her mother's cloak, some homemade soap and her hairbrush.

The full moon cast a soft glowing light on the river. Tes moved slightly downstream, conscious of Deavon being not far away. Sitting on the bank, her feet submerged in the startlingly cool water, she watched her moonlit silhouette dance amongst the ripples. Rising, she let her dress slip from her shoulders and then forced herself to walk into the icy water until she was waist deep. She scrubbed at her hands and arms, her soft, young skin goose-bumping as she contemplated dipping fully into the water. Reaching up, she felt her dirty hair and made the decision. Before she could change her mind she quickly descended, the coldness drawing her breath as the water passed her shoulders causing her to pause slightly before continuing under.

Broaching the surface of the water; she strained to take in a deep breath as the coldness bit at every nerve in her body. To help herself settle to the frigid water she swam a short distance in a gentle breast stroke fashion. After a few minutes she returned to the shallows and washed her hair before walking back to the bank. Decided the cool night breeze on her wet skin was far worse than the freezing water she quickly dressed and brushed her hair before returning to the fire.

Deavon's eyes followed her as she approached. "Cold?" he smiled.

"Very," replied Tes. "But refreshing. I wouldn't want to go in later in the night. I'd freeze to death." As she said the last word she fell quiet; sitting again near the fire she held her hands to the comforting warmth of the flames.

"I'm going freshen up also," Deavon said as he walked toward the river. "Keep a sharp ear out for anything approaching."

Tes leant her head against her clasped hands as she watched him go. *He's a brave man,* she thought to herself as she looked back to the fire. *He put his life on the line for me and he's cut and hurt.* She realized she'd been self absorbed; all she had been thinking about was Giddy and her own concerns. Picking some cloth out of her bag, she tore it in strips, boiling them in the pot of water.

When Deavon returned from the river Tes insisted he sit and let her tend his wounds. He protested briefly before removing his shirt and submitting to her ministrations.

Running her hand over his biceps, she found the cuts; swabbing them and then patting them dry before moving onto his torso. Gently she ran her fingers over the wounds on his chest, exploring, before moving down to a cut on his toned stomach and bathing it gently.

Deavon watched her as she worked. "Tesania," he said softly.

Tes' head jerked up as she heard a shrill whistle, her eyes whipping to Deavon as she rose. "Giddy!" She started to run. "It must be her!"

Giddy materialized from the moonlit woods as Tes ran toward her. She winced as Tes, with arms outstretched, threw herself against her.

"Giddy!" Tes exclaimed. "You're alive."

"You didn't think a mere beast could kill this old goat did you?" Giddy asked in obvious pain.

"You're hurt!" said Tes worriedly as she released the soldier. "Come to the fire."

Deavon stood aside as they returned. "Well met," he said to Giddy with a nod.

"Well met," replied Giddy with an exhausted smile.

Tesania sent Giddy to bathe at the river. When she returned she tended her wounds, the worst being the cut in her side. Tes then searched Giddy's pack, finding a plain-woven dress, she handed it to her, insisting that she wear it. Giddy was far from comfortable as Tes started to plait her hair, but decided to let the girl have her way.

"What do you know," said Tes playfully when she'd finished. "The goat is actually beautiful! Isn't she Deavon?"

Deavon's eyes flicked from Giddy to Tes. "Very," he said before looking quickly away.

Giddy looked from Deavon to Tes then back to Deavon again. "Why, thank you kind sir," she said, smiling.

Deavon shifted uncomfortable. "Tell me. Why did you leave us in the hills?" he asked.

Giddy looked sheepishly at him as she answered, "I know I should've stayed with you." Her eyes moved to the fire. "I was caught up in the battle." She paused, looking back to Deavon. "Guess I just wanted to kill the beast," she finished, shrugging her shoulders.

Deavon nodded his head. "And? Did you?" he asked.

Giddy smiled. "I'm here, it's not," she replied brazenly.

"Come on Giddy, tell us what happened?" pushed Tes impatiently.

"Ok, ok, I will," Giddy laughed. "When the beast ran, I followed. It ran for a few hundred yards or so down the track then veered suddenly into the woods." She looked from Deavon to Tes. "I followed, chasing for a long time, it was all I could do to keep it in sight. We ducked tree branches, jumped rocks and scrambled over boulders. Eventually it tripped and stumbled, slamming into a tree." Adjusting her position, she continued, "It was on its feet in a flash, spinning around to meet my sword just as I was about to plunge it into its back." Her hand moved in unison with her words as she relived the fight. "The beast thrust, I parried, it went on for what seemed like minutes." Pausing, she shook her head before continuing, "Those beasts can fight, I'll give them that." She smiled at Tes. "Ugly though, aren't they?" She threw her hand to her wrinkled nose. "And they smell!" she laughed. "Anyway," she said as she started back on her story. "Finally I drew its measure, wounding it a few times. It grew more and more enraged, losing its discipline as it started to slash and thrust recklessly. I drew back, waiting for my chance. When I went to a high guard, it charged. I sidestepped, slitting its throat on the pass."

Pausing for a long while, she stared at the fire as she relived the last moments of the fight. After a short time, she continued, "When it was done I was exhausted. I sat for a while against a tree and rested. Eventually I found my way back to the track and then to you."

"I called you. All the way down!" Tes accused. "Why didn't you answer?"

"Didn't hear you," Giddy shrugged. "Maybe I was in the fight when you passed or too far from the track. Don't know."

Deavon listened to Giddy's story. "Sounds like it was a tough fight. Next time though, stay together!" he said seriously.

"Yes boss," Giddy saluted. "At least we don't have to worry about it sneaking up on us in the night," she said as she winked at Tes.

"I'll take the first watch tonight. You two get some sleep," suggested Deavon. "Tomorrow, we'll remain here. After today I think we've earned a rest."

10 BATTERED AND WORN

Tesania awoke early, the weariness of the previous evening having drained from her body. Humming, she cheerfully strolled to the river for fresh water, watching as two stately swans gracefully glided toward the far bank. She thought it a glorious morning. The sun warmed the earth whilst a light breeze gently swayed the trees. Frogs vocalized along the river in a croaky, uncoordinated song, whilst a flock of birds circled above. Kneeling at the river's edge, Tes looked at her reflection. She thought she looked somehow, older. Gone was the girl who helped her mother cook and clean in their small village home. She looked now at a face that had suffered loss, seen battle, drawn blood and knew death. Reaching down, she touched her watery cheek causing her image to flee on the ripples.

~

Deavon awoke a short time after, groaning as he pried himself from his blankets. His wounds and bruised muscles sent intense messages to his brain as he walked past the fire. He had remained awake for a good part of the night, deciding to let Tes sleep through before waking Giddy in the early morning for her turn at watch. His gaze fell on Tes at the river.

"Pretty isn't she?" Giddy asked as she walked up behind him.

Deavon didn't answer for some time. Eventually, he said, "She's very young."

"I think she ceased being young yesterday; when she slipped that sword into the beast's throat," she said with an insightful smile. "What do you know of that sword of hers anyway?"

Deavon shook his head as he looked at Giddy. "Not a lot. Apparently it's been passed down through her family, but that's all she knows. It's obviously very old, but even so, the blade is still keen. I don't doubt that it's been magically enhanced after yesterday, it was plain to see. I'm hoping the mages in Wyvern City may know something of it. I guess we shall see."

~

Tes walked toward them as he finished. "Good morning," she called cheerfully. "I'm making tea if you want some?" she offered as she stoked the embers while adding more wood.

"Good morning, Tes. "I'd love some tea," replied Giddy. "How do you feel this morning?"

"I feel fine," Tes smiled. "You?"

"Sore," laughed Giddy. "But I'll live."

They ate a simple breakfast of bread which Deavon toasted on the glowing coals of the fire, and cheese. As the morning wore on Tes sorted her soiled clothes and headed to the river to launder them. Deavon ranged out to collect wood for the fire. Giddy cleaned her weapons and armor before joining Tes by the river.

Tes tried her best but couldn't remove the bloodstains from the dress she had worn the previous day; she was however managing to make them fade.

Giddy watched the soap bubbles drifting lazily down river. "So, what happened at your village, can I ask?" she inquired, looking at Tes.

"You can," replied Tes as she stopped washing and looked thoughtfully across the water. When she'd retold the tale of the massacre she went back to scrubbing her stained dress.

"And you met Deavon in the woods outside your village?" Giddy questioned.

Tes didn't look up this time. Continuing to scrub, she replied, "Yes, It was a lucky meeting, I suppose." She looked at Giddy. "He's going to help me kill Trannyth."

Giddy sat up quickly. "You're going after Trannyth?" she asked with eagerness igniting in her eyes. She looked away at the river for a few seconds before looking back at Tes. "Sounds like fun! I'm in! If you want me?"

"If she wants you to what?" asked Deavon as he approached from the camp.

"Help kill Trannyth!" Giddy replied as she looked up at Deavon. "I'm coming with you!" She looked from Deavon to Tes. "Can I?" She paused before adding keenly, "You'll need my sword! I can help you get across the mountains!"

Before Tes could reply, Deavon said, "I can't see the King, or his advisor's, letting either me, or you," he said gesturing to Giddy, "go on an ill advised quest over the mountains. Or to take on a well protected mage." He paused looking at Tes. "Especially one the caliber of Trannyth!"

Tes looked at him incredulously. "You said you'd help me!" she erupted, confusion in her eyes.

"I said! I would talk to my superiors and ask for their advice. Never did I say I would accompany you on a suicide mission to Trannyth's Keep!" Deavon said angrily. Looking from Tes to Giddy, he turned and stalked away.

"My offer still stands; I'll hunt Trannyth with you," said Giddy with a mischievous smile.

Tesania ignored her as she picked up her washing and walked away.

As Tes hung her clothes, Deavon approached. "Would you like to start learning to use a bow?" he asked tentatively. Tes was still angry from his earlier remarks but sullenly agreed. Giddy set up a target on a nearby tree, then sat aside to watch. Deavon handed his bow and an arm guard to Tes. "Now remember, this bow is made and adjusted to suit me, you won't be able to draw it fully, so don't try." He handed her an arrow and showed her how to take her stance. "Now place the nock of the arrow over the bowstring, that's it. Rest the shaft on the arrow rest," he said pointing to the small projection on the bow. "Ok, now draw it back as far as you can."

Tes pulled with all her strength but couldn't draw it near as far as she had seen Deavon do.

"That's far enough," he said. "Now, use the bow sight to aim at the target, good. Don't forget to hang onto the bow," he said with a smile. "Let it fly when you're ready."

Tes strained as she held the draw, she found the target and positioned it dead centre of the sight. Twang, she let go, the arrow flew, it performed a somersault then flopped to the ground four feet in front of her. Giddy roared with laughter, Deavon put his hand to his face to hide his grin. Tes turned slowly, fixing Giddy with a glare. "Show me how you do it then!" she said, holding the bow out in front of her.

"Ok," said Giddy rising and taking the bow. Picking up Tes' arrow, she nocked it to the bow. Drawing it, she quickly aimed and let the arrow fly. It flashed through the air, hitting a tree, four feet higher and six feet wide of the target. It was Tesania's turn to laugh, Giddy joined in, falling to the ground and shaking with laughter. Deavon shook his head as he picked up his bow. "I can see why you're so good with your sword," he teased Giddy. "You'd never survive with a bow," he laughed.

Tes practiced for half an hour. When her weary arms couldn't draw the bow any longer she asked if they could stop and rest. Deavon took his bow and went hunting; Giddy produced a hook and line from her pack and headed toward the river. Tes cleared the camp before setting off in search of mushrooms and herbs.

When she returned to the campsite the others still weren't back. She must have dozed, as the next thing that she knew Giddy had returned with three small fish. "How do these look for our midday meal?" Giddy proudly asked.

"Tasty," said Tes. "I love fish." She stoked the fire and warmed Deavon's pan before adding the fish. Humming lightly, she tossed in some of her herbs; the heady aromas drifted along the breeze.

Deavon arrived, drawn in by the delicious smells; he carried a plump fowl. "Our dinner," he said as he hung it on a branch. Rubbing his stomach, he sat down and accepted a plate of fish. "Smells good" he said as he looked at Tes.

"Giddy caught them, I only collected the herbs," Tes smiled.

They ate in silence, enjoying the change from dried meats and stew. When they'd finished, Giddy turned to Tes. "Would you like to duel with me a little?" she asked eagerly.

Tes stared at her, eyes wide open. "With swords?" she asked.

"Only training, I won't hurt you," Giddy laughed. "Although after what I saw yesterday it's me who should be worried."

"Ok," Tes replied nervously. "But I have no training at all, what happened yesterday was all the doing of the sword."

"We shall see?" said Giddy as she stood to retrieve her weapons.

Deavon agreed to act as the referee. "Go easy on her Tes," he laughed. Giddy pierced him with a sneering glare.

Tes stood with her sword held out front, the blade showed no sign of life, it didn't even hum. She wondered if she could fight Giddy without its help as she nodded to Deavon when he asked if they were ready.

"Fight!" he said.

As she fended the first soft blow from Giddy her sword burst into life. It hummed; its fire flaring along the blade excitedly. Tes felt the magic flow through her as she looked at Giddy. Instinctively she attacked. Giddy defended with all her strength and ability, lucky to keep Tes' blows out.

"Stop!" roared Deavon after a flurry of blows had driven Giddy back five paces.

Tes reluctantly lowered her sword, battle lust coursed through her veins as she stood drawing deep breaths.

"Can you just defend?" asked Deavon. "Or does the sword encourage you to always attack?"

Tes had wondered the same thing. "I don't know," she answered.

"Let's find out," said Giddy excitedly, always up for a fight.

"Tes, you'll need to try to be defensive; can you do it?" asked Deavon.

She didn't know, the sword had led her to attack on previous occasions. "I'll try," she nervously replied.

Giddy walked toward her, gently starting to duel. Slowly she built up her tempo, slashing and thrusting, eventually attacking with all her guile. Tes at first easily, then with some urgency blocked every attempt Giddy made.

Deavon soon called them to stop. He offered the hilt of his sword to Tes. "Try this one," he suggested.

Tes exchanged swords, noticing with alarm how much heavier Deavon's sword was as she took guard once more. Giddy attacked slowly again; easily she slipped through Tes' defense, careful not to hurt her in the process. Deavon looked at Tes. "May I use your sword against Giddy?" he asked.

"Yes," replied Tes, happy to stop fighting.

Tes' sword remained dead in Deavon's hand as he took guard. Giddy came at him, the sword remained inanimate, no magic flowed from it and the fire never came. He asked Giddy to stop then returned the sword to Tesania. "It appears it only serves you," he said with raised eyebrows and a questioning smile.

The rest of the day was spent relaxing. Giddy talked of her training with the sword and life in the army. Tes and Deavon told the story of their trip so far, since they had met, until they had arrived at the troop's camp the two days ago. Tes eventually asked Giddy if she was married.

"I've had many boyfriends," she replied coyly, with what for Giddy would pass as a shy smile. "None that I would want to marry, or for that matter, would want to marry me. Besides I'm a warrior woman," she said flexing her muscled arms. "Not somebody's wife."

Tes laughed. "It's getting late, let's make dinner," she suggested hungrily.

Deavon mounted the fowl on a spit and placed it over the glowing embers, turning it periodically. Tes produced the mushrooms and more of the herbs she'd collected earlier. Giddy dug an old but still edible onion from her pack. Tes caught some of the dripping fat from the bird in the pan before adding the sliced mushrooms, onion and herbs. The result was a mouth-watering dish of soft succulent meat with crispy charred skin finished with the herbed mushroom and onion sauce. As Deavon washed the plates, he suggested they all get an early nights rest. Tes insisted on taking the first watch.

~

In the soft grey light of the early morning, the trio packed and started on their way. Rilmir lay some four days away and Deavon was keen to reach it as quickly as possible. The journey was without difficulties. Deavon hunted fresh food while Tes collected colorful winterberries and other tasty treats along the way. The travelling companions chatted, discovering each other's pasts, and ambitions. In the early evenings Tes practiced her archery and at Giddy's insistence she also used Deavon's sword to practice her fighting techniques. "You may not always have your own sword," she had said. By the time they neared the fork of the Lyiera and Tarmikos Rivers they had become fast friends.

They waited for half an hour for the old wooden ferry to make its way to their side of the river. As Deavon had rung the ferry's calling bell, he explained to Tes that it was the only way across without travelling many miles farther upstream. Tes didn't mind waiting. Whilst her legs had now grown more accustomed to the long days of walking, she still enjoyed a rest. She also looked forward to talking to someone other than Giddy or Deavon.

The ferryman waved as he came closer to their shore. Tes saw that he was a hunched little man with grey, receding hair. His face looked like old leather, a wart sprouting three hairs sat rooted in the very centre of his chin. As the ferry ground to a halt on the shallow river bottom, he boomed out, "Well met! You'd be wanting the ferry then?"

"Well met," replied Deavon. "Yes, we require passage across the river, all three of us," he said as he took Tes and Giddy in with a wave. He passed three small coins to the ferryman. "I trust that will suffice."

"Surely," said the little man. "Let's be on our way." He stood aside to let the traveler's board and then pushed the ferry away from the bank with a large wooden pole before moving to the hefty rope that ran through the three large blocks mounted on the deck. He heaved, the ferry started to glide slowly across the water. As they entered the main stream, the current tried its best to drive them down river. Deavon went to help, asking, "What news is there to tell?"

"Not too much I'm afraid," replied the ferryman. "Rumors of attacks by some kind of beasts abound, don't know how true they are though."

"Oh, their true alright!" said Giddy quickly. "We dispatched four in the hills, only three days ago." Her face was aglow with triumph. "Didn't we Tes?" she asked looking over at Tesania.

"We did," Tes looked out over the water as she tentatively replied, conscious of not sounding boastful.

"Really?" the little ferryman asked dubiously.

Giddy rolled her eyes at him as Deavon replied, "The beasts do exist. And yes, we did encounter four of them in the Lyiera hills a few days ago. They were, as Giddy so eloquently put it, dispatched."

The ferryman was stunned, his eyes showing alarm. "And they're that close to us?" he asked anxiously.

"I'm afraid so," replied Deavon. "Although those particular four won't cause you any problems," he said with a disarming smile.

Giddy cut in, "My troop, you'll remember, crossed on your ferry a week or so ago. They're on patrol. You shouldn't have any troubles here."

"That's a relief," answered the little man. His worried look dissipating as a smile spread across his face. "It's getting late; you'll be wanting some lodgings I suppose?" he asked, looking at Deavon. "The wife cooks a mean roast," he boasted with pride.

The ferry bucked as it hit the opposite bank; Tes nearly fell, throwing a hand out and catching the rail just in time. The three travelers thanked the ferryman and headed toward the small roadhouse run by his wife. "Greetings," said a small, plump woman as she bustled from the kitchen to meet them. "How may I help you?"

"We require lodgings, three rooms please," replied Deavon

"Will you be wanting meals as well?" asked the little lady with a hopeful smile.

"Please," answered Deavon with a nod. "We hear your cooking is the best around," he stated with a charming smile.

"Why thank you, I do try," she said as she beamed at Deavon. "I'll show you to your rooms. My name is Annie by the way." She led them to a small door at the back of the room. "The rooms are small, but the beds are comfortable," she said as she showed them into a little hallway with three rooms leading off each side. "We have a lovely bath in the room at the end there," she pointed. "When Jarit, my husband, returns from the ferry I'll get him to warm some water and you can all have a good soak. Make yourself comfortable. I'll be in the kitchen if you need anything. How does a roast joint for dinner sound?" she asked looking around their faces.

"Sounds lovely," replied Tes keenly. "And so does the bath."

After storing their gear in the cozy little rooms they all headed to the sitting room at the front of the building. Jarit arrived home from the ferry and stoked the fire before heading off to heat the bath water. Annie brought them some tea and homemade biscuits. They relaxed, not talking much. Tes watched the fire while anticipating her bath while Giddy fiddled with her hair.

Delicious smells from the roast started to seep under the kitchen door, making Tes realize her hunger. As she contemplated the meal ahead Jarit came back to the room announcing that the bath was ready. Tes looked at Deavon and Giddy keenly.

Deavon chuckled and motioned to her as he said, "Go on, off you go."

Tes jumped from her chair and made her way quickly to her room to collect her soap, brush and clothes. The bathroom, when she entered it, was warm and well laid out. Steam drifted lazily above the plain, oval shaped bath. She ran her fingers over the water, thinking it a touch too hot, but having not had a real bath for a long while she couldn't wait any longer. Laying her soap and brush on the wooden shelf that sat over the edge of the bath, she quickly undressed. Slowly she dipped her foot into the water, waiting to adjust to the heat; eventually she managed to get both feet in the water before lowering herself down. Her skin cried out as the water enveloped her. Ignoring it, she reached for the soap.

A short time later she was used to the heat and luxuriated in her newfound cleanliness. Remembering after a short while that the others had to also bathe she reluctantly decided she should get out. Rising from the bath, her skin pink and raw, she dressed and brushed her hair, returning utterly refreshed to the front room. "Giddy, it's amazing!" she gushed as she sat down. "It feels so good to be really clean."

"I'm about to find out for myself," laughed Giddy as she rose and headed toward her room.

Deavon took his turn after Giddy, emerging just as Annie called them to the table. The roast was heavenly, the meat fell off the bone, baked yams and honeyed carrots garnished with herbs completed a very filling meal. As they retired to the fire Jarit appeared with three servings of berry pie. "The missus' signature dish!" he boasted as he proudly presented them with a flurry.

Tes tried her first ale as the night wore on, deciding half way through to ask for a cider instead. "How can you drink that stuff?" she asked Deavon and Giddy with a shudder.

"Like this," replied Giddy as she tilted her head back, draining her tankard before slamming it down on the table. Deavon laughed, Tes rolled her eyes.

Deavon asked Annie to wake them early as they moved to their rooms. "I certainly will," she replied. "And I'll have your breakfast ready when I do. Goodnight."

"Goodnight," yawned Tes as she found her door, the half tankard of ale having made her sleepy. She discovered, happily, that Barit had used a warmer on their beds. Pulling the covers up to her chin, she quickly fell to sleep.

~

A soft knock at her door woke Tesania from her deep slumber, she mumbled an answer and then lay for a while sleepily trying to remember the dream she had been having. She knew it involved Deavon but that was all she could recall.

Reluctantly she slid her feet from under the warm covers, the coldness bit immediately, causing her to draw them quickly back under. She lay for a few seconds and enjoyed the warmth. Knowing she needed to rise, she set herself, threw the covers back and rolled into a sitting position, regretting it instantly as she put her feet on the icy cold floor. Rolling on her side and reaching as far as she could, her fingertips barely touched her boots, after a few moments she managed to flick them closer and was able to pick them up. She dressed quickly; wearing only light clothes with her heavy cloak draped over her shoulders, knowing the sun would quickly warm the day. Hair brushed, she opened her door just as Giddy walked past. "Good morning," she said cheerfully.

"To you too," replied Giddy as she sniffed the air. "Can you smell that ham? Let's go before Deavon scoffs it all," she laughed.

Their breakfast, though small, was delicious. Fried ham, eggs, sunny side up as Tes liked them, fried tomato halves, toast and honey. Tes thanked Annie profusely as they rose to get their gear; the little lady delighted that she'd made them so happy. Deavon paid her as they left, Jarit waved from the ferry as they turned and headed once more toward Rilmir.

The roads became more travelled as they neared the city. More and more farms began to appear as they walked. One farmer let them spend the night in his breezy old barn. Tesania slept poorly as two horses shuffled and a calf continually lowed. "We should reach Rilmir by tonight," Deavon said as they started out the next morning.

Giddy and Deavon spent the day warning Tes of the dangers of the city and that the people she might encounter may cause her harm. She did not want another episode like they'd had in Lyiera with the thief Burrit, but she felt she was much wiser and worldly now, saying indignantly, "I think I can handle myself!"

Giddy laughed. "That statement just proves you haven't got a clue about a big city. Stay close to Deavon and I. We'll look after you."

Tesania sulked as they walked along, she did not think she needed looking after at all, but kept it to herself. After a while she asked, "Can we get some horses? It would save our legs, and we could get to Wyvern City much quicker." She had never ridden a horse but thought they looked like fun.

"I'd already thought of that," replied Deavon. "As we are on the King's business, I'm sure we would be able to organize some." He looked at Giddy. "The army have a few; don't they?"

"Don't look at me," said Giddy in a defensive tone. "I'm just a soldier. You think I can just walk up and say, I'll have those three horses over there please, oh, and while you're at it, please saddle them up and provision them for us, there's a good chap?"

Deavon laughed. "I guess not. The Council would, I'm sure, organize some for us, once we tell them of our need for haste."

Giddy scoffed, "The Council don't do anything, unless it's for their own sakes."

"Well, I am a King's Ranger," informed Deavon. "They'll listen to me."

"Oh, la-d-da," grinned Giddy. "Look at me. I'm a King's Ranger," she said in a posh voice as she pranced off up the road. Tes burst into laughter; Deavon shook his head while still managing a smile.

The imposing outer walls of Rilmir came into view when the three were still many miles away; Tes was amazed at the sight of it. "How many people live there?" she asked.

"Thousands," replied Giddy. "The rich quarter is moderately nice, the rest though is," she looked at Deavon,

"How do you say? Blah!" she proclaimed with her tongue out and eyes bulging.

Deavon once again shook his head. "You have such a way with words, Giddy," he laughed.

The late afternoon sky began to darken as they entered the worst sector of Rilmir through the city's western gate. The houses were gloomy; people rushing everywhere, beggars clawing at their clothing. On the side of the cobbled street sat filthy men and women selling disgusting looking food from dirty stalls. Laundry hung from windows and across the streets on sagging twine. Tesania held her hand to her nose as a man, begging for coins, came up to her and breathed his rancid breath in her face, his brown, rotting teeth made her feel ill. Deavon pushed him aside.

The houses were squalid. Children ran about, poorly dressed and with no shoes on their feet. Sewerage ran down the side of the street in a crude gutter, a little boy floating a homemade boat on the tide. Tesania cringed. "How can they live like this?" she asked, turning to Deavon. "How can the King let them live like this?"

Giddy moved out in front to push the beggars and peddlers away. Deavon walked behind Tes, careful that their packs and belongings stayed intact. "It's the way of the world Tesania," he said, sadness in his voice. "Many of these people choose to be here. The King gives handouts and tries to improve their standards, but they waste it on beer or gambling." He looked about. "Thank the stars we weren't born here."

Tesania felt ill, but still her eyes streamed with tears of compassion. A little girl approached shyly and offered Tes a filthy, worn-out doll. "You keep it, little one," she said in an emotional voice as she looked into the little girl's eyes. She reached toward her pack to get the girl some coins for a new doll.

Deavon gripped her hand and stopped her. "No, Tes," he said gently. "It won't help her. It'll just be wasted."

Tes buried her head in Deavon's chest; he gently wrapped his arms around her. Giddy returned to them, placing a comforting hand on Tes' shoulder as she held the beggars and thieves at bay.

Tes settled and pulled away from Deavon. Touching the girl on the cheek, she said, "Take care little one," and slowly walked away. She felt crushed by what she saw. She thought of her beautiful village, the little boys and girls running around, happy and plump, her father handing them toys made in his smithy. Even Lyiera seemed lovely compared to this horrible place.

Deavon pushed her along, not wanting to expose her to the horrendous sights and sounds any longer than need be. As they neared the centre of the city the people and surrounding buildings changed, becoming cleaner and more upbeat. Tes though, remained morose, lost in thought.

They passed the central market as the stall owners were packing up for the day. "I need to report to my headquarters," said Giddy as they walked into the upper class area of the city. "Where will you be staying? I'll meet you there in the morning."

"The Rangers Arrow Inn," replied Deavon as Giddy disappeared into the crowd. "Come on, Tes, let's get indoors," he said as he gently gripped her arm and led her toward the Council chambers. "The Inn's near the eastern gate, past these buildings," he advised her as they walked. He worried that she was still so upset, she walked along, seemingly dazed.

As they moved past the Council buildings, Tes looked to Deavon and said, "I'm going to save that little girl one day," conviction resonating in her voice.

"Maybe," he said tenderly. "There is however not much we can do now." He led on quietly as Tes slowly came back around.

"Do you have to be a ranger to stay at the Rangers Arrow?" she asked worriedly.

"You do actually," he laughed. "But don't worry, I'm sure they will let you in if I tell them you're with me." As he noticed Tes blush, he quickly added, "Travelling with me, should I say."

Tesania laughed.

11 RILMIR CITY

Deavon asked Tesania to stay at the inn as he left to attend the Council the following morning. They'd retired early the previous evening after eating a small meal.

Tes felt relaxed as she explored. The inn was much larger than the two previous establishments she'd stayed in. The walls held many animals' heads as trophies. The woodwork was polished with oils and gleamed while the whitewashed walls reflected the flickering fire. A luxuriant rug tucked under the feet of plush arm chairs covered the floor.

She approached an immaculately dressed staff member, asking if there was a place to wash her clothes. He politely asked her to follow and led her to a well-provisioned washroom that opened onto a small courtyard containing numerous hanging lines. "Thank you," Tes said politely as she left to get her laundry.

Humming as she washed, she tried to force the images of the little girl from her head. She turned her thoughts to the journey ahead. *What would it be like to attend the King's court? What fabulous people would she meet?* As she envisioned a stately lady walking through a throng of admirers the little girl's head appeared on the shoulders. Shuddering, she decided to concentrate on the soapy water.

Deavon returned shortly after. "I've spoken to the Council; they've agreed to provide us with horses and provisions. We're here for the day though I'm afraid. At least we'll be able to attend to some chores."

"I've already done mine," Tes beamed.

"Well, looks like you get to relax while I work," he laughed.

"I wonder where Giddy is?" Tes asked uneasily as she looked at the front door.

"She'd need to debrief with her headquarters, and then arrange to be detached so she can accompany us. It takes time, with the chain of command being what it is," he answered as he walked toward his room.

When he returned Tes chatted to him as he washed his clothes, finally asking about Rilmir and how it compared to Wyvern City. "Wyvern City's much larger than Rilmir," Deavon replied. "It's the King's City and therefore is kept in much better order than the other cities of Eldanal. There's still bad sectors though," he said, looking at her. "There always will be where people are involved."

Tes nodded. "Is it near the sea?"

"The city sits on Wyvern Harbor. Many boats and majestic ships sail from the docks. The Royal quarter of the city is exquisite, avenues lined by trees, fountains, beautiful stately buildings." He smiled at her. "You'll see when we get there." He finished and hung his last piece of clothing. "Let's get a cup of tea," he suggested.

They sat in the large, comfortable chairs, sipping their tea as they watched the crackling fire. A knot of wood exploded, sending embers dancing across the floor, racing one another to see which could get to the rug first only to fall short on the protective tiles where they glowed in defiance before slowly petered out.

Late in the morning Giddy arrived, making a fuss with the door attendant, demanding to be let in. Deavon waved to the attendant who reluctantly let her pass. Giddy fixed him with a triumphant glare as she headed toward Tes and Deavon.

"Morning," she said with a nod to each of them. "Bad news I'm afraid." she looked guiltily at Tes before saying, "The bosses have decided I can't go with you."

Tes sat forward quickly, anxiously asking, "What do you mean you can't come with us? You said you'd come all the way to Wyvern City!"

"Tes, I'm in the army." Giddy defended. "I have to do what they say. They want me to lead a troop. Can you imagine it? They want me!" she said stabbing her thumb to her chest, "to lead a troop. I can't believe it." She flopped back in the chair with a dreamy grin on her face. "I'm sorry, Tes. But it's every soldier's desire to be promoted; I can't turn it down."

Tes looked down at her lap. "I understand," she said sadly. "It's just that I..," she paused before looking up at Giddy with a wry grin. "I actually enjoy your company. Only the stars know why?" she said, tilting her head back and pretending to look to the heavens.

Giddy laughed. "You'll be all right," she said. "You have Deavon here to look after you and the road to Wyvern City is well travelled. There won't be any beasts to worry about."

"What's your mission?" asked Deavon curiously.

"There've been rumors of beasts in the Issdale Forest. We're going down to have a look. They want me to lead because I'm the only soldier who's seen, let alone killed a beast. I guess they think I can do it again," she laughed.

The three friends sat and talked. Giddy eventually rose, saying, "Well, I have to go, being the boss now I have to tend to provisions, make sure my troops don't get too drunk, you know what I mean," she winked.

Tes hugged Giddy at the door of the inn for a long time. Giddy patiently waited for her to let go before giving

Deavon a quick hug as well. "Goodbye," she said tenderly. "Look after her Deavon."

As Giddy disappeared into the throng of people traversing the street, Tes yelled, "Goodbye Giddy, I'll miss you!" Turning to Deavon with a tear in her eye, she said quietly, "Let's go inside."

Later in the day Deavon offered to show Tes the markets in the centre of the city. The stalls were numerous, selling everything imaginable, fruit and vegetables, livestock, arts, crafts and jewelry. There were food stalls by the dozen and even a butcher plying his trade on a large table that ran with blood. Tes spent hours examining all sorts of wares, cooing excitedly when she found a lovely headband in one of the jewelry stalls. Placing it on her head she turned to Deavon. "What do you think?"

Deavon thought it beautiful, silver chain chased through a single strand of softly woven wool, strings of autumn colored leaves hung on either side of her head, beaten from various metals blending perfectly with her dark hair while glinting different hues in the afternoon sun. In the centre hung a small string of handmade beads with fiery colors of red intertwined with blacks and browns. As she moved, they appeared as if they might be on fire. "Beautiful," he said simply.

"How much, for the headband and the matching necklace, please?" she enthusiastically asked the merchant.

"Twelve kings head coins, for both," replied the eager man.

Tes started to reach for her coins. Deavon placed his hand on hers, stopping her before she could open her pack. "Come now!" he said acridly to the merchant. "Twelve coins is much too steep a price for these trinkets." He took the headband from Tes' head and placed it back on the table. "Let's go Tes, this man means to rob us." He guided her by the arm as they started to walk away.

"But I want them," Tes argued. "I don't mind paying that much."

"Listen to the young lady," implored the man. "She obviously knows quality." He held the two pieces of jewelry toward them invitingly.

"Quality are they?" Deavon asked scornfully. "You get the street urchins to make them for you, pay them a pittance and then have the effrontery to ask twelve coins!" He once again started to walk away, Tes, bewildered, followed.

"Kind Sir, ten coins, it is the best I can do," called the man anxiously.

Deavon stopped. Without turning, he said, "Six coins, that is all they are worth."

"Please sir, eight coins and you are getting it for my cost." Deavon took another pace away from the man, "Seven Sir, seven kings head coins and they are yours."

Deavon stopped again, smiling triumphantly at Tes, he said, "Go and pay the man."

Tes almost ran back to the stall as she dug in her pack and retrieved seven coins, handing them to the man as he passed her the jewelry. "Thank you," she said, beaming. The man scowled as he turned away.

"I'm sorry," Deavon apologized as they walked away. "But he saw you as a soft target, I had to step in."

"That's ok, thank you," she responded, happily holding the band up to the sun. "I love it."

Deavon pushed her hand down, saying, "Wrap them and put them away; securely."

After purchasing supplies for the journey ahead they headed back to the inn. The evening meal, served in front of the flickering fireplace, was utterly filling. Tes sipped some cider while staring into the flames. Her thoughts ran from where she had been, the new friends she had found and where she might find herself after entering Wyvern City. Yawning, she stood and said, "Goodnight."

~

Early the following morning Tesania nervously stepped up to her horse. Brown with white socks and a diamond on its forehead, it towered over her.

"Easy, Nellie," Deavon said as he ran his hand down its nose. "Tesania has never ridden a horse before; you'll have to be nice to her," he explained to the horse as he motioned Tes to approach. The horse sensed her reluctance and shuffled its feet nervously. "Take the reins, that's it, now put your foot in the stirrup. Easy girl. Now, reach up to the pommel and pull yourself up. Good, well done!" he enthused to Tes as he patted Nellie on her flanks to settle her down. "She's as nervous as you," he laughed as he looked up.

"She won't buck me will she?"

"That one has a good soul," said the stable hand as he stood holding the reins of Deavon's large black stallion. "She won't give you a hard time once she's used to you. Now Prince Kasimar here," he said motioning toward the horse he held. "He's a whole different kettle of fish. He'd buck you off and then turn around and run you down if you upset him," he laughed as he handed Deavon the reins to the stallion.

Tes nodded as she concentrated hard on keeping Nellie from turning back toward the barn.

Ominous black clouds built on the horizon as they coaxed their mounts through the eastern gate of the city. Tes held tightly to the reins with one hand while the other gripped the saddle's pommel. The horses gait jostled her as she tried to find her balance. Eventually, as she found her rhythm, she started to enjoy the ride.

Deavon started at an easy pace, explaining as they went the art of riding a horse. As Tes became more accustomed to it they picked up the pace. "Looks like we may get wet," he stated as he looked at the clouds.

The day wore on as the skies thickened. Stopping for a short break, Tes gratefully dismounted, rubbing her legs as they sat. "I didn't know riding a horse could be so painful," she complained, looking over at Deavon as they rose to remount.

Producing two juicy looking apples, he replied, "It takes some time to get used to it. Here, give this apple to Nellie and she'll love you forever." He tossed the apple to her. "Hold your hand out flat though, like this, or she might take your fingers as well," he demonstrated as he held his own apple out to Prince.

Tes nervously held her hand out, Nellie, smelling the offering, walked forward a pace and nipped it out of her hand. Tes beamed a smile at Deavon. "She loves it." She stroked Nellie on her neck as she looked into her eye. "You're a good girl, aren't you?" Nellie pushed her with her nose. "I haven't got any more apples," Tes protested while holding her hands out as evidence. "See," she laughed.

As they mounted, a splatter of rain hit Tes on the chin. She looked up just as the heavens opened with a deluge of rain. The light dimmed further; it was almost as if it was the twilight, thunder clapped in the distance, the rain, it seemed to Tes, was growing heavier.

They rode on in silence; both lost in their own thoughts. Tesania felt dreary while water cascaded down her back. Every part of her was wet. A river of water ran from the end of her nose, her hair clung to her face and neck. She was miserable and cold. Nellie started to struggle, the road having turned to mud and become treacherous. Deavon led the way onto the grass shoulder where he hoped the horses could find a better footing. He yelled to Tes, the roar of the rain almost drowning him out, "There's a roadhouse, a few miles, we'll stop there."

Tes could only nod. Her mind wandered back to the steaming hot bath in the roadhouse near the ferry, she decided she would give anything to be back there, right now, laying back, bubbles tickling her nose.

They trudged on for what seemed like an eternity. Deavon had slowed the horses to a dawdling walk. The rain continued unabated. Tes looked down at Nellie's neck. On the odd occasion that she looked up there was only a wall of rain ahead. Finally on one of her quick glances she caught a glimpse of light in the distance. Looking toward Deavon and almost screaming, she called out, "I see a light!" as she pointed ahead.

Deavon looked up, straining to see. Turning his head to her, he nodded. "The roadhouse!" he yelled back.

As Deavon tied the horses to the hitching post outside the roadhouse Tes removed their packs and carried them onto the porch. Opening hers, she despaired to see everything was wet through.

The roadhouse door creaked when she pushed it open and moved inside. Immediately Tes felt the warmth that the roaring fire radiated throughout the room. She wanted nothing more than to run to it and warm her hands. However, aware that she was dripping puddles of water on the floor, she stayed near the door.

A man rose from a chair in the far corner. "A horrendous day for travelling," he said dryly as he approached them. "I take it you will be wanting a room?"

"Two please," replied Deavon. "And stables for our horses."

"The stables are around the back, plenty of room, there's grain in the barrel at the far end. I'll show you to your rooms. I can lend you some dry clothes, if you wish?" he offered as he turned and headed for a door at the back of the room.

Tes started to follow. Deavon caught her by the sleeve. She looked at him, wondering why he had stopped her. "I'm cold," she said, shivering.

"So are the horses, but they can't get themselves unsaddled," Deavon admonished as he headed for the door.

Tes thought of poor Nellie, still standing in the pouring rain. "We'll be back soon," she said to the man. "Do you have a bath that can be heated up?"

"We certainly do," he replied. "I'll start the water heating right away," he said politely as he turned away.

Tes jubilantly walked back into the rain; she could handle it a while longer, since she knew that a hot bath was on its way. As she untied the reins Nellie shoved her with her nose. "I'm sorry girl, I almost forgot you," she said apologetically as she led the way to the stables.

Deavon pulled the huge wooden doors open, the smell of hay assaulting Tes' nose. Both horses whinnied and nickered as they recognized the stable would be their temporary home. Once inside, Nellie shivered before shaking her whole body, water sprayed everywhere. "Does that feel better?" Tes laughed as she started to undo the saddle.

Forty-five minutes later the horses were unsaddled, cleaned of mud, brushed, fed and settled. "Ready?" asked Tes as she and Deavon stood at the door. He nodded, Tes ran, Deavon turned to close the stable door. Tes burst into the roadhouse, Deavon not far behind; dripping water again they looked at each other. Tes couldn't help laughing. The roadhouse keeper came back into the room and scowled at the new puddle on his floor. "Your bath is ready," he said. "I have laid out some clothes in the washroom for you."

"Don't even bother," Deavon said emphatically as Tes turned quickly toward him. "It's my turn to go first." Tes pouted as she slowly turned away. "Ok, I give up, you can go first," he smiled as he knowingly succumbed to her game.

Tes spun back around, treating him to a gleeful smile. "Really? Thank you, thank you, thank you," she said exuberantly, managing, just, not to run.

Tesania hung her things by the fire after her bath while Deavon took his turn. The roadhouse keeper made them comfortable before retiring to the kitchen to prepare the evening meal.

"I hope it's not raining tomorrow," Tes said hopefully as she sat snuggled in an overstuffed chair by the fire.

"We'll have to stay here if it is," replied Deavon disappointedly. "We can't keep travelling in that," he gestured toward the window, the rain still falling heavily.

Other travelers arrived, as wet and bedraggled as Tes and Deavon had been. After a fine meal, they all sat by the fire talking for many hours into the night.

12 JOURNEY'S END

Tesania peeked out of her bedroom window the next morning. Grey clouds still dominated the sky while patches of azure had begun to find their way through. The rain had ceased; the ground though, remained wet and heavy.

When she arrived at the table for breakfast Deavon was talking to one of the other travelers. "Good morning Tesania," he said brightly. "Looks like we can be on our way."

"I looked out my window. It seems to be clearing," she replied happily. "Good morning to you all," she said politely as she nodded to all at the table before sitting down. Breakfast was a platter of delightful winter fruits. Tes enjoyed every succulent mouthful.

The sun broke through as they saddled their horses. "A much better day for a ride, hey girl?" Tes asked cheerfully. Nellie nickered as she excitedly moved about, ready to be off. Deavon handed Tes' pack to her. "It's a shame they didn't all dry," she said in a frustrated voice as she attached it to the saddle. "We'll have to remember to air them later this evening."

The road remained slippery with mud but the mid morning sun soon started to bake it dry. By mid-afternoon they were making good headway. Nellie seemed to enjoy the day as much as Tes, regularly nipping Prince's hindquarters when she thought him to slow. Prince, more than once, looked around, evil in his stallion's eye.

As they crossed the Wyvern River via an arched stone bridge, Deavon said, "We can stay in the Roadhouse just up ahead tonight. Wyvern City is only a few hours away. We should be able to reach the gates by mid morning.

Tes nodded; glad that she would soon be able to get off Nellie's back.

With the horses tended, they hung their clothes in the dying sunshine; a light breeze ensured they would dry in a short amount of time. Tes was exhausted from a full day in the saddle. Deavon suggested they retire early.

~

Tes pulled herself into the saddle excitedly the next morning. "I can't believe I'm going to see the King's City," she said as Deavon mounted Prince. "I can't wait."

Deavon spoke to her of what she might find in Wyvern City, some of the etiquette required in court, of his friends and his dwelling. Tes absorbed it all, paying particular attention to the Court. The day passed quickly as they talked. Tes saw a wall in the far distance. "Is that it?" she asked enthusiastically, standing in her stirrups to get a better view.

"Yes," replied Deavon, equally enthusiastically, he found her excitement contagious. "We'll be there soon, stay close."

The walls loomed above them as they entered the city. The gates were huge, towering high above them. The streets, unlike Rilmir were perfectly paved and clean. Colorful bunting flew from poles as far as Tes' eyes could see. Shops lined the street, tables overflowing with goods outside their busy windows. People, their children suitably behaved, walked along well-maintained paths.

The traffic on the street was meager, making it easy for them to proceed. Tes looked around, no beggars, no urchins, the difference amazed her. Eventually they came to an inner wall, the gates this time manned by soldiers. "Well met," Deavon greeted as they approached.

"Well met," replied the soldier. Recognizing Deavon, he waved them through.

As they proceeded through the royal quarter the houses became more opulent. One, Tes thought, was at least as big as her whole village.

The palace loomed on the horizon. It was, to Tes, beautiful. As they approached, she took in the huge building. Manicured gardens surrounded a stunning lake, which in turn surrounded a fountain, rising twenty feet into the air. Statues lined the avenue leading to the front entry of the palace; giant pillars reaching up to support the ornately carved facade. What seemed like hundreds of windows punctuated the three-story building; two accommodation wings ran off on either side.

Deavon smiled at the look on Tesania's face. "Big isn't it?" he asked.

Long before they reached the palace, Deavon turned down a side street. "The stables are located down here," he said as he turned in the saddle to look at Tes. "We need to hand the horses in to the stable master. Then I'll need to report to my superiors and tell them what I know of the beasts. Meanwhile, I'll take you to my friend, Ayana's, house. She'll, I'm sure, allow you to board with her whilst we stay in Wyvern City."

Tes smelt the stables well before she saw them. As they rounded a bend in the street a large building housing hundreds of horses came into view. As they drew nearer a groom approached them. "Well met," he said brightly as he reached for Nellie's bridle.

"Well met," replied Deavon cordially as he dismounted. "These two fine animals are from the stables at Rilmir. You'll be able to care for them, I trust?" he asked as he helped Tes dismount.

"Most certainly," the groom replied. "Do you wish them to stay here for your return? Or should I send them back with the next travelers?" he asked as he started to lead them away.

"Send them back, we won't be returning that way. For now anyway," Deavon replied as he reached down for his pack.

Tes called to the groom as he led the horses away, "Wait a minute please." Walking to Nellie, she stroked her side as she looked into the horse's eye. "Thank you Nellie, I enjoyed your company. Goodbye." As she walked back to Deavon she turned her head to the groom. "Oh, and that's Prince Kasimar," she said as she pointed to the large black stallion. "He's a real a sweetie." Prince turned his head toward her, his ears pricked, snorting as he kicked his hind legs in the air.

"I think you upset him," laughed Deavon as they walked along the avenue.

13 THE ROYAL CITY

The royal quarter of the city was expansive with houses lining the perfectly cobbled streets and boulevards. Tesania peered inside elaborate carriages as they trundled past; the exquisite clothes worn by the occupants astonishing her. One stately carriage conveyed a beautiful lady with blond curls cascading over her slender shoulders; her azure dress delightful; it seemed to Tes that it took up half the carriage by itself. Affluently dressed men rode on magnificent horses. Couples strolled along the paths of the many lush parkways, the women, with gorgeous dresses, held colorful parasols to keep the sun at bay. Tes looked from one dazzling sight to another, awed by the opulence, keenly aware that her own clothing was that of a poor village girl.

"Ayana lives in an apartment. It's not too far away now," Deavon explained as they walked along. Recognizing Tes' awe and realizing that she must feel very out of place, he added consolingly, "She's similar in size to you. I'm sure you would be able to borrow some of her dresses whilst we're here." They entered a broad avenue; manicured gardens filled the centre of the street, elegant trees lining either side.

"It's so beautiful!" Tes exclaimed wondrously. "And the people." She watched as a couple strolled by with an immaculately dressed little girl holding her father's hand. "I'd heard stories of the Royal City, but never could I have imagined." she paused, turning around to take in all the sights again, "This!"

Deavon laughed as he lead her into a small pathway leading to a large building, explaining as he knocked on a carved redwood door that Ayana lived in the ground floor apartment at the back. As they waited, Tes adjusted her hair as best she could. She stood nervously, afraid, not wanting to make a bad impression.

Deavon watched her fiddling. Reassuringly, he said, "Ayana is a very good friend and a lovely person; she won't be concerned with how you look after long days of travel. Just be yourself and she'll have no choice but to like you."

Tes looked at her feet with a slight blush. "I'm nervous," her voice quivered slightly as she spoke. "These people are much better than me!" She looked up at him. "I should have stayed in Rilmir!" Embarrassed, she quickly turned away.

"What makes them better than you?" Deavon asked irritably. He gripped her shoulder and turned her back toward him. Looking into her eyes he frowned as he questioned her, compassion mixed with anger. "That they have money? That they live in this place? That they wear pretty dresses and travel in fancy carriages?" He released her shoulder as he turned away. "I know many of these," he paused briefly, "people! that you call better than yourself. I assure you, I would rather spend time with you than with most of them!" He turned back to her, his anger abating. "These people may not yet know it, but, one day it will be they who will be nervous about meeting you." As he watched Tes' hurt and confused expression, he realized that perhaps he had said too much. He started to apologize, stopping abruptly as the door opened. Addressing the resplendently dressed porter, he cordially asked, "If the Lady Ayana is in, could you please inform her that her friend Deavon wishes to visit upon her, with a," he looked at Tes and smiled, "friend."

"Certainly, sir," replied the porter with a gracious bow. "The Lady is in. I will advise her of your request immediately. Please wait here. I will return shortly."

Deavon turned to Tes, concern in his eyes. "I'm sorry Tesania. I didn't wish to upset you, but, never think that these people are better than you, they're far from it!" he said in a resolute manner, tempered with tenderness.

Tes stood silently as she looked into Deavon's eyes, she could see that he meant what he said. "I understand.," she said as she looked away. "But it's hard for me. Remember I come from a small village, this is all new." Looking back to him impishly, she declared, "I'll look them in the eye, as I would an equal!" confirming it with a purposeful nod of her head.

The porter opened the door as she finished. "Lady Ayana wishes me to bid you enter," he gestured for them to follow as he turned. They entered a large whitewashed hallway with portraits adorning the walls. The porter led them to the door at the very end and softly knocked.

Tes tried to peer into the room as the door opened. The porter performed a flourishing bow and announced, "Your guests, milady."

"Thank you," replied a soft feminine voice. "You may go now." As the porter moved from the doorway Tes strained to see Lady Ayana but only caught a glimpse of a soft, embroidered dress. When the Doorman had retired, the Lady excitedly ushered them in. "When did you get back?" she asked delightedly as she threw her arms around Deavon and pecked him on the cheek. "I thought you would be away for months, in that village you were going to help?" She stood back, holding Deavon's hands in her own as she rapturously looked into his face.

Deavon beamed. Tes looked at his face; suspiciously she turned her gaze to Ayana. *She's beautiful,* she thought. Flowers woven into her perfect plaits adorned her soft blond hair. Her face was aristocratic and refined. A fitted lacework bodice accentuating her gorgeous ruffled taffeta skirt, the soft blue contrasting exquisitely with her alabaster skin. Hollowness clawed at her stomach as she wondered if they were more than just friends.

Deavon released Ayana's hands as he softly replied, "The beasts attacked the village before I arrived. All the villagers were killed." He stopped, embarrassed, he turned to Tes. "I apologize for my rudeness," he uttered. "Tesania, this is my friend, Ayana. Ayana, meet Tesania," he said grandiosely as he swept into an elaborate formal bow.

Tes shook her head, amused by his bow she laughed as she held her hand out to Ayana. "You can call me Tes if you like," she struggled to say. Looking toward Deavon, she said, "That was so funny!" Ayana covered her smile with her hand, amused.

"What?" Deavon asked with feigned hurt in his voice.

Ayana led them to a sweeping open veranda. A large table dominated the area. The paved floor of terracotta blending elegantly with the array of flowers that hung from manicured vines. An imperious old oak tree sat in the centre of the garden, causing the late winter's sun to cast dappled shadows across the entire area. From a fountain depicting a little boy playfully pouring water from an urn emanated soothing babbling noises that made Tes think that she was in the most relaxing house in the world. Lush green grass ran right to the feet of orange and mandarin trees, pregnant with luscious, ripe, fruits. "It's beautiful!" Tes exclaimed as she took a seat at the table opposite Deavon. "Do you live here all the time?" she questioned Ayana wondrously.

Ayana laughed amiably at Tes' reaction. "Yes. I am lucky. My parents own this apartment, but they spend most of their time in our country manor, not too far from here, just a few miles outside the city." As she spoke a maid arrived. "Excuse me," Ayana apologized to Tes. "Our guests will be staying for their midday meal; we shall be dining in the courtyard here. Please bring us some refreshments in the meantime." The maid nodded and then scuttled away. Returning her attention back to Tes, Ayana inquisitively asked, "Tell me of your village, and of your travels?"

Tes spoke for what seemed like hours, Deavon cutting in periodically to embellish the story and fill in any blanks. Ayana listen intently, often with astonishment on her face, she nodded, asking many questions as she looked from one traveler to the other during the epic tale. When Tes finished, Ayana looked at her searchingly. "And why is it that you came to Wyvern City? What is here for you?" As Tesania looked dejectedly down at her glass of juice, Ayana carefully said, "Please don't misunderstand me. I am not saying that you should not be here. I wish only to know what your plans are?" She turned to Deavon. "You must have had a reason to bring her this far, otherwise, I'm sure you would have left her with the authorities in Rilmir?"

"I seek revenge!" Tes whispered tersely, barely audible to the others at the table.

Ayana was taken aback. "I'm sorry?" she said, astounded. "Did you say revenge?" Looking at Deavon, she asked, "Revenge on whom?"

"Trannyth! The man who murdered my parents!" Tes looked searchingly into Ayana's eyes. "You understand! Don't you? He must pay!" She looked away quickly as she saw Ayana's confusion. "I don't expect you to understand!" she said bitterly.

"Tesania, I have only just met you; I don't know you or what you are capable of doing. Yet I must say that it is foolish for you to think that you can defeat Trannyth." She turned abruptly to Deavon. "You don't go along with this. Do you?" she asked bewilderedly.

As Deavon shook his head and started to answer, Tes cut him off, disdain clearly in her voice, "He also thinks I'm foolish!" She glared at him, daring him to say otherwise.

Deavon stared at the table. After a few moments he looked guiltily at Ayana. "I brought Tes to Wyvern City..," he looked back down, "Because," he paused, thinking. "Because of her sword. I believe that the King's Mages should be advised of it and be allowed to study it, to learn its secrets." His eyes flicked quickly to Tes then back down to the table.

Tesania sat in her chair with arms crossed, seething as she glowered at him. Eventually she shook her head and looked away. Ayana watched them both. Reaching over, she cupped her hand over Tes' clenched fist.

Deavon scowled at the table, eventually he looked straight into Tes' eyes. "I also wish to help you rebuild your life." He looked embarrassedly away, aware that Ayana was watching him intently, an insightful smile radiating from her face.

Tes' face softened as he spoke. Looking at him, she sulkily replied, "I'm going to kill Trannyth, whether you like it or not! You can help me if you want! If you don't, I'll find somebody else who will!"

Ayana squeezed her hand, as if to ask her to stop. "That's enough of that for now. Our meal will shortly be served. I'm sure you would wish to bathe after?" She released Tesania's hand as she turned to Deavon. "You will need to report to your superiors I should think."

Deavon nodded. "Yes, right after our meal." he looked questioningly at Ayana. "We hoped that you may be able to offer Tesania a place to stay, for a few days at least. Maybe help her settle into city life?"

Ayana paused fleetingly as she thought it through. Turning to Tes, she said cheerfully, "I would love for you to stay with me; we can find you some lovely dresses to wear." A sudden thought came to her, excitedly, she said, "The King's Winter Ball is tomorrow night. You will be going, won't you Deavon? Tesania can accompany you." she turned to him, her face aglow. "Won't you?"

Deavon laughed. "It doesn't look as if I have a choice now, does it?" he bantered.

Tes smiled shyly. "I think I'm more scared now than I was when we faced those beasts in the hills," she laughed nervously.

"Oh, you'll be alright, I will help you with all the things you need to know," Ayana said enthusiastically. "And I have an absolutely exquisite gown for you to wear." Obviously in her element she spoke of the Ball throughout their meal, who would be attending, what people would be wearing, who might be with whom. It was all over Tes' head as she sat lost in her own thoughts and worries. *How could a simple village girl hope to attend a King's Ball and not look a complete fool?*

Deavon stood. "I must leave you now, Tes. Ayana will look after you. If you should require me, for any reason, send a message to the Rangers Barracks and I'll come when I can." He embraced Ayana and thanked her for helping Tes before starting for the door. Stopping, he asked, "May I take your sword, Tes, so I may show it to the mages?"

"Yes," Tes replied reluctantly. "Can I be sure it'll be safe? And that I'll get it back?"

"I guarantee it. Personally!" he responded sincerely as he leant to take the sword. "I'll see you at the Ball." He paused; looking back at Tes with an ardent smile before turning and opening the door.

Tesania immediately felt lost; in a strange house with a woman she barely knew. Deavon had been her constant companion since she'd left Aryd Village, her adviser, in some ways her strength. She realized, as her stomach tied in knots, that he had come to mean a great deal to her. Already she missed him.

Ayana asked one of the maids to prepare a bath for Tes. "While you bathe I will find some clothes for you to wear. Give all your clothes to the maid, she will have them laundered." She studied Tes for a short while, deciding she could hardly wait to see her sashay into the Ball with Deavon. *Oh what a fuss you will cause*, she thought gleefully.

14 FRIENDSHIP FOUND

Tes rose from the warm soapy water of the bath. Clean and refreshed, she retired to the palatial bedroom that the young maid, Kailyn, had said would be hers during her stay. She sat on the end of the huge canopied bed, her hand caressing the luxurious, midnight blue, dress that had been placed for her to wear. It amused her that she had no idea how to put it on. Eyes and hooks ran along the length of the opening in the back with laces that she couldn't possibly begin to tie. There were hoops in a white petticoat and others that she assumed to be underskirts.

As she sat wondering, Kailyn bustled in. "Aren't you going to dress yet?" she asked in a curious voice.

Tesania looked at her, bewilderment written on her face. "I don't know how!" she embarrassedly replied. "I come from a small village; I've only ever worn simple dresses that I could just pull over my head." She shook her head in wonderment. "I can't believe that ladies wear these beautiful things all the time."

Kailyn tutted as she picked the underskirts from the bed. "After a day in these you may not ever want to wear them again," she chuckled. "Being a lady is not all fun and games; they have to work hard to be as beautiful as they are." She looked toward the door, ensuring that no one was listening, winking as she said, "Some of them have to work really hard, if you know what I mean." She giggled joyfully at her own joke.

Tes imagined the old crones from her village wearing the gorgeous dress that lay before her, unable to resist, she fell back, laughing uncontrollably.

"Shh, shh," giggled Kailyn. "I'll get in trouble if we laugh too much." she couldn't help herself though, as her giggles turned to uproarious laughter.

Tes eventually controlled herself, tears rolling down her cheeks as she lay on her back looking at the elaborate floral moldings in the ceiling plaster. Shaking her head, she glanced over to where Kailyn stood. Fighting to keep from laughing, Tes sat up. "Well, I guess we'd better get started," she said as she stood and reached for the dress.

Holding it against herself she performed a pirouette, the skirt billowed and fluttered. Tes caught her reflection in the large mirror mounted on the wall. Stopping abruptly, she stood and stared, lifting the skirt outwards, cocking her head and swaying her hips from side to side. She sighed dreamily as she turned back to Kailyn. "I never could have imagined I would wear a dress like this," she enthused. "In my life!"

Kailyn looked at Tes fondly. "Come on," she said as she reached out to take the dress. "We must start with the stockings, then the petticoat, then the underskirts." Noticing Tes' flustered face, she giggled, "I'm sorry, I get excited. Let's take it one garment at a time shall we?" As Tes gratefully nodded Kailyn had her sit on the bed and started to help her dress. She babbled gaily as she proceeded, telling Tes of the maids and servants and their roles within the household. Finally, she pulled the back of the dress together, cheerfully warning, "Now, I'm going to pull the laces tight. Are you ready?"

Tes nodded, not expecting much more than a tug. She was astonished to feel Kailyn's knee in her back as she drew the laces tighter and tighter. Her breathing restricted, Tes squealed in pain, protesting loudly as she spun her head and scowled at Kailyn. "That's much too tight, and it hurts," she chided.

Kailyn adopted a look of pure innocence. "It's not my fault; it's how the dress is secured. Lady Ayana often has two of us pull her dresses in!" she declared as a playful smile grew across her face.

Tes relaxed as she looked into the glowing face of the maid; she liked Kailyn and didn't want to hurt her feelings. "Tie it as loosely as you can will you, please, I beg of you!" she feigned breathing difficulties as she spoke, fanning her face with her hand. Kailyn broke into renewed fits of giggles. Tes managed to suppress the urge to join her. "I can't believe this. I feel like a horse is sitting on me. If this is being a lady I don't want to know about it!" Tes burst into laughter as she finished, cringing when a stitch suddenly clawed at her side.

"What is going on in this room?" boomed an angry voice. Kailyn stopped giggling immediately and stood aside, head bowed with her hands clasped at her front.

Tes whirled to see who had spoken. An elderly lady, Tes assumed to be the head maid, stood glowering at Kailyn. Tes' head swung from one to the other. "Kailyn is helping me dress," she interrupted, feeling that she should come to the young girl's aid.

The head maid took Tes in with a glance, scowling, she cautioned, "Kailyn is a member of this household's staff. She will behave in a manner that is befitting of her position." She looked at Kailyn. "Is that clear!" she snarled.

Kailyn continued to look gloomily at the floor. "Yes Madam," she replied morosely.

Tesania couldn't believe what she heard. Jumping to Kailyn's defense she interjected irritably, "Kailyn was sharing a joke with me. Surely she's allowed to laugh!"

Kailyn looked at Tes quickly, concern and warning in her eyes. "Please don't!" she implored.

"See me in my rooms, immediately you have finished dressing this..," she again looked at Tes; a sardonic grin crept onto her face as she mockingly said, "Lady!"

Tes blazed, "You mock me! You think me not good enough to be a Lady! If you want to play games, then it is I who should look down upon you, in your lowly station!" She glared at the head maid, watching as she withered under her stare. "Leave us," she commanded scornfully, dismissing her with a negligent wave. The head maid glared threateningly at Kailyn as she turned on her heel and stormed away.

Kailyn shook uncontrollably. "You shouldn't have done that," she said sadly. "She'll punish me now and make my life even more unbearable." As she started to cry, Tes rushed across the room and held her comfortingly in her arms.

Tesania held Kailyn tightly as her tears slowly subsided. Keenly aware that she had placed the girl in an untenable position, she softly said, "I'm sorry Kailyn, but I couldn't let her speak to you that way." She held her at arm's length as she continued, "I'll speak to Lady Ayana, tell her what happened. Surely she'll intervene on your behalf."

Kailyn wiped the tears from her eyes with the backs of her hands as she looked up at Tes. "It won't help. That.., that witch will make sure I'm punished, even if Lady Ayana tells her not too." She moved around behind Tes and grasped the laces in her hands; gently she started to tie them in place, careful not to pull too tightly. "I wish I could leave this place. But I have nowhere else to go," she sniffed.

"Surely you could move to another household?" Tes asked. "There must be many positions for a maid in this enormous city."

Kailyn held back more tears as she blurted, "Yes, but my father signed a contract with Lady Ayana's father. I'm bound here until it expires." She sighed, "So you see I am stuck with that nasty woman for another two years, and then my father may renew the contract."

Tes was taken aback. "So you're a slave?" she asked in confusion.

"No, my father gets paid while I'm here, and I get a small allowance and lodgings. There, you're all finished. I must go now and see the.., witch," she added with a sad smile.

"I'll talk to Lady Ayana, straight away, I promise," Tes called after her.

Tes hurried from her room, holding the skirts high as she headed for the veranda where she'd last seen Ayana. "I would speak with you urgently!" she said as she threw herself into a waiting chair.

"You look lovely," Ayana smiled as she looked at Tes. "What is it you wish to speak with me about, so urgently?"

"The maid, Kailyn, was helping me dress," Tes started with a worried look on her face.

"Yes, and..?" asked Ayana as she nodded for Tes to continue.

"And, she made a joke, about..," Tes stopped abruptly, realizing that she may be about to cause Kailyn more trouble. "She made a joke," she continued cautiously. "I laughed, a lot, and she joined in. It was my fault! She told me she would get into trouble, but I laughed anyway. The head maid came." Tes looked guiltily at Ayana. "She yelled at Kailyn, I interposed, she got angry and..," She looked down, embarrassed. "And she implied I wasn't a lady." Looking back at Ayana, regret in her eyes, she said, "I put her in her place, and dismissed her. I'm afraid she'll take it out on Kailyn." Pleadingly she added, "It wasn't Kailyn's fault, it was mine, I made her laugh. It was me who talked down to the head maid. Why should she be punished? Why should the witch..?" she paused, apologetically starting again. "Why should the head maid be allowed to punish her for laughing? Please help Lady Ayana!" she implored.

Ayana sat and listened as Tes recounted her story. "Calm down and tell me everything that happened, including the joke."

Tes took a few deep breaths before starting from the beginning. Ayana stifled a laugh when she retold Kailyn's joke. "I have to agree there," she had said. Tes told her of how the head maid had talked to Kailyn and herself, and how she had questioned her own right to be a lady. Ayana shook her head as Tes finished. "You need to understand the hierarchy of a household such as this. The maids would run amuck if there was no discipline imposed upon them." As Tes looked down dejectedly, Ayana continued, "However; I will not have my guests talked to in this way," she said angrily as she rang the small, silver summoning bell.

Tes' head whipped up. "And Kailyn; what of her? All she did was laugh with me!" she questioned, hopeful that the girl may gain a reprieve.

Ayana shook her head as she sadly said, "I will speak with her, but she must maintain the discipline that is set out by the head maid." As she saw Tes' head drop once more, she added, "I will not punish her. I agree that she was not doing anything terribly wrong. I fear though that the head maid, despite my wishes, will make her life unbearable in the future." As a maid arrived she said, "Let me deal with this as I see fit." Turning she spoke to the maid. "Please ask the head maid to see me in my chambers immediately, I then wish to talk to Kailyn." As she stood to leave, she said, "And please bring some refreshments to my guest," she smiled gracefully at Tes, making a point of her next words, "Lady Tesania."

15 PAIN OF THE BEAST

The banmora looked proudly over his harem, six females in all, two already showing the first signs of pregnancy. The spring sunshine had brought a delectable range of flowers and young shoots for them to feast on. They grazed through the days, his females grunting and swaying back and forth, alerting him when they had found a particularly tasty morsel, stepping aside as he approached, allowing him to eat. They wandered the forest in the foothills of the mountains, moving daily to fresh pickings and new delights. His life was simple, defending his rights to the harem he found easy, his size and cunning set him apart from the other males, their attempts to succeed him only led to their own failure, sometimes death. He lay, one beautiful spring night, with his favorite female as she searched his fur for insects and ticks, causing him to drift off to sleep.

As the sun broke over the northern horizon the banmora stirred, an unfamiliar sound causing him to jerk his head upright. Searching the forest he saw three strange animals, he had seen ogres many times, but these were different; he knew instantly that he should fear them. Struggling to his feet he voiced a withering snarl and stalked toward them, one foot at a time he slowly moved forward, crouched low, ready to strike.

He made his way between the intruders and his harem, protecting them his main concern. The intruders raised the sticks they carried; light springing from the end of one of them, striking the banmora on his hindquarters. Blinding pain wracked his body as the spell took hold. Snarling, he ran at his attacker, not understanding the danger, another spark hit him, then another.

The intruders laughed as he crashed to the forest floor, writhing in pain. His females huddled in a circle, not knowing anything better to do. He had always been their protector. As the pain subsided he lurched to his feet. The intruders hit him with a small spark; he darted forward then started to turn. Another spark hit him on the side, turning the other way he was hit once more, this time on the other side. He quickly realized that if he didn't walk where they wanted him to he would be bitten by the pain. Involuntarily he went where they directed, his females following meekly behind. Two days later they were herded into a pen inside a dark cave, his harem cowering at his side, he let out an agonizing roar as he realized there was no more he could do for them.

~

Pain wracked his body as he lay bound to the cold slab of rock a few days later, his shrieks echoing throughout the underground cave before fleeing into the starlit night. Writhing as a thousand years of evolution forced itself upon his mind and body in seconds, tissue torn, bones warped out of all proportion, his animal instincts squashed aside as Trannyth's thoughts were imprinted in his brain. As the terrible pain subsided he lay quietly, aware that he was no longer a simple banmora, his muscles twitching as he watched a mage approach and release him. Slowly, as he tested his new form and muscles, he rolled off the slab and stood instinctively at attention.

"Do you understand me?" a mage questioned.

The beast lowered his gaze. Looking directly at the mage, he nodded.

"Very well. You will be henceforth known as Kragh," the mage said. "Kreash here will take you to your new commander."

Kragh followed the other beast out of the cave, the rock plains were littered with small fires. Beasts, male and female, by the hundreds sat tearing the flesh off bones with their sharp ogre like teeth, their guttural conversations intermingling; his newfound speech synapses not yet able to decipher their full meaning. They approached a small group of beasts near the cave entrance. Kreash turned to Kragh. "This your unit, Kreatch Commander, he train," he said as he pointed to Kragh's hairy chest.

Kreash walked away as Kragh found an unoccupied area near the fire and sat down. A fellow beast next to him grunted and shoved a bone with raw flesh dangling from the torn joints at him. Still bewildered and unsure of his new existence, he shook his head and stared at the fire.

The next day was hell for Kragh. Human trainers forced him to fight and run and fight some more. By the end of the day he was exhausted and fell to the ground, sleep overtaking him in minutes. The next day proved better as he came to like the feel of the viciously curved sword in his hand. Fast and agile, over the next weeks he learnt the swordsman's art at an astonishing rate, soon able to best the other beasts in his unit; even Kreatch, his commander, was obliged to give quarter under Kragh's accurate onslaught.

Mealtimes created a conundrum for Kragh, years as an herbivore banmora made the unappetizing raw meat thrown in front of him almost inedible; even his newly found Ogre idiosyncrasies didn't drive him to eat much. Standing one night, he walked into the craggy rocks that surrounded the camp. Finding a lone, bushy plant he sat and started to pick the juicy green leaves. Memories flooded back of his days in the foothills, his harem of females tending his every need as he wandered from bush to bush picking the tastiest morsels of young budding leaves for himself; he longed for those days again.

He could feel the thoughts of Trannyth controlling him, telling him that he was a mere soldier, to do as he was instructed. He felt his past life and memories being quashed. Every minute he fought against it, determined not to become what these man-things wanted him to be. As he walked back to his unit he determined to show no sign of his inner turmoil. Sitting by the fire he snatched up a piece of rancid meat, grunted and tore at its end.

16 A GENERAL IDEA

Deavon was greeted warmly by his fellow rangers when he entered the barracks. Gratefully he opened the door to his room and tossed his pack onto the bed. It was a small room, unadorned with stone walls, just large enough for a bed, table, cupboard and a chest. Deavon, nevertheless, thought of it as home. He quickly washed, dressed in fresh clothes and with Tesania's sword in hand walked back out the door. He strode through a labyrinth of echoing hallways as he made his way to the offices housing the headquarters of the Rangers. "Well met," he said to the secretary as he neared the general's office. "Is General Legana in please?" he asked. "I have urgent need to speak with him."

"Well met," replied the secretary. "The General is in. I shall let him know you wish a meeting. Deavon isn't it?"

"Thank you," Deavon nodded. He took a seat against a wall. A massive tapestry, depicting a battle scene involving rangers and ogres, dwarfed him. As he sat, he studied Tesania's sword, wondering at the intricate molding. *Where did it come from? When it was forged? Who had forged it and why?* As he slid the blade back into the scabbard, the secretary returned.

"The general will see you in a few moments; if you would kindly wait."

"I shall; thank you again," Deavon cordially replied. He watched as other rangers came and went, delivering messages, debriefing from missions. Many greeted him as they passed by. One approached him with a broad smile.

"Well met, Aldan," Deavon said cheerfully as his friend thumped down next to him.

"Well met," Aldan replied as he clapped Deavon on the shoulder. "I thought you'd be away for months. At least until summer?"

"Things have changed I'm afraid," replied Deavon as he fiddled with the sword. "I can't explain now, I have a meeting with General Legana in a few moments. Are you free to share an ale after I see the general?" As his friend nodded affirmatively, Deavon went on, "I'll tell you of my journey then; what I can anyway," he said with a conscientious grin.

The secretary approached. "The general will see you now," he said.

Deavon excused himself from Aldan and headed for the general's door. Pausing with his hand on the handle, he took a deep breath, gathered his thoughts and entered. The general sat busily studying a parchment that took up most of his desk. Deavon stood to attention, just inside the door, waiting to be recognized. General Legana read on for a few moments before looking up and gruffly saying, "What are you waiting for Deavon; take a seat." He waved irritably toward a chair that sat on the opposite side of his large, ornately carved desk. "Tell me. What of your mission?" he asked as he leaned back in his chair, waiting to hear Deavon's report.

Deavon quickly passed over his outward journey as he made his report. As he spoke of reaching the forest outside Aryd Village and meeting Tesania he expanded on the detail. He told of the beasts killing all in the village, how Tes had survived and met him in the woods. The General sat forward, taking particular interest in Tesania's sword. Deavon started to explain its apparent power that only Tesania could wield whilst passing it over the table to him.

He spoke of the battle in the hills with the four beasts, of Giddy and Tes' role in their defeat. Glossing over the details of the journey from there he finally told of how he had brought Tesania with him, to Wyvern City, as he thought the King's Mages may wish to see her and the sword. He, however, chose not to tell the general of Tes' desire to exact revenge upon Trannyth and the beasts.

The general sat for some time examining the sword; seemingly lost in thought. He looked up at Deavon. "And you say this girl.., Tesania, can fight like a warrior with this sword.., but not at all with a normal sword?" he asked, eyebrows raised.

"That seems to be the case," Deavon replied. "It also burns with fire when it perceives her enemies are near. Without it, we would probably be dead," he said as he looked down at the lifeless sword in the general's hands.

"Berton!" called the general loudly as he placed the sword on the desk. A few moments later the secretary poked his head through the door. "Send urgent summons to my staff to meet in the morning, in the planning room. Also send for the army generals and their staff, as well as the Archmage and his people." As Berton turned to leave, the General called, "And also, please invite the King. Inform his advisers it is a matter of urgency; concerning the beasts."

Deavon was astonished. "Why are you calling an urgent meeting with all these people?" he asked cautiously. "I've brought no real news, except of a wiped out village, a few dead beasts and a girl with a sword."

The general tapped his chin with his forefinger, looking at Deavon evenly as he said, "A girl with a sword, you say." He shook his head at Deavon. "I say, a girl with a magic sword. We need to find out what this sword is capable of, and quickly. Where is the girl now?" he asked anxiously.

Deavon had known that Tesania's sword would draw attention, but he hadn't imagined that the general would be this interested in it. He looked at the general's questioning face as he answered, "She's with my friend, Lady Ayana, staying at her apartment."

"Fine, fine, keep her there. Nobody else is to know of this sword, do you understand?" he commanded. As he sat in thought, he suddenly asked, "Who else does know of the sword and its powers?"

Deavon replied quickly, "There are only two; the soldier who fought the beasts in the hills with us who's now on assignment in the Issdale Forest, and Lady Ayana."

The general looked at Deavon apologetically. "You will understand more after tomorrow." He stood, his demeanor changing to that of the host. "Will you share some wine with me?" he asked as he produced a bottle and two earthenware goblets.

The general questioned Deavon more on Tesania as they sipped their wine. He remained confused as to how a family of village blacksmiths had come to possess a sword of this magnitude and managed kept it secret through generations. "Surely the girl knows of its history?" he questioned again. "It's obviously old and couldn't have been forged in a village smithy. It would require an accomplished sword smith to produce something this balanced and light," he marveled as he drew the sword and held it out in front of himself, studying its length.

"Agreed," replied Deavon, remembering when he had wielded it. "It obviously has something to do with her bloodline though," he frowned. "Why else would the magic only come forth for her?" he asked thoughtfully. "There's obviously something in her family's past that we don't understand," he suggested, wondering at what it could be.

"The mages may know more. Let's hope so anyway," suggested the general. "I'm sure you have much to do. I'll see you in the morning."

Deavon, realizing he had been dismissed stood and reached for the sword before heading for the door. The General interrupted, "You can leave the sword," he said.

"But I promised Tesania I'd look after it," he said quickly.

The General looked at him. "I said you can leave it. You may go," he said dismissively as he looked back to the parchment on his desk. Deavon, with no choice, turned and left.

Later he sat miserably in the large mess hall attached to the Rangers Barracks. The ale he was drinking with Aldan wasn't enjoyable. As he listened to his friend recount his mission to the mountains his thoughts strayed to Tesania and her sword. *What have I got the girl into? She's now exposed to the prying eyes of all the King's departments. The mages will want to question and test her. They wouldn't allow her to keep the sword, of that he was now sure.* He lamented as he absentmindedly pushed the tankard around the table that he should have told her to hide the sword and left her at Lyiera. There at least she could have rebuilt her life in peace.

He shook his head, knowing that he could not have done it, his duty dictated that he bring a sword like that to the attention of his superiors. As he sat mulling, he had to admit that there were other, more personal, reasons that he had brought her all the way to Wyvern City. He jumped as Aldan asked if was listening. Apologizing profusely, he excused himself and retired to his room.

17 A MEETING OF MINDS

The planning room buzzed as twenty-six people milled about, all greeting one another at the same time. Deavon walked to the far end of the table, reaching his seat as the King's arrival was announced. Suddenly quiet, the entire room turned to the door as the courtiers entered. Strutting like peacocks; they formed two lines along the room. The King paraded down the centre waving cordially and nodding as he went. As he reached his chair at the end of the long oak table, he turned and looked around the room before performing a regal bow and taking his seat. The other members of the meeting quickly found their positions, the courtiers, interested only in the pomp and ceremony, filed out the door.

Chairs dragged across the flagged stone floor as General Legana called the meeting to order. He bowed deeply to the King "Welcome, My Lord," he said, waiting for the King's approving nod before moving on. Turning, he walked along the length of the table. "Gentleman," he started. "As you are aware, Trannyth's beasts are creating havoc throughout Eldanal." He paused as the gathering murmured. "The army," he swung his arm, taking in the gathered army generals, "have sent forth troops of soldiers. As we know, they haven't had much success." He held his hand in the air as the army generals started to protest. "My intent is not to point out any flaws with our esteemed colleagues of the army. I make this point because I believe that hunting the beasts down, group by group, will be impossible. Even when we do manage to eliminate a group Trannyth will just send more." Again he paused as the room erupted. Smashing his closed fist on the table, he thundered, "We must strike!" He strode purposefully along the length of the table. "He thinks he is safe in his Keep. He thinks he can't be attacked!" Spinning on his heel, he retraced his steps. "I believe that a small group can cross the mountains, penetrate his defenses and eliminate him. Once he and his mages are gone we can mop up the last of his beasts."

The gathering clamored, the Archmage stood. "What makes you think you can destroy Trannyth with a few rangers?" he asked condescendingly. "Trannyth is beyond anything this Kingdom has ever faced." He looked around, seeing that the majority agreed he continued. "He is a mage of immeasurable strength. You do not stand a chance!" he said as he sat with a flourish, convinced his point was made.

General Legana turned; an insightful look on his face. "A few days ago my rangers delivered two of Trannyth's mages that they captured above Orash." He paused as astonishment rippled through the room. "These mages have been.., ah.., questioned," he said with a mirthless smile. The gathering chortled, knowing full well the methods that the rangers employed to, 'question'. It appears that our friend Trannyth has made a fatal mistake." He again allowed the din to settle. "Apparently, according to our guests in the dungeon, he has crafted an orb." The Archmage scoffed. Ignoring him the general continued. "The orb is used to convert simple Banmoras, with the life force of a captive Ogre, into what we know as beasts. If we can destroy the orb, we destroy Trannyth!" he announced exuberantly.

The room once again erupted. The Archmage protested vehemently that it was ridiculous, "Destroying the orb may kill the beasts, but certainly not Trannyth. He will resurface with a new orb and beasts almost immediately!" he bellowed, his cheeks quivering as he looked at the General triumphantly.

The General remained unfazed, knowing he still held an ace up his sleeve. Waiting until everybody had once again taken their seats, he continued. "The Archmage is correct as always," he said as he graciously bowed before him. The Archmage gleamed in victory, looking toward the King for his approval. The General smiled. "However. Trannyth, as I have stated, made a fatal error." he looked directly at the Archmage. "He infused a part of his own life force into the orb." Spinning on his heel, he strode to the far end of the room. "Now I am sure the Archmage will correct me if I am wrong, but, I believe if the orb should be destroyed, Trannyth, in fact anything that has its life force imbued in the orb, will be destroyed along with it!" He turned, looking triumphantly into the eyes of the mage.

The Archmage sat quietly for more than a few seconds as he digested this new information. Aware that he had been outplayed and made to look foolish, he stood and glared around the room; the meeting falling ominously quiet. With a seething voice, he asked, "And how is it that you plan to destroy this orb?"

"I plan to simply, smash it," the General shrugged.

The Archmage once again scoffed, "If this orb exists at all, and if it is made with magic, it can only be undone with magic; and I mean strong magic. You are wasting our time!"

The general pondered the words as he slowly walked to a small table set against the wall. "I believe that I have come into the possession of a weapon that can accomplish the task," he said as he threw back the black material covering the table and grasped Tesania's sword.

Deavon leapt to his feet. "General Legana, I must protest." He stormed to where the general stood. "That sword belongs to Tesania of Aryd Village. It's not yours to offer, or to wield."

"You forget your place, Deavon," the general said coldly. "Please retake your seat."

Deavon reluctantly walked back to his chair as the general walked toward the King, offering the sword. "My Lord; this sword is enhanced with magic, I have had it confirmed overnight by one the mages' of my esteemed colleague, the Archmage here," he said with a victorious grin. "It has very powerful magic imbued into it." He grinned, clapping his hand down onto the Archmage's shoulder. "That, my friend, is how I shall smash it."

Deavon couldn't control himself. Again he rose to his feet. "It won't work!" he yelled defiantly at the general. "The sword only works for the girl. You can't, nor can any other, call its power. It's useless to anyone; except her!"

As the King stood the room went deathly quiet. "Enough!" he warned. "We must work together to bring Trannyth to justice and rid Eldanal of his hordes." He held the sword up, pointing it at the Archmage., "I want this fully investigated. Find out what magic is in it and how it works." He turned to Deavon. "Who is this girl that owns the sword?" he asked. "And where is she?"

Deavon, whilst having been in the same room as the King before, had never met or spoken to him. He nervously recounted finding Tes in the woods, the journey, the battle with the beasts and arriving in Wyvern City. "She's staying with Lady Ayana; a friend of mine."

"I know Lady Ayana well," replied the King. "Tell me. Why did you bring this girl to Wyvern City? Why not just bring the sword and leave her at Rilmir? She could have been summoned later if she were required."

Deavon felt trapped. He knew that he must tell the truth to the King, to do otherwise was unforgivable. Cautiously he said, aware that he was possibly putting Tes in the path of danger, "Tesania is the only one who can wield the sword. I thought it best that she be here; for when it's examined by the mages."

The King, sensing that Deavon was holding back, asked, "Is that all? There is no other reason that you brought her all this way?"

Deavon didn't wish to tell them of Tes' fixation on Trannyth, but felt he was in a position where he had no choice. He looked directly at the King. "She's adamant that she's going to kill Trannyth. She wishes to avenge the death of her parents." He paused, feeling foolish. "When I saw the power of the sword I told her I would talk to my superiors and ask for their help."

"So the girl is willing to take on the task of destroying Trannyth?" the King asked carefully.

Deavon winced. "She's only a girl, sixteen years of age. What can she do?" he asked, horrified.

The King started to walk to the door. "She is a subject of Eldanal. If she is the best chance we have to defeat Trannyth, I will command she go." He spoke to the general, "I want to see a realistic plan for this mission, and I wish to meet this Tesania. See that she is presented to the palace tomorrow!" Turning to the Archmage, he said, "I want that sword examined immediately; we need to know its origin I think, before we can understand its full power."

Deavon stood, dumbfounded. "Tes, what have I done to you?" he mumbled as he started for the door.

18 A DRESS FOR A BALL

Tesania returned to her room, propping at the door as she saw Kailyn sitting on the end of her bed. Rushing to her, she gripped her hands and sat down. "Tell me. What happened? Are you ok?" she asked quickly.

Kailyn beamed. "Lady Ayana said I'm to be your lady-in-waiting while you stay with her." A tear of joy ran down her cheek as she looked at Tes. "I'm to devote all my time to you. Isn't it delicious?" she asked as she started to giggle.

"Shh," Tes said. "The head maid might come again!" She looked quickly at the door to emphasis her point.

Kailyn shook her head. "No; the witch was told to leave me alone! Isn't it wonderful?" she gasped.

Tes watched the exhilaration in the young girl's face. She was pleased that Kailyn was so happy, but also confused. "Tell me, please, what's a lady-in-waiting?" she asked.

Kailyn burst into laughter. "I see I have a lot to teach you," she said as she gained control of herself. "I've been appointed to attend your every need, your personal assistant if you like. And guess what?" she asked conspiratorially as she looked toward the door. "I don't have to do any of my old maid duties while you're here." Without waiting for Tes to answer she erupted delightedly, "Isn't it just like a dream?"

Tes felt Kailyn's hands shaking slightly in her grasp. "That's wonderful," she said whilst looking down at the bed, uncertain of why she would need her own maid. "We could be more like, just friends, if you want," she suggested hopefully.

"I like that," replied Kailyn. "Friends!" She peered happily into Tes' face. "We'd better start getting you ready for the Ball," she said as she stood and headed for the cupboard. "Your bath is ready. Whilst you bathe I'll prepare your gown," she suggested enthusiastically.

Tes sat, confused. "But it's early. We have hours before the Ball, don't we?" she asked.

Kailyn shook her head and laughed. "That's exactly why you need me," she teased. "Trust me, we'll need every minute. Lady Ayana would already be bathed and starting to dress, as we speak."

Tes shook her head in wonderment. Kailyn bustled over. "Come on, come on, go! I'll be waiting for you when you return," she said as she laid a gorgeous gown on the bed. Tes gasped and moved toward it; Kailyn blocked her way, hastening her from the room.

A short time later Tes appeared back at the door. Kailyn took her hand and led her to a white dressing table adorned with intricate gold inlay. There were pots of powders, vials of perfumes, pads of colored blush, brushes, hairclips and other implements that Tesania had never seen before. Kailyn appeared to know what was to be done, so Tes sat back and let her work. She hummed lightly as she brushed Tes' hair, placing clips at rapid speed. As she started to make ringlets, Tes intervened. "I would like my hair straight please. I don't want any fancy styles. Just part it in the middle and let it fall over my shoulders."

Kailyn shook her head. "No, no, this is how all the ladies in Wyvern City wear their hair," she said as she started to curl more strands.

Tes reached back, gently holding Kailyn's hand. Looking at her in the mirror, she said, "I'm not a Lady of Wyvern City. I'm from a small village. My mother always brushed my hair straight. I prefer it that way!"

Kailyn looked aggrieved as Tes released her hand. "But it's the accepted way for it to be done. You won't look like all the others," she said uneasily.

"That's just it," Tes replied adamantly. "I'm not, and do not wish to be, like all the others!"

"But, you'll stand out, you'll be different!" Kailyn said incredulously.

Tes sighed. "I am different, Kailyn! I don't care if I stand out. If they don't like it, I don't care!" She looked in the mirror impatiently. "Please just brush it straight!"

"Very well; I will," Kailyn said sulkily. "But I still think we should do it the same as all the others."

Tes sat quietly, thinking of her mother as the girl brushed her hair. It had only been two weeks since the beasts had attacked, yet it felt like a lifetime ago. She thought of what she might be doing now, probably helping her mother prepare a meal or watching her father in the smithy. How odd that the chain of events had led her all the way to the King's City, where she was about to attend a Ball held by the King and Queen themselves. A tear ran down her face as she glanced to the heavens, mumbling, "I hope you're proud of me mother."

"There," Kailyn said as she stepped back. "It's very plain though," she remarked, tut tutting as she shook her head.

Tes studied herself in the mirror, pleased with what she saw, but aware that the girl was right; it was plain. A thought came to her. Rising, she rushed to her bag. Rummaging through, she finally stood with a small package in her hand, handing it to Kailyn as she sat back down. "Try these," she said cheerfully.

Kailyn slowly opened the parcel, drawing her breath sharply as the jewelry that Tesania had bought with Deavon at the markets in Rilmir tumbled out. "They're beautiful," she exclaimed. "Where did you get them?"

Tes explained the markets in Rilmir and how Deavon had bartered with the man. "I'd almost forgotten them. Quickly, put them on!" she begged.

"But we have to do your face first."Kailyn frowned. "We have to put the powder on, then the blush, then the.., oh, you'll see," she laughed.

"What? You mean I have to have all that?" she asked as she pointed at the table in front of her. "On my face?"

Kailyn giggled. "Yes, you do. How far away was this village of yours?" she teased.

Tes laughed as she turned toward her. "Come on then, get on with it."

Many hours later, Kailyn stood back, admiring her work. "There!" she said proudly. "All done."

Turning to the mirror, Tes was amazed. Her face was perfect, her skin like porcelain, blush highlighting her cheekbones, lips painted a soft red, her eyes sparkling, the eyeliner dramatically ensuring they would be the centre of attention. She could never have believed that she could look so beautiful. Smiling at Kailyn, she said, "Thank you, you've done a lovely job." She spun in her chair. "Do you think my friend Deavon will even recognize me?" she asked happily.

"I think he will," replied Kailyn. "And I think he'll like what he sees." She walked to the bed. "Especially when you are wearing this gown."

After much pulling, pushing and grunting, Tes stood before the mirror. The burgundy red gown was made of the finest silk, the soft neckline of the fitted bodice and bell shaped sleeves adorned with pearl sequins over delicate lacework appliqué. The sumptuous, floor length, multi layered skirt trimmed with satin ribbon resting on petticoats and a satin hooped underskirt. As she stood, stunned at her own image, Kailyn approached her from behind. Carefully, she placed Tesania's jewelry over her head, adjusting it so that it fell daintily amongst her hair. As she finished securing the matching necklace, she stepped back, cooing, "Lady Tesania, you're so beautiful!"

19 ENEMY FOUND

Deavon stood at the top of the stairs leading to the grand ballroom watching the seemingly endless line of carriages discharging their elegantly dressed occupants. Some greeted him warmly as they passed, most simply nodded. As Ayana's ornate family carriage neared the lush red carpet where the footmen were disembarking the passengers, he started to fidget, adjusting his clothes and brushing away stray fibers. Looking back toward the carriage he grew confused as he saw the exquisite creature, in glorious burgundy red, daintily offer her hand to a footman. He quickly looked down the line once more, certain that he had mistaken this carriage with Ayana's.

His head jerked to a stop as he recognized the jewelry worn on her head. His eyes whipped back to the radiant smile greeting him, beaming from the face that he had been so eager to see. "Tesania?" he gasped as he started toward her. His mind ranged back to the pretty young village girl he had met in the forest only a few short weeks ago, yet here she was now, a woman of immeasurable beauty.

~

Tesania took the footman's offered hand and stepped from the carriage. Her excited eyes scanned the crowd of nobles as they dallied on the stairs, gossiping and exchanging pleasantries. She quickly recognized Deavon standing to one side at the very top of the stairs. He looked confused and his head turned for a split second before whipping back to her. She beamed at him, wanting to run to him, but aware of Kailyn's last minute instructions, 'A lady should always wait to be escorted,' she waited.

Ayana alighted and stood beside her. Tes ignored her, her attention locked on Deavon as he reached the bottom of the stairs with a peculiar look in his eyes. As he reached them he stopped directly in front of her. Offering him her gloved hand, she performed a small curtsy as he lightly took it and bowed his head to impart a small kiss. She watched his face; he didn't seem to know what to say.

Finally, he stammered, "You look beautiful." He then just stood there, looking into her eyes.

Ayana coughed suggestively. "It is nice to see you Deavon," she said. "Perhaps we should move away a little, to give the footmen room to do their duty."

Deavon, red faced, apologized profusely as he greeted Ayana, "I'm sorry. You too look beautiful this evening." He offered his arm to Tes. "Will you walk with me?" he asked.

Ayana smiled as she watched them slowly walk toward the stairs, his right hand resting over Tesania's arm. She turned; accepting the arm offered her, by her cousin.

At the top of the stairs a courtier asked them their names. "Deavon and the Lady Tesania," Deavon replied before guiding Tes through a magnificent vaulted archway. Tes looked around, amazed by the grandeur of the building and the decorations. As they approached the main ballroom the courtier bid them wait. Walking to the small podium set inside the room, he boomed out, "My Lords and Ladies. I present the Ranger Deavon and the Lady Tesania."

The murmur of voices in the room lowered as many of the guests, not recognizing Tesania's name, turned to see whom the newcomer was. A ripple of excited whispers erupted as they saw her enter. Deavon proudly walked Tes along the polished marble floor to where the King and Queen sat regally on their golden thrones. Tes panicked as she realized that she was about to be presented to the King. Not knowing what she should do, she watched the lady in front of her. As Deavon bowed deeply, she followed with the same elegantly performed curtsy. The king nodded, taking particular note of Tesania whilst the Queen smiled graciously. Deavon led off to the left, the formalities now complete.

Tes shook as she stood looking around the room. Elaborately carved pillars of marble supported huge frescoed ceilings. A small string orchestra played light frisky tunes as servants carried trays of drinks and small canapés. Ladies dressed in flowing gowns whispered and tittered behind their daintily gloved hands. She shook her head in wonder as Lady Ayana approached. "Isn't it, so lavish?" she asked.

Ayana laughed lightly. "It is indeed." She looked to Deavon. "Well, aren't you going to fetch refreshments for your date?" she asked teasingly.

Deavon looked at her, confused, his face turning red as he realized her meaning. "I'm sorry," he stammered as he rushed off to find a waiter.

Laughing as she turned her attention to Tesania, Ayana said, "I am sorry, I could not help but tease him."

Tes looked at the floor shyly. "I don't think this is a date." Her head whipped up. "Is it?"

Ayana looked at her seriously. "I think Deavon harbors feelings for you; that much is obvious."

"I hadn't noticed," Tes said defensively as Deavon returned with four glasses in his hands.

"Champagne?" he asked as he held a glass toward Tes. "It's very nice."

Sweetness filled Tes' mouth whilst tiny bubbles tickled her nose. "Mm, delicious," she said as she self-consciously watched Deavon smiling down at her.

"Careful," Ayana said. "It may get you drunk."

Tes turned and once again surveyed the room. She noticed an area with many different colored tiles that made an elaborate design on the floor. The area was empty. Looking toward Ayana, she asked, "What's that area for?"

Ayana looked to where Tes pointed. Turning back she said, "For dancing of course."

Tes' heart skipped a beat. "For..," she gulped, "dancing?" Her stomach clenched, in all the excitement of coming to the Ball she had completely forgotten that the Ball was a dance. She felt the blood drain from her face as she stood frozen. Barely breathing, she looked toward Deavon, fear in her face.

He leant toward her. "Fear not," he whispered into her ear. "We'll sit for the first few. You can watch the others and learn a little. If you feel up to it we can dance later, if not that's ok too." The look of relief on Tesania's face made him laugh. "Come on, let's get something to eat."

He took her hand and led her to a table that Tes thought might collapse under the weight of food. There were silver platters and bowls containing all sorts of food. Roast meats and vegetables, soups, stews, fish cooked in all sorts of ways, salads and desserts of types Tesania could not have believed. Already squeezed into her dress and aware that eating too much might make her explode, she sparingly picked at the food as Deavon devoured a full plate. As she sat and watched the regalia around her, she realized that the wonder had now worn off. feeling totally out of place, she became aware of the looks and whispers of many of the groups around them and was certain that they were mocking her.

Ayana glided toward them and sat beside Tes. Leaning over, she spoke softly, "You are the talk of the Ball." She stopped abruptly as she saw a tear come to Tes' eye. "Not in a bad way!" she exclaimed. "They're all talking about your beauty, they think your dress and jewelry are exquisite. You have made quite a first appearance my dear."

Tesania looked at Ayana searchingly, certain that she too was mocking her, but finding only a genuine smile. "Really?" she asked shyly as a smile started to replace the frown on her face. "I thought they were all making fun of me."

"Quite the opposite; I assure you," Ayana said as she patted her hand. Deavon sat in the background, his face alight with pride.

Tesania's mood changed as she watched everybody and everything that went on around her. A young couple approached and introduced themselves. Tes was enraptured with them, the way they spoke and their elegant clothes. They politely excused themselves as a page called the attention of the gathered guests and announced that the dancing was about to begin.

Tes once again started to worry, sure that she would embarrass Deavon if she didn't dance, and certain that she would if she did. As the music started to play she looked toward the dance floor. She couldn't believe it, she knew the dance; she could remember laughing as her father whirled her mother around the kitchen table in their home. Looking at Deavon, she said, "I would like to dance."

Deavon looked at her, confused. "I thought you didn't know how to dance," he said.

Tes jumped to her feet, grabbing his hands and pulling him toward the dance floor. "Come on," she said excitedly. "I know this one."

"Tesania, stop." Deavon adjusted his clothes and stepped up beside her, offering his hand, held shoulder high in front of him, palm down. Tes placed her hand on his as he led aristocratically toward the other dancers, many couples parted, allowing them to step through to the middle of the floor. Deavon turned toward her, bowing in response to her curtsy and started into the robust dance. Tesania whirled and dipped enjoying every nuisance of the dance, aware of the attention on her and relishing it. She smiled and laughed a tinkling laugh.

As the dance went on Tes became aware of a blond woman slowly maneuvering closer to them. She tried to ignore her but the other woman's malevolent eyes never left her. As Deavon sent Tes into a dizzying twirl, the woman deftly slid her foot backward. Tesania's foot caught on the woman's shoe, sending her sprawling across the floor. The other dancers stopped and stared; the blond woman glared triumphantly at Tes.

Tes moved quickly from a feeling of embarrassment to confusion and then to anger as she looked at the woman. Deavon quickly approached her and held his hand out to help her rise. When she found her feet she lithely stepped around him. "It would be in your best interest to watch where your feet fall in future!" she growled at the blond woman before turning and walking from the floor.

The woman let out a lilting laugh as Tes left, then turned to Deavon and asked for the next dance. Deavon shook his head. "I think not, Lady Caitriona," he said in disgust as he walked after Tes.

Tes sat at the far end of the room facing the wall. Anger still coursed through her as she turned and glared at the dance floor once more. Seeing Deavon approaching she stood and moved toward him. "Who is she?" she demanded. "And why would she trip me?"

Deavon looked back to where Lady Caitriona still watched him. Scowling, he turned back to Tes. "I warned you about her type," he said. "Her name's Lady Caitriona, the daughter of Lord Dalgliesh." He led Tes back to her seat. "She has chased me for some time now, but her father has forbidden it. He insists she marry a rich merchant." As Tes' eyes flew up accusingly, he defensively said. "I don't want to marry her! She chases me!"

Tes studied her hands as she thought about what he said. "So she wants you, but you don't want her?" Slowly Tes looked toward the dance floor, Lady Caitriona watched her as she danced, a vindictive smile on her face. Tes leant forward, embracing Deavon and affectionately kissed him on the cheek. Lady Caitriona's smile quickly fled, replaced by a baleful frown. Tes laughed gaily, her stare never leaving the blond woman's eyes. Lady Caitriona excused herself from her partner, holding her handkerchief to her face as she ran from the floor.

Deavon freed himself from Tes' grasp, saying seriously, "I think you may have just created an enemy."

"I don't think we were ever going to be friends anyway!" Tes replied.

"Ayana will stay for many hours yet. If you wish I'll walk you home?" Deavon suggested.

"That would be nice. I think I've seen enough Lords and Ladies for one night."

The cool night air prickled at Tesania's skin as they left the ballroom. She placed her arm in the crook of Deavon's elbow and walked quietly toward Ayana's villa, happy just to enjoy the night and Deavon's company. As they knocked on the door to the apartment, Deavon said, "The King wishes an audience with you tomorrow morning. I shall collect you straight after breakfast."

"The King? Wants to see me? Why?"

"My general told him of your sword. I think he wishes to meet you, to try and solve the mystery of where it came from?" Deavon said evasively.

Tes looked at him in wonder. "I can't believe it! I get to talk to the King, personally!" As she turned toward the open door, she said, "I can't wait. See you in the morning." Pausing, she turned and gave him a light kiss on the cheek. "Thank you for the lovely evening," she whispered.

20 THE TASK AT HAND

Tesania sat patiently in the grand hallway of the King's Palace. The guard at the carved doors had been expecting her and Deavon. He politely asked them to talk to the hunched little man seated at a table half way down the immense hallway. She was mesmerized by the opulence of the grand hall. Two tiers of windows reached to the extravagantly painted ceilings and the flagstone floor was magnificent. There were numerous gilded frames depicting long past Kings covering the walls. The sheer splendor of it still hadn't sunk in as she sat waiting, looking from one wonder to the next.

~

Deavon sat calmly. He had seen the palace many times. His thoughts were focused on how he might be able to extract Tes from the predicament he had landed her in. Her sword held the key. If he could persuade them to try to unlock its power for another to use then Tes could remain here, safe. He shook his head, trying to clear his thoughts, and then looked at Tesania, smiling as he watched the childlike joy on her face. He knew that underneath the young exterior lay a cunning, headstrong and determined woman who would jump at the chance to eliminate Trannyth. He made a decision as he watched her, if she were to go, then he would do everything in his power to make sure that he would be there, all the way, to protect her.

~

A page approached, bowing deeply as he informed them that the King was ready to see them in his stateroom. Asking them to follow, he glided toward what Tes thought was a wall, where he stopped and tapped twice before pushing the wall open to reveal a sparingly furnished room.

A single table ran down the centre with a throne-like chair at the end where the King sat waiting for them. Tes looked around the table; about thirteen men sat in various garbs. She recognized the ranger and army uniforms, but of the others she had no idea; she assumed them to be lords and mages. One man, in a plain brown robe appeared to be a monk. As the page introduced them the men rose and bowed to Tes, all but ignoring Deavon.

The King said, "Sit. At the end of the table there will be fine."

As Tes sat and adjusted her dress there was a murmur amongst the gathering. "Silence!" said the king. Tes looked up to find the his eyes boring into her. Feeling uncomfortable, she looked toward Deavon. He offered no comfort as he stared grimly at the table.

The gathering sat quietly for some time and watched at her. Eventually she drew the courage to talk. "May I ask why I have been summonsed here today?"

The King reached to the floor beside his chair, Tesania recognized her sword instantly as it came into view. Placing it on the table, he asked, "It has come to our attention that this sword belongs to you. Is this correct?"

"Yes," Tes mumbled. "It was my father's."

"What do you know of it? Where does its power come from and how is it that only you can draw upon it?"

"I don't know," Tes stammered. "It's been passed down through many generations. That's all I know." She looked down at the table, abashed at not being able to answer the King's questions.

"Please tell us the story of your father, what you know of his ancestors, how he came to live in the village of..," he paused, thinking. General Legana leaned across and spoke softly. Nodding, the King continued. "Thank you. How he came to live in the village of Aryd. How you came to be in possession of the sword and how you came to know of its powers?" He watched Tes' overwhelmed expression. "Take your time. But please, do not leave anything out."

Tes' mind whirled as she tried to remember the stories her father had told her in her youth. Mostly she believed them to be fairytales, made up to entertain his young daughter. Looking hesitantly at the King, she said, "As I have said; I know little of the sword. As far as I know my father was born in Aryd Village, my mother too. His father was a blacksmith as was his father before him." Rubbing her finger along the edge of the table as she thought back, she continued. "The sword has always been kept in my father's closet. He used to bring it out every now and then to clean it. He was always amazed at the feel of it and how the blade maintained a keen edge." She looked around the room apologetically. "I'm sorry, that's all I know of its past." She went on to explain how the beasts had attacked her village and the massacre of all the people, how she had left the next day and met Deavon in the woods. Her eyes glowed as she told them of the sword igniting into internal flame as they battled with the beasts in the Lyiera hills, and how it had filled her with the knowledge and ability of a warrior.

Deavon broke in, describing how they had tested the sword, finding that the magic would only work for Tesania.

The King listened intently, running his hand over the hilt of the sword as they spoke. "I can tell you that the Archmage here had his people study the sword throughout the night. They found that it is indeed imbued with magic; very powerful magic. It seems it is from ancient times. The spells required to make something like this..," He drew the sword and let it reflect the sunlight streaming through the window mounted high in the wall. "like this magnificent sword do not exist." He looked scornfully at the Archmage. "Or are beyond the mages' of today. Are they not?"

The Archmage quickly averted his eyes as he reluctantly nodded. He knew better than to try to justify himself in this situation.

The King turned his attention back to Tes. "Tell me, Tesania of Aryd Village, what would you have me do with this sword, and indeed, with you?" he asked poignantly.

Deavon groaned as Tes' wooden chair crashed backward. She stood; fire in her eyes. "I would have you do nothing with me!" she said defiantly. "And the sword is my property. I will do with it as I please." She glowered at the King as the room erupted with protests.

Deavon placed a calming hand on her forearm, exerting downward pressure, hoping she would come to her senses, apologize and sit back down.

Tes twisted her arm, freeing herself from Deavon's grip. As she looked at the shocked faces of the men at the table, she went on. "From the day Trannyth's beasts attacked my village Took my family. My friends. My life! I've had but one goal." She drew her breath as she looked back at the King. "I, with the help of my sword, am going to kill Trannyth; and his beasts." Tes took in every incredulous face as she stood silently for a few seconds. "I realize that you think me a mere girl from a small village, how could I possible kill Trannyth?" Her hand cannoned down on the table; the sound reverberating throughout the room. "You're mistaken!" she scowled at each and every one of the gathered men, daring them to say otherwise. "I realize that I can't hope to accomplish this alone; therefore I have come to Wyvern City to ask for your assistance." She stepped out to the side of the table and walked toward the King. "Get me to Trannyth and I'll do the rest." As she grasped her sword she fixed the King with an obstinate stare. "With or without your help! I will have my vengeance!"

As Tes turned and purposefully walked to her seat the gathered officials erupted once more. The King watched Tes as she sat. Motioning to the others to be quiet, he said, "Silence!"

He continued to watch Tesania as the room quieted. "You are in the presence of your King," He growled. "By now, normally, you would be a guest in my dungeons as a reward for your insolence." The gathering once again erupted, a lord rose. "The girl is an upstart! My daughter, Caitriona, was attacked by her at the dance last night. Surely she should be dealt with harshly."

~

Tes flared once more. Deavon managed to hold her down, as he himself rose. "Lord Dalgliesh. Lady Caitriona did indeed meet Tesania last night, it was however, she that perpetrated an attack, tripping Tesania as she danced." He glared at the lord, aware that he was putting himself in danger by defending Tes. "Tesania, with a great deal more grace than Lady Caitriona, did not cause a scene, and certainly didn't attack your daughter. To suggest otherwise is ludicrous!"

"You dare to call me ludicrous!" bellowed Lord Dalgliesh in a trembling rage. "I will see you in chains for this. You have insulted me, and my daughter. I will not stand for it!"

"If the truth is an insult to you, then yes, I am guilty of that!" With an effort Deavon controlled himself. Turning to the King, he said, "My Lord; I am certain that Tesania meant no offence. She has, since the very first day I met her in the woods outside her village, expressed her desire to avenge her parents' death by killing Trannyth. In truth, I thought it foolish." He could feel Tesania's cold stare on the side of his face. Ignoring it, he went on. "I decided to bring her to Wyvern City because of the sword. I felt that you and the Archmage would wish to study it, find its origin and maybe use it against Trannyth." He looked down at Tes; she sat with her arms crossed, laid back in her chair, glaring at him. He quickly looked away. "Since that time I have come to know the real Tesania. She is not just a girl from a village. Within her lies a determined courage. I can assure you, Your Majesty, that it was her inner strength and determination, uncontrolled I admit, that you witnessed here today. Certainly I believe she meant no insolence toward you." He bowed as he retook his seat, quickly glancing at Tes, warning her not to intervene.

~

Lord Dalgliesh blustered, looking to the other men gathered at the table for backing. "My family has been besmirched, my daughter attacked! Are we going to sit here and let these two.., two commoners talk to us like that?" The table erupted; the Archmage and his supporters agreed with Lord Dalgliesh, demanding disciplinary action be taken. General Legana and the army generals argued, just as hotly, that the battle against Trannyth took precedent here and the girl was only showing her desire for revenge. Insults and shouts flew across the table like confetti. Lord

Dalgliesh, red faced, screamed at General Legana, "My daughter wants her destroyed!"

"Enough!" roared the King. As the room settled, he turned to Lord Dalgliesh. "Am I to understand your motives here today are led by your daughter's desire for petty revenge?" He stared scornfully at the Lord. "Does your daughter direct you in all your dealings?" He waited for a response, when the lord merely stared at him he went on. "Do not forget, I was at the Ball, I witnessed your daughter's underhanded act. Tesania here is the one who was aggrieved, not her." As he turned away, he hissed, "Sit down!"

Lord Dalgliesh remained standing. Trembling, he said, "My Lord. Lady Caitriona is of noble blood. This upstart," he said, pointing a shaky finger at Tesania, "is a commoner. Surely Your Majesty would not put her above my beloved daughter."

"These proceedings are about the war against Trannyth, yet you stand there and make speeches about your precious daughter," the King roared. "If she is more important to you than the safety of our very Kingdom, then you should go to her, now, and teach her some manners. Perhaps your wife could tutor her in the art of dancing without placing her feet under others!" He glaring at the lord.

"My Lord, I certainly did not mean to suggest that the war against Trannyth is trivial."

"It is obvious to all," the King said as he scanned the room. "That your daughter's position in court is uppermost in your mind. I will only have members here who are dedicated to the eradication of Trannyth. You should go to your daughter. Now."

"My Lord, I…"

"Leave! Now!"

Lord Dalgliesh stalked from the room, fixing Tes with a malignant stare as he passed.

The sword flashed to life in her hands, vibrating insistently. Tes eyes met Deavon's and then shot to Lord Dalgliesh as he stormed out the door. The sword settled when the door slammed shut, returning to cold, hard metal.

The King walked along the length of the room. "Trannyth must be destroyed." He turned and looked around the table. "I ask you, what alternatives do we have to achieve this? General Ardel, can we send your army over the mountains, or indeed the rangers?"

A large man stood and cleared his throat. "My Lord, we have run many scenarios for an en-mass attack by the army. The problem is always the mountains. The passes are far too narrow for us to pass enough men through; there are also far too many areas where just a few of our enemy could hold us up for months. We cannot hope to place enough men on the far side to mount a successful attack."

The King shook his head. "Archmage Edana?"

"My Lord, Trannyth has trained his mages in the forbidden ways. My people cannot hope to match him alone. We would need to have a hundred mages in place for the battle. Alas, we also have the problem of crossing the mountains in strength."

"General Legana?"

As he stood, General Legana turned toward the King. "The rangers have the same problems as the other branches of your forces, Your Majesty," he replied. "I have put forth the plan to send Tesania, with her sword, to accomplish this goal." Tes gasped as she shot forward in her chair, her head whipping from General Legana, to the King, to Deavon. Deavon touched her hand and frowned at her to remain quiet. "A small party should be assembled, consisting of the Girl, two Rangers, two Soldiers, and at least two mages. A Party this small could slip unseen through one of the mountain passes.

The King walked back to his chair as General Legana spoke; he stood in thought for a moment before looking at Tes. "Tesania of Aryd Village, subject of Eldanal. I ask you to perform a duty for your King and your people." He paused as he watched Tesania's eager face. "I task you to travel to the wastelands, where you are to destroy Trannyth's orb, and thus Trannyth and his beasts." He looked at her solemnly. "There is much risk involved in this endeavor. We will provide you with a small party to help you cross the mountains and then penetrate Trannyth's Keep."

Tesania nodded eagerly.

"There is, of course, a high possibility that you and your party may perish on this mission. Do you accept?"

The room became deathly quiet as all attention turned toward the girl at the end of the table. Tes sat in deep thought. That she wanted to go she did not question, but to place others in danger was another thing entirely. She looked at Deavon, knowing he would insist upon accompanying her, aware he would be in dire danger. She remembered her parents, slain on the ground. She thought of Annie, the small plump woman who ran the roadhouse by the ferry, in danger if Trannyth were not stopped and imagined a horde of beasts clamoring at her door. She wondered what Rilmir might be like in the future, picturing the little girl slain in the filthy street, her worn-out doll clasped in her small, blood covered hand. She looked toward the King. "I swore that I would avenge my parents. My desire hasn't changed. I accept your task," she said simply as she fleetingly glanced at Deavon before turning her attention to the sword in her lap.

Excitement rippled through the room, the King called them to order. "General Legana, General Ardel, Archmage Edana. You are to formulate a plan over the next two days. Decide whom you are going to send on this mission and have them summonsed to Wyvern City. I want them assembled within four days."

As he spoke a chair rasped across the floor. The man Tes had assumed to be a holy man rose from his seat. From his cowl emanated a soft voice, "My Lord, I believe that we should know more of this sword before we commit it, and indeed, the girl to a perilous battle with the likes of Trannyth."

"What do you suggest?" the King asked.

"The Monks of Udoros have extensive texts and scrolls from ancient times. Maybe there is magic, as yet unknown, in the sword that may be unlocked. Knowledge is power, power is knowledge." The darkened hood turned toward Tesania. "The sword, as we know; only works for this girl. There is something in her blood that the sword recognizes. It is obvious that she comes from a line of warriors, long past." He paused as he turned to the King. "She may, it is possible, even hold the blood of nobility." He waited for the commotion to settle before saying, "I believe also that a monk should be a member of the party that is to be sent on this mission, to represent our branch and offer advice and prayers where required."

The King considered the monks words. "It would be wise to follow your advice. The Monks would also hold detailed maps of the mountains; we may be able to discover a little known pass that Trannyth has not covered." He looked toward the two Generals. "Make sure to include Unastine City in your planning for the mission. The more we know of the sword and the landscape that lays in the path of Tesania's party the more chance the mission will have for success."

He stood and addressed the room, "I am sure you are all aware that the matters discussed here today need to be held with the utmost of security. Archmage Edana, as you have not yet managed to identify the spy in your ranks you may be able to use it to our advantage. Spread false leads to throw Trannyth's people off the party's track." As he walked toward the door, he said, "You will reconvene here this afternoon. Have your plans ready by then." Pausing beside Tesania, he said, "The people of Eldanal thank you for agreeing to take on this task. Indeed, I thank you." With that, he strode out the door.

General Legana stood. "Gentleman, gather your most trusted advisers. We will meet in two hours time. Deavon, please return Tesania to Lady Ayana's apartment." As Deavon started to speak, he held up his hand. "I know what you are going to ask. I have already decided who will be going on the mission." As he passed, heading toward the door, he winked. "Don't worry, you're one of them. I want you at the planning meeting."

As the room emptied, Deavon turned to Tes. "Well, you got your wish, we're going after Trannyth. Are you happy now?"

Tes remained in her chair, staring at the table. "No, I never wanted you to be placed in danger." she looked up pleadingly. "Tell them you can't go, that you won't go. I couldn't bear it if you were hurt."

Deavon squatted next to her. "If you go, I go; it's as simple as that. I too could not bear it if you were hurt. I could not sit here in safety whilst you risked your life." He rose and placed his hand under her elbow. "Come on, let's get something to eat, I'm sure Lady Ayana will be having her midday meal soon." Tes gripped her sword tightly as they left the palace; she had her wish and was about to go after Trannyth. Why then, did she feel so hollow?

21 PLANS ARE AFOOT

Deavon approached the meeting room slowly, trying to collect his thoughts, aware that the generals could be overzealous with their plan making. It would not do for Tes to simply charge over the mountains, sword in hand. Trannyth was cunning and they would need to use all their guile to even get close to him let alone destroy his orb. As he entered the room he sat in his chair, watching silently as the participants of the meeting arrived.

General Legana led the meeting, calling them to order, he started as he walked toward Deavon. "I believe the first order of business here is to appoint a commander for the mission. I nominate Deavon here," he said placing his hand on Deavon's shoulder. "He is a King's Ranger, knows the girl well and most importantly she trusts him." He slowly scanned the room. "Does anyone object to this?" Apart from a small murmur, the room remained quiet. "Very well, Deavon, from this moment forth you are the commander of this mission. Your task is to get the girl, Tesania, to the wastelands without being detected. From there you are to mount a clandestine mission to infiltrate Trannyth's Keep and destroy his orb."

The room grew increasingly rowdy as the gathered men expressed their doubts about the mission. "Gentlemen!" continued the general. "The King has ordered this. It is possibly the only way we have to quickly rid Eldanal of this menace. We must all work together to make sure it has every chance of success. General Ardel, have you decided which two soldiers will be accompanying Deavon?"

"Yes, I have sent for two of my best soldiers. They will be here in four days."

"Very well. Archmage Edana?"

"Naisa is in Wyvern City. The other mage I have chosen is currently on assignment in Carella City, he will not be able to join the mission until a later time. They will have to travel anyway, so the delay, I believe, will not be a problem."

"I think it would be more prudent if you had him here for the start of the mission; don't you?" asked General Legana.

"In an ideal world, I would agree. He is however on an important mission that must be completed. I would choose another, but Elddyn is the best man we have for the party. For the success of the mission I would recommend no other."

"So it is then, if he is the best man for the job we will have to make do." Looking around the room, he paused on the monk. "Your Holiness?"

The holy man stood and perused the room before speaking. "I have consulted with my Lord. He has divined that a monk by the name of Tean should accompany the mission."

"Very well, the mission will include Deavon and another ranger, I have chosen Aldan. He is an accomplished ranger with many successful missions to his credit. I believe, Deavon, that you are familiar with him?"

Deavon sat forward, excited by the news that his friend would be joining them. "Indeed I am familiar with him, an excellent choice, I would say."

"So we have our two rangers, our two soldiers who are on their way, the mage Naisa and the mage Elddyn who we will pick up at some point along the journey. That makes six by my count. With the girl, and the monk Tean, that makes eight in total."

Archmage Edana stood. "Eight! That seems ludicrous. How can eight people, talented though they may be, hope to fight Trannyth and all his minions?"

"We do not plan to fight them," General Legana replied calmly. "The small number will allow stealth over the mountain ranges. When they reach Trannyth's Keep they will need to find a way to enter and destroy the orb." He looked at Deavon apologetically. "I am sorry I can give you no more help than that. Even if we sent an army they would never manage to cross the mountains unopposed and thus would fail."

"I can see the advantages of a small group," said the Archmage. "I cannot, however, see how they will breach Trannyth's Keep."

"As I have said, they will have to reconnoiter the area when they get there. There has to be some way in." As the Archmage retook his seat, the general went on, "It is not the best plan, I admit it. It is, however, the best we have." He looked at each of them in turn, asking, "Do you agree?" As he reached the last member, he nodded. "It's unanimous then, we proceed." He turned to his aide. "The map please."

The aide spread a large paper map of Eldanal on the table. General Legana took a thin length of rod from the aide as he approached the map. "I have arranged for the party to board the King's Ship, Triumph. She will convey them to Udoros. A dispatch has already been sent in regard to the sword. It is my hope that the monks will have already found any references they may have to it by the time the

Triumph arrives." He paused. "Are we all agreed at this stage?" As the majority murmured yes, he continued. "The farthest pass over the Britath Mountains from Wyvern City is the Draon Pass, above Carella City. I believe that Trannyth would expect any attack to come from Wyvern City itself and will therefore have the most defenses set at the Orash Pass. We will be laying a false trail of rumors. It is hoped that any spies that Trannyth has in the King's City will feed him this misinformation and he will concentrate his attention on the wrong area. Any questions?"

Deavon raised his hand. "What lies beyond the Draon Pass? What can we expect once we reach the wastelands?"

"The Western Wastelands are basically plains of rocks and dead trees; there is not much else there. You will find many small caves and crevices, if you choose carefully you will be able to light a fire at night without being observed. As you get closer to Trannyth's Keep you may need to travel at night to avoid detection. Any other questions?" The room remained quiet. "Very well, the Triumph will remain in Udoros until the party is ready to leave. The Captain of the Triumph will then sail to the harbor of Carella City. There the party will disembark and join up with the mage Elddyn. After re-provisioning they will head up into the pass."

He walked toward Deavon. "The main task is to eliminate the orb; this in turn will eliminate Trannyth and his beasts. We believe that the other mages will be in disarray after that and will disband. The army will be posted on this side of the mountain passes to mop them up as they try to sneak back to their former lives. If the orb proves unreachable then the secondary target is Trannyth. His death should cause havoc amongst his followers, although another will soon rise to take his place. So the destruction of the orb is of the utmost importance." He reached forward and placed his hand on Deavon's shoulder. "I wish I could offer you a better plan my friend. This one is a long shot, but I am afraid that under the circumstances it is the best we can do." He turned and walked back to his seat. "Are there any more questions, or indeed suggestions?"

General Ardel stood. "It seems to me that we are placing the fate of the whole of Eldanal in the hands of a small group of people. You have said yourself that the mission has little chance of success. The girl herself is untested. How do we know she is up to the task?"

Deavon stood quickly. "Tesania is far from untested. As yet there have been only four beasts killed by any of the King's forces. She has accounted for one of them herself and I freely give her the credit for the one that I managed to kill. She'll be there when she's needed, this I confidently promise to you."

"A pretty speech," replied General Ardel. "But to place the fate of our entire Kingdom in her hands?"

General Legana rose once more. "Gentlemen, we don't have many options at this stage. To not send the girl would be just as ludicrous. Nobody else can ignite her sword!" He sat down slowly and looked at Deavon. "Besides, if she perishes, then no harm is done, we are simply back to where we already were."

Deavon jerked forward in his chair. "No harm is done!" he blustered.

The General scowled at him and then looked around the room. "I suggest we call this meeting to an end. The party is to be ready and assembled on the docks at sunrise, four days hence." Returning his gaze to Deavon, he said, "You and Aldan need to plan for your journey. Make sure you have everything you may need. I trust you will inform Tesania?"

"I will," Deavon replied between clenched teeth.

"Very well then Gentleman. Unless there are any more questions, this meeting is concluded."

22 A FRIEND'S HEART BROKEN

Tesania sat quietly on the end of her bed while Kailyn gently pulled a brush through her long hair. Deavon had left a short while ago, having informed her of the meeting and the plans that had been agreed upon. It worried her that her desire for revenge had now put seven people's lives at risk. Deavon had assured her that all the travelers understood the risks. She still felt guilty, even though she only knew Deavon. "I'll be leaving in four days," she said wistfully.

Kailyn gasped. "Where're you going? I thought you'd be staying with us here?"

"The King has asked me to go on a quest."

"What? The King! Asked you?" Kailyn asked incredulously.

"Yes, well. You could say I kind of asked for it."

"What quest? Where? Do you have to find some new type of material for the ladies dresses? Ooh, I know; some new and exotic fruit for the Queen's Birthday dessert?"

Tes giggled as she turned to the girl. "You have spent way too much time in the City, my dear. There are much more important things going on in Eldanal, some very dangerous."

"I'll come with you!" Kailyn stated brightly.

"I don't think so," Tes said quietly. "We'll be travelling rough, sometimes sleeping in caves. It wouldn't be at all what you're used to."

"I've been camping many times, with my father, when I was a girl," Kailyn replied defensively. "Besides what could be so dangerous?"

Tes decided to tell her a little of the mission, surely it couldn't hurt. "Deavon and I, along with a few others, are going on a ship; it will take us to the island of Udoros, where the monks live. There we will study my sword."

"That doesn't sound very dangerous," Kailyn scoffed. "I've always wanted to sail on a ship, they're so majestic. I've decided, don't argue, I'm coming along."

"You can't; I wish you could," Tes said as she shook her head. "That's not all of it, from there we're going to Carella and then over the mountains."

"Why would you want to go over the mountains? I don't understand. What could possibly interest you over there? It's only wastelands, isn't it?"

"We're going after Trannyth!" Tes blurted out, regretting it immediately. "I'm so sorry, I shouldn't have told you," she said worriedly. "You have to keep it a secret. Don't tell anyone, please!" she implored.

"Don't be silly," Kailyn said. "Of course I won't tell anyone." She leant forward and quickly looked at the door. Whispering, she said, "That doesn't stop me though, I'm coming along too."

Tes groaned and threw herself back on the bed. "I've already told you. You can't come. It's far too dangerous."

"You're only a few years older than me, you're still a girl too. If you can go then so can I!"

"It's different for me, Kailyn. I have a reason to want Trannyth dead and I have the means to do it. I must go, not only for my parents but for all of Eldanal. Your life is here, with Lady Ayana, among pretty dresses and parties."

Kailyn looked at Tes as if she had sworn. "You think my life here idyllic? I don't get to wear the fancy dresses or go to the parties. If I do it's as a waitress, not a guest. The moment you leave here I'll be under the control of the witch once more. Do you truly think it would be better for me to stay with that, while you get to sleep under the stars and have grand adventures?" She looked down at her lap before whispering, "I would rather go with you." Her head whipped back up to face Tes. "I can help you. If that puts my life at risk then that's fine with me!"

Tes sat up and gently took the girl's hands in her own. "But it wouldn't be fine with me. I couldn't stand it if something should happen to you."

A tear ran down Kailyn's cheek as she stared at Tes' hands. "But I want to be with you. I don't want to stay here."

"When I return in a few months I'll ask Lady Ayana if you can be appointed to me permanently. That way, in my absence the head maid can't make your life a misery. Maybe she could grant you some leave. You could go home and see your parents?"

"Maybe?"

"I'll go and talk to her now."

~

Tes knocked lightly on the library door and waited until Lady Ayana's light voice called, "Enter." Walking into the room she stopped and stared at the huge polished mahogany bookcases. There must have been books by the hundreds. Lady Ayana sat at a beautifully carved wooden table with a leather bound book open in front of her. She looked up as Tes approached. Smiling, she said, "Hello, my dear."

Tes looked around the room once more. "Your library's magnificent," she said.

Lady Ayana's smile broadened. "Thank you, I do love to read. I try to expand my collection every chance I get." She looked at Tes. "You seem to have something on your mind. Let me guess. Deavon told me you will be leaving us in four days time?" She waited as Tes nodded her head in affirmation. "And you now wish to speak with me about the maid, Kailyn. Am I correct?"

"Yes,' Tes answered. "I worry that the head maid will make her life unbearable, even though you may tell her not to. Couldn't you tell her that Kailyn is still my lady-in-waiting, even in my absence?"

Lady Ayana shook her head. "I cannot. How can I justify a young maid sitting around all day doing nothing whilst the others work. It would not be fair."

"Send her away then, to her parents, for a holiday!"

"That I also cannot do. Her father accepted money in exchange for her loyalty to this house. I cannot, in-fact, will not send her back there. It would set a precedent. Any young maid who is not happy with their treatment would be asking for the same concessions." She touched Tes' arm. "All I can promise you is that I will keep an eye on things. If the head maid is causing her undue stress I will step in. Upon your return we will talk further about her being assigned permanently to you; if you can afford her."

Tes thanked her and walked dejectedly from the room. She made her way slowly back to the expectant Kailyn with the sad news. "I tried," she said as the girl threw herself on the bed in tears. "Honestly. But you have a contract, or rather your father does. You have to stay here." She laid her head on Kailyn's shoulder and rubbed her back. "I'm sorry," she said. "When I come back I'll see about having your contract transferred to me permanently. How does that sound?" Kailyn continued to sob.

The day wore on slowly. After the midday meal Tes returned to Lady Ayana's library, asking if she could borrow a book. She browsed at the rows of spines, passing the volumes of history and poetry, finally selecting, 'The Britath Mountains, by Ernal Tenrad'. She asked Kailyn to bring her a drink in the courtyard, deciding to enjoy an afternoon in the sun.

The book engrossed her; she read pages of stories about the author's travels through the mountain regions. He described the trees, the birds, the paths and the crisp clean air. It reminded her of her own pristine village.

At the back of the book there was a pull out map; she spent an age studying it, trying to memorize all the names. As the light faded to dusk, she stretched. Rising, she started for her room.

"We'll have to find a store that sells clothes," Tes said as Kailyn produced another tight fitting dress from the cupboard. Tes groaned. "In my village we wore normal clothes to dinner. I can't even eat in these things."

Kailyn giggled. "There's a lovely dress shop a few streets away, Lady Ayana always shops there."

"Not a dress shop, you ninny," Tes laughed. "I'm going on a quest; on ships and over mountains. Do you really think I would be able to climb a cliff with one of these on?" she asked as she grabbed the hem of the dress in Kailyn's hands.

"Perhaps not. We'd need to go into the other parts of the city to get travelling clothes. We can go tomorrow if you like?"

~

Tes spent the next few days preparing for the journey ahead. Kailyn sulked as they packed the last things in her bag. "Well, that's it then," Tes sighed, taking her friend into her arms. "I'll see you in the morning. You can come down to the harbor if you like."

23 SHIPPING OUT

Tesania walked dejectedly up the long hill leading to the harbor, Deavon continually asking her to keep up. She looked back, concerned about Kailyn. The girl had disappeared. Tes had searched Lady Ayana's apartment but there was no sign of her. The head maid said that she hadn't seen her at all since the previous evening. Tes had so wanted to say goodbye; she considered Kailyn to be her friend and wanted to thank her for her help. She hoped that she hadn't run away or done something equally as bad.

Trudging along, her spirits rose as the swaying mastheads of the ships in the harbor slowly materialized from behind the crest of the hill. "I've never seen a ship," she said to Deavon, her excitement for the journey starting to return. "I can't believe we're going to sail on one. Have you ever?"

"Yes, many times," Deavon laughed, already enjoying being back on the road with Tes.

As they crested the hill, Wyvern Harbor came into full view. Masts from several moored ships cluttered the horizon like a forest of dead trees. Small boats with colorful sails rushed in and around their giant cousins. Tes drew a large breath of sea air as she watched flocks of seagulls circling the little fishing craft unloading their morning's catch. Deavon pointed to one of the smaller ships, tied along the expansive main wharf. "That's the Triumph. She'll be taking us to Udoros."

Tes studied the ship as they walked down the hill. It rode up and down on the tide and three masts towered above its decks. Tes could see men busily carrying supplies from the dock onto the ship. She marveled as one man swung himself onto the ropes and quickly ascended the front mast. Rising up and up, he stopped at the very top and then shimmied out along the curled up sails, eventually stopping and working on a rope that ran through a large wooden block. "I couldn't go up there," she said to Deavon.

"Me neither. I think it takes a certain type to do that job," he laughed.

"Deavon, over here." A man called as they neared the gangway. Deavon headed directly toward him. Tes recognized his uniform and assumed him to be the other ranger joining them. Deavon shook his hand warmly. "Aldan, this is Tesania. Tes, this is my good friend Aldan. He'll be accompanying us on our mission."

"Well met," Aldan bowed.

"Also," replied Tes with a curtsy.

"Are the soldiers here yet?" Deavon asked as he looked about.

"They arrived a few minutes ago, along with the mage. They're stowing their gear on board."

"Let's go aboard. We'd better report to the Captain," said Deavon as he walked toward the ship.

Tes looked up into the masts; feeling dizzy, she quickly looked away. An officer greeted them as they stepped on board. "May I ask your names and your reason for boarding the King's Ship Triumph?" he asked.

"Deavon, Tesania and Aldan. We're on a mission for the King. This ship is to sail us to Udoros."

The officer unrolled a scroll and studied it for a few moments. Nodding, he said, "We're expecting you. I'm Dayl, first lieutenant of this fine vessel." Looking along the deck he barked at a seaman, "You there. Take these passengers below, the steward will show them their cabins." He looked at Tes and smiled. "I'm afraid the cabins may be a bit small and uncomfortable for a lady. My apologies." He turned to Deavon. "The Captain wishes to speak with you immediately, he's on the poop deck."

Tes followed the seaman as he disappeared down a hatch in the middle of the deck; the stairs were narrow and steep. They walked along a few feet before again descending stairs. The light grew dingy as a few lanterns tried unsuccessfully to chase the shadows away. The seaman walked quickly along the narrow passageway, Aldan had to duck to pass under the beams of the deck above. A cabin opened out before them; tables with long wooden benches lining the room. Another sailor stood in a little alcove on the left. "Lieutenant said to bring these here people to you."

"Fine, fine," the man said as he bustled out of his room. "I'm Tasis; I'm the steward for this here wardroom." As he shook both their hands, he said, "The capt'n has allocated some cabins for you and y'r party." He disappeared down another passageway as he spoke. "Y'r two friends arrived here earlier, took the best ones." He stopped before a tiny doorway. "This one be y'r's," Tasis said to Tesania.

Tes had to duck to get through the door. The room was like a cupboard, small and musty. She walked to the bed; it too was small, made of a length of wood hung from the wall by chains. She placed her hand on the mattress and pushed, it was as hard as the wood below it she thought.

The joints in the wooden planked sides of the cabin were stuffed with fibers; it creaked as the ship shifted. Tes reached over and touched it, her hand came away wet. She shivered, deciding to spend as little time as possible in this dingy hole. As she lifted her pack onto the bed a voice came from behind her. "I didn't know I would have to look after some kid on this journey."

Tes stood bolt upright. Slowly she turned to face the doorway. A soldier stood there, hands on hips. Tes glared and slowly moved forward. "Do not assume me to be some kid. I could take you in battle; any day!"

The soldier laughed. "You think so? You're a mere slip of a girl. I'd take you down in a second."

It was Tes' turn to laugh. "You talk tough, for a mere foot soldier."

"Now that hurts!" said the soldier. "Besides, I'm a captain."

"Where is your troop then..? Captain."

"I had to leave them to come and babysit you!"

Tes nearly choked. "Babysit!" she blustered. "You go too far!" Turning to the bed, she grasped her sword. "Shall we settle this on the deck?"

"I see you haven't changed," the soldier said.

Tes grinned, threw the sword back onto the bed and rushed to the soldier. "Giddy! I'm so glad to see you. Are you really coming on the mission?"

"I'm standing here aren't I?"

"I can't believe it. Deavon didn't tell me."

"Don't be too hard on him," Giddy laughed. "I'm not sure he even knows I'm here."

"When did you get here? What happened on your mission? Did you find any more beasts?" Tes asked all at once.

"Whoa! Let's get settled in first. We can talk about that later," said Giddy. "For now, come and meet Raim."

Tes followed Giddy farther down the cramped passageway; she was overjoyed to see her friend once again. Giddy knocked on a cabin door and stood aside to let Tes pass. The room was twice the size of Tes'; she didn't even have to duck to get through the door. A man stood and shook her hand as Giddy introduced them. She studied him. Short, muscled, brown hair, dressed similarly to Giddy; she decided that she liked him immediately.

"They'll be casting off soon, let's go up on deck," suggested Giddy.

Tes introduced Aldan to the two soldiers as they passed his cabin. They attempted to retrace their path through the ship but became hopelessly lost until a seaman offered them help. He happily led them to the hatch to the main deck. Tes had to shade her eyes from the sun as she came out of the gloom of the below decks.

Lieutenant Dayl bellowed commands along the deck; groups of men ran for the ropes supporting the masts and scampered up to the top sails. Tes watched as they untied and slowly dropped the canvas, letting them flap in the light breeze. Another shouted order sent other men to the ropes holding the ship to the dock, with a great deal of effort they hauled it in and lowered it through a hatch in the deck. "Heave away," Lieutenant Dayl bellowed over the port side of the ship. Tes ran to the rail and watched as a rowboat, with ten men, pulled taught on a rope and slowly started the ship turning away from the dock. As the ship turned downwind to the breeze more seamen ran to the substantial array of ropes that came down from each mast and started pulling, the sails boomed as they caught the breeze. The ship slowly started to move; the masts and ropes creaking and groaning. Tes turned toward the back of the ship, noticing for the first time a woman standing near the main mast, staff in hand. "Hello, are you going to Udoros too?" Tes asked.

"I am indeed. I am to accompany a ranger called Deavon. You don't happen to know where he is, do you?"

"He's with the Captain. You must be the mage that's coming with us? My name's Tesania."

The woman bowed slightly. "Indeed, I am known as Naisa."

Naisa walked across the swaying deck and leant against the rail next to Tes; the ship had gained speed and was proceeding gracefully down the harbor. "I've never been on a ship before," Tes said excitedly as the breeze whipped her hair around her face. "I love it!"

"You may not when we get into the open seas," Naisa laughed lightly.

They slipped past a large ship at anchor in the heart of the harbor; she was huge compared to the Triumph, almost twice the length. Tes counted the cannons on her deck, "one, two, three.., twenty eight all up," she said. "Is it a war ship?" she asked a passing seaman.

"Na Miss, the Lady Roslyn, she be an armed merch'nt."

"Thank you," Tes beamed.

"Weren't no problem t'all miss," the seaman said as he tipped his hat and bustled away.

Tes took in everything as they traversed the busy harbor. Little sailing boats zipped around while birds squawked and squabbled behind fishing boats. The shoreline became less inhabited as they headed out between the points of land guarding the harbor and headed out to sea. Lieutenant Dayl snapped more orders to the crew; more men scampered up the rigging and started to unfurl more sails. The ship heeled as it turned, the sails flapping for a heartbeat before the wind caught the canvas and sent the ship careening along the Eldanal coastline.

~

The evening meal consisted of salted fish and pickled pork. Tes dabbled at it with her fork before pushing it aside. Since they had gained the open seas the constant motion of the ship had made her feel ill. Deavon sat at the head of the table; oblivious to the ships movement, he attacked his plate with abandon. She looked around at her new companions, Giddy, as always, acted as if she hadn't a care in the world, bantering and teasing at every opportunity. Aldan, big and bearded, obviously a good friend of Deavon, he seemed well natured, always ready to laugh, but Tes thought this might be a facade, sensing an underlying ferocity. Raim, the other soldier; Giddy appeared to know him well. He was small in stature but well toned and obviously fit, quiet, he had so far kept to himself. Naisa, the mage was impeccably neat, obviously conscious of her appearance. *Not beautiful,* Tes thought, *Homely maybe?* The mage daintily picked at her plate, carefully patting her lips with a piece of cloth after each bite. Finally she turned her attention back to Deavon, the leader of their little group, composed and reliable. "So this is it," she whispered as she looked down at her shaking hands. "Two more to pick up and then off to confront Trannyth."

"Sorry?" asked Giddy.

Tes looked up quickly, she hadn't meant for the others to hear; yet all of them were watching her expectantly. Coughing, she embarrassedly said, "I was talking to myself, don't worry about it."

"But we do worry about you," Giddy teased. She looked about the table. "Don't we."

"Leave her alone, Giddy," interjected Deavon. "We have a hard task ahead of us, everyone here has been selected because they have the abilities and," he looked at Giddy, "sheer hard headedness to succeed."

"I'm not arguing boss; all I asked is what she said."

"I said; once we pick up the monk we'll be off to get Trannyth." Tes looked directly at Giddy. "I admit it. I'm a little scared, if that's ok with you?"

"C'mon Tes, you know I was only teasing," Giddy assured her. "We all get scared sometimes, I'm sure when we're sneaking past a few hundred beasts even Raim here will be a tiny bit scared." She dug the little soldier in the ribs. "Won't you?"

"Not if your there to protect me," quipped Raim.

Giddy laughed uproariously. Tasis scowled at her from his little alcove.

Deavon broke the silence that followed. "Perhaps we should know a little more about one another.., I am a King's Ranger. I hail from Orash where my family owns an estate. I joined the rangers and have been stationed at Wyvern barracks for the past five years." He looked at Aldan to continue.

"Also a King's Ranger. I was born in Rilmir City, left home when I was eighteen to train as a ranger. When I graduated six years ago I was appointed to the King's Rangers in Wyvern city also. That is where I met Deavon."

Naisa folded her cloth and carefully placed it aside before smoothing her robes. Eventually she looked around the table. "I am a Mage of the Sixth Degree in the Order of Rynem. I come originally from Aliaga, where my parents live. When I was four I was identified as talented, at six I was taken to the Mage's Guild in Carella where I studied the ways."

Tes gasped. "They took you away from your parents at six? I can't imagine what your mother must have felt."

"I fear my mother was glad to be rid of me. A family of twelve children is hard to feed at the best of times, my parents were poor farmers and their land yielded little." She bowed her head in silent memory. "So you see it was a blessing for them when the mages came to declare I was to be taken." She took a deep breath and looked back at Tes. "After I reached the fourth level of Rynem I was sent to Wyvern City where I was attached to the Archmage's office. There I have continued to study and attained my current rank."

Aldan whistled. "Sixth degree in the order of Rynem. We'll leave Trannyth to you then shall we?" he asked light heartedly.

Naisa bowed her head. "I fear that Trannyth is too powerful, even for the Archmage. He has studied the forbidden ways; they afford him powers I can only dream of."

"Maybe you should study these forbidden ways," suggested Giddy. "Then the mages could take care of the problem that; let's face it, they themselves allowed to be created."

Naisa smiled indulgently. "You obviously don't understand the ways. The forbidden ways are exactly that for a reason. It is magic that is destructive and cruel. It is used to create havoc and pain, to torture and maim. Trannyth has stepped beyond even these bounds and used it to create abominations." She shifted in her seat uneasily. "If we allow the Guild to teach others, even as a defense, then we are no better than he. Forbidden magic seduces the mind. How long do you think it would be until there were more, maybe even hundreds of Trannyth's type threatening our world? No! I will not dabble in the forbidden ways and nor should others, that is final!"

"Easy, I was only asking a question!" Giddy said indignantly.

"Whomever created Trannyth is irrelevant," Deavon cut in. "Naisa speaks wisely. We shouldn't use the forbidden ways, even in defense. That's why this little band has been put together." He looked at Raim. "How did you come to be in the army?"

Raim sat forward slowly, picking up his fork and stabbing his leftover food as he spoke. "I come from a long line of soldiers, my father, his father, his father before him and so it goes on." He dropped the fork with a clatter and lay back in his seat. "I didn't have much choice. When I was sixteen my father took me to the barracks in Rilmir and signed me on. Don't get me wrong, I enjoy it, three squares a day, accommodations for free." He looked around the gathered faces. "Besides if I wasn't in the army I'd be walking behind some plough for a pittance in wages."

"Do you intend to be in the army your whole life?" Tes asked.

"I plan to." He looked at Giddy sideways. "I'm working toward becoming a general."

"And I'm going to carry a little podium around so he can stand on it and look his soldiers in the eye," teased Giddy.

"My first command as general will be appointing you to follow my stallion with a manure scoop."

"I'll scoop it all right, but you'd better duck when I do!" Giddy countered.

"How do you know Giddy?" Tes interrupted.

"We trained together. I've had the misfortune of being stuck with her in the Rilmir barracks ever since."

"Watch it!" said Giddy. "Truth be known, when we're not on duty he follows me about like a lost puppy."

Raim laughed. "Well not quite like a lost puppy, but it helps to have Giddy along when you go into some of the seedier bars in Rilmir. For some reason the thugs leave us alone."

Giddy fluttered her eyelids and adjusted her hair. "It's the affect I have on men; I can't help it, born that way you know."

"It's more like the boot prints you leave on their britches."

"Now, now. Tesania here thinks I'm an angel. Don't you Tes?"

Tes smirked. "Yes Giddy, that's exactly what I think!"

"I'm really hurt now," Giddy blustered.

Aldan groaned. "It's going to be a long journey," he sighed to himself.

Giddy beamed. "It will be. I do try my best." She looked around the table. "My turn I suppose. I grew up in the village of Estom. I had no desire to work in the fields like my parents so I ran away and joined up in Rilmir. I have never, and will never, look back."

"Do you also wish to become a general?" asked Naisa.

"I'm a Captain now. That'll do me for the time being. Besides, when Raim here is a general he'll give me all the cushy jobs, special envoy or something like that."

"You wish," replied Raim. "As I've already said, you'll be mucking out the regimental stables."

"Let's not start that again," Deavon pleaded. "Tes?"

Tes looked about the expectant faces; self-consciously she blushed. "I come from a small village called Aryd, near Lyiera. My father was the blacksmith. She looked at the ceiling wistfully as she remembered the smells of the smithy and the sounds of her father hammering at the anvil.

"Mother and I used to help him sometimes; or I wandered the fields to collect herbs and mushrooms. I loved the village. I had no plans to leave and join the army or rangers. That all changed the day the beasts arrived and took it all away." She looked from face to face. "You all know about my sword. It holds magic. The King thinks it can destroy Trannyth, hence I am here."

Deavon watched her closely, it was the first time he'd heard her speak of her parents and Trannyth without passion, she hadn't even declared her desire for revenge. It worried him a little. Was she getting cold feet? "Tell us more of the beasts and the day they attacked your village."

Tes shuddered, not really wanting to relive it again. Starting slowly she recounted the day of the massacre. As she continued, her anger grew, "..., I swore revenge, Trannyth will pay!"

Satisfied that she still held her desire to achieve the mission, he stood. "Tes has seen what a marauding band of beasts can do; not many live to tell that tale. Giddy, Tes and I have encountered them in battle." he paused to let his words sink in. "Don't take them lightly, they're well trained and they fight like demons," he said as he stood. "It's late; we should all get some rest. I'll see you in the morning. Goodnight."

24 FRIEND OR FOE

Captain Oneida paced the fo'c'sle deck as the Triumph drove toward the clouds gathering on the horizon. "Shorten the sails, bear away three points to the east," he barked at the Boson. They had run smoothly throughout the night, the flat seas conducive to making sail and he'd had all available canvas set. As the first winds from the approaching storm started to pluck at the waves he turned and headed for his quarterdeck. "No avoiding it I'm afraid. Have the decks cleared, secure all lashings please number one."

"Sail ho!" cried a lookout from above.

"Where away!?" shouted Oneida

"Dead astern, hull down. I have her royals now. She's standing directly toward us, coming up fast."

"Very well." *If she carries royals she must be a big one,* he thought; his main concern though wasn't the new arrival.

"Mast head there, can you make her out?" he bellowed after half an hour.

"She's under full sail. Looks like the Lady Roslyn."

"The Lady Roslyn? She wasn't due out of port until tomorrow. I wonder what she's up to?" he asked himself more than anybody. With the knowledge that the approaching ship was friendly, he relaxed, turning his attention back to the now ominous clouds. The Triumph's pitching became more noticeable as the seas picked up; she shuddered as her bows crashed into the waves.

"She's altering course to weather us," reported Lieutenant Dayl as he lowered his telescope. "She's in a hurry, that's for sure."

"She'll have to drop some sail soon I should think. That storm is coming up fast and the wind is starting to back." He looked up at his own rigging. "Have the men furl the mains'ls, reef the tops'ls. Be ready to close haul them when the wind backs up fully."

"Yes sir," replied Dayl. He strode down the deck as he bellowed the orders.

~

Tesania gripped the railing with all her strength; she felt quite ill as the ship lurched through the sea. Deavon had brought her on deck to meet the Captain. She tried her best to keep her balance but found that the railing was the only thing keeping her from stumbling like a drunken fool as the deck heaved and rolled.

"Captain Oneida, I would like to present Tesania of Aryd Village," Deavon said as they approached.

Captain Oneida didn't turn; he continued to watch the Lady Roslyn, still under full sail. "What is that fool doing? Get me my telescope, on the double," he snapped at the boson's mate. Turning to Tes, he bowed. "My apologies, well met." Telescope now in hand, he turned back to the rail and scanned the big ship's rigging before moving down to her deck. "My God! They're raising the gun ports. She means to attack us!" he exclaimed. "Lieutenant Dayl, belay my last order, get those mains'ls back up, hurry man! Cox'n, bear away, sou' east."

"Why would they want to attack us?" Tes asked quickly.

"I've no idea," replied the captain. "But I'm not waiting around to find out."

"She's reefing her sails and coming about to meet us," cried the lookout, having to yell to overcome the quickening wind.

"Very well. We'll maintain our present course for now Cox'n."

"Shall we clear for action?" asked Dayl.

"I don't intend to fight her!" snapped the Captain. "She out guns us three-to-one. Our best chance is to lose her in that storm."

Tes tried again, "Please Captain, I don't understand. Why would the captain of that ship want to attack us? They were in Wyvern Harbor; surely they must be friendly?"

"Indeed. I've shared many an ale with her skipper. I know not what is in his mind."

"Is she a King's vessel?"

"She isn't, she's a private merchant, belonging to a Lord Dalgliesh."

Deavon looked sharply at Tesania. "I fear we may know the reason for their aggressive nature," he said.

The captain turned, anger contorting face. "Why would the captain of a merchant ship want to attack you?" he asked. "And why was I not warned that my ship and crew may be in danger?"

A squall suddenly hit the ship as Deavon prepared to answer, rain whipping over them, driving into their clothes and soaking them in seconds. Raising his voice to be heard, he said, "Lord Dalgliesh holds a grudge against Tesania here. In truth the fault lies with his daughter but he can't see that. The King dismissed him over the matter. It would appear that he has asked his captain over there," he motioned with his chin, "to avenge his daughter's, so-called, honor."

The Captain raged, "And this simpleton over there obeys him? He dares commit an act of piracy for the sake of some girl's precious honor?" He stormed over to the stern rail, glaring at the other ship, only just visible now through the rain. "I will see you in chains; and your precious lord too!" he bellowed as he shook his fist.

Tes held onto the rail for dear life, the ship tossed and heaved in the roaring wind and waves, the rain slashing at her exposed skin, water pouring from her drenched hair.

"Why don't you go below?" yelled Deavon.

Tes shook her head. She had no desire to be cooped up like a bilge rat, not knowing what was happening, waiting for the other ships cannons to bite into the Triumph's side. "I'm alright. I want to stay!" she yelled back.

"She's catching us sir!" cried Dahl.

Tes strained to see through the mist and rain. She could just make out the masts and sails in the distance. The big ship was nearly up to them, her larger sails allowing her to move faster through the water.

"Send the men to their stations please, Lieutenant," the captain said calmly. "Prepare to bring the ship about." Walking to the wheel he looked around and watched the sea and then bellowed, "Quickly now, Cox'n!" The ships great bow started to slowly come around; the men at the rails expertly handled the ropes and lines, allowing the sails to come slowly around. "Meet her!" yelled the Captain. The Triumph's rudder dug into the water, stalling her swing as she settled onto her new tack. "Well done men!"

The Triumph ran on her new heading, the other ship though came about to meet their new course and started to catch her once more. The Captain spoke to his lieutenant, "We can't out sail her, she's just too darned big. We'll have to out think her."

"Without this storm we would have no chance," Dahl said as he watched the other ship. "If we can just hold out until dark."

"Agreed," the captain grunted. "We'll have to hold her off, somehow." He scanned the clouds ahead. "We'll run on this tack for a time, you can send the men below."

Tes watched as the men rushed for the hatches, shivering at the thought of poor Giddy and the others in the damp wardroom, glad now that she had stayed on deck. "I can't believe that they'd send a ship to sink us," Tes yelled into Deavon's ear. "All over such a silly thing, and it was her fault."

"Power, greed, ambition, Lord Dalgliesh suffers from all of them," Deavon replied. "He's spent many years positioning himself and his daughter in the King's court only to see it crash down before him. He's too arrogant to see that it was his own doing and therefore transfers his anger to us, or more specifically to you. If we get out of this," he said motioning toward the other ship, "the King will be informed of his treachery. He won't stand for an act of piracy against one of his ships."

"What will happen to him?"

"Lord Dalgliesh, I fear, may have all his assets confiscated. He and his family may very well be banished from Eldanal."

Tes fell quiet as the ship shuddered into the storm; deciding that she didn't understanding the world of lords and ladies at all. She looked up as Lieutenant Dahl's cry reached them, "She's drawing closer again, Captain!"

"Very well," replied the Captain. "Call the men back to their stations." As Dahl started to leave the Captain gripped his arm. "Tell them to act casually. Let's not give the Lady Roslyn reason to think we're going to come about any time soon. When I call for the tack I want them to be quick about it. Hopefully we'll surprise them and gain some sea on them."

Dahl grinned as he turned and rushed for the companionway.

"Prepare to come about," yelled Captain Oneida. The men, who had been sauntering along the decks as Lieutenant Dayl had instructed, dashed for their positions. "Now!"

Tes turned and watched the Lady Roslyn as the Triumph shuddered and came about. The other ship remained on its course while its officers gesticulated wildly toward their crew.

A satisfied smile grew on Oneida's face as the big ship struggled to come around onto the same tack. The Triumph settled now on its new heading, picked up speed as it thrashed through the waves.

"That's done it!" Captain Oneida yelled triumphantly. "By the time they can build up speed again we'll be well hidden in these squalls. "Cox'n, bear away another few points. Let's get as far away from her as possible." Already the Lady Roslyn was falling away, disappearing behind a sheet of rain. "He's expecting us to make for Udoros. Let's give him another disappointment. Make a course for Estom Harbor." He turned to Tes and Deavon. "My apologies, but we will be a few days late."

Tes nodded, aware that avoiding the Lady Roslyn was paramount to their safety.

"Why don't you two get below? We'll be beating into this for hours; there's no use all of us being miserable."

"Thank you for saving us!" Tes yelled to the captain as Deavon took her arm to help her navigate the pitching deck.

Captain Oneida simply removed his hat, placed it against his breast and bowed his head before turning his attention back to the wind.

25 CALM WATERS

The Triumph rode gently at its anchor; they had made the secluded Estom Harbor sometime during the night. Tes lay in her bunk, grateful that the storm appeared to have passed. The travelers had been thrown around their cramped quarters as the ship heaved and rolled; no one managing much sleep.

Giddy tapped on Tes' open door. "The captain wants to have a meeting with us in his day cabin. Deavon's gone on ahead."

"I'll be there in a second. Is everybody going?"

"Yup, he's putting on breakfast for us," replied Giddy as she looked around to see if Tasis was in earshot; not seeing him, she whispered, "It has to be better than the muck that's served down here."

"Giddy!" gasped Tes.

"Can't help myself," Giddy laughed. "C'mon, hurry up. Let's go!"

The day cabin was huge compared to their cramped quarters, the morning sun streaming through the gallery windows highlighting an intricate red carpet under the beautifully carved oak table that bulged with platters of fruits and meats. Tes turned to Giddy. "You were right, I apologize."

"No need," Giddy grinned. "The bosses always live the highlife; it's just the way it is. Don't waste it! Dig in."

Tes filled her plate with fruit; there was even a pot of fresh cream. As she sat to eat, a cabin boy offered her some tea.

"Tes! Try the biscuits, they're divine," mumbled Giddy through a mouthful of crumbs.

"I will," Tes laughed as she turned to Lieutenant Dahl. "Will we be here long?"

The Captain, overhearing her question, answered for him. "We'll be setting sail after breakfast. I plan to sail down the western coastline of Udoros and come into Unastine from the south."

"You're not worried about the Lady Roslyn? That she might still be out there looking for us?" asked Deavon from his seat opposite the captain.

"I shouldn't think that he'd expect us to come that way. The last he saw of us we were still on a heading that would take us straight to Unastine. There's no way he could find us here or suspect us to take the alternative route. By the time we reach into this breeze and round the southern rocks off Udoros it'll be at least two days. By then he surely will think we've fled back to Wyvern City. I'd like to see the look on his face right now. He knows we'll report him, he can't go to any of the King's ports, he must be livid," the captain laughed as he crammed a small cake into his mouth.

The adventurers ate heartily of the fine fare. Tes chatted happily with the captain about the ship and the seas. After a short while the captain interrupted and drew the attention of the first lieutenant. "Mr. Dahl; please have the ship made ready for sea. We'll be weighing anchor in one hour."

"Yes sir," replied Dahl as he rose, bowed to the ladies at the table and left.

"He looks a good man," said Deavon as he watched the first lieutenant go.

"A fine man," muttered the captain to no one in particular.

"I might go up on deck. I love watching them set the sails," said Tes. "Giddy, Naisa, you coming?"

"Sure am," replied Giddy as she rose. "C'mon Raim, come up too."

"We all should go up," said Deavon as he stood. "Thank you, Captain Oneida, for the wonderful breakfast."

"Yes, thank you, it was delicious, the best I've had since I was at home," said Tes as she walked to the door. The rest of the travelers muttered their thanks as they followed to the deck.

The group stood against the rail at the stern of the ship and watched as the men of the Triumph made her ready to sail.

"Man the capstan," bellowed Dahl in his now familiar resonating voice.

A group of sailors scuttled to the front of the ship, grasped handspikes from the mast and inserted them through holes in a wooden drum mounted on the deck. Other men disappeared below decks.

"Why did they go below?" Tes asked the Boson's mate as he strode past.

"To the cable tier," he told her. "The men at the capstan pull the anchor cable in; it goes down through the deck and gets dried and stored. Rope doesn't like to stay wet."

"Thank you," Tes replied. She'd only half listened, her mind already focused on other activities going on about her.

Captain Oneida had come on deck and was standing beside the huge ship's wheel. Lieutenant Dahl shouted from the front, "At short stay."

"Very well, keep it coming please Mr. Dahl," replied the captain. Watching the wind carefully, he bellowed, "Ease away the mains'ls sheets, hands aloft to off gaskets, loose the heads'ls, look alive there." Men ran to the ropes and slacked them to allow the sails to drop from the yards.

"Anchors aweigh," a sailor called.

"Sheet home the mains'ls; rudder hard over, draw the heads'ls sheets," roared the Captain as he stormed forward. "You men, get it home." As the Triumph caught the gentle breeze she came about. "Set your course to weather the starboard headland," Captain Oneida called to the helmsman. The men still worked at the capstan, others waited with hooks to catch the anchor and haul it onto the ship. Captain Oneida continued to bellow orders, sending the men to set the tops'ls, topgallants and the courses. The Triumph came alive. No longer wallowing at anchor she picked up speed and rode the rippling waves to the open ocean.

Tes watched on, enjoying the wind in her hair as the ship slipped out of the harbor. As they passed the heads Lieutenant Dahl informed them that a pod of dolphins was dashing and cavorting at the bows. Tes raced forward to watch. Mesmerized, she leaned over the rails, delightedly calling Giddy and the others to come and look.

As they watched the playful dolphins a commotion broke out behind them. A boy was dragged out of the hold and thrown to the deck, a large man stood over him. "I'll teach ye to stow away in me stores locker," screamed the ship's sail maker as he walked forward, gripping the back of the boy's shirt and lifting him from the deck. "Capt'n Sir. I found this 'ere stowaway," he said as he again threw his captive across the deck. The boy groaned as he hit the side of the mast.

"Handle it please Mr. Dahl," said the captain as he turned his back on the cringing boy.

"My whip," Dahl called to the Boson's mate as he walked to the shaking stowaway. "You have come aboard a King's ship without permission. That makes you in the eyes of the King's law a stowaway, subject to the punishments decided by the ship's captain; or in this case, me." The Boson's mate arrived with the cat-o-nine tails, handing it to Dahl with an eager grin. The Lieutenant raised it above his head, the tails whistled through the air as he brought it down on the boy's back. Screaming as the whip bit deeply into his skin, the stowaway scrambled down the deck, Dahl placed his foot in the small of his back and forced him to the deck. "Stay! Or your punishment will be worse."

"Deavon, Aldan, stop them… Please! They're hurting him!" pleaded Tes.

"It is not our business. The boy stowed away and now he has to pay the price," said Aldan nonchalantly.

"Giddy?"

Giddy held her hand up. "Wait."

"Wait!" Tes said. "For what? For them to hurt him, maybe kill him!"

"They won't kill him, Tes," said Deavon. "As Giddy said. Stay out of it."

"No! I will not stay out of it!" Tes cried as she rushed forward and threw herself in the way of the lieutenant's upraised arm. "I won't let you do this. It's cruel. All he did was stow away. That doesn't give you the right to treat him like this."

"But it does," Dahl sneered. "Stowaways are treated this way for a reason. If we…"

He was interrupted by the stowaway on the deck. "Lady Tesania, please don't let them hurt me!"

Tes' head whirled around at the sound of the voice. Kneeling, she placed her hands on the boy's shoulders, turning him to look at her.

"Stand aside while I give the boy what he deserves!" roared Dahl.

Tes stood, turning slowly to face the lieutenant. "That, I will not.., cannot do."

Lieutenant Dahl reached forward and shoved her aside.

Tes lost balance for a few moments before looking back into the Lieutenant's eyes as Deavon and Giddy rushed forward. Holding her hand up to stop them, Tes growled, "Never.., touch.., me.., again!" As Dahl lowered his hand, she continued. "You see. I can't let you, because this is not a boy." She knelt down and pulled the floppy hat from the stowaway's head. "This is my lady-in-waiting, Kailyn, and I assure you sir, that whilst I am on board this ship she will not be harmed!"

Lieutenant Dahl looked to his captain, at his nod he turned back to Tesania. "As you wish. It certainly wasn't my intent to hurt you, please forgive me for manhandling you. As for the girl, she may go free if it is your will." He turned to a nearby seaman. "Tell Tasis we have another guest, every courtesy will be extended to," he looked scornfully at the dirty creature curled on the deck and sneered, "her."

Kailyn gratefully took Tes' offered hand and rose, tears staining her cheeks, blood starting to slowly seep through her shirt as she looked from Lieutenant Dahl to the sail maker. "I didn't mean to cause any trouble. I just so wanted to go with Lady Tesania; on her adventure. They wouldn't let me, so I snuck on board. I'm sorry," she sniveled.

Tes glared at the sail maker, daring him to say something. When he lowered his eyes, she said, "Let's go to my cabin, you can get cleaned up." She turned her attention to Lieutenant Dahl. "I trust you have a doctor? Please have him come to tend her wounds."

Deavon stepped aside as Tesania helped her friend to the companionway. Looking at Giddy he shook his head. Giddy grinned and shrugged. "Give them some time. We can talk to her later."

Kailyn sank gratefully onto Tes' bunk. Tes fussed over her, making sure she was comfortable before pouring some water into a dirty mug. "What possessed you to run away from Lady Ayana? You'll be in such trouble."

"I couldn't stay there. Besides, I wanted to come with you; nothing was going to stop me!" Kailyn stated defiantly.

"The mission I'm on is very dangerous. You can't come. Don't argue.., it's too dangerous!"

"I don't care! You need my help. I can cook for you.., for all of them!"

The ship's surgeon arrived. Tes stepped from the room to allow him to examine Kailyn's back. He lightly washed her wounds and covered them with a wad of cotton. "Let the girl get some sleep. Be sure to keep the wounds clean; they should be redressed every day," he explained to Tes as he handed her some clean wadding and left.

"The evening meal will be in a few hours. I'll wake you then," Tes whispered as she gently closed the door.

~

Kailyn picked at her food. Her back throbbed painfully from where the whip had bit her. She was grateful that Tesania had intervened so quickly, shuddering at the thought of more lashes. She sat now as they discussed her future.

"I will not go back!" she stated, after Deavon had said she should be sent back from Unastine on the first available ship.

"She could accompany us as far as Carella; couldn't she?" asked Tes.

"To what end?" asked Deavon.

"I could help Tesania," said Kailyn. "When you go into the hills I could cook for you, help to set camp, collect wood. I'll do anything, just please let me come."

"There are many of us who can do exactly that," replied Deavon.

Tesania leant forward and touched Deavon's arm. "Please let her come to Carella."

Kailyn sulked, looking up quickly as Deavon scowled and said, "Very well. She can accompany us as far as Carella, and there she will be sent back to Wyvern City."

"Thank you, thank you, thank you," Kailyn bubbled, her appetite suddenly returning.

26 CHANGING OF THE GUARD

Serran held a scented piece of cloth to her nose as her troop of beasts marched past her; she found their stench unbearable. They had been marching for four days now and she was pleased to see the Draon pass ahead. Trannyth's orders were to replace the troop of beasts that had been guarding the pass; she looked forward to setting camp and a good rest. She wondered for the thirtieth time that day if she had done the right thing joining Trannyth and his mages. She enjoyed the dark ways. The feeling of power that rushed through her as she cast a spell. But she hadn't signed on to babysit these foul, stinking beasts. Sighing, she moved off after them, having to walk at a faster pace than she cared for to try and keep up.

As the day wore on they came into the pass. Gnash, the troop's commander, cracked his whip over the back of the trailing beasts, driving them on. The pass became steep whilst the surrounding trees crept in, making the way unbearable for the short little mage. Gnash called a halt to the group, pointing the butt end of his whip at a particularly large beast; he motioned for him to carry Serran. After a brief period of refusal the mage submitted and allowed the beast to hoist her onto his back. As her face came against the coarse hairy shoulder she inhaled a lungful of the dreadful smell she abhorred. Fighting against the stench, she fainted. The company commander lashed her to the beast's back and barked at them to continue the treacherous climb.

Barely aware of her surroundings, Serran's mind retreated into the past. Her mother's face came to her, smiling and beautiful, her father came into the room after working all day in the fields; he opened his arms as she rushed to him, twirling her around the room, her legs flying in an ever higher circle. Oh how she loved her parents. Memories rushed back of the day she left for the Mages Guild in Carella. Her parents, as proud as they could be, her mother brushing away tears, had seen her off at the gate. She arrived at the Guild with grand plans, first to pass her tests and then to become one of the highest ranked mages in all of Eldanal. As her schooling went on she passed, but with only average marks. Many of her fellow classmates could cast stronger, faster spells than she. Upon graduation she left Carella and headed to a lowly posting in Rilmir. Unable to cast high level spells, stuck with mundane tasks, she soon felt disillusioned with her life. Other mages in her quarters started disappearing for long hours during the night. One day she followed them to an inn on the far side of town and as they sat at a table she walked up to them and asked why they came all this way just to have a drink. Surprised as they were at her sudden appearance, they had no time to react before a dark voice asked, "Who is this mage?"

Serran jumped at the insidious voice. "I.., I am a mage of the King," she replied nervously.

"I didn't ask who you worked for," said Trannyth in a low voice as he stood and walked toward her. "What is your name?"

Serran felt fear rush through her body as the dark robed mage approached, emanating hate and evil. "My name is S.., Serran," she replied as he reached out and touched her hair.

"Tell me.., Serran. What do you do for your King?"

Serran didn't answer for a time, she looked around the faces of her friends; none of them offered her any support, preferring to look at the table or the floor. "I do whatever is asked of me, as do we all," she replied simply.

"Why?" Trannyth asked in a low voice.

"Because that is my station. The Archmage's office instructed me to come to Rilmir when I graduated."

Trannyth laughed mockingly. "And you just came? Like a dairy cow called to the morning milking. To spend your days as a lowly forge mage, forgotten by those that think they are better than you?"

Nervously Serran shuffled toward the door. She wanted to remove herself from the presence of this mage and the thoughts that started to arise in her own head. "I must go," she said and turned to leave.

"Stay!" Trannyth commanded. In a whisper he continued, "I can show you powers you could only dream of. The Archmage is a fool. His rules only hold us back. Imagine what you could become if only you could use the ways as you wish."

Frozen at the door, Serran fought inside her own mind, knowing this was against everything she had pledged to obey, weighing up the consequences of non obedience to the laws of the Mages Guild. As she stood in total confusion she heard Trannyth hiss, "Sit." Without another thought she turned and walked to the table, the gathered mages shuffling along the bench seat to make room for her. From that day on she was bent on doing Trannyth's will.

~

Jolting awake, Serran was unceremoniously dumped on the ground by the beast that had carried her up the hill. Instinctively she brought the scented cloth to her nose, cringing as she smelt her own hands and arms, the stink of beast all over them. Scrambling to her feet, she retched and stumbled to a nearby stream. Without thought she threw herself into the water, scrubbing at her skin.

27 MONKS OF UNASTINE

Rays of sunshine speared through the soft, cotton like clouds as the Triumph rounded the Unastine headland and headed towards her anchorage.

Tes and the others carried their belongings to the deck. Lieutenant Dahl said he would have them delivered to the shore during the day. Kailyn excitedly climbed down the swaying rope ladder into the little boat that waited to transport them. A gathering of monks had appeared on the dock, apparently awaiting the small party.

"I wonder who they are?" Tes asked as the oars of their boat clawed them steadily toward the shore.

"Emissaries from the Monastery I should think," replied Naisa.

"Yes, word was sent ahead for them to prepare for our arrival," interjected Deavon.

The boat bumped into the wharf as a sailor tossed a rope around an old weathered stanchion. The monks stood back, faces cowled, hands hidden inside their oversized sleeves. Raim jumped lightly from the boat, turning to help the others to alight. A small hooded monk approached as the last of the travelers stepped ashore.

"Greetings," he said in a monastic tone. "I am known as Brother Matthias. The Abbot has requested that I convey you directly to him. Please follow." He turned and started toward the huge stone monastery; seemingly gliding, his aides falling in behind.

Tes looked at Giddy; shrugged, placed her arm through Kailyn's and said, "Let's go." Before happily setting off after Matthias. They looked in wonder at the huge stones that made up the impressive building before them, all seemingly carved to fit the exact spot they were in. Huge arched windows with stained glass depicting angels and gods reflected the sunshine in a dazzling display.

Matthias led them through the grand arch and into a hallway that seemed to go on forever. The further they proceeded, the more the light faded; soon only the evenly spaced candles mounted in the walls showed them the way. Gone was the cozy, warmness of the stone walls. The hall had taken on an austerity, cold and dark. Tes turned to Deavon. "We must be underground?"

"I know not," replied Deavon with a shrug.

"It's getting cold," Naisa commented as she drew her cloak around herself.

Giddy called to the monks leading the way, "Where're you taking us? This is hardly hospitable."

The monks kept up their pace; Matthias' voice came out of the near darkness ahead of them. "The air in these tunnels, whilst cold, is dry. It is the perfect place to store our many texts and scrolls." As he spoke they stopped before an elaborately carved door. The monk pushed it open and ushered the travelers through. They entered a well lit room, filled with rows of shelving, scrolls and parchments congesting every visible space, overflowing from tables, stacked high on the shelves. Monks sat at the ancient tables, studying and transcribing.

Tes gazed in wonder at the enormity of the room, almost losing her balance as she leaned back to see the uppermost shelves. "It's amazing," she mumbled as she returned her attention to the tables. At the far end of the room was a podium, upon that sat a huge stone table, also overflowing with paper. Between stacks she could make out a very old, hunched man; his pure white hair was a mere ring around the back of his head, leaving his crown bald. Standing, he walked around the table and approached the party, his sandaled feet scuffing on the worn stone floor. His robes, nearly as ancient as he, were held in place by a frayed piece of rope tied around his waist.

Brother Matthias bowed as the old Abbot approached. "The travelers have arrived." He reported. "I have brought them directly to you as you instructed."

"Yes, yes, I can see that. Thank you. Have their luggage taken to their cells." He took a small step back as Giddy and Raim stepped forward and half drew their swords. Raising his shaking hand, he said, "Fear not, we are not meaning to detain you, we of the brotherhood refer to our dwellings as cells." Giddy relaxed, an embarrassed smile spreading across her face. "I trust your journey was satisfactory?" the abbot asked. "We did expect you a few days earlier."

Deavon stepped forward. "We were beset by err.., pirates. Luckily for us our captain was able to out sail them." He moved to the side. "May I present our party? I am Deavon, this is Aldan.., he went on to introduce the entire party, leaving Tes till last.

"So, this is our special lady with the sword?" the Abbot said with a glint in his eye. "May I?" he asked as he held his hand out to take the sword.

Tes looked nervously at Deavon; at his nod she unclipped the scabbard and handed it to the curious little man.

"Ahhh.., such workmanship. It is obviously not of Eldanal. The intricate design would concur with our studies." He looked searchingly at Tesania, seemingly trying to see into her soul. Turning his attention to Deavon, he said, "We have devoted much of our time in the last few days to learning of this sword and its past." He swept the room with his hand. "Most of these learned people have spent many hours scouring our texts." He walked toward the centre of the room, placing his hand on a young monk's shoulder. "Nikaus here stumbled upon the answer, only last night. It appears your young lady has quite a history." He handed the sword back to Tes. "But enough for now; I am due at afternoon prayers. Settle yourselves in, we shall meet later." Turning his back on them, he instructing a young apprentice to escort them to their cells.

"A strange little man," said Kailyn.

"You live a life of servitude to the Lord, hunched over a million parchments, and see if you wouldn't be a little strange," chided Naisa.

Kailyn glared at her. "I do live a life of servitude, except I'm hunched over a mop or a pile of dishes."

Tes grabbed her hand. "Hush, Naisa has a point. Don't take it personally."

Their rooms, it seemed to Tesania, were exactly as the Abbot had called them, 'cells'. About six-foot by seven, adorned only with a lumpy straw mattress on the cold, hard, floor. No furniture, nor amenities, just cold grey stone. She dumped her bag on the mattress and quickly left, determined to spend as little time as possible in there. The others seemingly had the same idea; most of them were already standing in the afternoon sunshine on the lawn outside their accommodations.

Giddy shuddered as Tes approached. "The cabins on the Triumph look like luxury rooms now. Those cells are horrible." She shuddered again.

"How long do you plan to stay here?" Aldan asked Deavon.

"Captain Oneida will have the Triumph re-stocked and ready to sail by tomorrow. The sooner we can be on our way, the happier I'll be." He looked around the old monastery. "We need to pick up our new companion, Tean. I'm sure we'll be introduced tonight. In the meantime let's explore this wonderful building." He headed off; Giddy and the others following. Tes however remained, touching Naisa's arm and asking her to stay. Kailyn stood a few feet away.

"May I ask..," Tes paused, slightly nervous. "How do you know if you have magic, or can learn magic?" she asked quickly, looking away.

Naisa smiled. "It's in your blood, or it isn't. It's as simple as that."

Tes looked quickly to Naisa's luminous eyes. "Do you think I have it? Can you tell?"

"I can't tell by looking at you," Naisa laughed. "It would seem that there is magic in you, the sword senses something." She looked at Tesania's nervous face. "We could try some simple spells if you like. If you can succeed at them it would confirm that magic is in your blood, if you fail, then it is not."

Tes nodded enthusiastically. "Let's"

Naisa sat on the manicured grass, commenting that it felt like a cushion. Tes sat next to her, anxious to try. "Now, firstly, a few ground rules. Magic is a gift that can help you in many ways. But used incorrectly it can harm you.., and others. Do you understand?"

Tes nodded. "Like Trannyth you mean?"

"Yes, like Trannyth. But he is an extreme case. There are other ways that magic can harm. Used incorrectly it is very dangerous. Some spells can kill when you mean to help. It must always be treated with the greatest respect."

"I understand, like fire, it can help you cook, but it can burn down your house too?"

Naisa laughed a peeling, musical laugh. "I guess you're right. Let's start with a simple spell. Touch your forefinger to your thumb.., that's it." Leaning over, she picked up a leaf from the lawn and placed it in front of Tesania. "Concentrate your mind onto the leaf. Summon it to you; channel the thought through your fingers." The leaf didn't move. "Desire it; want it with all your heart." Still the leaf didn't move. Naisa frowned. "Relax, clear your mind and try again."

Tes drew in a deep breath, closed her eyes and tried to relax. She had hoped that the magic would show itself instantly. Disappointment coursed through her. Trying to force it, she opened her eyes and stared at the leaf, studying it, learning its shape and color, wanting it. She focused her desire, closed her fingers and summoned it with all her being. The leave resolutely refused to move, then, as she was about to give up, the tip of the leaf started to tremble, a small quiver growing through it, the edges curling upward. She was elated; the leaf was starting to move. It flipped into the air, stood for an instant, then dashed to its summoner. Tes watched in dismay as the leaf flew to the raised hand of Kailyn.

Kailyn stared in wonder at the leaf in her hand and then looked up at Tes and Naisa. "I did it," she whispered disbelievingly. Looking back at the leaf she sent it into the air, freezing it and then drifting it toward Tes before eventually landing it in her lap. A look of pure elation came across her face. Jumping to her feet, she ran to Tes. "Can you believe it?" she squealed. "Me, with magic. I never would have thought."

Tesania looked at her own hand, no leaf, seemingly no magic. Disappointment raged through her. After a few moments she looked into her friends excited eyes. A smile spread across her face. Standing quickly, she embraced Kailyn. "Clever girl. Who said you were a simple maid?"

Kailyn broke her embrace. Stepping back, she focused on the leaf once more and sent it dancing away, making it summersault and jig until it disappeared among the trees. Her joy was plain to see. Tes stood back, Naisa placed her arm around her shoulder. "Well that was unexpected. It looks like I'll have a student on this journey; would you like that Kailyn?"

Kailyn beamed, looking from her hand to Tes to Naisa and back again. "Of course I would!" she gushed excitedly.

"Back to you, Tes. Did you feel anything? Did the magic flow through your blood?"

Tes looked at Naisa, sadness in her eyes. "No."

Kailyn's smile dissipated as she realized Tes' loss. "I'm so sorry. Here I am celebrating while you're upset." She walked to Tes and embraced her.

"It's Ok, enjoy it. Not everyone can be a mage."

Deavon and the others approached, wondering what the fuss was about, as Naisa started to explain Tes wandered away, preferring her own company for a while.

~

Their meal that night was sparse; a simple vegetable broth accompanied by freshly baked bread. Giddy complained she would waste away to nothing. Naisa appeared quite content.

Brother Matthias approached Deavon. "The Abbot wishes to meet with you, please follow." He led them through a high arched doorway and down a well-lit hallway before opening a door to the left. The room they entered was large and well furnished. Tapestries depicting religious history adorned the walls while a large wooden table filled the centre of the room with plain benches running down either side.

Tes and the others positioned themselves at the table as the Abbot arrived, followed by a tall, thin, monk. "Good evening," he said as he glanced around the room. "May I present Brother Tean. He will be accompanying you on your mission."

Tean looked at each of the travelers, nodding his head in greeting to each before taking a seat next to Aldan.

The Abbot took his seat at the far end of the table. Clearing his throat, he looked at the group, now eight. "We have much to discuss." After shuffling a few parchments he continued. "As you are aware. The king sent a messenger to us a few days ago, tasking us with discovering the origins of the young lady's sword." He looked directly at Tes. "I can tell you that we have had some success in our task. It appears that the sword is many centuries old. The first accounts of it are recorded in the Tenule Chronicles." Tes turned the sword in her hands as he spoke. "The sword was forged in the far reaches of Aliaga, during the Tiadath wars. It has been forgotten over the centuries that a race from across the seas invaded the land of Aliaga, intent on laying the land waste, moving through the country like a plague." He stopped abruptly as a fit of coughing overcame him. A monk standing to the side rushed over with a mug of water, the Abbot took it from him and drank deeply. "My apologies," he said as he waved the attentive monk away. "The invaders were skilled warriors. Aliaga's army was being decimated; every day brought the enemy closer to the capital. At the time, Aliaga was not governed by Eldanal, being a Kingdom in itself. The ruler of the time was at his wits end. His advisers could offer no recourse against the oncoming foe. And so the kingdom collapsed and the King's City of Estel was overrun."

"So what does that have to do with my ancestors?" Tes asked, confused.

"Patience, my dear," the old monk admonished. He shuffled more papers, knocking a few onto the floor. "Here it is!" he exclaimed as he waved a parchment in the air. He studied it for some time, the travelers waiting expectantly while Giddy yawned. The Abbot finally cleared his throat and continued. "A rebel group was formed, led by a warrior named Rodus. They gathered in the south-western hills. Daily more groups from the shattered army joined them. Stories grew of a mage that stood at the rear of the Tiadath armies, streams of light emanating from her upraised hands, coiling toward her massed soldiers, giving them unnatural strength and abilities."

He looked up from his parchment, gazing at Tes. "It is no wonder, now that we look back, that Aliaga's army was decimated." Shaking the parchment he apologized, "I digress. Many months passed as the rebels grew in strength. Rodus, however, knew that the cause would be lost once again when battle was joined. One summer's evening he summoned the gathered mages to his fire. One of their number was Aliaga's Archmage, a powerful man, well skilled in the ways. Over many days they discussed the Tiadath's mage, determining that the only way to regain control of their beloved Kingdom was to eliminate her and then her armies." He paused and looked around the room.

"Where did these Tiadaths come from?" Giddy asked; her curiosity piqued at the talk of war.

"The world is a very large planet. On the other side there are many lands and many peoples. We believe that they came from there," replied the Abbot. "It is not known how the Tiadath managed to land so many men on Aliaga. It is hinted in the chronicles that it may have been by the use of magic. We have no way of knowing that, I am afraid," he said as he spread his hands in apology. "What we do know is that Rodus and the Archmage contemplated ways to achieve the destruction of the Tiadath mage. Deciding that she was far too skilled in the ways to be defeated by magic alone, they devised a way to imbue your sword with magic," he said as he gestured toward Tesania. "Their aim was to create a weapon that would be dismissed as harmless by the enemy mage. She would falsely believe that her protection spells would protect her from the primitive sword, however, that sword, with the contained magic, would be capable of cutting through that protection, allowing her to be mortally wounded."

Deavon turned to Tes. "That would explain the power in your sword."

"Yes, quite," the abbot continued. "It was many days before the gathered mages came to Rodus with their spells. Rodus, a skilled blacksmith, set about forging the sword. Melting down the best quality armor they could gather, he hammered and folded and hammered again."

"The sword doesn't appear as if it was made in a field," Aldan said as he pointed out the elaborate scabbard. "I would think it had many hours of quality craftsmanship put into it."

"Indeed," The Abbot replied as he glanced down at the sword. Perhaps it was worked at a later date, when he had time and a well set-up smith shop."

"Are we sure this is the same weapon?" Deavon asked.

The Abbot considered his question for some time as he took another sip of water. His eyes moved from the sword to Tesania. "I would say so," he replied. "The sword can be traced to Aryd where Tesania was born. It only answers to her bloodline which we can trace back through the blacksmiths of the village. "I believe indeed it is the sword forged by Rodus in the fields."

Deavon nodded while Tes ran her hand along the scabbard in deep thought.

The abbot returned to recounting the story of the Tenule Chronicles. "It seems the Archmage cast spells on the steel as the sword took shape, slowly building the magic until the day it was complete. Fearing the sword may fall into enemy hands, three mages gathered around the sword as Rodus ran the keen edge across his arm. As his blood glistened on the polished blade a final spell was cast, locking the magic in the sword, only to be called forward by his hand."

Tes sat forward quickly. "How is it then that I can call forth its magic, if it was locked to this Rodus, as you say?"

"I shall explain in a moment," the Abbot replied. "By now the rebels had grown in number to more than a thousand. A plan was devised to draw the Tiadath army, and thus their mage, to do battle once more. They started lightning strikes on Tiadath strongholds, moving in small bands, then disappearing like smoke. The enemy mage came from the capital with her army. She expected to confront only small rebel groups, so it was limited in number. As they came to the plains at the foot of the hills, a light gathering of the rebel soldiers greeted them. After a small skirmish they turned and fled into the hills, following a ravine as they ran, stopping intermittently to reengage, ensuring the enemy soldiers continued to follow. As the last of the Tiadath soldiers entered, so too did their mage. Rodus sprung the trap," The Abbot said as he snatched his hand closed. "The rebel army rose from their hides; as one they surged down the hills. Rodus and the group of five mages made directly for the enemy mage and joined in battle against her. Spells hissed as they struck and counter struck at each other. She easily blocked the five mages spells. Rodus made his way behind the Tiadath mage. The

Archmage was the only mage left alive to face her now; the other four having fallen. She cast a spell that penetrated the Archmage's defenses. As she gloated Rodus' sword penetrated her side, the magic of the sword shattering her magical defenses.

"With the mage dead, the Tiadath army quickly fell. It was only a matter of weeks before Rodus and his swelling army arrived at the gates of Estel. Routing the invaders, they freed their King from the dungeons and restored his throne. The King, fearing the popularity and strength that Rodus now held among his people, ordered him arrested and the sword seized. Rodus, with a few of his loyal people, fled Aliaga, never to be heard of again. The King ensured the sword and its story became like a fairytale, believed by children but scoffed at by grown men. Over time, even the fairytale was forgotten."

"So.., this Rodus is my forbearer?" Tes asked nervously.

"That appears to be the case. It would seem that Rodus sailed to Eldanal, set up a blacksmith's shop in the Village of Aryd and lived out his days in peace. The sword was passed from generation to generation, until it reached you. The spells that were cast on the sword by the Aliagian mages were never recorded. With the death of the five mages went the knowledge of exactly what magic the sword contains. It is obvious to us now that when they cast the spell, they linked it to his blood, therefore the magic will come forth for any of his line. Hence you."

"And so it is," said Naisa. "Centuries on, we have no way to combat another renegade mage, and the sword comes forth to do battle once more. Poetic don't you think?"

"Lucky I would say," said Giddy. "It's just like a King, the army pulls him out of the can, Tes' great, great, great granddad puts his life on the line, and what thanks does he get? Exile, that's what. It's just like them, I tell you."

The Abbot spoke once more, "That is all we can tell you of the sword, its history and its magic."

Deavon thanked the Abbot for his help as the meeting broke up. "We'll be spending the night on board the Triumph, so as we can sail on the morning tide. Thank you again for your hospitality and research."

"I wish we could help you further," replied the Abbot. "Tean here," he said, "will be of great assistance to you in your coming journey, I am sure. Be safe."

28 MISLEADING INFORMATION

"My Lord, our people in Wyvern City report that an attack by a battalion of rangers is imminent."

Trannyth scoffed, "They wouldn't dare. They know we have the passes covered. How can they hope to come through the mountains?" He sat quietly in thought. The mage that had delivered the news stood patiently with his head bowed. Trannyth stood and walked to the window, the Britath Mountains barely visible in the distance. "Did those fools in Wyvern City happen to find out where they intend to cross?"

"Orash pass is their intended crossing point," the mage replied.

Trannyth whirled and fixed the mage with a hostile glare. The mage took a step back, head bowed. "And you believe this to be true?" Trannyth asked scathingly.

"My Lord, it is what our spies have said. What can I do?" the mage groveled.

"You can use your own intelligence," Trannyth raged, spittle flying across the room. "The rangers are not fools. They would not attempt a crossing over the Orash path where they know they would be held up for weeks, months even. Their losses would be unacceptable to their generals. They would rather sit on their hands than risk embarrassment in front of their precious King... No, they have another plan." He turned back to the window. "Have all the passes across the mountains reinforced. I want every pass covered by mages and beasts. See to it immediately."

"My Lord," the mage said as he bowed and backed from the room.

Trannyth watched the smoke rising from the workshops in the caves. His plan was coming together, his beasts were causing havoc in Eldanal, village after village reported to have fallen. But the banmora numbers in the hills were exhausted, causing his mages to have to range long distances to procure more. He turned and looked over the sea of tents that housed the beasts in training. Smiling, he mumbled to himself, "Well, King of Eldanal you may be, but for how much longer?" Turning on his heel, he strode to the door.

29 CARELLA CITY

Captain Oneida watched with joy as the mains'ls boomed before the wind, the Triumph had sailed swiftly along the southern coast of Eldanal and was now running before a freshening southerly breeze toward Carella on the western coast. Unastine and the monks lay four days behind. The weather had held, allowing them swift progress. He had lookouts set at all times, fearing the imbecile captain of the Lady Roslyn might still be lying in wait. He liked the travelers in his care, but was keen to reach the City of Carella and unload them, wishing to return to Wyvern City and personally present his complaint to the authorities as soon as possible.

~

Tesania and the others sat at the table in the wardroom, maps covering every inch of the worn old wood. "Captain Oneida assures me that we'll reach Carella by tomorrow evening, assuming the winds hold," said Deavon as he placed his finger on the uppermost map. "The mage, Elddyn should be waiting for us at the Mage's Guild. I plan to be in the city for as little time as possible." He looked around the group. "I feel it would be prudent if we kept to ourselves; no one should learn of our mission. Especially in Carella. Trannyth is sure to have spies."

"We'll need to re-stock our supplies; there'll be no other chance to do so once we start to ascend the mountains," interrupted Aldan.

"Agreed. Make a list, take Naisa with you and tell anyone who asks that you are travelling to Orash Village to visit friends." He looked to the map. "The Draon Pass is a hardly used track so it may be dangerous. We'll need ropes and hooks." Looking up, he said, "Giddy, Raim, can I rely on you to purchase these in Carella?" Giddy nodded, her face serious. Deavon continued, "The pass will be overgrown, many places will merely be ledges on the side of cliffs. It's imperative that we stay together and help each other." He looked around the table. "I would rather take extra time than lose someone. Agreed?"

"Agreed," they all murmured.

"We should still have a scout," said Raim. "Trannyth may have guessed that an attempt might be made to cross the mountains this way."

"Wise words," replied Deavon as Giddy dug her finger into the little soldier's ribs. Deavon shook his head as he returned to the map. "The pass will bring us into the wastelands some four to five days to the west of Trannyth's Keep. After the first few days we'll need to travel at night as Trannyth is sure to have patrols guarding every approach. There are many caves and fissures in the wastelands, this will allow us a safe haven each day; if we position ourselves correctly we will be able to light a fire. There'll be game along the way. If you go after something though, make sure you let the rest of us know. We don't want to be separated. Understood?"

Giddy raised her hand. "Excuse me boss. What do we do when we reach this Keep? Surely it's heavily guarded, possibly even impenetrable."

Deavon sat back in his chair. "We don't know what the Keep even looks like at this stage. Once we get within sight of it we'll need to scout it out, see where there are weaknesses in the defenses, guard changes, etc... There has to be a way in."

"Good plan," Giddy quipped.

Deavon smiled. "Best I can do Captain. You all knew this would be tough." He scanned their faces. "If anybody can get in, it's us."

"It will be difficult," interrupted Naisa. "There will be many protection spells on the Keep. It may take days for Elddyn and I to dismantle them, even then it may be discovered that the protection is weakening."

"I think it'll be necessary for us to find a way in that doesn't involve dismantling their spells. We won't have time to spend days," replied Deavon. He looked slowly from one traveler to the next. "There will be eight of us, skilled in many varied w..."

"Nine," interjected a small voice from the corner of the cabin.

Deavon paused, sighing as he looked to the girl who had spoken. "Kailyn, we have had this conversation. You'll be returning to Wyvern City on the Triumph. It's already been arranged with Captain Oneida."

"No!"

"Kailyn," Tes interrupted as Deavon started to reply. "It's far too dangerous for you!"

"I don't care!" Kailyn almost screamed. "Stop telling me I'm useless!" She stood and stormed to the table, a tear of frustration rolling down her reddening cheek. "I can help you. I can cook, collect wood." She looked around frantically now, aware that the Deavon was showing no sign of changing his mind. Her eyes met Naisa's. "Tell them," she pleaded. "Tell them that my magic is growing... That I

224

can help." She collapsed into an empty chair, looking down at the table in despair.

Deavon stood and walked slowly toward the despondent girl. "We can't afford to have an untrained girl among us. The path ahead of us is fraught with danger; many days of hardship await us. We can't..."

"The girl in fact speaks the truth," interrupted Naisa. "She is strong in the ways, gifted even." She looked gently at Kailyn as the girl raised her head, hope in her face, having finally found an ally. "She learns quickly. Already she can summon fire and levitate. Just today we started on some simple combat spells." She looked at Deavon and stated simply, "Kailyn may prove useful."

Deavon returned to his seat, lost in thought. Coming to a decision he turned his attention to the expectant group. "We shall put it to a vote. Should Kailyn accompany us on our journey?" Starting at the far-left side of the table, Deavon asked them each for their vote.

"Naisa?"

"Yes, I believe she can be of advantage in the trials to come."

Kailyn sat quietly, a smile threatening to invade her face.

"Raim?"

"No."

"Giddy?"

"Let her come. The less cooking I have to do, the better."

"Got to agree with that," Raim shot at Giddy.

Before Giddy could answer, Deavon went on. "Aldan?"

"No, she'll be a burden on us. The mission is hard enough."

A frown crossed Kailyn's face.

"Tean?"

They all looked to the thin monk; he appeared to be in a trance. After a few moments his eyes refocused. "I have consulted with my Lord. My answer is yes."

Kailyn smiled at him before looking at her trembling hands where she counted the votes on her fingers. She looked up at Tesania hope written on her face.

Deavon looked to Tes. "Tesania?"

Tes sat for some time, looking at her fidgeting hands. She wanted her friend to come along, but the thought that she may be harmed appalled her. She looked up and searched Kailyn's eyes; there wasn't any fear, only excitement. Turning slowly to Deavon, she voted, "Yes."

Kailyn couldn't help herself, jumping to her feet and emitting a small squeal. "Thank you, Tesania." she looked around. "All of you. I promise you won't regret it."

"It appears my vote is null and void," said Deavon from the far end of the table. "Kailyn, it appears you will be accompanying us on our mission. Be warned though, you must obey all orders, whether it is from me, Giddy, Aldan.., whoever, no matter what you think. Your life..," He watched her closely as he continued, "and ours, may depend on it. Do you understand?"

"Yes," replied Kailyn. "I won't let you down."

"See that you don't. Naisa, continue to teach the girl at every opportunity. Giddy, I want her trained in basic combat; I fear she may need it."

"Yes boss," replied Giddy eagerly. "Give her your sword Raim. Let's go up on deck."

"Looks like the meeting's over," laughed Aldan as he watched Giddy, Tes, Raim and Kailyn head out the door.

As the fiery sun kissed the horizon, casting its last light of the day across the darkening ocean, the Triumph rounded the point of land protecting Carella Harbor. Lieutenant Dahl bellowed orders at sailors racing along the deck while others scurried up the rigging, the sails already starting to flap, allowing the bite of the water to slow them down.

Captain Oneida approached Deavon. "Will you be staying aboard tonight?"

"I think not," Deavon replied as he watched the last of the sun disappear beneath the waves. "I'd like to meet our new companion tonight."

"Very well," the Captain replied, reaching out to shake Deavon's hand. "Best of luck on your journey." turning to Tesania, he bowed. "It was a pleasure to meet you Milady. Fair thee well." As Tes smiled and curtsied in return he spun on his heel and ordered a boat to be unlashed and lowered to convey the party ashore.

A few minutes later the last of the travelers stepped into the rocking boat. Tes found a seat at the front. As the oarsmen pulled toward the shore she looked back, a pang of regret passing through her as she watched the Triumph ride gently at its anchor. She had enjoyed the voyage. With a sigh, she turned her attention to the port of Carella. Ships and boats of all sizes littered the harbor. Most were settled in for the night, showing little sign of life aside from the odd light from an open porthole. The huge wharf that they were heading for was made of hewn rocks as wide as two carts that protruded one hundred feet out into the choppy waters. The boat bumped against some old worn steps, barnacles and oysters fought over every square inch of the ones near the water making it a perilous jump from the pitching boat. Tes leapt and was caught by the strong arms of Deavon. She paused for a second as their eyes met. Noticing Giddy watching she quickly looked away as he passed her further up the stairs. Forming a chain, they managed to get their entire luggage ashore without mishap.

Kailyn huddled close to Tesania as they left the wharf and walked along the seedy wharf side street. It was lined with raucous bars and brothels, the decayed old buildings looking as if they had been built during the days when Rodus had forged Tesania's sword, centuries ago. The stench of unwashed bodies and sewage pervaded everything. Tes followed Kailyn's lead and held the hem of her cloak to her nose. She flinched as a man approached her, dirty and disheveled, with his hand out begging for money. Aldan quickly stepped between them. "Be on your way stranger, we wish no trouble tonight."

"I was only asken 'em for some money," the drunk slurred as Tes and Kailyn moved away. "Man needs ta drink."

Aldan laughed. "I think you've seen too much drink tonight, and the sun has only just set. Be on your way," he said as he rested his hand suggestively on the pommel of his sword.

The man, not too drunk to recognize the danger, turned and stumbled away. Aldan grinned as he hurried to catch the others.

Deavon took the lead as the breeze started to stiffen. Giddy and Raim walked on either side of Tes, Kailyn, Naisa and Tean, Aldan fell in at the rear, thus they passed through the streets without further interruption.

Kailyn started to complain that she was tired as they moved into an obviously more affluent area of the city. Entering a square with an elaborate fountain dominating the centre, Deavon came to a stop. "The Mage's Guild is on the western boulevard. Naisa and I will proceed there and collect Elddyn." He looked around the gathered faces. "Aldan knows this city well. He'll take you to the Roundhouse Inn. It's not far, but keep together, speak to no one. We'll meet you there in an hour or so."

The cool spring breeze lifted dust and litter from the sparsely lit street, swirling it around the travelers before darting between the well-mannered rows of houses. Tes pulled her fluttering cloak closer, positioning the hood to protect her face as best she could. Kailyn positioned herself behind Aldan, somewhat protected behind his large frame. "It's not far now," Aldan called, having to raise his voice to be heard as the breeze quickened to a surging wind.

Tesania tried to study the surrounding street and its buildings as she pushed into the wind; the light allowed little detail to be seen. Rows of neat houses lined both sides of the cobbled street, all the same size, many with the glow of the evening fire emanating from the lower floor windows. Tes squinted, trying to make out more detail, deciding in the gloom that the houses all appeared to be the same whitewashed color. Neat gardens with hedged paths led from the street to the ornate front doors, probably locked and barred now for the night. She thought of the families that might be inside; a little girl playing with her dolls in front of the roaring fire, her brother teasing her, mother knitting a warm scarf while her father smoked a pipe and sipped wine from a fine glass while reading an old worn book. Shuddering as the wind blew her cloak wildly in the air, Tes came back from her thoughts. A large building stood before them, light glowing invitingly from the windows, a sign flapping and creaking in the wind. Tes read, 'The Roundhouse Inn, Est.608.

Aldan opened the door and ushered them through. The room that greeted them was warm and inviting, a fire danced and crackled in the central fire pit. On the far wall a large joint of meat dripped and sizzled over a brazier of glowing embers; the smell permeating the room, making Tes' stomach rumble, reminding her that she hadn't eaten for many hours. Grateful to be indoors, the travelers quickly removed their cloaks, shaking them out as the Innkeeper approached. "Greetings, welcome to the Roundhouse. How may I assist you? A meal perhaps?" he asked with a hopeful glint in his eyes.

Aldan smiled at the Innkeepers keen face. "Better than that," he laughed. "We seek lodgings, and meals and ale.., lots of ale!" He paused as the Innkeeper rubbed his hands together. Laughing once more, he added, "There will be three more joining us, so that will make nine." After making a point of looking around the room he returned his attention to the eager man. "You look busy though. Perhaps we should make enquiries elsewhere?" he teased while slinging his cloak back onto his shoulders.

"No, no; we have many rooms," the Innkeeper almost begged. "It would be our pleasure to have you and your fine friends stay with us. Our ale is the finest in all Carella, you won't regret it." He looked at Aldan expectantly whilst wringing his hands nervously together.

"What say you?" Aldan asked as he turned to Tesania, winking as a wry grin crossed his face.

"Well.., the roast does smell delicious, and that wind..."

"Yes, Yes, it would not do to take these splendid ladies back into that wind, they would be much more comfortable in our cozy Inn," the hopeful man interrupted.

"Very well," Aldan said as he turned. "Innkeeper! Board and lodgings for nine, if you please."

"Certainly sir, you won't regret it," replied the man, his crooked, yellow teeth showing through his thankful smile. "Rose," he called to a pretty little waitress. "Please make rooms ready for our guests." As she scurried for the stairs, he started toward a large table at the back of the room. "If you would have a seat, Rose will light the hearths in your rooms, by the time you have eaten they will be waiting for you, cozy and warm."

Giddy threw her belongings in the corner before dragging a chair out with her foot and sitting down. "I hope the ale's as good as he says it is."

"Oh, it is," replied Aldan. "I've stayed here a few times in the past. Remember though, that we leave early on the morrow, a hangover does not sit well with a long day's march," he cautioned.

Rolling her eyes at him, Giddy turned to Raim. "Takes more than a few ales to give us a hangover, does it not?"

Raim laughed heartily. "Aye; that it does."

"Still," suggested Aldan. "Let's keep it to just a few."

"Ok, ok, I'll be good, just get the first one ordered," Giddy begged with an exasperated smile. "Please!"

Tes took her seat at the other end of the table, Kailyn settling in next to her. "I don't drink ale," she whispered in Tes' ear.

Making a sour face, Tes said, "I don't drink it either, I tried it in a roadhouse near a ferry we crossed on our way to Wyvern City." Shuddering at the memory of the bitter drink, she flicked her eyes toward Giddy. "I don't know how she drinks it; disgusting stuff."

"What is?" asked Giddy, her attention now turned toward the two girls.

"Ale," retorted Kailyn. "How can you drink it?"

"An acquired taste, I must agree. But truly it's the nectar of the gods, once you do get used to it."

Tes shook her head. "I can't see it. I don't think I would ever get used to that..," she poked her tongue out, remembering the taste, "stuff! Kailyn and I will stick to cider I think." Kailyn nodded her head emphatically.

Giddy laughed uproariously, rocking back in her chair. "Each to their own," she managed to say between labored breaths.

Rose, having returned from tending their rooms, carried a board to the table; Tes smelt the aromas of freshly baked bread before she could see it; combined with the smells of the roasting meat, her stomach again began to clench with pangs of hunger. As Rose placed the board on the table Raim and Giddy dove for the steaming, golden, loaves, tearing them apart, dipping them in the accompanying flavored oils before quickly devouring them. The others, sensing they may miss out, quickly grabbed for the remaining morsels. Giddy, through a mouthful of food, called to Rose as she retreated to the kitchen, "Ales, all round." Noticing the frown on Tes' face, she added, "And two ciders for the young ladies, if you please."

~

As Giddy started on her second ale of the night, cold wind burst through the front door. Deavon stepped through; Naisa followed and then came a tall, lean man. Dressed in the robes of his profession.

Deavon quickly closed the door, removing his cloak as he looked about the room. Spotting his companions, he gestured to Naisa and the new arrival to follow.

Tes studied the mage as they approached. His robes were of the deepest black with a simple burgundy sash tied around his waist. Reaching up, he slowly slipped the cowl from his head revealing short cropped blond hair, hooked nose and square chin. Tes' attention though, was caught by the glistening earring in his right ear. Directly below this was a tattoo of a lightning strike running from his ear and disappearing beneath his robes. Forcing herself, she dragged her eyes to his, deep and dark, they flicked from one companion to the next. Tes exposed when he rested his attention upon her; she felt his eyes bore into her very soul. Shuddering, she broke the contact and looked away. Kailyn leaned over and whispered in her ear, "I don't like him, he's creepy."

"Shh," Tes admonished quickly. "We don't even know him." She glanced quickly toward the newly arrived mage as she spoke, looking just as quickly away. "Besides the Archmage said he's the best mage to help us."

Kailyn scowled, peeking around Tes to see the mage once more. Sitting back, she sulkily stated, "I don't care. I don't like him!"

"Keep it to yourself," Tes whispered as she lightly kicked Kailyn under the table.

Deavon stood at the table now. "Our latest and last member, Elddyn, has joined us. Welcome to our little group. As you can see, we're a mixed lot. Over there is Giddy."

Giddy slid her chair quickly back, jumped to her feet and bowed. "At your service."

Deavon shook his head, turned to Elddyn and continued. "You'll get used to her; most of us just ignore her."

"Hey," interjected Giddy.

"Sit down Giddy; please," begged Deavon. As she reluctantly obeyed, he went on to introduce the others, finally coming to Tes. "And this is our last member, Tesania of Aryd village."

Elddyn again fixed his gaze on Tesania. "The sword carrier," he said in a quiet voice. "Strange that magic of such magnitude should manifest itself through a simple village girl."

Giddy's chair crashed back this time as she stood quickly, hand on sword. "I would not judge the girl too quickly if I were you," she said quickly. "She wields that sword.., and the magic better than you think."

Elddyn raised a placating hand. As his sleeve slipped down his arm a tattooed serpent became visible, winding its way from his palm to his elbow. "I did not intend to offend; it was merely an observation. A curiosity, if you wish."

"You suggest that she's a simple village girl. Is that not insulting in itself?"

Tes stood slowly. "Giddy, I'm sure he meant no harm. He can't possibly know of the sword's history, or, for that matter, how it came to be in my possession."

Giddy slowly sat, fixing Elddyn with an icy glare as she did so. "I've seen Tes in battle; I've seen the magic in her sword. Don't underestimate her!" she said in an irate tone.

"Indeed," Elddyn replied as he took a seat. "I believe we may have got off on a wrong note... As I said, I meant no offence. I am here to provide my best efforts to help the girl succeed in her mission."

"The Girl's name is Tesania!" replied Tes abruptly. "But you may call me Tes."

"I'm starved," Deavon said in an effort to change the atmosphere at the table. "And a quality ale is well overdue... Innkeeper!"

Rose approached the table, a huge wooden tray balanced expertly on her hand. Tes leant forward in expectation as the roast meat came into view; steam drifted lazily from carrots, potatoes and another vegetable that Tes thought might be squash. The Innkeeper approached with a large carving knife; well worn; it bowed in the middle from the wear of repeated sharpening.

~

Full and content after eating her fill, Tes shoved her plate aside. Looking to Kailyn, she smiled as the small girl struggled to finish her serving. "Don't worry about it; leave it if you wish."

As Kailyn placed her fork on the plate, Raim reached over. "No need to let it go to waste," he grinned as his fork stabbed a piece of the remaining meat.

"Tch, Tch," said Giddy as she pinched his stomach. "Getting a little podgy aren't we."

Raim laughed through his mouthful. "Just because I beat you to it. You know.., jealousy really doesn't sit well with you."

"Jealousy," snorted Giddy. "If I wanted it, I'd take it."

"One piece left," Raim said as he pointed at the plate with the end of his fork. "Take it.., if you can."

As Giddy snatched her fork from her empty plate, determination written on her face, Deavon reached across the table, stabbed the meat with his fork and shoved it in his mouth. "You're both too slow," Deavon laughed as he sat chewing, a grin spreading across his face.

Naisa stood. "I'm retiring to my room. Goodnight to you all."

"A good idea indeed," replied Deavon. "Everybody is to be ready to depart at dawn; we have a long day ahead of us tomorrow." He gazed around the table, stopping at the two soldiers. "Raim, Giddy; that means you too."

"We'll just have one more boss," Giddy replied as she raised her hand to attract Rose's attention.

"Now!" Deavon barked light heartedly.

Giddy saluted. "Yes boss. Come on Raim, we've been ordered to our beds." she leant over and whispered in his ear, loud enough for the others to hear, "He thinks he's our daddy."

"Go!" laughed Deavon.

As the group of nine headed for the stairs, Deavon called to the Innkeeper and arranged an early morning call and breakfast. Tes and Kailyn shared a room; Kailyn drifting to sleep almost as soon as her head touched the pillow. Tes lay awake for some time, listening to her friend's light breathing, thinking about the task ahead. Admonishing herself, she snuffed out the candle on the bedside table, rolled into her blankets and drifted off to sleep.

30 ENEMY WITHIN

The chill morning air caused the traveler's breaths to hang on the soft breeze. Tes pulled at her cloak, trying to keep warm. Their breakfast had been a substantial affair, fried ham, eggs, toasted bread and scalding hot tea. Deavon now led the way through the still sleepy city as birds started their morning songs. Listening intently, she caught the call of an eagle, far away in the skies. She had always found birds fascinating, spending many hours watching them by the river near her village. Forcing her attention back to the road, she walked on, Kailyn at her side.

Carella slowly revealed itself as the light grew. Not as beautiful as Wyvern City Tes thought to herself, but certainly cleaner and more ordered than Rilmir. Shuddering at the memory of that far away city, with its filthy streets, thieves and beggars, she cast it from her mind and concentrated on the buildings at hand. She surveyed the rows of pretty gardens as they passed; spring flowers opening as the first morning rays of the sun tickled them awake. Pleased to see that she was not the only one silly enough to be out in the morning cold, she watched as honey bees industriously started their day. The gardens fronted neat dwellings; their whitewashed walls making them all seem the same. "Boring."

"What?" Kailyn asked.

"The houses," Tes replied, indicating with a lift of her chin, regretting it straight away as the cold instantly found its way to her exposed neck. "They're all the same; boring," she shrugged.

"Oh," said Kailyn, looking around, as if for the first time. "I hadn't noticed."

Tes smiled as she gently nudged her friend. "Tell me of your family. Where were you brought up?"

"Nothing really to tell."

"Surely there's something?" Tes pressed. "What about your mother? Is she pretty?"

"Very," Kailyn replied softly as her thoughts turned to her childhood, her mother singing lightly as they mixed dough for the daily bread in the family kitchen, wisps of hair escaping from her linen cap, the sun's morning light streaming through the open window and picking out the beautiful auburn tones. Looking at Tes, a tear in her eye, she sighed, "I miss my mother so much."

Tes placed her arm around the young girl's shoulders. "I miss mine too." They walked along in silence for a few minutes, Tes eventually asking, "Where is your home?"

Kailyn shrugged. "Just a few miles from Wyvern City, on the Wyvern River. My father farms sheep."

"You couldn't stay on and help him with the farm," Tes asked in confusion. "Surely he needs help."

"He does," Kailyn replied. "But my three brothers are there for that." She shook her head. "I however am a girl, ideally suited for servitude as a maid. At least that's what the man that came to negotiate with my father said." She paused for a few moments, remembering the night the man had come. "I couldn't do anything. I wasn't even allowed in the room." Looking abashed at Tes, she said, "I snuck to the door and listened. The man said I'd be well treated and would learn the world of ladies. My heart skipped a beat when I heard father agree. When my mother started to cry I ran back to my room... I begged him in the morning to reconsider, but he said it was too late... The contract had already been signed. My mother cried every day that week. Then, one-day a carriage came to pick me up. My father..., I don't know.., maybe he couldn't face what he'd done.., didn't even say goodbye."

Tes drew her closer and kissed her on the top of the head. "I'm sure he didn't want you to go." She gripped the girl's chin, drawing her face around to look into her own. "Look on the bright side. You're on a grand adventure which you would never have even known about if you'd stayed at home," she smiled.

"Oh, I miss my family," Kailyn replied. "But I don't regret it. Besides I got to meet you."

"And me," added Giddy from close behind them.

"And you too, Giddy," Kailyn laughed, her tears receding.

The Northern wall of the city followed the winding path of the Carella River. The shops that sat just inside them were in the process of setting up their outside displays for the start of the day's trade. The group split; Giddy, Raim, Aldan and Naisa headed for the general store to buy rope and provisions. Tes and the others took a seat on a worn bench near some well kept stables and rearranged their packs to accommodate the new supplies.

Shortly after, re-provisioned and keen to be on their way, the group approached an ancient cobblestoned bridge which would take them past the city outskirts and finally toward the wilderness and Trannyth. Tes looked back, knowing this may be the last civilized place she would ever see in her short life. With a sigh, she turned and walked quickly after the others.

By late afternoon, when Deavon called a halt to make camp under a copse of weepy old willow trees, they had made good headway. Kailyn's feet hurt, but she had bravely walked on without much complaint. Raim had kindly taken her pack after their midday meal, carrying it for the rest of the day. They camped beside a creek. The water, sweet and fresh from the mountains, rumbled and bubbled through the trees. Raim quickly pulled a line and hook from his pack and headed upstream to try for some fresh fish. Deavon cleaned out the old ring of stones that had been used by the many travelers before them who had also found this place an ideal camping spot. Aldan and Giddy ranged out to collect fire wood while Tes and Kailyn explored the surrounding woods for mushrooms and herbs. Tean used a branch broken from a nearby tree to sweep a large area clear of twigs and leaves, providing a smooth area for all to sleep. Naisa settled down to help Deavon with the fire, a spark jumping from her fingertips, causing a flame to slowly start licking at the dried leaves and kindling. Elddyn sat, offering no help, his back to the others.

"That one scares me a little," Kailyn whispered as she looked back at Elddyn. "I don't know what it is."

"I know," replied Tesania. "He doesn't say much, but he watches everything I do. I'm sure of it."

Kailyn shivered. "Creepy," she said.

Tes laughed. "Shh. I'm sure that the Archmage wouldn't have sent him on our mission if he wasn't trustworthy."

"I suppose so," replied Kailyn, a little sulkily. "Still I'm going to keep an eye on him." She glanced back to the camp. "There's something... I'll work it out.., eventually."

Tes looked at her friend seriously. "You be very careful."

"I will," Kailyn smiled. "I can be very sneaky."

"I'm sure you can," Tes laughed once more.

~

The aromas of frying fish drifted through the camp as the travelers sat near the fire. Kailyn feverishly practiced lighting the end of a small twig with her emerging magic. Tes watched the flames flicker around the embers of a log as she thought of her parents and the village she had left behind, seemingly so long ago. Giddy stared at Elddyn, her dislike open and plain.

"If you have something to say, say it," suggested Elddyn as he turned toward Giddy.

"Nothing to say," Giddy shrugged. "I just don't like you."

"Harsh words from somebody that only met me one night ago."

"Oh, believe me, it only took a second," Giddy sneered.

"Who are you to judge me?" Elddyn bristled. "You're a lowly soldier!"

Raim sat bolt upright, his hand reaching for his sword. Giddy reached across, touching his arm and shaking her head. Tes watched on, knowing that Giddy would enjoy the game of goading Elddyn. Deavon listened disconcertedly.

"A soldier yes," Giddy hissed. "Lowly.., maybe. But I'm sure you could slither under me… Without any problems!"

Elddyn stood, tightening his cloak around his shoulders as he glared around the gathering and then stormed into the night.

Deavon shook his head. "Do you have to Giddy? We have to travel together for many weeks, maybe months. I'd prefer we all got along."

"He doesn't try to fit in," Giddy retorted. "Mark my words; there's something evil about him. Kailyn agrees… Don't you?"

The young girl sat perfectly still as the groups attention turned to her. She continued to stare at the twig in her hand, eventually raising her head, looking from Giddy to Deavon and swallowing before replying, "He makes me nervous. I agree there's something.., odd about him." She looked quickly back to her twig.

"Naisa?" Deavon asked. "Do you know anything about him?"

"He's well regarded by the Archmage..." She paused, thinking. "He's a fifth degree mage."

"So you outrank him?" Tesania asked.

Smiling, Naisa replied, "Not as such. Rank is not decided by the degree you reach in the order of Rynem. I have no more control over him than Giddy here has over Raim. However," she continued quickly before Giddy could interrupt. "He is very skilled in the ways. His knowledge of the forbidden ways will help us greatly when we need to face Trannyth."

"Whoa!" said Deavon. "He's studied the forbidden ways. How can that be?"

"When Trannyth fled the Mages Guild, Elddyn took it upon himself to learn as much as he could to stop him. The Archmage put a stop to it immediately when he found out. But knowing that the best defense is knowledge, he didn't expel Elddyn from the Guild, swearing him to secrecy while forbidding him to study any further."

"How do we know we can trust him?" asked Aldan. "He studied the forbidden ways, just as Trannyth did before he chose the dark path. Why's he any different? Surely the forbidden ways can seduce him as well?"

"There is truth in what you say." Naisa replied slowly. "The Archmage didn't take the decision lightly. A panel of highly ranked mages was convened to decide if Elddyn could be trusted to hold the responsibility of the knowledge and be able to resist the urge to wield it. Remember, he had only just started to study, he is by no means an expert in the forbidden ways, not like Trannyth." She paused as she looked back at Giddy. "After much deliberation and testing it was decided that he would stay on at the Carella Mages Guild where he is closely monitored."

"So, even the Archmage and his people don't trust him?" Giddy asked as she nodded into the darkness where Elddyn had disappeared. "He seems more likely to be evil than good to me!"

"He's a high level mage; his study has been impeccable..." She looked into the darkness, seemingly not sure if to continue. Coming to a decision, she spoke quietly, "You may not like this, but.., he was a friend of Trannyth when they studied together in the Mages Guild."

"Great," sighed Giddy. "An evil mage, studied in the forbidden ways, a friend of our enemy, the one we're going to try and kill." Turning her attention to Deavon, she asked, "Do you believe this? An enemy within our own ranks. I knew it!"

"We don't know that for sure, Giddy. Let Naisa speak."

"So while I'm fighting Trannyth I'll have his friend watching my back.., or will he be aiming for it?"

"Giddy! Let her speak!"

"Their friendship didn't last long. Trannyth is brutal and cruel, when he started to stray toward the forbidden ways Elddyn distanced himself from him. Trannyth became more detached and sadistic as he slipped further from reason. Elddyn was often a target of his malicious pranks. Any friendship they'd had was lost."

"I still don't trust him. Believe me when I say that we will regret the day he walked into that Inn." Giddy said ominously.

They settled into an uneasy silence, as the fire died down to a scattering of glowing embers they prepared their sleeping rolls. Raim wandered out to take up the first watch, Elddyn had still not returned.

31 THE DRAON PASS

A few days later the Britath Mountains loomed ahead, barring their way. "The Draon pass is through those two peaks there," Deavon said as he pointed toward two jagged looking spires. "It'll be tough going in some parts. Everyone stay together and make sure the person behind you keeps up and remains safe." He looked around the small group. "Kailyn and Tes, stay close to me. Raim take the point, Aldan take the rear." He adjusted his pack. "Everyone ready..? Right, let's go." Turning, he started into the foothills. Tes looked at the steep climb ahead, sighed, smiled at Kailyn and started after him.

When the sun passed its zenith they had made their way deep into the pass, Tes was pleased that the going, so far, had been surprisingly easy. Kailyn started to sing a lullaby, soon Tes and Giddy joined in. It was almost an enjoyable day in the hills.

Soon enough though, the surrounding vegetation grew in upon them as the track became steeper, eroded earth formed small cliffs whilst gnarled tree roots protruded from the ground, threatening to trip the unwary travelers. Tes groaned in frustration as yet another thorny branch gripped her clothing and pulled her to a stop. She had to concentrate hard to navigate the many hazards; combined with the physical climb she soon found herself exhausted. "Can we please stop?" she implored of Deavon.

Deavon looked back at the two young girls; Kailyn too appeared at her limit. "Here isn't the best place to stop. We should shortly come upon a clearing where we can rest." He walked down the track toward them and took both their packs, hefting them onto his shoulder. "Come on; we should find a clearing soon." he said with a smile as he turned and headed back up the track.

Aldan stood close by, waiting for them to proceed. He well understood the rigors of the mountains and allowed them a few moments before gently ushering them on.

Tes grimaced at Kailyn who stood rubbing her shoulders. "I guess we'd better go," she sighed.

They trudged on, slipping and sliding as the mossy ground became soaked from rivulets of water running from beneath the thick, brambly forest. All the travelers had fallen at some stage, their clothes now filthy and damp. It seemed like hours since Deavon had said that the clearing wasn't too far away. Tes fought her weariness, dismissing the pain of her many scratches and bruises as she pushed on, regularly stopping to reach back and help Kailyn past a particularly hazardous obstacle. The forest grew denser as they proceeded, soon the canopy of the trees blocked out most of the light, creating an eerie atmosphere where any sound echoed amongst the giant trunks and branches. As Kailyn fell once more, Tes cried out, "Enough!" as she collapsed to the ground next to her exhausted friend.

32 MUNDANE TASKS

The monotony wore on Serran. For weeks now she had been stuck in this god forsaken mountain pass. The beasts entertained themselves when they weren't on guard duty by practicing their swordsmanship and wrestling each other. She lay back against a tree far to the back of the camp, happy to not be anywhere near the smelly creatures. Writing had proven fruitless; she had no imagination for such things. The small number of books she had brought along had long since been read from cover to cover. Apart from her lonely walks along the streams edge, where she would sit and watch the multi colored butterflies flit from flower to flower, there was nothing for her to do. She took to preparing her own meals as the beasts usually tore their catch from the days hunting to pieces and ate it raw. Wild mushrooms and herbs were plentiful along the banks of the stream, collecting them as she walked back to camp each day made her meals a time to savor.

Days drifted into weeks as the pass remained quiet. Serran wondered if it was a waste of time. Surely no army would try to cross these steep inhospitable climbs. Still, every day beasts were sent out to scout the pass, returning at dusk with nothing to report. Finally the day came when their replacement was due to arrive and Serran couldn't wait to depart. Her bag was packed. Her flimsy tent cleaned out and swept with a branch broken from a nearby bush. She sat happily humming to herself as she waited, feet immersed in the cool mountain stream.

A beast rushed toward her, sword drawn, grunting and gesturing wildly at the camp and pass leading down the far side. She rose as it approached. "What is it?" she snapped, irritated at being disturbed.

The beast ground to a halt, panting only slightly as it replied in its guttural voice, "Man-things come up pass."

"How many?" Serran asked quickly as she rushed past the beast, anxious to get her staff.

"Scout see one man-thing, hear others, not far."

"Where is your commander?"

"He gathers others, prepares attack."

Serran was out of breath when she reached the gathered beasts. "Where are they?" she asked quickly of the commander.

"Few miles, Kreght see only one, others not far, they stop rest."

"Is it an army?" Serran asked Kreght with some alarm.

"No," was his simple reply.

Anger erupted in Serran's face. "Well how many then? What are we up against? Are they soldiers? Rangers? What?"

"Man-thing wear brown," replied Kreght.

"Did he wield a sword or a bow?" Serran erupted impatiently.

"Sword," the beast replied. "Just man-thing."

"They must be soldiers, maybe it's an attack." She spun on the commander. "We must stop them, at least delay them until our replacement troop arrives to back us up."

The beasts were ordered down the track, a scout leading the way. Cautiously she turned each bend of the track as her keen animal senses took in every sound and smell.

33 A CHANGE OF PLANS

Deavon sighed and turned back to talk to Tesania and Kailyn as they lay collapsed on the forest floor. "Giddy, go on ahead and tell Raim that we've stopped here." Deavon too found the going hard, so he was gentle as he approached the two girls. "We have to press on. We can't risk not finding a clearing to set up camp." He looked around. "Here would be most uncomfortable I should think," he smiled at them both.

"We can't go on," Tesania protested. "Kailyn's exhausted and my legs feel like they'll explode."

Deavon stood and called to the others, "We'll rest here for a short time. Aldan set a guard. Naisa? Can you do anything to help these two along?"

Naisa loosened her pack and produced a small vial of clear liquid. "This will help soothe your aching legs at least," she said as she leant over and handed it to Tes. "You only need a few drops."

Tes removed the cork stopper and turned to Kailyn. "Open your mouth," she instructed as her mother would have when she was a little girl.

Kailyn grimaced as the drops splashed onto her tongue, twisting her head and wiping her mouth, she exclaimed, "Eeeew, that's horrible." She looked aggrievedly at Naisa. "You could've warned me!"

Deavon and Naisa laughed, Elddyn scowled. "It's just fermented lungis berries. The taste will go in a few minutes."

Tes sniffed the vial tentatively.

"Just do it!" commanded Elddyn irritably.

"Why should she?" asked Kailyn, jumping to Tes' defense.

Elddyn fixed her with an icy stare. "Can you still taste it?"

Kailyn thought for a second, explored her mouth with her tongue and exclaimed. "No, no I can't!"

"And do you still feel exhausted," the mage pressed on.

Kailyn sat still, not wanting to give the horrible mage the satisfaction of being right. She couldn't however deny that her legs felt much better, her body no longer ached as much as it had; she felt almost invigorated.

"Bah," Elddyn sneered as he stood and walked toward Aldan. "Why bring silly little girls on a journey such as this?" he muttered.

"You dare call us silly little girls," Tesania flared as she jumped to her feet, weariness forgotten. "Who do you think you are?"

Elddyn ignored her and kept walking up the track.

"I'm talking to you!" Tes said, her voice oozing contempt.

"Let it go," said Deavon as he touched her arm. "He meant nothing by it."

"Meant nothing by it," Tes snapped as she whirled on Deavon. "He all but said we shouldn't be here." As she fixed her eyes on Elddyn's back she scornfully jeered, "It's you who shouldn't be here."

Elddyn stopped dead in his tracks. Slowly he turned, mirth in his face. "And why, pray tell, do you say that?"

Tes knew she shouldn't say it, but the look on the mage's face goaded her beyond reason. She looked straight into his eyes, her own filled with contempt and said, "You are a traitor..."

Deavon grabbed her arm. "Tesania, that's enough!"

Elddyn's smile disappeared as he watched Deavon intervene. "No. Let her speak... Let her tell us all," he said, his smile returning as he swept his arm around, half turning to take in Aldan. "How this..," he looked her up and down, "Woman! Wise beyond her years. Comes to this conclusion!"

Tes tore her arm from the rangers grasp as the mage mocked her. "You are Trannyth's friend. You studied with him. You work, even now, with him to further the forbidden ways!"

Elddyn walked slowly toward her, his face playing with emotion. "I am no friend of Trannyth. I abhor him.., and everything he stands for!"

Tesania stood her ground and smiled. "A pretty speech indeed; did Trannyth write it for you?"

"Arrgghh!" the mage screamed in frustration as he raised his staff. Tes' hand went to her sword, but not before she heard the sound of Deavon's weapon slipping quickly from its sheath.

Tesania's head whipped around to Deavon. "My sword!" she exclaimed. "It's vibrating!"

Giddy appeared from the trees, sliding to a halt. Looking from Deavon's sword to Elddyn's raised staff, she said, "You boys will have to play another day. Beasts are coming down the track."

~

Raim had walked ahead of the others all day. He liked being the scout and happily watched the branches around him for any movement, often smiling as a bird took flight or a tiny creature scuttled away. His instinct told him his fellow travelers were no longer following so he climbed a tree and perched in the lower branches where he had a view of the meandering track further up the pass. Withdrawing his knife, he started to whittle a piece of fallen wood he had found on the forest floor.

"Where're you off to then?" he asked with a mischievous smile as Giddy walked past a short time later, oblivious to his hiding spot.

Recognizing his voice instantly, Giddy turned and started to climb the tree. "The others have stopped for a while. Deavon wants you to wait till they catch up."

"Problems?"

"Tes and Kailyn are having a hard time of it, not used to the harsh outdoor life like us, eh," she said jokingly as she poked him in the ribs.

"It's a tough climb, even for we highly trained soldier types," he laughed back.

"It'll be hell for them over the next few days," Giddy said. "Deavon may want them to move fast but I don't think they'll be able to."

"The mages will struggle too I'll wager," replied Raim.

"Yes," Giddy somberly agreed.

Raim looked at his friend seriously. "Do you think we have a chance of pulling this off? I mean, really?"

Giddy thought for some time before answering. She was always a willing participant in any adventure that presented itself, but even she had harbored similar thoughts over the past weeks. "We have to. Don't we?" she asked simply as she looked at him.

"That's not what I asked," Raim laughed lightly.

Giddy went silent; staring at the mountain. After some time she spoke again. "Tesania is tougher than she looks. I've seen her wield that sword against the beasts; it has powers that we can only imagine. If..," she paused in thought for a few moments, "If, we can get her near that orb or even Trannyth, I think we have a chance."

"Getting into a heavily guarded keep won't be easy."

"We'll find a way," Giddy replied unconvincingly. "We have to."

Raim sat up quickly, almost losing his balance in the tree.

"What is it?" asked Giddy, immediately looking up the track.

"I thought I saw movement," Raim replied as he relaxed. "It must have been an animal or something."

Giddy looked at him slyly. "You do know the beasts are animals.., right?"

Raim grinned. "Sure I know. I don't..." he stopped abruptly. "I think we have visitors. Up the track, about half a mile, near that old rotting stump," he pointed. "Watch!"

Giddy sat forward and watched for a few moments. As she was about to look away a movement drew her attention. "I see it!" She watched a little longer, gripping Raim's arm as a black haired beast inched its way around the bend in the track. "Beasts! I'd better warn the others!" she said quickly as she started down the tree. "Try to slow them down!" As she leapt onto the track and started to run she looked over her shoulder. "And don't do anything foolish. I want to see you at the bottom of the pass in one piece; got it?"

Raim saluted as Giddy disappeared around a large tree. He had no intention of getting himself killed, but he knew he had to do something to give the others a start.

He watched the beast as it slowly made its way down the track. When he was certain it was a scout and no others were close behind, he slithered down the tree and walked a short way up the track, backing into a thicket that allowed him a view of some thirty yards in the direction of the approaching beast. Gently breaking some berries from the bush, he crushed them in his hand before rubbing them on the branches surrounding his hiding place, the fragrant smell drifting over the track. He hoped this would hide his scent from the beast, at the very least help him remain hidden until he could spring his trap. Adjusting his position until he felt sure he couldn't be seen, he settled in to wait.

~

"How many?" Deavon snapped as he quickly forgot the angry mage and walked toward Giddy. "How far away?"

"Raim and I spotted what appeared to be a scout, about ten minutes up the track."

"No idea of numbers?"

"None." She shook her head. "When we saw the scout I came straight down to warn you." She looked at Deavon angrily. "I wasn't going to wait for a whole troop to come down, was I?" she asked defiantly.

Deavon dismissed her anger, asking, "Where's Raim?"

"He stayed to slow them down," Giddy replied, concern written on her face. "You get these people out of here. I'm going back to help him," she said as she drew her sword and started up the hill.

Deavon reached out and grabbed her arm. "It would be best if we all stayed together!"

"Raim's up there..." She used her free hand to loosen Deavon's grip. "Alone!"

"He knows what he's doing," Deavon replied as he looked around the others. "We must go back down the track; we don't know how many beasts are coming. Tes, Kailyn, Naisa, Tean.., you go first, as fast as you can now... Go!" As they moved off, fear in their faces, he turned to the rest. "Giddy, you and I will take the rear. You two guard the others. With your life," he growled at Elddyn and Aldan. "Move out."

The group moved quickly. Tes and Kailyn crashed down the track, jumping roots, scrambling down crevices, brushing the overhanging branches aside. Naisa was somewhat slower, older and hampered by her staff, she fell behind. Aldan and Tean followed close behind her, helping when they could. Elddyn moved with surprising alacrity, offering no help to anyone, interested only in himself. Deavon and Giddy held back, allowing some distance to grow between themselves and the others. "We have to give them a chance to escape," Deavon said as he looked at Giddy's excited face.

"Agreed. Raim will only stall them for so long before he pulls back. I'd like to be here when he does," Giddy replied.

"We have to keep moving down; Raim will be coming quick so he'll catch us."

Giddy scowled. Her instincts told her to move toward her friend. She knew though that Deavon was right. She walked down the path, continuously looking behind and listening for any hint of pursuit.

~

Tesania and Kailyn slowed and came to a halt after what seemed like an hour. Both had torn clothes, blood seeping from hundreds of scratches received from the surrounding branches and bush. "Wait for the others," Tes gasped, holding her side as a stitch set in.

Kailyn gratefully sank to the ground, leaning against a huge tree, she shut her eyes. "Will they kill us?" she asked between ragged breaths.

Tes grimaced. "Not if Deavon and Giddy have anything to say about it."

"But surely they can't stop a whole troop of beasts, even with Raim."

"They can, and they will, even if they have to..." Tes trailed off.

"They have to what?" Kailyn asked quickly. "Die! Is that what you mean?"

Tes looked at her friend gently. Looking away, she said, "I didn't say that. But I think they would, to save us."

Tears ran down Kailyn's face as she listened to Tes talk. "They won't though... Will they... Tell me they won't die!?"

"Who?" asked Naisa as she stumbled over a tree root and fell to her knees beside Kailyn. Her hair matted to her face by sweat.

"Giddy and Deavon and Raim," Kailyn sobbed.

Naisa smiled softly. "I think the beasts will be the ones dying. Those three are tough."

Aldan arrived with Tean and Elddyn close behind. "Come on," he said. "There's no time to stop!" Reaching down he helped Naisa to her feet.

Tes looked with trepidation up the track before turning and setting off once more.

~

The beast scout crept along warily, her senses told her that no danger presented itself in the near vicinity, yet she maintained her vigilant descent. The track opened into a long straight section, she stood for a few moments studying the trees on either side. Cautiously she walked on; one step slowly after the other. The smell of the forest, flowers and berries clouded her senses. Stopping after thirty or so steps, she sniffed the air, the smell of freshly crushed berries assaulting her nose. As she grunted, thinking the smell was out of place, a flock of birds screeched and fluttered from a nearby bush. Satisfied that the birds were the cause of the overpowering smell, she started to walk on. She thought she heard a noise behind, it was the last thought she would ever have.

Raim emerged from the bush as the huge beast walked past him. Silently he reached up, stretching to reach as he slid his razor sharp knife across the beast's throat. Gurgling blood as it tried to scream, the beast fell to its knees. Turning her head, the beast looked mournfully at her attacker as the final light faded from her eyes.

As the beast collapsed, Raim wiped the bloody knife on its coarse hide, turning his head as the rancid smell hit his face. Certain that the other beasts would continue en-mass once they found their dead companion, he started to run. He didn't move at his full speed, aware of the need to conserve energy, he settled into an easy pace.

When he neared the place where Tes and Kailyn had collapsed earlier he heard the thunderous roars and snorts of the beasts as they came across their dead scout. Pausing to try and ascertain their numbers, thinking there was at least a dozen, he shrugged and moved on. Slipping and sliding, making no effort to conceal his presence, it wasn't long before he came across Deavon and Giddy.

Brushing aside a heavy overhead branch, he came face to face with Giddy's sword point. Halting abruptly, he grinned and said, "That's a nice welcome to give an old friend."

Giddy dropped the sword point to the ground, stepped in, placed her left arm around his neck and pulled him into an embrace. "Is that better," she asked slyly.

Deavon ignored their banter and asked Raim immediately, "Did you see how many? What of the scout?"

Raim leant against a tree, gratefully accepting Deavon's proffered water bag. "The scout's dead," he said, sliding his thumb across his throat. "I didn't see the others, but judging from the commotion when they found their friend, I'd say a dozen or more. Hard to say, more than we can handle, that's for sure." He looked around. "Where are the others?"

"Gone, I sent them on ahead. You, Giddy and I will have to slow the beasts down to give the others a chance to get out of the pass."

"We can't take them head on; there's too many of them. We'll have to skirmish them all the way down," Raim replied.

"How long before they get here?" Deavon asked as he bent his bow and set the string.

"Hard to tell. Won't be long," Raim replied as he looked back up the slope.

"Let's move back to the small clearing a bit further down. We can set some kind of trap there."

Giddy took up the rear as the trio moved off. They moved at a good pace, aware the beasts would be coming as fast as they could now that the game was afoot.

As they reached the little clearing, Deavon motioned for the others to stop. "I'll take up a ranging position some hundred yards down," he said. "See what you can set up here."

As he bounded away, Giddy looked about. "Give me some of that rope," she called to Raim.

As he quickly untied the rope from the side of his pack, Giddy pulled at a branch. It was a young branch, green and full of sap. It bent easily at first, then as she pushed it around and over the track the tensile strength started to build. Grunting as Raim reached her, they pushed together. Raim tied the rope off to the end of the straining branch, passed it through a fork in a nearby tree and fed it down the path, Giddy held on with all her strength as he tied it off. Slowly and cautiously she let the branch go, ducking under it as the rope took the strain. Raim reached into his pocket, grinning as he tossed her the piece of wood he had been working with his knife whilst he sat lookout in the tree. Giddy looked at the sharpened end, smiling as she realized his meaning and wedged it into the trap.

They just had time to hide when the first beast came lumbering into sight. "Let two through," whispered Giddy. The beasts were spread a few feet apart, as the second one passed Raim cut the rope holding the young branch back, it cracked like a whip and slithered rapidly through the branches as the trap snapped shut. The third beast in line took it full in the face, the sharpened spike embedding itself into its eye. With a roar of pain it flailed about, its sword singing through the air. The beasts behind it halted and then started to back up as their stricken companion stumbled toward them. The two that had been let past before the trap was released turned and looked at the commotion. Thinking an attack was coming from the rear they started back up the track.

Deavon smiled at the twang his bow made as he loosed his arrow. It flew true; embedding itself in the beast's back as it sliced between two ribs and cut its heart in two. A moment later his second arrow was on its way. The second beast had seen the arrow strike its mate and turned just in time, the arrow cutting a ragged line across the bridge of its nose as it flew on and struck a tree. Enraged, the beast charged blindly down the track. In its haste; it failed to see Giddy standing behind a tree, blade in hand. A few seconds later it saw no more, its head cleanly removed. Giddy stood exultingly looking at the beheaded beast, Raim pushed her shoulder. "Go, before they come through," he yelled. As he looked back at the confused beasts, one of them raised its sword and slashed the wounded beast blocking their way. As it fell to the ground, writhing, the others let out a piercing cry and started down the track.

Giddy and Raim raced past Deavon as he let two more arrows fly, the lead beast took both, one to its upper right arm, the other to its leg. Screaming, it stumbled, collapsing after a few steps and tumbling down the track. The beasts behind it had to stop as it wedged between two close growing trees, they roared and grunted, trying to move their fallen companion's heavy bulk as Deavon and the others fled.

~

Tes landed flat on her face as her foot snagged another protruding root. She slid a few feet before crashing to a halt against a rock. Her hair was drenched in sweat, dirt and blood covered every bit of her exposed skin. She cried out in pain as she tried to rise, her shoulder collapsing under her weight. Kailyn fell to her knees beside her. Reaching over to Tesania, she gently helped her. "I can't go on," Tes mumbled.

"We have to," Kailyn replied breathlessly as she fearfully looked back up the track. "They're coming."

"Exactly!" Tes almost screamed, delirium taking over her senses. "We're running while Deavon and the others stand and fight." She shakily gained her feet and started back up the hill, her battered body only allowing her to move slowly before she stumbled and fell. Determined, she started to crawl.

Kailyn walked tiredly toward her. "They're doing it to protect us. We have to go. That's what Deavon wanted."

"I don't care what he wants!" Tes snapped. "We have to go back!"

Kailyn placed her arm over Tes' shoulder as Naisa arrived. She stopped abruptly at the sight of the two girls on the ground, causing Tean to cannon into her back. Both of them crashed to the ground, limbs sprawling in all directions. Aldan managed to stop in time, Elddyn not far behind. "Why have you stopped?" Aldan asked urgently. "We have to move on!"

Naisa had managed to right herself and sat against a tree. "We're exhausted," she replied. "Can't we rest a moment?"

"The beasts won't be resting. Let's move!" Aldan roared.

"But Deavon and Giddy and Raim," Tes implored. "We have to help them!"

"The best way we can help them is to get out of the pass." Aldan reached down and pulled Tes to her feet. "They'll be alright; they're all fine warriors,"

"They might die!"

"Then don't let their deaths be in vain!" Aldan yelled. "Deavon ordered us out, so out we are going." He turned Tesania and pushed her down the hill. "Move!" he shouted at the others.

Tes was too exhausted to argue and she knew Aldan was right. Moving in a daze and not really aware of her surroundings she stumbled on. After an interminable time she broke from the woods. Green grass met her stare as she abruptly stopped. "Where to now?" she asked as Aldan ground to a halt beside her.

"We can't follow the track, it's too obvious. There's a creek a bit further on. We can move along that without leaving tracks." He started off once more and the others fell in behind.

~

Giddy paused, picked up a fallen branch and wedged it across the path at ankle level between two trees. She smiled with satisfaction as she heard the anguished scream of a beast a few moments later. "Hope it broke its leg," she called out to Raim. She quickly calculated in her head, ten beasts had come upon them where they had laid the trap, they had accounted for four, maybe five if the tripped beast had broken its leg. The odds were getting better; but they were still in for a fight.

Deavon raised his hand above his head, motioning both ways as he dove into the bush to the right.

Raim and Giddy took his meaning immediately, both diving off to the other side at the same instant. They lay still, not daring even a whisper.

Twenty seconds passed before they heard the pounding feet of the beasts approaching. Giddy held her breath as the first beast beat past, oblivious to their smell in its haste to catch its prey.

The trio waited until the beasts had all rushed on down the track before Deavon stepped out, took aim and sent an arrow on its way. It flew straight at the last beast, piercing its neck just as it was about to disappear around a bend in the track. It uttered no sound as it fell dead in the middle of the track. "We make a stand here!" Deavon said fiercely to the others. "They can't get around to flank us. It's our best chance."

Raim took his stance, two hands on the sword raised over his shoulder. Giddy adjusted her grip and stood comfortably by his side.

They waited for the beasts to come roaring up the track. Looking at each other nervously as the track remained empty, Giddy grinned. "They don't know we're behind them."

They all started to laugh. Deavon sobered quickly. "But now they're behind Tes and the others. Let's go!" he said as he charged off, jumping the dead beast, flicking the arrow shaft protruding from its neck with his boot. They followed the beasts, trying their best to catch them. Giddy came up beside Deavon. "Do you think they'll catch the others?" she puffed, ducking under an overhanging branch at the last second.

"We would hear them if they had. Aldan will be driving the others on."

"What if they do catch up to them? Can they hold them off?"

"Aldan has Elddyn and Naisa to help him. Tes can hold her own, if she has to." He looked grimly across at her. "Let's hope it doesn't come to that," he wheezed between breaths as he strove for an extra bit of pace.

~

The beasts bounded down the track; unaware that another of their troop had perished on the end of yet another of Deavon's arrows. They had only one thing on their mind, revenge for their fallen companions. The lead beast started to think it strange they hadn't caught the man-things yet, they could only have a short lead on them, they could not have moved on too far while he and his companions pulled the fallen beast from between the trees after the ambush. The track however remained empty ahead of him, no attacks came, no traps sprang out from the surrounding trees. His mind could only think that the enemy was racing ahead of them. Onward they pushed, maintaining a daunting pace, stepping lithely over any obstacles that got in their way, easily vaulting logs and snags, spanning furrows left by the rains in one easy step.

On and on they ran until they too broke from the woods. Halting, the leader looked around, scuffed his foot on the disturbed ground, snuffling as he smelt the air. "Man-things" he grunted. Without another word he started to move again, heading away from the pass along the track where he was sure the enemy must be. After a short while he stopped. Water tumbled across the track before merrily jumping over stones and pebbles in a little creek bed. He snuffled once more, looking around warily. Bending down he snuffled at the edge of the track, shrugged and took a drink before grunting at his troop and moving on along the track.

~

Aldan let them finally step out of the water that ran along the little creek bed. He had insisted they walk in the water to hide their tracks and dissipate their smell. He lay now in a copse of trees some five hundred yards from the track. Making sure he was well hidden, he waited, watching for movement, ready to call Deavon and the others when they appeared.

Tesania sat trembling on the ground, Tean pushed one of her feet back in an effort to force out the cramp that had seized her left calf. She moaned as pain wracked her body, her shoulder ached, every muscle in her legs wanted to follow her calf's lead into cramp. Kailyn lay still on the ground, wrapped in a ball; she made neither movement nor any sound. Naisa sat exhausted, her dank hair hanging limply, eyes unfocused. Elddyn sat, as always, away from the others. Also exhausted from their ordeal, he had dropped his staff before collapsing to the ground. Tean seemed relatively untouched, his thin frame was bloodied and torn from the mad dash down the pass but otherwise he seemed in good spirits.

"Any sign of them yet?" Tes grimaced as she called up to Aldan.

"Not yet," Aldan replied. "They may still be trying to hold back the beasts."

"Do you think they'll be ok?" Tes whimpered as she pictured the beasts attacking Giddy and the others.

"Shh," Aldan hissed. "Someone's coming."

Tes managed to ignore her aches, rolling over and crawling up the little incline where Aldan had set up his observation post. "Where?" she whispered as the track came into view.

"Keep your head down," Aldan said as he placed his hand on her head and pushed her back down to where she could only just peer over the clumps of grass. "I saw movement behind those.., here they come.., beasts," he said as he pulled Tesania down the slope.

"Beasts?" Tes asked incredulously.

"Everyone stay down. Don't make a sound, don't even cough," Aldan said as he looked around the group with wide eyes, his forefinger pressed to his lips. Slowly he crawled back up the incline. Carefully he raised his head, making sure not to make any sudden moves. He watched as the beasts ran up to the creek bed, cringing as they stopped. He ducked down quickly as the lead beast gazed in his direction. Turning to the others, he whispered. "Four beasts, they've stopped at the creek, maybe they smell us. Be ready to move." After he had counted thirty seconds he dared to raise is head once more. The beasts were drinking. With bated breath he watched, exhaling as the lead beast moved off along the track. Waiting to see that they continued along the track and didn't make a turn toward them he watched them for some six hundred yards before it wound through a field of boulders, obscuring them from his view.

Turning to the others he announced, "They're gone. Went straight down the track."

They all looked at each other; no one spoke.

Tean tentatively asked the question they all dreaded, "What of the others?"

"If the beasts made it through, then surely they have perished," Elddyn stated without emotion.

"Not necessarily," interjected Aldan as Tes twisted to face the mage, cringing as her side went into spasms of cramp.

Tes swung back, ignoring the pain. "You think they're alive?" she asked as hope spread across her face.

"Maybe. There's any number of reasons that the beasts may have got ahead of them. Maybe Deavon and the others diverted into the woods and are making their way down as we speak."

Tes eyes grew thoughtful. Suddenly she looked up. "They could be injured. They might need our help." Bending down she snatched up her pack.

"Where are you going?" Aldan asked quickly.

"Back up the pass, to search for them," she replied as she limped toward the creek.

Aldan stood quickly, blocking her way. "You are not. I forbid it!"

Tes looked at him incredulously. "You forbid it? Deavon's up there, maybe wounded, he needs our help!" She moved to go around him.

Reaching out to stop her, he said quietly, "The beasts have only just gone through; they may double back at any time. Besides, how are we to know if there are others still in the pass waiting for us to attempt just such a foolhardy rescue?"

Tears started to brim in Tes' eyes. "But we can't just leave them up there." She spun, looking from Tean to Naisa and then Elddyn. "Surely even you don't want to leave them up there injured, alone!"

Tean stood and embraced her. "The Lord will provide for them, if it is his will they will rejoin us," he said calmly. As he released her he knelt, clasping his hands he said, "I will consult my Lord."

Elddyn scoffed. "What good will that do? If they're dead, they're dead."

Tes glared at him. "Just shut up!"

"Keep your voices down," Aldan muttered. "The beasts could come back at any second."

"Don't you see?" Tesania sighed as she turned back to Aldan. "That's exactly why we have to go and look for them. If they're injured and the beasts come back they'll surely kill them."

Aldan shook his head sadly. "If they were injured, the beasts wouldn't have left them alive; they'd be dead already."

"No!" Tes screamed, not caring who heard it.

"The beasts!" Aldan hissed.

"I don't care. Let them come!" Tes cried, tears flowing down her face as she weakly drew her sword. "I want them to!"

Kailyn slowly stood, staggering as her weary legs took her weight. "Tes, he's right. It's too dangerous."

"But they might be alive..." She dropped her sword as she sank to her knees in dismay. "We have to try," she whispered in a small, defeated voice. Tes looked into Kailyn's eyes as the young girl knelt beside her. "Deavon and Giddy. I can't lose them, not now, not after all we've been through." She fell into Kailyn's outstretched arms, sobbing, tears running freely down her face.

~

Deavon told Giddy and Raim to stop as they came out of the woods. "We have to assume the beasts have gone on after the others. We can't catch them, so let's hope Aldan has something up his sleeve."

Giddy stood bent at the waist, holding her side. In-between ragged breaths, she said, "I don't know how much farther I can run."

Raim had collapsed to the ground, totally spent, his sword tossed aside. "We won't be much good in a fight like this anyway," he managed to get out.

"All the same. We have to move on," Deavon said as he started to walk in the direction of the beasts.

Giddy sighed. Reaching down she took Raim's arm and helped him up. "No rest for the wicked," she grinned and followed Deavon down the track while Raim retrieved his sword.

It wasn't long before they reached the little creek; gratefully sinking to their knees they drank deeply. As Deavon stood he heard raised voices off in the distance. "Shh," he said to Giddy and Raim urgently, holding out his hand to emphasis the point. "Did you hear that?"

"Hear what?" Giddy asked as she looked about.

As they listened, Tesania's scream of, "No!" drifted toward them.

"It's them," Deavon yelled as he jumped into the creek and started to run, with sword raised, toward the sound "The beasts must be upon them! Hurry!"

~

Aldan heard the rushing footsteps in the water. "The beasts are upon us, fight for your lives!" he yelled as he drew his sword and turned toward the attackers.

Elddyn quickly found his feet, moving to the back of the area they were in, he raised his staff, preparing an offensive spell to meet the first beast that showed its ugly face.

Naisa took up a similar position on the other side. Tean stayed where he was, kneeling in the middle of the little clearing, his mumbling reaching a crescendo.

Tes and Kailyn moved faster than their aching bodies liked. Kailyn, unarmed except for a small knife, moved behind a tree. Tes snatched her sword and took up a stance that Giddy had taught her. For a split second she wondered why it didn't hum or glow as the beasts approached, too late now as the footsteps drew near. The attackers charged over the top of the little mound. Stopping dead in their tracks as they saw who opposed them.

"Deavon!" Tes cried as she dropped her sword and ran to him. Throwing herself into his open arms, she gripped him with all her remaining strength, determining never to let go.

Deavon couldn't believe he had found them all, safe and unharmed. He bent down and kissed Tesania on the head, whispering, "I'm so glad you're safe." Giddy and Raim moved around shaking everyone's hand as Deavon extracted himself from Tes' embrace. "We can't stay here; the beasts will still be looking for us." He looked around the bedraggled, exhausted group. "We can rest when we're safe. For now we need to move as far away from the track as we can get." He put his arm happily around Tesania's shoulder and started to walk. "I thought I'd lost you," he said as he smiled down at her.

Tes slipped her arm around his waist, happy as could be.

34 DRIVEN

The whip, travelling at over fourteen hundred feet per second, cracked against Kragh's back. He winced as the tip sliced through his hide, but ran on, refusing to show any sign of pain. They had been on training runs around the hills and rocks of the Keep for two days now, only allowed to stop for a short break at noon, or a drink at the occasional puddle or streamlet they came across. The commander insisted they keep a lively pace. When any of the troop started to drop off his whip would whistle through the air, more times than not aimed at Kragh, even when it was others that were at fault he bore the brunt of the abuse. Larger than most of the beasts, gifted at swordsmanship, athletic and strong, the commander had quickly picked him out for extra attention. He bore it with no obvious sign of rebellion, always looking downward as the commander flew into rages over the simplest things, standing in front of him; face only inches away, spittle flying in strings.

Behind Kragh's calm exterior a battle raged. Always a leader before he was transformed, he had fought off many lesser males to ensure the safety of his harem. Yet now he was forced to follow this weak individuals command. He kept to himself in the rare moments of rest that they had, preferring not to engage in the simpleton conversation the others enjoyed. He reveled in the fighting; it was one of the only enjoyable parts of the otherwise monotonous days. His sword felt like an extension of his being, during practice he wielded it like a well tuned instrument, continually besting his counterparts. During the nights, when he could, he stole a few minutes by himself, wandering into the rocks. He had come to enjoy the quiet company of the plant in craggy rocks above the camp, carefully picking a few leaves, conscious of not overindulging and killing the brave little bush that so tenaciously hung onto life in such an inhospitable place.

Daily he managed to drive Trannyth further out of his head. Although he would have been considered clever by a scientist studying him when he was a banmora, his mind now had conscious thought of his destiny. As the controls on him lessened he started to think of the day when he could steal a few of the females away and escape into the mountains. He tried to take one aside and talk to her, finding to his dismay that she was under Trannyth's total control, unable to see anything outside of what she was told to do. He quickly decided to halt any attempts at organizing an escape whilst they were so close to the Keep. He would watch and wait, taking his chance when it arose.

A few months after his painful transformation the troop sat around the fire, exhausted from yet another day's arduous training. As Kragh disgustedly threw aside the joint he had been gnawing on, a mage approached. Keeping his distance and positioning himself upwind, he said, "You have been assigned to me. We move out tomorrow morning." With that he turned on his heel and disappeared as quickly as he had arrived.

Kragh stole into the rocks in the dark of the night. Picking two luscious young leaves, he patted the little bush and growled, "Goodbye friend."

For four days the troop ran on, whip cracks and curses following threateningly behind. Keeping to the base of the Britath Mountains, they headed always east. Kragh looked longingly at the hills and forests, his heart yearned to break ranks and disappear forever amongst the dense foliage. Fleeting thoughts of escape crossed his mind, wondering in the quiet of the night if he could eliminate the commander, mage and other males and steal the females for his own. He knew full well that the females wouldn't help; they would side with the mage and protect him with their lives. Dejectedly he ran on, one day blending into the next.

On the morning of the fifth day they halted their relentless march eastward. The mage motioned for them to climb between two rocky outcrops. The way was narrow and thick with brambles; the footing hazardous as they labored up the steep incline. Kragh strained in the lead, shoving aside old fallen branches while pushing through the thick vegetation, grateful when he finally broke through into a small clearing. Nestled tight against the side of a cliff with a commanding view back across the rocky plains, it was big enough to easily accommodate them all. At the back of the clearing was a dark slit in the rock face, a cave entrance just big enough for Kragh to slip through. The packs they had been forced to carry were dumped on the ground and ripped open. Kragh sniffed suspiciously at the wooden torches that were revealed, heavily wrapped in oil soaked linen.

35 ORASH

Kailyn luxuriated on the smooth rock outcrop as the waterfall massaged her muscles, working every part of her still weary shoulders. It had been two days now since they had escaped from the beasts at the Draon Pass. They had walked for a few hours before coming across this idyllic little oasis, after a quick discussion it was decided that this would be a good place to lay-up and address their abused bodies. Deavon had said that they could spend two days recuperating, washing and mending their clothes while tending their wounds.

Tesania wore a sling over her right shoulder, Naisa had inspected it shortly after they had arrived, announcing, thankfully, that it was only bruised and that there was no break. She sat on the bank, hair still wet, chatting happily with her friend. Giddy approached, smiling at the two young girls from the high bank. "You two are lucky. You get to laze about all day while the rest of us have to hunt and cook."

"That's not true," Kailyn grinned up at her. "Just this morning I collected firewood with Tean. We got enough to last till we leave." She chuckled, raising her eyebrows. "I hope."

"And you?" Giddy asked Tesania teasingly.

"I went with Naisa to collect herbs," she replied defensively. "I can't do much else with my shoulder," she added while unconsciously rubbing the slings material between her fingers.

Giddy laughed. "Deavon wants to have a meeting. Get dry and come on in."

"Oh, about what?" Kailyn asked curiously.

Giddy shrugged. "I wouldn't know. Doesn't let me in on his little secrets does he?" she stated. "Let me see." she adopted a casual stance, put her right hand to her chin and looked up at the top of the waterfall, as if in deep thought. After a few moments she glanced back at Kailyn, her face bright, as if an epiphany had come to her. "Maybe it's about the mission, and getting over the mountains," she laughed.

Tes grinned at her friend. "She's very astute for an old dear, isn't she?"

Giddy blustered, "Old?" Lightly jumping across the rocks she came toward Tesania. "I'll give you old."

Tes laughed gaily. Jumping to her feet she ran off toward the camp, Giddy in hot pursuit. Kailyn reluctantly prized herself from under the ministrations of the waterfall and walked after them, smiling as she watched the fit soldier catch Tes and slap her lightly on the rear.

Nine travelers gathered around the coals of the fire. "How's your shoulder?" Deavon asked Tes.

"It's fine. I might stop using the sling tomorrow."

"And everyone else?" he continued as he looked around the group. After two days, they had all had sufficient rest and recuperation. Most still bore evidence of the rapid descent down the pass, scratches healing on their faces and arms, but apart from that they all looked healthy and ready to move on. After they all nodded and mumbled their answers, he went on. "It's safe to say that the Draon Pass is now out of the picture as a way across the Mountains. Trannyth will be sure to reinforce it as soon as he can. For that matter the other passes will also be heavily guarded. I see no other way to get through." He looked solemnly around the group. "We have to attempt one. The question is which will it be?"

"Surely there are other places to cross that Trannyth may not know about?" Elddyn asked with a sour look on his face.

Deavon shook his head. "The Orash and Draon Passes are the main ways to get to the wastelands. There are other passes, but they're only for the most hardened of travelers. Rumor has it that some parts require hours of traversing small ledges. We aren't equipped for that. Nor do I think our group could manage them anyway."

"So your whole plan was based on the Draon pass? Now that it's closed to us you have no alternative. Good planning," he sneered.

"I don't see you contributing anything," Giddy cut in. "Except your vile remarks!"

"It's not I that planned this farce," Elddyn replied.

"The only farce I can see around here is you!" Giddy snapped.

"Enough!" Deavon yelled. "Both of you!" Turning to Elddyn, he said, "This mission is fluid. We always knew that going through the Draon Pass was a risk. So it has failed, we have to find another way. Your negativity doesn't help. If you have something constructive to add, do so. If not, please remain quiet!"

"Here, here," Giddy muttered.

"The same goes for you, Giddy!" Deavon snapped.

"Me," Giddy asked defensively. "It was him who..."

Deavon sighed. "Enough!" Looking around the group he asked, "Does anyone have any knowledge of another way we might get through?"

As Tes looked at the others a sudden thought came to her. Looking quickly at Deavon, she ventured, "When I was at Lady Ayana's house I read a book..." She cast her mind back, trying to recall, smiling as it came to her, she continued excitedly, "It was The Britath Mountains, by Ernal Tenrad. I remember it now. It was about his travels through the mountains. He explored everywhere!"

"How does that help?" Elddyn sullenly asked.

Tes scowled at him. "It helps because he wrote of some catacombs under the mountain."

"Where?" Deavon asked quickly

Tes thought for a while, trying to remember the name and whereabouts that Tenrad had mentioned. Hesitantly, she said, "I believe he called it the Owara Caves. Somewhere in the foothills of the Rhaem Forest."

An excited air swept through the group as they realized that there may be a way to continue their quest to eliminate Trannyth. Tean spoke up, "I have also read Tenrad's writings. The caves he speaks of are unexplored. There is no way of knowing if they lead all the way under the mountain or are simply a dead end. Even if it does go through there may be many different paths to choose from." He looked around the group. "It could be a labyrinth for all we know."

Deavon thought quietly before speaking, "Still, it's an option. Maybe the only option we have. The Rhaem Forest itself is an obstacle. Many ogres make their home there, driven there as the lands they once inhabited are taken up by farms and villages. It's a dangerous place that most people avoid."

"We don't seem to have a lot of choice," Aldan said. "I say we try for the caves."

They all sat and watched Deavon as he mulled it over. Coming to a decision, he looked at Tesania. "We have to get you through, somehow. This seems our best chance." He stood and started to pace. "I suggest we proceed to

Orash. There we can replenish our supplies." He looked around the gathered faces noting that Elddyn was looking away, apparently paying no attention. "Are we all agreed? Does anyone have a better suggestion?" Elddyn quickly looked at him, but like the rest of them remained quiet. "Very well. In the morning we set out for Orash. My parents have an estate on the outskirts of town; we can set up camp there while we prepare for the caves."

~

Orash was like any other town in Eldanal, a main street of compacted dirt running through a myriad of shops and inns. Early morning shoppers bustled along the wooden walkways; a group of children chased a wooden hoop down the street as a bullock driver whistled and swore trying to get his wagon of flour to the loading platform at the general store. Whitewash adorned every building, the windows and doors were painted a soft, duck-egg blue, spring flowers hung from boxes attached to the walls, every building with the same colors, giving the town a pretty symmetry.

Deavon had warned them at the campfire the night before to keep to themselves as much as possible, stressing the need to keep their mission secret. "Trannyth's spies might be anywhere and could be someone as innocuous as a street urchin," he had said.

As they entered the general store to purchase provisions for the rest of their journey, a woman called, "Deavon?" from across the street. "Is that you?" she asked as she made her way over to them, stopping to let a horse and cart through. "I can't believe it's you," she gushed as she finally reached the little porch they were standing on. Reaching out both arms she took the ranger into an embrace.

"Hello, Jinee," Deavon stammered as he returned her greeting. "It's been a long time."

Tesania stood and watched the exchange, watching the woman's face as she withdrew from the embrace with Deavon and stepped back. Gripping his hands and feigning hurt with a pout on her pretty lips, she asked accusingly, "Why didn't you tell me you were coming?"

Deavon looked uncomfortable as he shuffled his feet, trying to remove his hands from her grip. "I.., we..," he started as he looked sideways at the group watching him. "It was a last minute decision. We're only passing through," he replied nervously.

"You must come for a meal!" she bubbled, obliviously unaware of Deavon's discomfort. "Mommy and daddy would be so glad to see you."

"I'll see," Deavon blushed, finally managing to extricate his hands from her grip. "We'll be very busy. I don't know that I'll have time to..," he looked again at the group. "To.., umm.., visit you." As he looked down at his feet, he quickly added, "Sorry."

"Don't be silly," Jinee smiled. "I will tell Mommy you'll be coming tomorrow night." She turned on her heel and started across the road. Looking back, she cooed, "Bye for now, oh.., and it was lovely meeting your friends."

Tes watched her go. "Who's she?" she asked as she turned to watch Deavon's reaction.

Deavon straightened. Adopting a dismissive attitude, he said, "Just an old friend. I did some schooling with her."

Giddy laughed. "An old friend hey. It looked to me like you used to be more than just friends," she teased.

Deavon ignored her. "Let's go inside. We'll need oil and linen. Naisa, if you could see to that. The rest of you replenish your supplies." He walked away from them toward the far end of the shop.

"Stay here. I'll be back in a little while," Tes said to Kailyn as she hurried after him. Slowing as she reached him, she asked quietly, "Do you like her?"

Deavon scowled. "We were just friends. Just because she comes up to me and asks me to dine with her parents doesn't make it any different," he bristled. Turning, he stormed away. "Got it!"

Tes felt sick. She hadn't meant to hurt him. Standing there in shock she thought to herself, *what had I meant to do?* All she knew was that when other women spoke to Deavon her stomach turned in knots. It hurt in her chest when he gave his smile to another. Confused, she wandered back to Kailyn, deep in thought.

"What was that about?" Giddy asked as she approached.

Tes looked up quickly. "Nothing!" she snapped as she ran out the front door.

Giddy looked from Tes to Deavon, shook her head and turned to Raim. "Hey, don't forget more soap. You can be a bit on the nose you know?" she laughed as she waved her hand in front of her face.

"Giddy, you are so hilarious," Raim replied with a sour look on his face.

"You know it, I know it, but the others, I do it for them."

"I'm sure they would live without it," he shot back.

"Possibly?" Giddy pondered. "Doubt it though." She looked out the door toward Tes, concern crossing her face. "Don't forget to get more salted pork," she said quietly.

~

Deavon's estate lay to the north-east of Orash. Lush green pastures greeted them as they walked along the worn dusty road that led to the homestead. Deavon led the way, keeping to himself. Giddy, Aldan and Raim followed, bantering with each other, talking of the adventures they'd had since joining the King's forces. Kailyn talked softly with Naisa and Tean; they talked of magic and what she would be able to achieve if she studied at the Mages Guild in Carella. Elddyn walked along by himself, refusing to enter into any conversation, scowling at anyone that came near him. Tesania walked at the rear, lost in thought, the occasional tear forming as she went over and over the events in the store. *Why did that girl have to come up to Deavon?* She so wanted to talk to him, but whenever she looked at him she couldn't find the courage.

The fields of crops gave way to an orchard. The trees wore shining dark green foliage that dripped with the bright colors of ripening oranges and lemons. As the orchard opened onto an expansive vegetable patch, the shingled roof of the homestead and barns came into view. Deavon halted. "It might be best if just Aldan and I go ahead to the homestead at the moment. We'll be back shortly," he said. "Help yourself to some fruit." With that he turned and started up the track, talking quietly to Aldan as he went.

Tes watched him go. Her emotions were out of control. Her chest hurt, her mind whirled, jumping from one thought to another. As a tear ran down her face she caught Giddy out of the corner of her eye, watching her. Twirling on her heel Tes strode into the orchard, embarrassed, wanting to be alone.

Giddy watched her go. Sighing she turned and talked quietly to Naisa.

Tesania walked for a few minutes, eventually stopping and picking a fat, lush, orange before sinking to the ground. She looked up into the branches of the tree. Tears running freely, she moaned, "Why..? Why do I feel this way?"

She jumped as a hand touched her shoulder. "It's only me," said Naisa calmingly.

Tes turned and saw the mage, with Giddy at her side, standing with a compassionate look on her face. "I want to be alone!" she stated fiercely, turning her face to hide her tears.

Naisa settled down beside her, Giddy stood kicking at a mound of soft soil. "Do you have feelings for Deavon?" she asked directly.

Tesania looked up quickly. "No!" she stated flatly as she stared at the mage.

Naisa placed her hand on Tes' arm. "Come now. It's plain for all to see."

"What! That I'm a fool?" Tes said angrily as she tossed the orange aside.

"No one thinks you a fool," replied Naisa gently. "We see what's happening between you and Deavon. It's natural for two people to be drawn to each other."

Tesania looked quickly from Giddy to Naisa. "Two? He thinks I'm a silly village girl!"

Giddy scoffed. "Tes, we see the looks he gives you. I've seen it since the day we crossed the Lyiera Hills and killed those four beasts." She squatted down and looked into Tesania's eyes. "He harbors feelings for you, but he's scared."

"Scared.., of what?" Tes asked as she sat up quickly.

"That he'll get too close. That his feelings for you will cloud his judgment if we encounter more danger." She reached forward and touched Tes' tear stained cheek. "He fears mostly that he will lose you."

Tes looked back down to the mossy earth. "What about that woman at the General Store?" She looked quickly back up. "He has feelings for her.., doesn't he?" Her eyes flicked to Naisa, confusion written on her face.

"Tes, don't let your feeling turn to jealousy. Deavon has many friends, a lot of them women. You can't get upset every time he talks to someone. Besides he was trying to get away from her, he had no interest in what she had to say," Giddy assured her.

"Then why did he get angry when I asked him if he liked her?" Tes asked in a confused voice.

Giddy laughed. "You ninny. He was embarrassed by the girl, you could see he was aware of all of us watching, you especially."

Tes' face brightened. "So you think he likes me?" she asked quickly.

"Likes you, is an understatement," replied Naisa. "Again, it is there for all to see."

"I bet Raim and Aldan are oblivious to it though," Giddy laughed as she stood.

Naisa laughed as well. Tes grinned and held out her hand for Giddy to help her up. "So what do I do now?" she asked bewilderedly.

They walked slowly back to the others as Naisa and Giddy told her to let Deavon have some space. "He'll come to you when he sees reason. Don't worry," Naisa said.

"Shouldn't I go to him.., and apologize," Tes asked; a little confused.

Giddy laughed. "Take it from someone who has hunted many a man. Make him come to you."

Kailyn rushed up to Tes as they rejoined the group. "Are you ok?" she asked with a concerned look.

"Yes," replied Tesania with a smile. "Very much so!"

~

"Mother!" Deavon's sister called as she watched the two rangers come up the path. "Deavon is here, with his friend Aldan!"

Coming out of the kitchen while wiping her hands on her apron, Deavon's mother said, "Deavon? Where?" When she saw him she ran, embracing him, kissing him repeatedly on the cheek. "It has been so long," she said as she stepped back and took her son in. "Welcome home!" she said happily. "And Aldan, you are welcome too." She moved between the two big rangers, reached around their waists and said, "Come inside, I'll make you some tea." As she gently pushed them forward, a smile spread across her face. "Issy, run and get your father and your brothers. Tell them Deavon is here." As Issy ran off toward the fields her mother called happily after her, "And Aldan too!"

His mother bustled them into the kitchen. "Sit, sit," she said as she pulled two chairs out from the polished wooden table. "Tell me," she bubbled. "What are you doing here? And why didn't you tell me you were coming?" she asked with a feigned pout on her lips.

Deavon laughed. "Our visit is unexpected. We had to divert through Orash at the last... father," he said as he quickly stood and warmly shook his father hand as he entered the room and then embraced him. "How have you been?"

"I'm well son." He stood back and looked Deavon up and down. "You look well too, except, where did all those scratches on your face come from?"

"It's a long story, for another time. Aldan is here as well," he said as he turned and gestured at the big ranger.

"Ah, Aldan, you are always welcome," Deavon's father said as he walked across the room and shook Aldan's hand. "Are you staying for long?" he asked as he turned back to Deavon.

"Just tonight I'm afraid." He stopped as his brothers burst through the door, covered in the dirt and muck of running a farm. "Hey boys!" he called as he was greeted warmly by them all, wincing as they slapped him on his still weary and sore shoulders.

"Are you on a mission?" Issy asked, having followed her brothers in.

"Of sorts," Deavon answered evasively. "We're travelling with a small group."

"Where? I didn't see anybody else," Issy asked curiously as she hung her head out the door and peered down the path.

Deavon laughed. "They're down at the orchard. I didn't want to bring everyone else up until I had warned you all."

Deavon mother admonished him, "You don't have to ask to bring your friends here, you know that. Now go and get them, quickly, go now," she said as she chased him to the door.

Aldan laughed heartily. "Don't let the others see you treat him like that."

Deavon hastened to the others. "My parents have graciously offered their hospitality. If you would please follow me," he said regally as he bowed and swept his arm toward the homestead.

The group gathered their gear and headed off toward the house in a ragged line. Tes came last, flashing a shy smile, for only a split second, toward Deavon. He quickly caught up to her. "How're you feeling?" he asked nervously, feeling like he had just met her all over again.

"I'm fine," Tes replied. "My shoulder's much better now."

"I'm pleased to hear that," he said as he looked at her from the corners of his eyes. "Tes," he said as he griped her hand and pulled her to a stop. "I would like to apologize for my behavior in the general store today," he said as he looked at the ground and kicked a pebble from the dusty road. "It was just that girl, she has always, since the time we went to school together, tried to drag me into more than just friendship." He looked up at her quickly. "And then when she came over to me today, I was.., I was embarrassed to have you.., and the others," he quickly added, "there."

"I understand," Tes smiled shyly. "I overreacted too. Please accept my apology as well."

Deavon smiled. "I don't even like he..."

Tes put her fingers to his lips. "shh... Let's pretend she doesn't exist."

"You are wise beyond your years Tesania of Aryd Village," Deavon beamed. "Let's catch up to the others. They'll be wondering where we are."

Deavon's mother greeted them all at the door as they reached the homestead. "Come in, come in," she said as she ushered them in. "Issy get the spare chairs out."

Tes and Deavon were the last to arrive. "Mother, I would like you to meet Tesania," he said proudly.

"Tesania, what a lovely name. It's so nice to meet you." She said as she followed them inside.

As Issy dragged the spare chairs noisily across the worn old stone floor, Giddy elbowed Raim and nodded her head toward the corner of the room. A four foot high, wooden ale barrel rested against the far wall, its tap reflecting the firelight, winking slowly at the two soldiers.

The travelers managed to organize themselves in the now crowded room, Deavon's family squeezing in between. "Tea?" his mother called out.

As she went around the room with her eyes, everyone nodded yes. She stopped when she reached Giddy. "No?" she asked as the soldier shook her head.

"Tea would be nice, but my friend," she said as she pushed Raim with her shoulder, "and I, have been walking in the hot sun, all morning. We're parched," she replied as she gripped her own throat and ran her tongue along her lips to emphasis her meaning.

Looking at Deavon, his mother asked, "What on earth does she mean."

Deavon looked at Giddy and Raim, rolling his eyes. "They're asking for ale instead of tea, mother," he explained.

"Well why didn't the girl just say so," she asked, confused.

"Giddy is very shy!" Aldan cut in. "And I don't think the word, girl, is the right one to describe our Giddy."

Giddy glared at him as the others broke into laughter. "You'll keep, ranger," she said as she smiled and looked at Deavon's mother. "So. Could we? Have some ale, I mean?"

"You most certainly can. Issy, pour Giddy and Raim an ale please."

"And me too," Aldan called with a sheepish grin on his face.

"What brings you home?" Deavon's father asked. "And with all these people?" he added as he sat forward and looked around the room.

"Top secret," Giddy said as she took her ale from Issy.

"Giddy," Deavon warned as he turned to his father. "We're on a mission. Unfortunately I can't tell you any more than that."

"I understand," his father replied.

"One thing I would like to ask you though," Deavon said as he watched his father closely. "What do you hear of the Rhaem Forest these days? Are the ogres still causing trouble?"

His father shifted in his seat as he answered. "The ogres have been quite troublesome of late. They've formed into groups." He looked around the room, stopping on Tes. "Unnatural for ogres you see. They're normally a solitary creature that lives alone."

"So, will they attack us?" Tes asked as her eyes flicked to Deavon. "I mean if we do go into the forest?"

"Oh, I should imagine that if you're careful you won't have too many troubles from them," he said with a disarming smile. "They mainly come onto the farms to steal sheep and cattle. These were once their lands after all."

They talked for hours about the homestead, embarrassing Deavon with tales of his youth. After a meal, cooked by Issy and his mother, they sang a few songs as Deavon's father played along on his mandolin.

"Time we retired to our sleeping rolls," Deavon said as Giddy asked for more ale.

"You can all sleep here tonight," Deavon's mother said.

"You can't possibly fit us all in," Deavon replied. "We should all stay together." His mother shook her head, but before she could speak, Deavon added, "The barn will do fine. It's warm enough."

The group moved out into the star filled night. Deavon held back, wanting to spend some time alone with his family. Tesania stayed by his side as they returned to the warm kitchen. They sat for many hours talking, his mother particularly interested in Tes and her past. In the early hours of the morning Deavon thanked his mother for her hospitality toward his friends and ushered Tesania out the door.

His mother gripped his arm. "I approve," she said as she kissed him lightly on the cheek.

Deavon looked at her with a confused frown on his face. "Approve?"

"Of the girl," she replied with a happy smile on her face. "Tesania."

"I don't know what you mean," Deavon claimed as he looked to his sister for help.

She grinned at him, enjoying his discomfort immensely.

His mother squeezed his arm. "A mother knows dear. Deny it all you like, I see the looks." She kissed him once more on the cheek. As he walked into the darkness in confusion, she whispered after him, "When you want to admit it, I approve."

"Leave him alone dear," Deavon's father chided as he took her by the hand and closed the kitchen door.

36 RHAEM FOREST

Tesania clawed her way from the depths of sleep as the sounds from the barn slipped into her consciousness. Horses shuffled and nickered; piglets grunted and squealed while a rooster let out an almighty morning cry.

Rolling onto her back, she blinked up at the straw loft. Sunshine blazed through loose joints and knots in the timber walls, a million particles of dust floating in the needles of light creating a soft, dreamlike serenity.

The air was sweet as she drew in a deep breath, catching the subtle nuances' of the straw and bags of grain. She wrinkled her nose as she recognized the faint odor of manure. Raising her head, she gazed around the airy barn. Deavon and Aldan sat on a bale of hay, talking quietly as they checked over their gear. A dozen or so chickens clucked and pecked at seed that someone had scattered across the floor. Raim laughed quietly at one of Giddy's jokes at the entrance to the building.

One of the big wooden barn doors stood open, allowing a cool breeze to wander through the stalls. Tean knelt in an empty horse enclosure, cross in hand, mumbling prayers as he gazed to the roof above.

Tes shifted onto her elbow. Kailyn still slept beside her, Naisa and Elddyn were nowhere to be seen.

"Good morning, Tes," Deavon called as he slipped his sword from its sheath.

"Morning," Tes mumbled, rubbing sleep from her tired eyes.

"Did you sleep well?" Aldan inquired as he ran a honing stone along the length of his blade. The ragged, rasping sound echoed through the barn, Kailyn's head jerked up.

"Sorry," Aldan apologized to her, laying the sword aside.

"It's ok," Kailyn grumbled as she dropped her head back to the pillow and dragged her blanket over her face.

"Giddy has some water boiling on the fire if you'd like a mug of tea," Deavon advised Tes.

She smiled, her eyes still half asleep. "That would be nice."

Deavon headed toward the door. "Consider it done. What about you, Kailyn?"

"Huh?" Kailyn's muffled voice came from under her blanket.

"Do you want some tea?" Deavon laughed.

"I guess so," Kailyn mumbled.

Tes rolled over and whipped the blankets off her friend. "Get up sleepy head."

Kailyn regarded her through one sleepy eye. "Go away."

Tesania laughed and climbed out of her own bed. Arching her back, she stretched and yawned and then headed toward a pail of water with a cloth laid out over the handle. She blinked as the cold water hit her face, and quickly dried it with the cloth.

"Morning," Giddy called as Tes wandered toward the fire and took the mug of tea offered by Deavon.

"A beautiful day," Issy called as she juggled a laden tray toward them. "Mother baked you some fresh bread," she advised them as she lowered the tray into Aldan's hands. "I made the butter yesterday, so it's lovely and fresh."

Kailyn's head came up as the aromas of the bread drifted past her. She reluctantly dug through her pack, looking for her brush and then started pulling it through her hair.

"Thank your mother for us," Aldan said. "And thank you as well."

Issy smiled up at him. "It wasn't a bother. I was making butter anyway."

"Where's Naisa?" Tes cut in as she looked around the yard.

"She wanted to pick some fruit from the orchard. Elddyn went with her," Raim advised her as he pointed to the dark green trees in the distance.

"Lucky her," Giddy interjected at the mention of the surly mage. "Remind me why we bothered to bring him again?"

"Giddy," Deavon cautioned. "Leave it."

"Yes, boss," Giddy saluted before asking seriously, "What's the plan?"

Deavon took a sip from his mug as he stared into the fire. "I want to start for the forest this morning, as soon as we can get everyone ready." He peered through the door at Kailyn as she dragged herself onto her feet. "There's no use in delaying here."

Kailyn managed to snatch the last piece of bread as Raim was reaching for it. She blinked in the morning sun as her eyes adjusted to the light.

"We're leaving shortly," Deavon advised her as he handed her some tea.

"Ok," she nodded sleepily.

~

Deavon's parents and sister wished them well as they started across the little bridge that stretched over the Wyvern River.

"If you cut through the north-east paddocks you'll get there faster," his father called.

"Be careful dear," his mother's voice drifted to them as they drew out of earshot. "Look after Tesania, won't you."

~

The day wore on slowly while they walked across the fields. Tes talked with Deavon, eager to learn more of his childhood and his family. A grassy hillock shaded by a great elm tree allowed them to rest for a while and eat a little lunch. Tes sat with Giddy, Kailyn and Naisa while Deavon discussed the map his father had given him with Aldan.

With regret, the travelers moved on from their picnic spot and moved further toward the north-east. The deep green canopies of the Rhaem Forest came into view as the afternoon wore on. Tes pointed, showing Kailyn an eagle floating on the air drifts above fields that ran to the very feet of the trees.

As the sun kissed the western horizon, they set up camp at the edge of the forest, a rambling stream burbling from within the darkness of the trees.

Deavon snatched up his bow and quiver then headed for a calm area of water where the stream widened into a small lake. A gaggle of geese waddled down the bank, slipping into the water and paddling toward a patch of reeds. "Dinner is served," he grinned at Aldan.

Aldan followed along to watch the sport as the others set about collecting wood and starting the fire.

"That forest looks creepy," Kailyn shivered as she collected fallen twigs from the edge of the trees.

"It'll seem different in the light of the day," Tean assured her as he lifted a heavy branch and dragged it toward the camp.

"I hope so." Kailyn peered into the darkness between the gnarled trunks. "But I doubt it," she shuddered, shaking off the dread feeling that tightened her shoulders.

"The Lord will provide," Tean advised her. "All you need do is believe." He crossed himself and looked toward the sky.

"I believe," Kailyn murmured as she glanced back at the forest. "That in there, is creepy,"

Deavon, Aldan, Giddy and Raim shared the watch during the night. Apart from an inquisitive banmora the night passed without any notable incident.

~

"Why does the smoke always follow me?" Kailyn complained in the morning as she moved to the far side of the fire for the third time.

"The Lord wishes it so," Tean advised.

"What?" Kailyn's eyes moved to Tesania as she shook her head in confusion.

"Don't look at me," Tes sighed. "I don't know what he's talking about."

"I studied the movement of smoke for many years."

"Why?" Giddy laughed.

Tean turned toward her, his eyes glazing over as he stepped closer. "The smoke consumes our sins, it cleanses us and then the Lord delivers us absolution."

"So the smoke follows Kailyn.., because she has sinned?" Tes asked.

Kailyn shot Tes a worried look, her eyes growing wide with concern.

"Indeed, the smoke seeks her out by the will of the Lord."

"I knew he was insane!" Elddyn exclaimed. "In the heat of battle he falls to his knees and prays. What good is he to us?"

Deavon held his hand up to Elddyn. "Let him speak." He leaned forward and studied the monk's face. "And why does the Lord wish to cleanse Kailyn? Why does the smoke follow her?"

"The Lord decides all of our destinies. It is for him, and him alone, to choose who will fall and who will survive."

"I'm telling you, he's mad!" Elddyn cut in.

Kailyn shakily rose to her feet, a tear running down her cheek. "Are you saying I'm going to..," she swallowed and looked at the ground, "die?"

"Not at all, dear child. The Lord decides these things. The smoke merely cleanses you, and prepares you to face ordeals that may lie ahead."

"Are you saying I'm in danger?"

"The Lord obviously believes so; why else would he direct the smoke to cleanse you?" Tean replied without emotion.

"Bah!" Elddyn stood. "You're mad... Insane." He looked about the others, stopping on Giddy. Looking straight into her eyes, he asked, "Even you can't believe this... Surely?"

Giddy shook her head and looked away from the agitated mage toward Kailyn. "We're all in danger Kailyn. We face risks every day, and will face risks that Tean can only dream of when we get to Trannyth's Keep."

Tes went to Kailyn, folding her arms around her.

Tean fell to his knees. "I will pray for you."

"Enough!" Elddyn cried. "You've upset the girl enough with your stories. If the Lord you devote yourself to wants us dead, then so be it. But don't you ever try this rubbish on us again." He glared at the monk, the orb atop his staff glowing.

Tean ignored him as his prayers grew into a crescendo.

Elddyn turned to Deavon, then to Giddy.

Giddy turned away.

"This is insanity. This.., this monk is a risk to our mission. I suggest we remove him immediately."

Giddy spun back to him. "At least he helps around the camp. That's a lot..."

Deavon held up his hand. "Enough Giddy." He turned his gaze to Elddyn. "We'll all proceed to the Keep. Tean has skills that we may need."

"Like what?" Elddyn sneered.

"Healing skills for one. Knowledge of the wastelands for another. We're all here for a reason. You don't exactly fit into the group either."

Elddyn flared. "I don't try to scare young girls with stories of Gods manipulating smoke from a campfire."

"Enough!" Deavon commanded. "We go on as we are. Tes, keep an eye on Kailyn. We move out in five minutes."

The forest, though thickly wooded, was clear of brambles and undergrowth. Kailyn remained upset for hours after they started into the trees. Tes walked behind her and helped her over any protruding roots or rocks that they encountered.

At midday, they stopped for a well earned rest. Deavon studied his father's crude map. "If we stay on a nor'-nor'-easterly heading, we should arrive at the foothills somewhere to the west of the caves." He pointed to the map and ran his finger along the crude depiction of the Britath Mountains. "From there we head east until we see some sign of the entrance."

"The entrance could be well hidden," Aldan suggested as he peered at the map. "We might walk straight past it without even noticing."

Tean interrupted. "My studies of Tenrad's texts suggest the cave lies in a valley. The way is marked by three spires of stone. Tenrad referred to them as 'The Sentinels'.

"I remember that..." Tes said. "The Sentinels point to the caves. As I recall, he wrote that when standing to the south-west of them," she said enthusiastically as her memory of the book returned. "As the three become one; that is your path," she quoted.

"That doesn't help much," Elddyn interjected. "What do these spires look like? How do you expect to find them in this?" He threw his arm toward the thick forest. "We can only see ten feet in front of us!"

"Always the optimist, aren't you?" Raim shot at him.

Giddy slapped Raim on his shoulder. "You tell him," she encouraged, beaming at Elddyn.

"It's a legitimate question," Naisa said irritably as she stepped forward and stood beside Elddyn. "We have no idea where these Sentinels might be."

"Agreed," Deavon said, cutting the others off. "But..." he studied the map. "If Tenrad found it, then so can we." Folding the parchment, he shouldered his pack. "We'd better move on."

The forest marched on in front of them. Tree after tree lining their path. Clearings were few and far between. They camped that night in a cramped little area. Deavon didn't allow them to light a fire for fear of setting the surrounding leaf litter alight.

They ate sparingly from their supply of cheese and hard bread and set their bedding rolls between the crowded roots as best they could. As the last light of day fled from the woods, Tean approached Kailyn. "My wish was not to frighten you, but to enlighten you to the ways of the Lord. Sleep well child," he said as he leaned forward and kissed her lightly on the forehead. "The Lord is with you. Fear not."

The next day passed slowly for the travelers as they moved through the seemingly endless trees. The forest floor grew steeper, slightly at first where only the experienced members of the group noticed, but by mid afternoon, as they grew closer to the Britath Mountains, they could all feel the rise starting to gnaw at their tiring legs.

Deavon dropped his pack on the ground as they came to a wall of rock. He surveyed the rising cliff in front of him. Tes and Kailyn dropped to the ground thankfully.

A small waterfall cascaded down the cliff face. Not much of a waterfall, just a few inches wide, but enough to throw mist into the light afternoon breeze as it rumbled into the water below.

"We can set up here for the night," Deavon said as he walked to the falling water and took a deep drink.

The others slid their packs off and sank to the ground. Naisa removed her boots and slipped her feet into the cool water of the little stream that ran away from the boisterous fall. "Ah."

Tes and Kailyn looked at each other, silent agreement passed between them as they started to tear off their boots and crawled to the water near the mage.

"Oh, you have such good ideas, Naisa," Tes smiled as her aching muscles felt the caress of soothing water.

"Well I have been around a long time you know. When you get this old you learn a few things," Naisa laughed.

"You're not old."

"I am, compared to you two." She swirled her feet in the water. "Can you guess how old I am?"

Tes' face creased in concentration. "Umm, thirty," she guessed.

"No."

"Fifty," Kailyn offered, squealing as Naisa kicked water at her.

"I'm twenty-eight, and proud of it."

"That's not old," Tes assured her. "My mother was older than that."

"I should hope so," Naisa laughed.

Tesania grew quiet as thoughts of her mother came flooding in. She climbed to her feet and wandered to a tree at the far side of the clearing. Sitting with her back against the rough trunk, a tear rolled down her cheek as she picked up a leaf and started peeling small pieces off until only the stem remained.

She felt someone watching her, flicking her eyes up, she caught Deavon's eye. He smiled lightly and turned toward Aldan.

The clearing offered spacious sleeping arrangements after the cramped area they had endured the night before. Giddy and Raim headed downstream with their fishing gear. Deavon and Aldan headed east along the cliff face to see what lay ahead of them. Elddyn rolled out his bedding and lay down with his back to the clearing. Naisa gathered stones from the stream and set about making a fireplace while Tesania, Tean and Kailyn ranged out to collect wood.

~

The aromas of cooking fish drifted through the twilight air as the travelers enjoyed the soldiers' catch. Tesania picked at the bones of her meal, her thoughts still off with her parents as Giddy poured tea into her mug.

"Tes," Deavon asked as he looked around the clearing.

Tesania looked up at him, "Hm?"

"Where's Kailyn?"

37 TRANNYTH'S RAGE

Serran stood like a statue, her eyes riveted to the stony floor of Trannyth's Tower Keep. The evil mage stood with his back to her, staring out over the rocky plains, mulling over her report on the attempt by the King's soldiers to cross the Draon Pass. He made her stand for an eternity as he seethed.

She started, stepping back a pace, when he spun on his heel and barked at her, "You sent the beasts down the track?"

"Ye.., Yes, My Lord." Serran replied; her voice quavering as her body trembled uncontrollably. "I thought it best to attack them in the narrow pass."

"And where were you?" he taunted, stepping closer until his cowl touched her hair, his menacing eyes boring into hers. "Cowering at the top of the pass, hidden in your tent?"

Serran drew to her full five feet. "I am not a coward," she stated bravely, her arms mocking her as they continued to shake. "I could not hope to keep up with the beasts as they descended the pass."

"You failed me," he snapped.

Serran's voice froze in her throat as her jowls shook. "I.., don't.., see.., how..." she managed to stammer, her eyes falling back to the floor.

"So, you're saying there was nothing you could do?" he sneered.

Serran paused for a moment, her eyes darting to the other mages in the room and then snapping back to Trannyth. "I waited at the top of the pass for the reinforcements. They were due in that day."

"You allowed the enemy to escape," he raged. "Not one of them killed, while four of your beasts died, another had to be dispatched."

"Are you suggesting that I..," She looked down at her stubby legs "that I could have kept up with the beasts in full flight."

"I am suggesting.., that you didn't even try." Trannyth turned his back on her and walked toward the window. "You might have caught one of them… We could have learned who they were and what they were trying to achieve."

"My Lord, I assure you..."

"Get out of my sight!"

Serran glared at Trannyth's back for a split second, hatred flowing through her veins. She stepped backward, lowering her eyes as she turned and fled from the room.

Trannyth turned to the other mages. "Have her assigned to the caves," he commanded. "If she fails again, kill her."

38 LOST

Kailyn wandered into the forest surrounding the little clearing to collect wood for the fire. She hummed a lullaby as she searched, lost in thought as she turned Tean's words over in her head. *What had he meant?* she wondered. She moved deeper into the trees than she'd intended, absentmindedly collecting small branches as she went.

Does he think I might die? She shook his words from her head. *Don't let his raving get to you, Kailyn. He's crazy.*

Glancing up through the trees, she stopped. *Where am I?* She spun and looked back, not recognizing any landmarks as tree after tree marched into the distance, each appearing to look like the next. She turned slowly, panic rising in her chest as she realized she had no idea in which direction the camp could be.

"Tesania, Deavon!" she called into the trees. Listening, she strained to hear the slightest hint that they might have heard her. When no answer to her call came she threw the wood to the ground and looked frantically about, trying desperately to find her bearings. Fear clawed at her throat as she opened her mouth to call again. *Calm down Kailyn,* she berated herself. Swallowing, she drew a deep breath and tried to call again. "Giddy, Raim!" she yelled into the uncaring trees.

A tear formed in the corner of her eye as she realized they couldn't hear her. *How could I be so stupid,* she asked herself as she decided to walk in the opposite direction to where she had been facing when she'd stopped.

Stumbling on for what seemed like an age, she stopped occasionally to peer into the darkening woods and call for her companions. The only answers that reached her were the soft, broken echoes of her own voice.

The sun was setting fast as she slumped to the ground, starting to cry. Emptiness filled her heart as she accepted that she was lost, in an unknown forest, with no idea how to rejoin her friends.

Determined to at least try and find them while there was still some light, she stumbled to her feet and moved on. *They have to be close*, she thought as moonlight drove the last of the sun's rays from the forest. She felt her way through the forest, using her hands to guide the way through the darkness of the night. She tripped, falling awkwardly, the twig of a fallen branch digging painfully into her chin.

The pain eased quickly to a dull ache as she pushed herself up and leant against a tree. "How can I find them if I can't see," she whispered to herself as she banged her head lightly against the furrowed bark of the tree. Closing her eyes she breathed deeply, trying to calm herself.

A thought wormed its way into her subconscious, pushing through her despair as tears splashed from her cheeks. Her eyes flashed open. *Tes is right, you are a ninny,* she admonished herself as she snatched up a small branch and focused on the end. Smoke lazily drifted from the end of the wood as she squinted at it, willing it to burn, a smile growing across her face as it flashed into flame.

She sat for short time, contemplating the flames. It still amazed her that she could make an old piece of wood burn with only her will. She cocked her head as a noise drifted through the cluttered trees. It was faint, almost imperceptible to her straining ears.

Her knee hurt as she scrambled to her feet, rubbing it, she looked at the jumble of sticks that she had tripped on and wondered how she hadn't done more damage to herself. Stepping cautiously over them, she held her makeshift torch high in the air, the light from the flickering flames dancing and cavorting on the shadowy trunks of the forest.

The sounds grew louder as she lifted her pace and started to rush in the direction it seemed to come from, her heart pounding as she drew closer to reuniting with her friends.

A light glowed in the distance, illuminating the overhead branches. She began running, jumping over snags and ducking under branches as her spirits soared.

Voices and raucous laughs carried to her ears, her face creased in a frown. *They haven't even missed me.*

~

Tesania looked around in confusion. "She was here."

"I haven't seen her since she went to collect fire wood, with Tean and Tesania," Naisa said as she stood and peered into the dark woods.

"Didn't she come back with you?" Deavon asked Tes.

"We went in separate directions," Tean interjected. "I went that way," he pointed. "Tesania went that way and Kailyn went off in that direction."

Deavon stood and walked toward the trees. "Has anybody seen her since then," he asked, concern edging his voice.

"I haven't seen her since Raim and I went fishing," Giddy offered.

Tes went to Deavon's side. "I can't believe I didn't notice she was missing. We have to find her!" she said as she looked at Deavon. "I should have noticed."

"She shouldn't have gone off by herself. Who was watching her?" Deavon asked.

"No one," Tean replied. "She should be able to look after herself by now."

"Obviously she cannot," Elddyn quipped.

"Why do you always have to put your worthless opinion in the ring?" Giddy shot at him.

"She must be close," Aldan offered as he approached Deavon and Tes. "She wouldn't go far away from the camp."

"Kailyn!" Tesania called. "Kailyn, where are you!"

The silence of the travelers was matched by the silence from the trees, only the odd call from an owl or other night creatures drifted toward them.

Tes started for the trees. Deavon snatched at her hand and held her back. "It's too dark," he told her as he shook his head. "We don't want to lose anyone else."

"But she's out there alone," Tes protested. "We have to go and find her. She turned back toward the trees. "Kailyn, answer me!" she yelled as loudly as she could. Her voice echoed unanswered into the night.

"It's my fault," she said as she turned back to Deavon. "I should have kept an eye on her. I was too caught up in my own problems."

"It's not your fault, Tes," Naisa comforted her as she draped her arm over her shoulder. "We all should have been aware she was missing much earlier."

"The Lord foresaw this," Tean stated as he dropped to his knees. "I will consult him and ask him to forgive Kailyn and deliver her back safely unto us."

"Do you people not hear him?" Elddyn asked incredulously as he looked around the gathered faces. "He is insane."

"To believe in the Lord is not insane, Elddyn," Raim snapped. "At least he tries to help people."

"This is not helping Kailyn!" Tesania screamed at them. "She's out there somewhere. We have to find her!"

"Tes." Giddy walked toward her. "Calm down. There-"

"Calm down! She's lost in the forest, she needs us."

"I know Tes; we can't just go running in there after her," Giddy said to her calmly. "We need to wait until morning when we can see properly."

Tes shook her head and stared at the soldier. "We can't... I won't." Striding to the fire she snatched up a burning branch and stalked defiantly toward the darkness.

"Tesania! You will not go in that forest alone!" Deavon commanded her.

"You won't do anything to help her!" Tes accused. "So I have to." She turned away from him and started toward the trees once more, stopping abruptly as the fire on her branch snuffed out. Staring at the tiny ember glowing defiantly on the end of the wood, Tes spun around, searching the campsite. "How..?" she asked as her eyes focused on Elddyn lowering his staff. "Who do you think you are?" she seethed as she stormed back to the fire and shoved the end of the wood back into the fire.

"I'll go, Tes," Aldan interrupted as he reached out and took her branch from her. "You stay here."

"I'll go too," Naisa added as the orb on the top of her staff blinked into life, casting a soft glow of light around her.

"If we're going to go out, then we need to be organized," Deavon said as he walked toward his pack, taking out some of the oil that they purchased in Orash. "Raim, wrap some cloth around those bigger branches. Giddy, talk to Tean and Tes and see which direction Kailyn might have gone."

Raim took a handful of rags from his bag, twisting them tightly around some branches he recovered from beside the fire. He held them out as Deavon poured oil over them, soaking the cloth through. "These should give us a few hours," he advised Deavon as he leaned over the fire and touched the ends to the flames.

"Giddy, you take Tes and Naisa and head straight east from where Tean says Kailyn entered the trees." He pointed off to the east. "Aldan, you and Raim veer south east a few points. Elddyn, Tean, you're with me. We will bear off a few points to the north east."

"I'll go out alone," Elddyn interrupted from the fire. "We'll cover more ground that way."

"No! We go in groups," Deavon insisted. "There's safety in numbers."

"Why do I, have to go with that," Elddyn growled, pointing his staff at Tean.

"Kailyn is lost you pompous fool," Giddy snapped at him. "Get over yourself."

"You're with me Elddyn. End of discussion," Deavon ordered. He checked his sword and then addressed them all. "It's dark out there and we don't know where the girl is. Make sure you keep an eye out to both sides as best you can. She may be injured and lying on the forest floor."

Aldan stepped to the front of the group. "Moving through a forest at night is a dangerous undertaking. We have a clear sky. Set your direction by the moon and don't forget to allow for the time difference when you're making your way back." He looked along the dark forest edge. "She can't be more than an hour out. I suggest after that, if you've found nothing, you head back to camp."

"Can we just go," Tes said impatiently. "She could be hurt."

~

Kailyn stepped through the last trees before the clearing, "I'm back!" she announced. "You didn't..." Her voice trailed off as she confronted the campsite in front of her.

A large fire pit sat in the middle of the camp, a small stream bubbling past on the left while a crude hut, made from bark and sticks, stood to the right. Kailyn's eyes flickered around the camp, taking in the pile of rancid, rotting bones. Fear constricted her throat as she focused on the group of large creatures staring back at her from the fire.

The firelight didn't manage to highlight their features much, but her instincts screamed; *ogres*. Turning, she looked back into the dark forest and ran, the sounds of heavy footfalls thundering behind.

She screamed as a calloused hand gripped her shoulder and snapped her to a stop, her feet flying out in front of her as she crashed to the ground. Unconsciousness descended upon her as her head cracked against a root. Her last sensation was the rancid breath of the ogre as it bent down and shoved its hands roughly under her back.

~

Tesania followed Giddy closely, making sure she could always see the lithe soldier in the soft glow of Naisa's staff. "Kailyn!" she shouted. She had called her friends name so many times since they had left the camp, her throat now hurt. "Where are you? Can you hear me?"

Giddy spoke softly to Naisa ahead of her, "We'll have to head back soon. We would've come across her if she could hear us."

"Agreed," murmured Naisa as she glanced back at Tesania. "If she was disorientated, she might have gone off in any direction." She stopped, holding her staff high as she turned and surveyed the close growing trees. Her magical light tried vainly, but it was no match for the darkness that hid among the marching trunks. Visibility was no more than a few yards. "Tes, we have to go back," she advised gently.

Tesania shook her head. "No." She stepped past Giddy and Naisa as she stared into the sooty night. "She's out here; we can't leave her." She turned back to Giddy and Naisa, her face shadowed and drawn as she guiltily looked at the ground and whispered, "I can't leave her. It's my fault she's lost."

"Tesania," Naisa reached out and gently lifted her chin. "It's not your fault. None of us noticed she was missing."

"But she's my friend," Tes insisted, her eyes flicking from Naisa to Giddy and back again, pleading for them to understand. "I should have been looking out for her. She's too young to know any better."

"She's only a few years younger than you, Tes. She should know better than to wander too far into the forest and not keep her bearings," Giddy pointed out. "It's not your fault."

"We can't leave her out here," Tesania whispered as she turned back to the trees. "I couldn't live with myself if something happened to her." A tear ran from her eye, shimmering in the light of Naisa's orb.

"She'll find somewhere to spend the night," Giddy assured her. "And it isn't cold, so she won't have to worry about blankets." Reaching out, she clasped Tes' hand. "Come on; let's head back. First thing in the morning we'll come out again." She gently pulled Tes in the direction of the camp. "I promise."

"Deavon will want to search for the caves tomorrow," Tes said morosely as she allowed herself to be led back.

"I will kick Deavon all the way into the forest to look for her if I have to," Giddy reassured her. "Trust me;

everyone will want to find Kailyn, even that obnoxious mage, Elddyn."

Tes peered back over her shoulder into the night. "Where could you be Kailyn?" She asked in a small voice. "Please be safe."

39 OGRES' DELIGHT

Kailyn groaned; her head pounding as the wound on the back of her head plunged daggers of pain through her brain. She didn't move for a few moments, trying to recall where she might be. Her memory flashed images of trees into her confused mind, and a... she forced herself to focus, a fire. She thought it a peculiar dream where she could smell a rancid, sickly odor and the smoke from the imagined fire, and voices, strange guttural voices, drifting to her ears.

Her eyes flashed open. The rough ropes that bound her to the trunk of a tree cut into her arms as she tried to stand and run. Her eyes jerked fearfully about. A crude wooden hut, illuminated by the flickering fire stood a few feet away from her, the rough bark that made up the walls barely holding the whole structure together.

She cringed as her gaze fell on a pile of bones, some five feet high; maggots crawling through the rotting flesh hanging from the gnawed ends. She turned her face quickly away; recoiling as the foul breathe of an ogre choked her. It crouched next to her, its vicious teeth only inches from her nose, its murderous eyes staring hungrily at her as a sneer twisted its lips.

Kailyn shrank back as the ogre reached out a filthy hand and grasped her chin.

"Let me go!" she cried out in pain as the rough hand chaffed her skin.

The ogre ignored her, turning her face forcibly from one side to the other, inspecting her. "Man-thing, good food," it chortled as it saw the horrified look on the girl's face.

"My friends..," She glared defiantly into her captor's menacing eyes, ripping her head sideways to break its grip, "will be here any minute." Struggling against the ropes binding her tightly to the tree, she felt a warm trickle of blood run down her torn cheek.

"Grug say eat now." It ran its slimy tongue along its lips, leering at her as she turned her head away. "Me say eat tomorrow." He laughed as he poked at her side with a huge, blunt finger. "Tender."

"Get away!" Kailyn screamed. "My friends will kill you if you touch me!"

The ogre laughed as it stood. "Tomorrow," it said ominously as it lumbered toward the others by the fire.

Kailyn tried to control her breathing; it came in sharp, ragged bursts. Her mind screamed at her, *Think Kailyn.*

The ogres sat on logs and boulders that had been dragged into a circle around the fire. Kailyn counted them, seven in all, large and grotesque. She shivered and turned away, their gravelly voices grinding on her nerves as they laughed and cajoled one another. She cringed every time she heard them grumble, man-thing, sobbing as her imagination flashed images of her arms being ripped from their sockets, the ogres howling in delight as their sharp, yellow teeth tore her flesh from the bone. She shook her head violently in an effort to clear the visions from her mind, regretting it instantly as pain from her injured head seared through her nerves.

She sat morosely for some time, the conversation of the ogres drifting toward her as she tried to concentrate and find a means of escape. Her attention snapped fully to the hideous creatures when she heard one say, "Man-things hunt us if eat friend."

"She lie, Bellowa. No friend come."

"Bellowa not believe, Bulg," the big ogre female threw her hand toward Kailyn. "Why alone in forest?"

"She lost," Grug interjected. "Nobody care, we eat."

"Man-things many days," Bellowa pointed into the trees. "They not let young one in forest by self."

"Like Grug say." Bulg looked at Kailyn hungrily; a smile growing across his foul mouth as she quickly turned her head the other way. "Man-things not care, they many days from Bellowa and Grug. We eat."

They argued for an eternity, all except Bellowa wanting to eat the distraught girl.

Kailyn sat in silence, head bowed as they discussed her death. As the first tinge of the dawning day appeared through the trees, she could take no more. "They're closer than you think," she yelled at them. "They'll be looking for me now!" She glared at Bulg and growled, "There are many warriors; they will kill you." She threw her chin at the ogre that so wanted to eat her. "And Grug, and Bellowa, all of you!"

"She lie," Grug said as he heaved his bulk up and walked toward Kailyn, the ground shuddering at each step he took. "You alone." He stopped in front of her, grinning as he withdrew his knife. "We kill now, hang from tree then eat tomorrow." He stepped closer to her and brought his knife up in front of her horrified face, her eyes growing wide as the tip of the blade dug into her neck and she felt blood trickling down to her collar.

Her mind went into overload. "Bellowa, they will come and kill you," she screamed out.

"Grug stop!" Bellowa demanded as she rushed toward Kailyn, her footsteps rumbling like thunder.

Grug spun on her, his knife flashing out in front of him, dancing before her face. "Bellowa come no closer," he sneered. "Grug kill you too."

Bellowa's mate flashed to his feet and rumbled toward Grug like an avalanche, smashing into him headlong and knocking him to the ground a few feet away. "Brausa not let Grug kill Bellowa!" he roared.

Grug jumped to his feet with surprising alacrity and stalked toward Brausa, his knife extended out in front of him.

Brausa snatched up an old thighbone from the disgusting pile of waste, maggots flew through the air as he swung the makeshift weapon toward Grug, a slimy string of half chewed sinew whipping from the end.

Kailyn wretched as the stench from the disturbed bones engulfed her. She drew her legs in as close as she could get them as the ogres paced around each other, their huge feet cannoning down only inches from her own.

Grug lunged at Brausa, his knife missing the big ogre by a sliver as Brausa stepped quickly out of the way and cracked him across the back of his head with the decaying bone, sending him sprawling into a tree. He scrambled to his feet and turned, rage playing across his face as he blasted a savage cry at Brausa, spittle flying from his rotting teeth.

Brausa pointed the old bone at the angry ogre. "Grug no match for Brausa. Grug not hurt Bellowa."

"Grug kill Brausa, take Bellowa as mate," Grug sneered.

Brausa roared, his voice echoing through the trees as he charged at Grug, knocking the knife aside as he smashed his fist into the other ogre's face.

Bellowa rushed to the aid of her mate, Bulg drove his shoulder into her, knocking her sideways toward the fire. She rolled and regained her feet, snarling as Bulg stalked toward her. Her brother stepped in front of Bulg. "No hurt Bellowa," he growled.

Bulg threw himself forward, tackling the ogre that stood in his way, taking the feet out from under Bellowa as they crashed to the ground.

The remaining two ogres looked at each other; one threw out his fist and knocked the other off his log then threw himself on top of him, fists flailing.

Kailyn looked on in concern. The big, heavy bodies were only a few yards away from her and could crush her if they crashed on top of her. *Think Kailyn*, she screamed inside her mind.

Grug smashed his fist into Brausa's head and shoved him; Brausa regained his balance and drove his shoulder into Grug, knocking him backwards. He stumbled, trying to regain his balance as he looked fearfully behind him. His arms swirled in circles as he threw one leg out in front of him, like a tree felled in a forest, he crashed into the fire. Sparks cascaded into the air as Grug roared in pain, Brausa snatched at his kicking leg, trying to pull him out. The other ogres ignored him, intent on pummeling each other into oblivion.

Kailyn watched the crescendo of sparks reach into the sky. *Kailyn, you ninny!* she scolded herself. Shuffling her body around, she strained to flex her fingers and bring the thumb and forefinger together. She tried to block the snarls and screams of the ogres out, calming her mind and concentrating on the image of fire.

The ogres continued to tear one another apart, blood gushing from wounds. Bellowa had her fingers firmly implanted in Bulg's big, flat nose, yanking his head back with all her strength. Brausa had managed to drag the screaming Grug from the fire and slapped frantically at the flames that still engulfed him.

Kailyn's felt the heat on her back as the smell of burning rope crept up to invade her nose. She focused on her fingers, managing to concentrate her will onto the rope, relieving the burning sensation on her skin. She looked sideways at the ogres as fire began to lick along the rope; they were too engrossed in their battle to notice the smoke curling lazily above her head in the early morning light.

Whimpering as the fire bit at her skin, Kailyn strained against the ropes as the fire burned through them. Tears ran down her face from the pain, she fought with all her will to not cry out. Just when she thought she could bear it no more, the rope gave way and parted. Moving quickly, she pulled the burning ends away from her back and then pulled on the rope, drawing it around the trunk as fast as she could until she could struggle out of the coils that had fastened her tightly to the tree. With one last glance at the ogres, she crept quietly into the forest.

40 FOUND

Tesania didn't sleep at all after she lay down. She had come out of the forest dejected and full of grief. After tossing and turning for hours she climbed out of her bedroll and walked to the fire where Naisa was boiling water to make tea.

"We'll find her," Naisa assured her gently. "She can't be too far away."

"Then why didn't we find her," Tes responded. "She would have answered, if she could."

Naisa handed a steaming mug to Tes and laid a calming hand on her forearm. "She might have been asleep."

"We yelled loud enough," Tesania shot back.

"You did at that," Naisa laughed lightly. "The whole forest is probably still awake." They sat quietly for some time, lost in thought. Naisa eventually looked up at Tes. "She may have gone deeper into the forest. If she lost her bearings she might be nowhere near where we searched."

"We have to find her," Tes mumbled. "I couldn't bear losing her."

"We will find her Tes. Try not to worry and get some sleep."

Tes wandered toward her bed, knowing she wouldn't sleep until they had found her friend. She flopped down and stared at the stars, watching them in deep thought as they traversed the sky. "How could I let you get lost?" she whispered into the night.

The dawn light found Tesania dressed and ready to leave. She shook on Deavon's shoulder. "We have to find Kailyn," she explained as he looked at her sleepily.

"Yes," he replied as he rubbed his eyes. "I'm sorry Tes. I should have been up by now."

"Hurry, please."

Deavon went to the stream and washed his face while Tes roused the other sleepers. Giddy's bedroll was empty.

Tes looked around the camp, but couldn't see the soldier anywhere. "Does anyone know where Giddy is?" she asked as she walked to the fire.

A chorus of sleepy 'no's reached out to her. Raim however said, "She went into the forest," he pointed. "She's hoping to find some sign of where Kailyn might have gone."

Deavon looked into the sky. "It's only just dawn now."

"She wanted to get an early start. She's quite worried about the girl."

Tes turned toward the woods, a small smile on her face. "Thank you, Giddy," she whispered.

"I hope you told her not to go too far. I don't want two people missing," Deavon commented.

Raim laughed. "Like I can tell her what to do." He shook his head and squatted down to pour another tea for himself. "She's very experienced. I don't think we need to worry about her."

They finished their breakfast quickly. Tean put out the fire while the others packed their gear and hefted it onto their shoulders.

Deavon called them into a circle and drew a crude map on the ground with a stick he had recovered from the edge of the forest. "We know Kailyn went in this direction," he indicated, drawing an arrow pointing off to the east. "We break into three groups, the same as last night." Ignoring Elddyn's groan, he continued. "We have the advantage of daylight now, so we should be able to cover a lot more ground." He looked up as a whistle echoed from the woods.

Giddy came striding from the trees. "Starting without me?" she accused.

"Did you find anything?" Tes asked hopefully.

"Mostly, it looks like a stampede went through the forest last night," Giddy quipped. "You people really should learn to be lighter on your feet."

"Giddy!" Tes protested.

"I was just saying," Giddy objected. "Anyway, as I was saying, before I was interrupted. Most of the tracks out there are from us last night." She turned and held her arm out to the north east. "There's a single track, it's very light, so I would say it was Kailyn."

"You found her?" Tes asked excitedly. "Let's go and get her."

"Whoa," Deavon snatched at Tesania's arm and held her in place. "We need a plan." He turned to Giddy. "Can you follow the track?"

Giddy shook her head and looked toward Raim. "Can you please explain it to him."

Raim laughed lightly. "Giddy could track a mouse through a field of knee high grass, if she had too."

"Thank you," Giddy said as she looked down and toed her shoe at the ground. "I don't know if I'm that good though," she suggested coyly.

"Can you follow it, Giddy?" Deavon asked in exasperation.

Giddy looked at him like he was a simpleton. "Isn't that what Raim just said?"

Deavon sighed. "If we can follow her track; I suggest we all stay together."

"Let's go," Tes said impatiently as she tugged at Deavon's grip.

They filed into the forest, Giddy leading, Tes at her heels while the rest fell in behind. It wasn't long before Giddy stopped and knelt down. "You can see here," she explained to Tes. "The broken twigs on the ground, disturbed leaf litter." Standing, she started off into the trees. "It's the track of a single person. By the signs I would say it's definitely Kailyn."

"How would you know that?" Tes asked.

"An animal has a small footprint and spreads its weight over four paws. A person is much heavier and would cause a lot more disturbance on the ground," She explained, smiling back at Tes. "This is definitely our Kailyn's track."

Tes grinned, her spirits soaring. "How long before we find her?"

"No idea," Giddy responded. "She may have walked for half the night for all we know."

"I hope not," Tes murmured, doubt once again spearing through her mind.

"We'll find her, Tes," Giddy said over her shoulder. "It's just a matter of time."

~

Kailyn thrashed through the forest, ducking branches and jumping over roots as she fled the ogres' camp. She had no idea which direction she was heading but ran as fast as her legs would carry her, hoping she would stumble across Tes and the others.

It was only a few minutes before she heard the ogres' angry roars of discovery echoing through the trees, the crashing sounds of pursuit following quickly after.

Her heart felt like it would explode as she burst between the trees, adrenaline and fear flooding through her veins as the ogres cries grew closer. *Think Kailyn!* She ground to a halt, turned and quickly ran a hundred yards back along her own track before darting off to the right.

She managed to run for a few minutes before the sounds of the ogres barreling after her grew. Coming to a small clearing, she collapsed to the ground and held her breath, a smile crossing her face as she listened for the crashing ogres. *I fooled them!*

~

Bellowa puffed along behind the other five ogres, fitter, they were leaving her behind. She lumbered on, her eyes fixed firmly to the ground as she concentrated on keeping up the harrowing pace. Following the track was easy for her after the other five monstrous ogres had been through, flattening everything under their pounding feet. So it was with some surprise that she saw a faint track leading off to the left, not much, just some freshly broken twigs and disturbed leaves.

She stopped, drawing deep breaths as she peered suspiciously into the forest. Her curiosity gnawed at her and with a quick glance down the track the others had taken she made up her mind and stepped into the trees to follow the new lead.

~

Tesania and the others marched on for an interminable time, with Giddy stopping periodically to make certain she was still on the right path. "She sure did move a long way," she growled.

Tes searched the forest on both sides of the track they were following, making certain they didn't miss anything. She peered between two huge trunks, craning her neck to see and ran painfully into Giddy's back.

"Why did you sto..?" she started to ask Giddy as she felt her already fattening lip.

"Shh!" the soldier replied. She motioned around Tes to the others, waving her hand downward to warn them to stop and keep quiet. Gripping Tes' arm she guided her back the way they had come.

Tes looked back, but could see nothing untoward. "What is..?"

"Not now Tes!" Giddy whispered insistently.

The group moved back a few hundred yards. Giddy turned to Deavon. "A camp, the tracks lead directly toward it."

"I didn't see a camp," Tes said as she gazed back down the track in confusion.

"Nor did I, Tes," Giddy replied. "I smelt it."

"You could smell a camp?"

"Tes, trust me," Giddy assured. There is a camp not far ahead of us. And there's a rank odor of rotting flesh."

"Ogres!" Aldan announced matter-of-factly.

Tes stomach clenched as her head whipped around to the big ranger. "How do you know?"

"No one else would be this far into the forest, Tes," Deavon advised her. "Giddy, anything else you can tell us?"

"The fire is burning," she looked at Tes and gently continued. "And I could smell burned flesh."

"No," Tesania moaned. "Are you saying they've eaten her?" Her throat constricted, her mind reeling at the thought of her friend being dismembered by the giant ogres.

Naisa reached out and touched Tes' arm. "It's my understanding that ogres eat their meat raw."

Tes stumbled into the trees, falling to her knees she dry retched, coughing and struggling for breath as thoughts of Kailyn being eaten thundered through her brain.

Tean knelt next to her and placed his arm over her shoulder. "I am sure Kailyn is ok. It is not wise to jump to conclusions."

Tes turned her head toward him, tears running down her face. "They will pay if they've hurt her." Grimacing, she climbed to her feet.

"Are you alright?" Deavon asked as Tes approached the others.

"Yes," Tes mumbled.

Deavon looked slowly away; he was concerned about Tes but needed to organize the others. "We need to go into the camp," his eyes drifted to Tesania. "Either way, if Kailyn's there, we have to find out."

"Agreed," Aldan took over. "Deavon's father said that the ogres have been banding together of late, so it's safer to assume that we are facing more than one." He scanned the gathering. "I don't know about any of you, but I've been up against an ogre once in my life." He looked seriously at Giddy and Raim. "Believe me; if there are five ogres there we are in for a battle, ten and we'll be lucky to walk away alive."

"Can't Naisa and Elddyn stun them or something?" Tes asked.

"Sadly, no," Naisa advised her. "Ogres have incredibly tough skin. Elddyn and I could possibly account for one with a concerted attack, but five or more ogres are well beyond what we can handle."

"Raim," Deavon addressed the little soldier. "Do you think you can get close enough to have a look?"

Raim grinned and dropped his bag. Slipping his sword and dagger from their scabbards, he removed his belt and laid it on top of his pack. "Ready," he announced. "I'll be back shortly."

"Such confidence," Giddy teased. Dropping her own pack she started up the track with him, drawing her sword as she glanced seriously at him. "I want you back safe," she said. "I mean it, nothing stupid. Do you hear me?"

"I'm just having a peek, Giddy," he assured her as he rolled his eyes. "I don't plan on stealing the breakfast off their plates."

"All the same," Giddy frowned. "Come back safely." She stopped halfway to the ogres' camp and leaned against a tree. "I'll be here, if you get into trouble."

"It's just a recon, Giddy, I'll be back in a few minutes," he assured her. His face grew serious as he moved on, his training kicking in as his senses took in the forest. Stepping lightly, he crept toward the camp.

He froze as a low moan drifted toward him. Squatting down he analyzed the sound. *It isn't Kailyn*, he surmised. Remaining in his crouched stance, he moved forward, step by agonizingly slow step.

The stench of the rotting bones curled into his nose long before he could see into the camp. He stopped and drew three long breaths, acclimatizing himself to the foul odors.

The moan came again, long and guttural. *Something isn't right*. Raim shook his head. Deciding to ignore the sickly moans, he crept forward.

The camp came slowly into view. Raim took one step at a time, studying everything he could see before committing to another movement.

Quickly deciding the crude hut was unoccupied, he scanned over to the fire. One ogre lay on its back, moans of pain escaping intermittently from its bloated lips. Stepping closer, Raim came slowly upright, perusing the whole area before backing lightly into the trees.

"One that I can see," he told a relieved Giddy as he retraced his steps to Tesania and the others.

"Is Kailyn there?" Giddy demanded as he walked past her.

"It didn't appear so," Raim shook his head.

The others came toward the two soldiers as they approached. "Where's Kailyn?" Tesania demanded, her face creasing with worry.

"What's the situation?" Deavon asked as he waved Tes to be silent.

Raim snatched up his belt and ran the tongue through the buckle as he answered. "One ogre; appears injured." He slipped his weapons into their sheaths. "By the size of the camp I'd say there are a fair number of them, five.., maybe six."

"Any sign of Kailyn?" Naisa asked.

"None," Raim replied simply.

"What of the injured one?" Aldan asked. "How badly hurt is it?"

"Hard to tell. Looks like it's been burned."

"Definitely no sign of any others?" Deavon asked. "I don't want to walk into a trap."

"Just the one there now. I have no idea how far the others might be," Raim shrugged.

Deavon slipped his sword from its sheath. "Ok, Aldan, Giddy, Raim, Elddyn and myself go in first." His hand shot up to cut off Tes' protest. "When we've cleared the camp, we'll call you in."

"But I…"

"Don't argue Tes," Deavon growled as he started down the track. "Tean, Naisa, make sure she stays with you."

Tesania glared at his back as he went.

"He's right," Naisa soothed her. "It's best they clear the area before we go in."

Tes looked at her sheepishly. "I know. It's just that.., Kailyn…"

"If Kailyn's there, they'll do their best to get her out unharmed," Naisa assured her.

"I know," Tes said in a resigned voice. A thought came to her as she stood and looked down the track. Snatching her hand to her sword she drew it a few inches from the sheath. It was lifeless, no vibrating, no fire shooting along its length. "My sword doesn't seem to think there's any danger."

"All the same, we'll wait until they call us," Naisa insisted.

"I just want to find Kailyn," Tes explained, exasperation edging her voice.

"The Lord will decide if Kailyn returns to us or not," Tean mumbled. "He knows all; that is why he cleansed her with the smoke?"

"Just shut up, Tean," Tes snapped.

"Tes," Naisa warned.

Tes glowered down the track for a few moments. "I'm sorry, Tean. I'm just worried about Kailyn's safety. Maybe you could say a prayer for her."

"A splendid suggestion," Tean replied as he sank to his knees and closed his eyes.

Naisa grinned at Tesania

Tes allowed a small smile to creep across her face and then turned her attention back to the track. "Hurry up," she whispered impatiently.

It wasn't long before Raim came toward them, waving his arm for them to follow. "Deavon says to come on in," he called. "But be on your guard."

Naisa helped Tean to his feet and then walked toward the camp.

Tesania dashed off ahead and burst into the little clearing. A wall of sickening stench met her, stopping her in her tracks. Looking around frantically she stumbled to the edge of the trees and threw up.

"Are you ok?" Giddy asked as she approached Tes and pulled her hair up out of the way.

"The smell," Tes groaned apologetically.

"I've smelt worse," Giddy laughed as she helped Tes up.

"Seriously? Where?"

"Well there's Raim's room at the Rilmir barracks for starters," Giddy quipped. "And then there was..."

"What's Deavon doing with the ogre?" Tes interjected as she peered around Giddy's shoulder.

"It's pretty badly burned, and isn't talking too much," Giddy shook her head. "I don't think it'll survive."

"I want to see what they're talking about."

Giddy seized Tes' upper arm and held her back. "It isn't a pretty sight, Tes. Maybe you should let them talk to it alone."

Tes pulled Giddy's hand away. "I can handle it," she assured the soldier. "My father burned his hand once, in his smithy."

"Trust me; this is not the same."

Tes took a tentative step toward the ogre that lay prostrate on the ground. "I'll be alright."

Giddy shook her head and followed Tes to the fire.

Deavon looked up at Tes as she approached, her hand covering her mouth, eyes wide as she took in the horror of the burned ogre. "Maybe you should stay away, Tes," he suggested quietly.

"No," Tes said as she stared into the frightened eyes of the ogre. "The poor thing," she exclaimed, a tear trickling down her face as she knelt beside him.

The ogre grimaced in pain as it tried to turn its head toward her.

"Naisa!" Tesania called as the mage came into the camp. "Give me that vial of fermented lungis berries, the one you gave to Kailyn in the Draon Pass."

Naisa took the pack from her shoulders and rummaged through it, eventually producing the vial of clear liquid. Handing it to Tes, she instructed, "Only a few drops." Looking at the huge ogre, she added, "Maybe four in this instance."

Tes reached out and took the vial. Turning to the ogre, her face full of compassion, she uncorked the bottle. "This will make you feel better." She held the vial in front of the ogre's frightened eyes. "I'm going to put some of this on your tongue."

The ogre creased its eyebrows and groaned. "Grug no want," he said, wincing in pain.

Tes reached out gently, placing her hand on the big ogre's cheek where it wasn't burned. The skin was as rough as sandpaper as she gently stroked with her fingers. "I promise it won't hurt you," Tes insisted as her tears splashed onto the dusty ground. "It will take away the pain."

"It's just a dumb ogre," Elddyn grunted. "Who cares if it's in pain?"

"Stay out of it," Giddy warned the mage.

"We should be looking for the girl," Elddyn flashed back at her.

"We know that," Tesania snapped. Smiling gently at Grug, she said, "I'm going to put a little of this on your tongue. It will help you."

The fear in the ogre's eyes softened as it felt the compassion pouring from Tesania. Slowly it opened its mouth and slid its tongue forward.

Tes held her breath as the ogre's hot, fetid breath blew over her, resisting the urge to gag and turn away. She dripped four drops on Grug's slimy, trembling tongue.

Grug spluttered as the foul tasting liquid ran into his throat, groaning as his movements shot spasms of pain through his devastated body.

"It won't take long to work," Tes assured the ogre. "I promise."

The ogre's eyes watched Tes. After a few moments the grimace on its face relaxed.

"I told you," Tes smiled.

"Grug hurt bad," the ogre coughed.

"I know, Grug," Tes said gently. "Try to stay still." Standing, she walked to Naisa. "Isn't there something else we can do for him?" she asked.

"I have nothing to treat his burns," Naisa replied apologetically. "If we were in Wyvern City, I might be able to do something."

"It would be unlikely that a badly burned ogre would be present in the King's City," Elddyn laughed.

Tesania drew a deep breath, managing to ignore the obnoxious mage. "We can't leave him here like this."

"It would be best for all of us if Deavon puts it to the sword," Elddyn sighed.

Tesania swung on him. "I've had enough of you," she seethed. "If you have nothing useful to add," she growled as she stalked past him. "Then keep your mouth shut."

Giddy and Raim grinned at each other and then at the mage.

"Bah," Elddyn spat, spinning on his heel, he stormed toward the hut.

Tes knelt beside Deavon and smiled down at Grug.

"And the Girl escaped into the forest?" Deavon finished asking the ogre.

"Others chase her," Grug's body wracked with coughing as he raised his arm and pointed into the trees, the brightness in his eyes dulling noticeably.

Tes reached out and placed her hand on Grug's, smiling down at him.

What might pass as a smile crept over Grug's big ogre lips, he closed his eyes, coughed and lay still.

"He's dead," Deavon gently told Tes as he held his fingers to the ogre's chest. He stood, gripping Tesania's elbow, pulling her up with him.

Tes threw herself into Deavon's arms. She managed to hold back her tears in the comfort of his embrace.

"Come on," he whispered. "Kailyn is still out there."

"Kailyn!" Tes scrambled back from Deavon. Wiping her eyes, she looked guiltily at the others.

"It's ok," Giddy said as she walked to Tes and placed her arm around her shoulder. "Compassion is a valuable asset, Tes," she reassured her as she glared at Elddyn. "Never lose it."

"Looks like she was tied to this tree," Raim held up the ropes that Kailyn had managed to escape from in the early morning light.

"Clever girl," Naisa smiled as she saw the burnt ends.

"Tracks lead off directly behind here," Giddy said as she inspected the forest floor. Looks like several ogres went after her.

"Grug mentioned at least five names," Deavon said. "We need to get after her. We'll have to move fast." He tapped Giddy and Raim on their shoulders. "You two move off first. The rest will follow. Tes, Tean, I want you at the rear again."

He didn't need to tell the soldiers to move out; they'd already disappeared into the trees. "Don't get too far ahead," he called to them as he turned to the others. "Let's go."

They moved at a steady pace, Giddy slowing periodically to let the others catch up. After twenty minutes or so she stopped dead. "The track splits," she explained to Deavon when he asked why they had halted.

He searched the forest floor. "Any idea which way Kailyn went?"

"The one that heads straight out from here had a stampede go through," Giddy answered from where she crouched by the track. "The one heading off north-east had far less traffic. But, I would say, one ogre at least."

"Which one Giddy," Tes asked anxiously as she tried to regain her breath.

"I can't guarantee which way Kailyn went," Giddy shrugged apologetically. "Any tracks she may have left have been wiped out by the ogres."

"This way," Tean pushed past Giddy and headed along the north-east track.

"How do you know," Giddy called after him.

"The Lord spoke to me," his reply drifted back to them.

"It's as good as a guess I suppose," Giddy shrugged as she set off after him, easily overhauling him and taking the lead.

Tes had only moved a few hundred yards along the track when Giddy came crashing back toward them. "Ogres up ahead," she reported breathlessly.

"Did they see you?" Deavon asked quickly.

"I didn't get that close," Giddy shot back. "Definitely ogres."

"How many?"

"Don't know," Giddy replied as she drew in deep breaths. "At least two. I heard them talking."

"There are ogres up ahead," Deavon explained as he turned to the others. "They wouldn't stop if they hadn't caught Kailyn."

"We have to get her," Tes pushed forward.

"We will Tes," Aldan gripped her shoulder. "Just let us work out a plan first."

"They might be..."

Deavon cut her off. "We know that at least five ogres came after her, the majority split off and went east. So we have at least one, possibly two ogres up ahead."

"The best plan would be all out attack, eliminate them before they know what's happening," Aldan suggested.

Deavon nodded his head. "Agreed." He looked around the group. "Giddy, Raim, Aldan. We'll approach the ogres quietly. When I give the order, start the attack, as fast as you can get in there." He jerked around as he heard a sword slip from its scabbard behind him.

Tesania stood with her sword in hand, breathing heavily as she looked up the track.

"No, Tes," Deavon said gently. "You stay here with Tean and Naisa."

Tes ignored him as she stared at her sword. "I don't understand," she looked up at Deavon. "My sword is dead."

Deavon frowned at her. "We don't have time for that, Tes. Stay here with Naisa." He turned to the others. "These ogres are big and ferocious. Use your weapons to keep them at arm's length, and back one another up."

Giddy's eyes were alight as she adjusted her gear. "I'm ready," she announced as she shifted her weight from foot to foot.

Deavon sighed. "Stay with us Giddy. No running off after escaping ogres. Got it?"

"Yes, boss," she saluted.

"Right," Deavon said as he started off. "Let's go."

They stepped cautiously through the trees, weapons at the ready. An ogre's voice drifted to them after a hundred yards or so. "I can only hear one," Deavon whispered back at the others as he motioned them to stop. "It's talking, but I can't hear any others."

"Don't know," Giddy shrugged as she started to creep forward. "Let's find out shall we."

Deavon shook his head in exasperation at Raim.

"Don't blame me," Raim said defensively. "I have absolutely no control over her."

"I wish you did," Deavon snapped as he crept after Giddy.

Giddy moved fifty yards and went to ground, motioning the others to follow. As they crawled up to her, she whispered, motioning with her hand. "Ten yards, that way. I heard Kailyn's voice. She's definitely alive," she grinned.

Deavon quickly suppressed the feeling of relief flooding through his body. "Let's make sure she stays that way," he growled. "On the count of three, we go."

"One.., two..., Giddy!" Deavon whispered urgently as the soldier jumped to her feet and sprinted toward the ogres. "Go!" he said urgently to the others.

Giddy crashed from the trees, pausing for a split second as she identified the single ogre sitting on the forest floor and charged toward it with sword raised.

"No," Kailyn screamed as she pounced in front of Giddy.

Giddy slid to a stop, almost toppling over the girl. "Move Kailyn," she yelled as she reached out to shove her out of the way.

The ogre had gained its feet and backed away, its teeth bared as it thundered an ear splitting bellow.

Kailyn spun around, pushing her back against Giddy as she held her hand out to the ogre. "Bellowa, stop," she pleaded. "I promise they won't hurt you."

The ogress stared warily at Giddy. "Man-thing hurt Bellowa with sword."

"Giddy," Kailyn turned to the soldier. "Please put your sword down. You're scaring her."

"I'm scaring her!?" Giddy laughed nervously as Deavon and the others came up behind her. "She's doing a pretty good job of scaring me too," she said as she lowered her sword, motioning to the others to do the same.

"She saved me," Kailyn announced. "If it wasn't for her, I'd be dead." She shivered and whispered, "Eaten."

"Bellowa save man-thing," the ogress repeated her as it stared at their swords. "Bulg say eat."

Deavon slid his sword into his scabbard, keeping his hand on the hilt. He motioned with his head for the others to do the same. "It's good to see you safe," he said as he reached out and touched Kailyn's cheek. "And Bellowa; it appears we owe you a debt."

"Bellowa no want anything. Bellowa want man-things leave her and Brausa live peace."

"We have no desire to harm you or br..."

"Brausa," Kailyn interrupted. "He's her mate."

"...And Brausa," Deavon continued. "Kailyn is safe, that's all we care about. As long as you leave us alone, we will do you.., and the others, no harm."

"Raim, go and get the others will you." As the little soldier headed back into the forest, Deavon added, "You had better warn them about Bellowa here."

Tesania rushed into Kailyn's outstretched arms. "I thought we'd lost you," she cried. Drawing back, she asked, "How could you be so stupid and get lost?"

"Well I..,"

"Never mind," Tes beamed as she drew Kailyn back into her embrace. "I'm so glad you're safe."

"The Lord kept you safe," Tean announced.

"Bellowa kept me safe!" Kailyn snapped.

"The Lord provided the ogress to work in his stead."

"Don't," Kailyn warned him. "I don't want to hear it." She stalked away from him and approached the ogress.

"You'd better go back Bellowa," Kailyn suggested. "Brausa will be worried about you."

"Brausa no care about Bellowa," she announced.

Kailyn laughed. "That isn't what I saw last night." As the big ogress nodded her head, Kailyn hugged her, her arms only reaching a part way around. "Thank you Bellowa... You saved my life!"

Bellowa patted her on the head. Kailyn felt like her head would explode with the blows that the ogress obviously thought were gentle pats. "Bellowa glad K.., Ka.., man-thing alive," she muttered.

"Thank you for saving my friend," Tesania called after Bellowa as she crashed away from them through the forest.

"We'd better move from here," Deavon suggested. "The other ogres might follow her tracks."

Tes and Kailyn walked together as they made their way north-east once more. "How did you get away from the other ogres in the forest?" Tes asked.

"I escaped from the camp by burning the rope with my magic," Kailyn said proudly. I could hear them chasing me, it was like rolling thunder. I ran into some trees and then doubled a short way back."

"Nice!" Giddy congratulated her from behind Tes.

"Thank you," Kailyn grinned. "Bellowa said she was the last ogre in line. She saw my track leading off to the left and followed it."

"Why didn't she call the others, or drag you back?" Tes asked in confusion.

"Bellowa knew that I couldn't be in the forest alone and that you would all want to kill them if they hurt me."

"So she did it to save her own skin?" Giddy questioned.

"And Brausa's," Kailyn chuckled.

"And Brausa's," Giddy laughed. "Love can make you do strange things. Can't it, Tes?" she teased.

Tes glared back at her. "Funny, Giddy, funny."

41 THE SENTINELS

Tesania yawned as she sat up in her bedroll. The dappled morning sunshine flitted across the clearing where they'd set camp. "Wake up," she said as she shook Kailyn's shoulder.

"No," Kailyn's muffled voice replied.

"Giddy," Tes called sleepily. "Kailyn won't get up."

Giddy grinned at Raim and nodded toward the sleeping girl. "I'm sure she'll be up in a minute."

"Did you hear that," Tes said to Kailyn.

"I'm tired," Kailyn replied.

The two soldiers crept toward Kailyn.

Tes shook her head and mouthed, "Don't."

Giddy nodded as she stooped at Kailyn's head with a mug of water.

Raim gripped Kailyn's blanket down near her feet and looked up at Giddy for the signal.

"You'd better get up Kailyn," Tes warned.

"No."

"Ok, I did warn you."

As Kailyn's head started to lift, Giddy nodded at Raim. He whipped the blankets off the girl as Giddy slowly let the water run from the mug and dribble onto Kailyn's face.

Kailyn spluttered as she clambered to her feet, Giddy and Raim ran in opposite directions, laughing as Kailyn rubbed her eyes and looked from one to the other. "I can't believe you did that," she mumbled, still half asleep.

"Tes warned you," Giddy advised her. "So it's your own fault."

Kailyn peered down at Tes. "It wasn't much of a warning," she accused. "You could have said. Kailyn! Giddy's about to pour cold water on you!" she grumbled sarcastically.

"Kailyn, it's good to see you're awake," Deavon smiled as he walked past. "Get yourself some breakfast and have Naisa redress those burns. I want to head out shortly."

The trees thinned as they headed due north. Deavon explained that he wanted to get back to the base of the cliffs before they started east again, "We'll have more chance of finding these Sentinels if we only have to search to the east."

Tesania walked behind Kailyn, watching her to see that she was alright after her escape from the ogres. Apart from a slight, almost imperceptible limp, she seemed fine. "You were lucky," she called ahead.

Kailyn looked over her shoulder and nodded. "If it was one of the other ogres instead of Bellowa, I might not be here now."

"Promise me you'll be more careful in future," Tes insisted.

"I will," Kailyn laughed back at her. "I never want to see another ogre in my life."

The Britath Mountains loomed above the canopy of the forest as they flashed through the wavering leaves. Tes strained to see the ash white cliffs, highlighted by bluish crags that seemed almost like bruises on the delicate skin of the mountain. "I'm glad we're not climbing over them!" she mumbled.

Deavon called a halt when they came face to face with a cliff. Tes leaned her head back and looked straight up. Feeling dizzy, she stumbled backward, shaking her head to fight off the nauseousness that clenched at her stomach.

"Have a rest," Deavon called to them as he dug in his pack and produced the crude map. "Aldan, let's walk a little and see what's ahead."

Tesania watched them go. "I hope we find them soon," she complained as she rubbed at a sore spot on her shoulder where her pack was chaffing.

"It can't be too much farther," Giddy assured her. Turning, she called out, "Tean! Any idea's where these Sentinels could be?"

"Tenrad's writings suggested that they're three days into the forest."

"And?" Giddy asked.

"And what?" Tean looked around the expectant faces.

"What do they look like? How big are they? How will we know that it's them?" Giddy pestered.

"Oh," Tean shrugged. "Three stone spires."

Giddy sighed. "And?"

"That's all I know," Tean replied defensively. "The book only mentioned stone spires."

"That helps," Elddyn sneered.

"Surely they must be visible," Naisa interjected quickly. "The word 'spires' suggests they're tall. Otherwise, he would have called them mounds, would he not?" she laughed.

Tes sat quietly, calculating in her head how far they had come. "We've been in the forest for three nights now," she ventured as she caught Giddy's eye. "We must be close."

"Yes, but we have been travelling north-east," Raim said.

"Not yesterday," Tes corrected him. "While we were looking for Kailyn, we were travelling east mostly all day."

"Agreed," the little soldier nodded. "But then, today we have travelled due north all day."

Tes sighed. "Still, we've been in the forest for three and a half days, travelling north-east for most of the time." She watched Raim as he calculated. "Agreed?"

"Agreed," Raim nodded. "We must be getting close."

"And we're travelling directly east along the cliffs now," Tes said excitedly as she jumped to her feet. "We must find them soon. Come on, let's catch up to Deavon."

The others watched her walk briskly after the two rangers. Giddy groaned and stood. "Let's go," she said. "We don't want to lose another one."

Tesania caught Deavon and Aldan after only a few minutes. "Did you find them?" she asked expectantly.

"Why didn't you stay with the others, Tes?" Deavon scowled. "I don't want anyone out in the woods alone."

"There's no ogres here," Tes assured him. "Besides, I knew you were close by."

"That's not the point, Tes," Aldan interrupted.

"The others are coming," Tesania pouted. "There isn't any danger."

"We don't know that," Deavon growled. "After Kailyn went missing, I thought you'd know better."

"You two came out alone!" Tesania flared.

"We're well equipped to handle anything that might come at us," Deavon replied quickly. "You are not."

"Anyway." Tes rolled her eyes, dismissing his arguments. "Did you find them? They must be close."

"Not yet," Deavon replied, shaking his head as Giddy and the others approached. "Why did you let her come out here alone?" he shot at the soldier.

"Hey," Giddy held her hands up. "We came straight after her. It's not like we just let her run off and forgot about her."

Deavon glared at her for a moment. "It's important that we keep the girls safe. You should know better."

"I can fend for myself," Tes snapped. "Don't treat me like a child."

Deavon stared at the ground. "I'm not treating you as a child," he insisted. "I'm trying to ensure your safety."

Giddy stepped forward and placed her arm around Tes' shoulder. "I'll look after her for you," she grinned. "I promise boss."

"It's for her own good, Giddy," Deavon declared.

"I know it," Giddy chuckled. "Consider it done."

"I said, I can fend for myself," Tesania mumbled, shrugging Giddy's arm off.

"We know you can Tes," Deavon relented. "We're close to the caves. From here on in we have to be doubly vigilant." He turned and looked along the cliff walls. "It stands to reason that Trannyth may know of these caves too."

Tes' head shot up, she looked into Deavon's eyes, trying to decipher his inner thoughts. "Do you think he might have the caves blocked?"

"Count on it," Elddyn sneered at her.

Tes turned to him. "How do you know that?"

"I'll tell you how he knows," Giddy exclaimed.

"I am not in league with Trannyth!" Elddyn roared, contempt oozing from every pore as he glared at Giddy and then snapped his eyes to Tesania. "If I was, you would be dead by now."

"And so would you," Giddy taunted as she laid her hand on the hilt of her sword.

Elddyn spun about and shouted at Naisa, "What's the use?"

"Calm yourself," Naisa suggested. "You do yourself no favors talking as you do."

"These..," he turned toward Giddy and Tes, "these simpletons don't get it."

"Watch yourself," Deavon warned as he stepped forward. "Tesania is no simpleton," he growled.

Giddy coughed, holding her hands up and pointing at herself. "And?"

Deavon scowled, ignoring her, he went on. "We're on the threshold of the wastelands. We can't afford these petty arguments anymore." He glared around the group. "No more. Do you hear?"

"It stands to reason," Elddyn said calmly, "that Trannyth would indeed know of these caves. He would have mages at least covering the exit on the far side of the mountains. Most certainly beasts would be stationed with them, or indeed within the caves themselves."

Deavon's anger had subsided. Nodding his head he agreed with the surly mage. "We can't afford to underestimate Trannyth. It's imperative, for the safety of everyone," he stated as he took everyone in with his gaze. "That we stay together as a group. That includes Aldan and I."

"Makes sense," Aldan nodded.

"Elddyn is probably right," Deavon suggested, ignoring Giddy's scowl. "We have to expect that the caves are guarded, or at the very least the exit to the wastelands is."

"They could be on this side of the cave entrance!" Kailyn said with a fearful quiver in her voice. "Couldn't they?"

"They may be," Deavon replied somberly. He thought for a moment and then issued orders to the others. "We stay together from here on. No one is to stray." He looked at Kailyn. "Not even to collect fire wood. When we find these Sentinels, we'll approach the valley where the cave is as if it is definitely infested with beasts."

"Sounds like a good idea," Giddy agreed.

"We move east from here. Everyone keep your eyes sharp for anything that looks remotely like stone spires. Any questions..? Good. Raim and I will take the front. Aldan and Giddy will bring up the rear. The rest of you keep to the middle, and try to keep the noise down." With one last glance at the others, he moved off, saying, "Let's move out."

The afternoon wore on. Tesania peered through every gap in the trees and into every fissure and valley that they passed. By mid-afternoon she craved a break. "Can we please stop?" she called to Deavon. "I need to rest."

Kailyn sighed and sank to the ground as Deavon called a halt. "I don't know that we'll find them today," he remarked as he looked up at the sun. "I think the next stream we come to should be our camp for tonight."

"Agreed," Aldan said as he dropped his pack on the ground. We can restart the search for the Sentinels when we're fresh and rested."

Tesania rubbed her calves. "I hope there's a stream nearby," she sighed.

Kailyn nodded her head vigorously as she pulled her boot from her foot and massaged between her toes. "I'd soak my feet in the cool water for hours," she moaned.

"What about collecting firewood," Giddy commented.

"Let Elddyn do it," Kailyn grinned.

Giddy laughed. "So no fire for the night. Is that what you're saying?"

"Elddyn is always happy to help out around the camp," Raim admonished Giddy.

Giddy erupted into laughter. "Sure he is," she said as she stared at the mage.

Elddyn scowled at her, stood and stormed into the trees.

"Elddyn!" Deavon yelled after him. "Stay together."

"I'll go after him," Naisa climbed to her feet and walked into the forest after him.

"I wish you wouldn't make so much trouble with him Giddy." Deavon shook his head at her. "It's hard enough on this mission."

"Me?" Giddy asked innocently. "It was Kailyn who..."

Naisa burst from the trees. "Come quickly," she breathed heavily.

"Danger?" Deavon asked as his hand flew to his sword.

"No!" Naisa assured him. "Just follow."

Tesania was on her feet and quickly running after Deavon as Naisa turned and retraced her steps. "What is it?" she called to the mage.

Naisa's voice drifted back to her, "Elddyn found something." She led them through the trees, stopping occasionally to find her bearings. "There he is," she pointed through the trees.

Tesania peered around Deavon. She could see Elddyn through the forest. He was standing with his back to them, craning his neck and looking upward.

"What have you found?" Deavon asked as he approached the mage.

Elddyn turned his head toward Deavon, a small smile passing his lips. "This might be one of your spires."

Tes walked around Elddyn, staring at the structure. Light grey stone rose into the sky, chipped and weathered, disappearing through the canopy of the trees with moss and ferns growing from every available crack and hole. "It's huge," Tes exclaimed as she reached out and touched it.

"It would appear so," Deavon replied as he leaned back and peered into the branches of the trees.

Tes walked around the stone spire, counting her steps as she went. "Twenty-three," she announced.

"Where are the others?" Kailyn asked as she looked up at the giant spire.

"Why couldn't we see it from one hundred yards away?" Raim asked as he looked back through the forest.

"The angle from ground level over the canopy of the trees would preclude us from seeing anything that wasn't at least twice the size of the trees that surround it. The further back into the forest the spire is, the harder it is to see," Tean advised him. "It's simple really."

"Uh, right," Raim shrugged as he looked at Giddy.

"I have no idea what he said," she laughed.

"Any sign of the others?" Deavon asked as he looked into the woods. "They must be close."

"None," Elddyn replied. "This one was hard enough to see, even from a hundred yards away."

"Tenrad said the Sentinels point to the caves," Tes said. We need to stand to the south-west of them." Looking at Deavon, she said, "Remember? When the three become one; that is your path."

"So if we head south-west from here we should find them?" Raim volunteered.

"What if this is the last one?" Giddy laughed at him. "What if the others are that way?" She turned and pointed.

"Well there is that," Raim replied sheepishly.

"Surely there would have to be a place where we can see over the trees?" Aldan suggested. "We'd need to see all three at the same time."

Deavon stood in thought as Tes tried to climb the spire, grazing her arm as she slid back down. "It doesn't look like we'll be able to climb that," she complained as she blew on her sore skin. "It's too steep." Stepping back, she looked into the canopy of the trees. "And far up."

"There must be another one further into the woods," Deavon muttered as he walked a little way into the trees. "Or at least a mound or something we can climb to see them."

"Surely we could just head north-east from this one," Naisa ventured. "The others have to be in line. Don't they?"

"Not necessarily," Tean explained. "Tenrad merely suggested that the three spires should be observed from the south-west. They may in fact point off in a different direction. Even a few degrees off directly north-east could make a difference when we get back to the mountains."

"I think it's safe to say that the others lie deeper into the forest," Deavon said. "This one is close to the mountains. The others must be further in."

"I kind of agree with Naisa," Aldan interrupted. "Why head into the forest to find two other spires when we are right here at the closest one? It would seem a waste of time. And effort."

Deavon turned toward him. "Searching along the mountains may prove fruitless. At least the spires would point the way."

"We've seen nothing like a mound or cliff within the forest that would even begin to get us that far up." Giddy said as she pointed into the air.

"Yes," Deavon agreed. "But as Tean explained, we wouldn't see anything above the trees unless we walked right past it or there was a clearing that allowed us to see into the distance."

"We're at the mountains. Why can't we see if we can climb a little and look backwards?" Tes suggested. "Then at least we could see how far it is to the other Sentinels and which direction they are."

Deavon beamed at her. "Tesania, you are wise beyond your years."

Tes smiled at him, her face heating into a blush. She turned away as he continued to look at her.

"I suggest we find a camp for tonight." Deavon explained to the others. "In the morning we'll search the cliffs for any sign of a valley. Failing that we'll need a volunteer to climb one of the cliffs to look across the forest."

"Raim loves to climb," Giddy grinned as she pushed him forward. "He'll volunteer."

"Thanks Giddy," Raim shot back at her as he stumbled forward.

"You know you wanted to," she laughed as Deavon walked past her, heading back to the cliffs.

"You didn't leave me with much choice," Raim accused her as he jogged past her and slapped her on her rump. "Let me talk for myself next time."

"You'd better run mister," Giddy yelled as she set off after him.

Kailyn smiled at Tes. "Do you think those two are..?"

Tes laughed. "No! Come on, we'd better catch up to the others."

Deavon led the way along the cliff face, his hand on his sword as he carefully scanned ahead. He suggested they camp by a small stream that bubbled from a pile of rocky debris at the base of the cliffs, pooling in an azure pond before babbling off into the woods.

"It's beautiful," Kailyn gasped as she sat at the edge and tore at her boots. "Tean, do you mind if I don't help with the firewood today? Please?" she begged the monk.

"Kailyn," Deavon called. "It was part of the reason we brought you along. Remember? You promised you would collect firewood every night."

Kailyn froze midway through removing a boot and stared at Deavon. "But I do it every time we camp," she complained. "I just want to soak my feet."

"You can do that after you've collected the wood," Deavon demanded.

Kailyn pulled her boot back on. "It's like being back with the witch," she complained sulkily to Tesania.

"Stay there. I'll get the wood if it's such a problem for you," Elddyn growled as he threw down his pack and walked toward the trees.

Kailyn watched him go, and then smiled at Tes. "Ok!" she grinned as she yanked once more at her feet.

The night was clear and warm. The moon reflected off the white cliffs, bathing the camp in a strange twilight. Tesania and Kailyn drifted into sleep as Tean told stories of the early kings of Eldanal.

Morning broke with the hint of rain in the air. Clouds gathered above the mountain peaks as a cool breeze ruffled the leaves of the trees.

Tesania dragged herself out of her blankets and walked to the fire. "Morning," she mumbled to Tean and Naisa. "Where's Deavon?" she looked around the camp. "And the others?"

"They went down the cliffs a little way," Naisa pointed. "They should be back soon."

"I thought we were supposed to stay together," Tes yawned.

"Deavon was comfortable that we were safe here," Naisa smiled. "And they can look after themselves. Tea?"

"Please," Tes replied as she watched the cliffs, hoping Deavon would return soon. "Did he say how long they'd be?"

"I think Raim's going to do some climbing. They might be a while."

"I wish they'd woken me," Tes frowned. "I would've liked to go with them."

"You were sound asleep," Naisa advised her. "Deavon went over to you, but decided to let you sleep."

"Well I wish he hadn't," Tes said peevishly.

"He does what he thinks is best, Tes," Naisa soothed as she reached out and patted her hand. "Don't be too hard on him."

"I'm not," Tes defended herself. "I just would have liked to have gone along."

"You'd better wake Kailyn up," Naisa suggested. "You know how long it takes her to get out of bed."

Tes packed her sleeping roll as she prodded at Kailyn, "Deavon will be back soon."

"So?"

"And Giddy," Tes warned.

Kailyn groaned. "Ok." Rolling over, she blocked the morning light from her eyes with her hand. "Tell her I'm up."

Tes laughed. "Tell her yourself. Here she comes."

Kailyn scrambled out of her blankets as Giddy walked toward them. "I'm up!"

Giddy frowned at Kailyn and then looked at Tes. "What's up with her?" she asked.

"Don't ask," Tesania grinned as she looked past Giddy. "Where's Deavon?"

"Coming, with the others," Giddy told her. "We found the other Sentinels."

"You did? Where?"

"Raim climbed a cliff. He's like a mountain goat you know."

"I can imagine. He'd probably climb a whole mountain to get away from you."

"Now, now, play nice," Giddy warned her. "Come to the fire when Kailyn's ready. Deavon will explain it to you then."

Tes chased Kailyn to the little pool. "Hurry up; I want to hear what they found."

"Well go, you can tell me later," Kailyn insisted. "I want to brush my hair."

"Ok," Tes said anxiously as Deavon walked toward the others. "I'll tell you later."

"Fine," Kailyn mumbled, watching Tes go.

"Kailyn doesn't want to come over," Tes reported to Deavon at the fire. "I'll let her know later."

"Fine." Deavon bent down and picked up a stick. "Raim climbed a cliff, about a mile down the way," he pointed along the cliffs and then began to draw in the sandy ground. "We're here, the Sentinel we found is here," he drew a circle. "Raim climbed the cliff here," he stabbed at the ground.

"My brave hero," Giddy teased Raim.

"Giddy," Deavon warned, "let me finish." Drawing two more circles to the far left of the first one, he continued. "The other two Sentinels are out in the forest."

"How far?" Tes asked.

"I would judge the second one to be about three miles inside the forest," Raim answered. "The other one would be at least that again."

"Any sign of a hill or something, where we might observe them from?" Naisa asked.

Raim shook his head. "None that I could see."

"There must be," Tean interrupted. "Tenrad wouldn't have written of it if he couldn't see it for himself."

"Agreed," Raim said. "But I couldn't see anything that remotely looked like a high point."

"Maybe he climbed a tree!" Tes offered. "He could see them then."

"Which tree?" Deavon asked.

"I have no idea," Tes replied, her face creasing into a frown. "There must be something."

"It'll take us at least half of the day to trek out to the outer one," Deavon estimated. "And then we have to find the high point. At least two days, I would think."

"Why not just search from this end?" Giddy asked. "Like I suggested last night."

"It would make more sense than wandering around the forest for two or three days," Raim agreed. "When I was up the cliff I could see the three Sentinels. If I drew an imaginary line along them, it would point to an area only a few miles away, maybe five at most."

"We could waste three days searching along the cliffs and still find nothing," Aldan offered. "I say the best bet is to go with what we know. Or what Tenrad knows, that is."

"And we might find it this morning," Giddy pointed out.

"It can't be that hard. Can it?" Tesania asked as Kailyn wandered over to join them. "I mean, we're at the cliffs. We know that the valley where the caves is in that direction," she gestured along the cliffs. "Surely we can find it. We only have to look one way and it will be obvious. Won't it?"

"Not necessarily, Tes," Deavon shook his head. "It might be a small entrance that's not readily visible. We might walk straight past it if we don't know exactly where it is."

"If it's that small, having the Sentinels point in a general direction won't help very much." Naisa said. "I think we should search along the cliffs. We know we're in the right area."

"You could be right," Deavon admitted as he scrubbed the ground with his stick. "We'll search along the cliffs today. If we fail to find the valley we can head into the forest tomorrow and try to find the high point to observe the Sentinels." He searched their faces. "Agreed?"

"I feel it's a wasted day," Aldan growled. "But you're the boss, so let's get going."

"Anyone else?" Deavon waited a few moments for any objections. "Right, let's move out."

Tesania walked with Kailyn. They searched in every nook of the cliffs. Giddy laughed at them as they investigated a small crack running up the cliff face. "Even if it is in there, I won't be squeezing through."

Aldan and Raim pulled vines and bushes aside to ensure they missed nothing along the way. Naisa and Deavon scouted ahead, watching for any signs of ogres or beasts.

By midday, no sign of a cave, or a valley, had been found. "It must be close," Tes complained as they ate some cheese and dried meat.

"It'll be close now," Raim assured her.

"I hope so," Kailyn sighed. "I'm bored with looking at rocks."

"I'll look," Tean offered. "You take a rest."

Kailyn thought about it, looking from Tes to Tean. "That's ok, Tean. I'll keep helping Tes."

"You can have a rest if you want," Tes told her. "I don't mind looking with Tean."

"It's ok," Kailyn mumbled. "I want to."

Tes laughed. "Why say you didn't then?"

Kailyn shrugged as Deavon called them to continue. "I want to stay with you. Come on," she said, dragging Tes up and heading back to the rocky cliffs.

Tesania looked up when light drops of rain splattered on her face. "We might get wet," she said worriedly as she scanned the darkening clouds.

Kailyn held her tongue out, trying to catch a drop. "wooks wike it," she mumbled.

"I can't understand you with your tongue hanging out, you ninny," Tes complained. "I hope we find some shelter. And soon," she added, wiping a splatter from her forehead with her sleeve.

Deavon came toward them. "We'll have to press on I'm afraid," he advised them, raising his voice to overcome the rising wind. "At least until we find some shelter."

Tes nodded and kept on, still searching the cliffs as she pushed into the wind. They walked for another hour, the rain growing heavier until it became a deluge. The wind whipped around their bodies, throwing their cloaks and clothing into a fluttering dance. Tes peered from behind her rain-drenched hair where it clung to her face, water running in cascading rivulets from her chin.

Deavon called a halt in the half darkness when the rain reached a roaring crescendo. "We have to move into the trees," he yelled. "I can't see any shelter along the cliffs."

"We'll get just as wet in there as here," Aldan shouted.

"I agree with Aldan," Giddy pointed along the cliff face. "At least this way we might find a cave or some kind of shelter."

Tesania and Kailyn stood next to Naisa, shivering as the incessant rain drove the temperature down. "I agree with Giddy and Aldan," Tes called to Deavon. "And we can keep searching as we go."

"Ok," Deavon conceded. "We go on. Is everyone ok?" he asked as he looked around the dripping group. At their grim nods he turned and led the way into the pelting rain.

Tes huddled close to Kailyn, her arm wrapped tightly around the young girls shoulders. "Have you ever been out in rain like this?" she yelled.

"Yes," Kailyn's beamed at her. "One day it rained like this at home. My brothers and I slid in the mud for hours. It was such fun."

"I bet your mother didn't think it was fun when she had to..."

Giddy held her hand up, her head cocked.

"What is it?" Tes shouted.

"Can you hear that?"

Tes turned her head from side to side. The only sound that came to her was the relentless beat of the rain. "No!" she shook her head. "Nothing, except the rain."

"Running water," Giddy pointed at the cliff.

Tes turned to the rocks, water streamed down the wall, splashing and puddling in every crease and crack. Shaking her head, she peered at Giddy through the rain and shrugged.

"Where the vines are growing," Giddy insisted, turning to Deavon and Aldan as they returned to see what she had found. "There's a rushing water noise coming from behind those vines."

"Let's have a look," Deavon called as he stepped forward and listened. Nodding his head at Giddy, he yelled, "You're right. Let's drag some of these vines back and see what's in there."

Giddy grinned and leapt forward, ripping at the vines and pulling them away from the rock face. She peered into the darkness behind, shaking her head as she looked back. "I can't see anything, but there's a lot of water going through. It looks like a small cave."

"Naisa," Deavon motioned to the mage who stood forlornly behind Tes, wet and bedraggled. "Can you use your staff to provide some light?"

Naisa shook her head and blinked, looking up numbly, she mumbled, "Umm, surely." Stepping forward she held her staff toward the opening Giddy had made in the vines. A soft glow emanated from the orb at the tip, chasing the darkness into the corners as Giddy poked her head through.

"A small cave," she reported. "I can't see how far it goes back. There's a waterfall at the back," she indicated, drawing her open hand down across her face.

"Can we all fit in there?" Deavon shouted.

Giddy shook her head, holding a finger up, she yelled, "One, at most."

"I'll see how far it goes back," Raim pushed past Giddy and poked his head into the cave. "Doesn't look like much,' he called back, grinning at Giddy. "See you soon."

"Don't go too far," Deavon called at Raim's feet as they disappeared into the darkness.

"I hope he finds somewhere dry," Kailyn's chattering voice complained into Tes' ear. "I'm freezing."

"I hope so too," Tes replied as Raim's head came back through the cliff wall.

"It's a short tunnel," he explained. "Only about fifty feet long. It widens past the waterfall."

"What's on the other side?" Tes asked as she knelt down near Raim and squinted into the cave.

"A valley," Raim called. "Full of trees."

42 OWARA CAVES

The dawn sun crept inexorably into the little cave where the travelers had spent the night. Tesania studied the trees outside the entrance, lush and green, glistening in the early morning breeze, their foliage still wet from the previous night's storm. Birds sang their morning song as butterflies and bees flitted industriously amongst small clumps of fragrant flowers.

The night had been cold and uncomfortable. Everything in their packs had been soaked by the incessant rain; nothing had been spared the insidious water. Deavon and Giddy had tried in vain to light a fire with the wet wood that Tean ventured out to collect. Even Naisa couldn't manage to make her magic flames take to it. Kailyn had sat shivering, her wet blankets useless. Eventually, Raim had taken some of the oil they had purchased in Orash and pooled it around the stubborn wood. The flames slowly overcame the moisture that fought obstinately against it, allowing the travelers to dry their belongings by the warm, flickering flames.

"Good morning, Tes," Deavon called from the fire. "It's a much nicer day by the look of it," he said, nodding out of the cave entrance.

"I hope so," Tes muttered, feeling her blankets and clothes. "My things are still wet."

"Hang them over the trees when you get up," he advised. "They'll dry in a few hours."

Tes rolled over and climbed to her feet. "Aren't we going to find the caves today?" she asked in confusion.

"Giddy and Raim have gone to scout the valley," Deavon replied.

"Why not all go?"

"Two reasons. First, we need to dry our gear. They will never dry once we enter the dark caves. I don't want to spend days in wet clothes," he laughed. "Second, we don't know if there are beasts guarding the caves. If we all go traipsing up there we'll be seen. Giddy and Raim can approach it more stealthily and report back their findings."

"I'll be glad of a rest anyway," Tes said as she gathered her blankets and pack, heading for the trees outside.

"I think we all will be," Naisa agreed. "The last few days have been draining, to say the least."

Tes managed to coax Kailyn out of bed with the smell of frying mushrooms. "Where did they come from?" Kailyn asked sleepily as she came to the fire.

"Just outside the cave," Tes smiled. "They're growing everywhere. Take your things out and hang them up. Deavon said we can stay here today and rest."

Kailyn's face lit up. "Oh, good, I'm so tired. I hardly slept last night."

The morning wore on. Tesania turned her pack inside out, sorting through her things as she chatted happily to Naisa and Kailyn. Midday came and went as they waited for the two soldiers to return. By mid-afternoon Deavon was starting to pace across the cave entrance, looking anxiously out into the forest. Relief flooded his face as a call came from Giddy, they still couldn't see her or Raim, but could plainly hear them coming through the trees.

"Did you find the caves?" Tes called as they came into view.

"Yes," Giddy replied. "A few hours north."

"Are you sure it's the entrance we're after?" Deavon asked.

"As sure as we can be," Giddy laughed lightly. "There wasn't a sign saying Owara Caves if that's what you mean."

"I imagine there isn't," Deavon laughed.

"The valley's narrow," Giddy explained as she leant her arm on Raim's shoulder. "My little friend and I searched along the valley walls. It's the only cave entrance we could find."

"So it's the Owara Caves?" Tes asked impatiently.

"Assuming we're in the right valley," Giddy replied seriously. "I would say so, yes."

"No sign of beasts?" Aldan asked.

"None," Raim answered. "If they were guarding the caves we would've seen some sign of them. I think it's safe to say they've neglected to take the caves into account. If they even know they exist."

Deavon nodded his head in thought. "It would appear so. Good news indeed." Turning to Tesania, he asked, "Could you cook some more of those mushrooms you collected? I'm sure Giddy and Raim are hungry."

"I can," Tes replied happily as she headed toward the fire.

"You two had better get your packs and gear dry. I want to head toward the caves first thing tomorrow."

They spent the afternoon chatting by the fire. As dusk drew in around them, Deavon suggested they all pack their things ready to move out in the morning. Tes rolled gratefully into her dry, warm blankets after the evening meal. To the soft sounds of Naisa singing a lullaby, she drifted slowly off to sleep.

~

The entrance to the Owara Caves was a disappointment to Tesania. She had walked with the others in the cool morning breeze to the foot of a cliff. Before it lay a mound of rubble, shale-like stone that had seemingly collapsed from the cliff face decades ago.

Raim scrambled up the slippery mound and pointed out a crack in the rock face. Not much more than two foot wide and five foot high.

"That's it?" Tes asked nervously. "It isn't very big."

"What did you expect?" Giddy laughed. "A grand hall with footmen to escort you through?"

Tesania blushed. "No! I just thought it would be bigger."

"I agree," Kailyn added. "Will it be bigger inside?"

"In some places it will be," Deavon advised her.

Trepidation clenched at Tesania's stomach as the realization sunk in at the task they had set for themselves. "So... We might have to... Go through something that small all the way under the mountains?"

"Maybe smaller," Giddy laughed as Tes' face grew paler.

"What! You're kidding... Right?"

"I wish she was," Deavon smiled. "We don't know what's ahead of us in there. All we can do is enter and find out. But first we need to make torches."

"Can't we just use Naisa and Elddyn's staff light?" Tes asked.

"For a short trip, I would say yes. We have no idea how long we'll be in these caves, or what lies ahead of us," Deavon advised her. "I'd rather be prepared. I want at least two torches in each pack."

Tean, Kailyn and Naisa followed Tes back into the trees to collect fallen branches. Giddy and Ream unpacked the cloth and oil from their packs while Deavon, Aldan and Elddyn climbed to the cave entrance.

Tesania and the others returned shortly after, helping Raim wrap the cloth around the wood and holding them out for Giddy to soak with oil. The pungent smell from the oil caused Tes' head to spin, coughing as the heady odor invaded her nose. Raim provided cloth for them to wrap the sticky torches in before they placed them into their packs.

"We went about one hundred feet in," Deavon slipped down the loose rock face as he called. "It opens out to a larger tunnel. We'll be able to walk freely through." Hefting his pack, he turned to the group. "It's essential that we stay together," he said, glancing from one face to another. "We don't know what's ahead of us, so one of the mages will need to lead at all times." He nodded to Naisa and Elddyn. "Ok?"

"I'll do what I must," Elddyn replied.

Looking sharply at Elddyn, Naisa said, "We'll both take turns."

"Good," Deavon continued. "We'll need to move slowly. I don't want anybody getting lost or falling down a crevasse. Understood?"

The group nodded. "Ok, let's go," Deavon said.

Tesania peered into the cave entrance, darkness stared back. "I don't think I like this," she whispered to Kailyn. "It's so dark."

"I agree," Kailyn shivered. "I wish I was at Lady Ayana's right now," she smiled weakly.

"We'll be ok," Naisa said as she ducked past them and entered the cave, the light from her staff managing to push the cold blackness away.

Tes followed her in, looking around the walls as Kailyn crowded in behind her. The rock was grayish, as it had been on the cliff faces. Reaching out, she dug at the wall with her finger, looking sharply at Naisa as it came away easily and crumbled to the floor of the cave like powder. "It's soft."

"Yes," Naisa replied, her own hand running down the wall. "And cool."

"You could move in further," Kailyn complained as the others pushed behind her to enter the caves.

Deavon came in last. "Ok," he called. "Single file. Naisa.., take your time."

The mage held her staff high and started into the uninviting darkness, cautiously at first, building to a quicker pace when she became accustomed to the dim light and could make out the floor ahead. "It's very smooth," she said to Tes over her shoulder.

"Yes," Tesania craned her neck, taking in the roof of the cave. It too was grey and smooth. "It's like somebody carved it."

"Indeed," Naisa replied. "I would think it's natural though."

Tes continued to study the walls as they pushed into the caves. Naisa paused periodically to point out jagged rocks to the others before continuing on. No other obstacles stood in the groups' way as the day wore on. Time seemed to stand still, the clinging darkness confusing Tes. Her stomach rumbled, telling her that it must be late afternoon. "When are we going to stop?" she sighed to Deavon.

"Soon," Deavon replied.

~

The cool caves caused Tes to sleep restlessly throughout the night. Aldan's light snoring echoed off the walls and bounced around inside her head. Tossing and turning, she managed a few hours rest.

Their breakfast was light. Deavon insisted on an early start so they could clear the caves as quickly as possible.

"I hate this," Kailyn complained to Tes as they followed Naisa deeper into the darkness.

"Me too. Hopefully it'll only be a few days."

"A few days!" Kailyn groaned.

The hours blended into one another, darkness pushing in on the travelers, seemingly pushing Naisa and Elddyn's magical light inward. Tes started to see shapes just beyond the light; shaking her head each time and admonishing herself for letting the perpetual night get to her. Still a gnawing uneasiness settled itself into the pit of her stomach, nudging at her, reminding her of the danger the cold caves might have in store.

"We've been lucky so far," Deavon smiled at Tes while they set up camp at a fork in the tunnel on the forth night. "The going's been easy."

"It has," Tes replied. "I can't stand it though. How much longer..? Before we reach the other side, I mean."

"Hard to know," Aldan offered as he studied the two tunnels ahead of them. "We could be out in a day or two. It depends if we choose the right tunnel," he motioned, "and what we come up against."

"I hope so," Kailyn muttered from her bedroll where she had collapsed. "I'm sick of darkness."

Tes ignored her, asking Aldan, "What could we come up against?"

"Chasms, cave ins," he offered. "For all we know this cave could lead nowhere and we might have to walk all the way back."

"Don't say that!" Tesania gasped, turning to Deavon. "He's joking... Right?"

Deavon laughed. "I hope he is." The smile fell from his face as he continued. "Unfortunately he might be right."

Tes slept fitfully that night, tossing and turning, trying to break through an imaginary pile of rubble, teased all the while by a dazzling shaft of sunlight that managed to find its way through the debris.

Deavon and Aldan agreed to try the tunnel to the left as it was larger and seemed to head in the right Direction. Tesania trudged on behind them, only half paying attention to the light that emanated from Elddyn's staff as he took his turn at the front. Her mind drifted back to her village. She imagined herself there, helping her mother feed the chickens, running errands for her father at the smithy.

The dark reality jerked her back into the caves as her foot caught painfully on a ridge of rock that rippled across the floor. She stumbled and crashed to her knees, crying out as skin tore painfully from her legs.

"Tes, are you ok?" Kailyn asked urgently, crouching down beside her.

"Yes," Tes replied as she sat rubbing at her skinned knees. "I was daydreaming."

The group huddled around her. "You could have warned her about the ridge," Giddy shot at Elddyn as he returned to them along the cave.

"She should have kept up and paid attention to what she was doing," Elddyn sneered in the soft light.

"It's ok, Giddy," Tes cut her off. "It's my fault. I wasn't paying attention." Groaning as she used the wall of the cave for leverage, she pushed herself up.

"Can you go on?" Deavon asked, concern filling his voice. "We could stop here a while if you need."

"Phht," Elddyn scoffed. "You mollycoddle the girl. It's just a scratch."

"You'd demand we stop if you fell," Giddy accused.

"And would you?" Elddyn snapped. "Hmm, Giddy... Would you let me rest if I fell down? Or would you tell me to get over it and move on?"

"If you fell down I would put you out of your misery," Giddy growled. "You filt..."

"Giddy!" Naisa stepped between the angry soldier and seething mage. "This solves nothing, leave it be."

Tes leaned against the chalky cave wall, her left leg throbbing, clothes askew. Slowly she stood upright and pulled her shirt into place. "I'll be alright," she assured Giddy while she adjusted her belt. "I can go..." She stopped abruptly, her head whipping around, her eyes meeting Deavon's. "My sword," she motioned. "It's humming."

"What?" Deavon asked sharply. "Are you sure?"

Tes rested her hand lightly on the hilt and then nodded. "It's faint. But it's definitely humming."

"What does that mean?" Kailyn asked nervously. "Are there beasts in the caves?"

"Possibly," Deavon replied slowly. "It could be any number of things though." He stood in thought for several moments. "Raim?" he asked the little man. "You may need to scout ahead."

"Not a problem," Raim's smile flashed dully in the soft light.

"But, won't the beasts..," Tes looked nervously into the darkness. "Or whatever it is in our way; they'll see the torchlight. Won't they?"

"She's right," Aldan agreed. "If it's beasts up ahead," he nodded toward the wastelands end of the cave, "they'll be after us the second they see the light reflecting off the walls."

Deavon nodded. "We can't just wander blindly into them either."

"I can dim my staff light," Elddyn offered. "Raim and I could scout ahead together and see what's in our way."

"And give us away," Giddy shot at him.

"For the last time, I... am... not... an... ally... of... Trannyth," Elddyn shouted.

"Keep your voice down," Deavon whispered urgently. "We know from experience that Tes' sword only reacts when danger is near. They can only be a few hundred yards ahead, one mile at most."

"It's settled then," Raim grinned at Giddy. "Elddyn and I are on scout duty."

"Ok," Deavon said. "Don't get too close to them. I want numbers, where they're situated, how big the area is, anything that might help us get around them safely." He looked from Raim to Elddyn. "I don't want any heroics, got it?"

"Yes, boss," Raim's eye glinted in the staff light.

Deavon sighed. "He's as bad as you Giddy."

"I'll take that as a compliment," Giddy laughed as she placed her arm around her friend's shoulders. "I want you back in one piece." As she stepped back she glared at the mage. "And keep an eye on him," she sneered. "Any sign of him betraying us..." a grin crept over her face. "Kill him."

"Have some faith," Raim laughed as he slipped his pack off and dropped it to the ground. "He didn't give us away in the Draon pass, so I don't think he will now."

"Thank you," Elddyn muttered as he stared triumphantly at Giddy.

"Ready?" Raim asked.

"Ready," Elddyn nodded as he fell in behind the crouching soldier.

Tesania watched the light of Elddyn's staff disappear into the darkness of the caves. "Do you think they'll be ok?" she asked to no one in particular.

"Raim will come back," Giddy assured her with forced sternness. "He had better, or Elddyn will answer to me."

Tes sank to the cold stone floor. "Naisa?"

"Yes, Tesania?"

"Do you have some potion I can put on my knees?"

"Oh, sorry," Naisa exclaimed as she dropped her pack and started rummaging through it to find her potions. "I was wrapped up in Raim and Elddyn."

"That's ok," Tes sighed tiredly. "I'm worried about them too." She looked at Deavon as Naisa administered to her scraped knees. "What if it is beasts?" she asked calmly. "Will we be able to get past them?"

Deavon frowned at her. "I don't know Tes. Let's find out what's up ahead and then worry about how to get past it."

They all fell quiet while they waited for the scouts to return. Tean walked into the semi-darkness and started a mumbling prayer. Aldan slumped against a wall and closed his eyes. Giddy pulled some cheese and a knife from her pack and carved small pieces off, absentmindedly placing them into her mouth. Kailyn helped Naisa treat Tes' knees while Deavon stared off into the darkness.

Time seemed to drag inexorably for the seven travelers as they waited for Raim and Elddyn to return. Half an hour seemed like an eternity to Tes. She chatted to the others, trying to fill in the time, talking about the sun and how much she missed it and how she would love to have a nice hot bath.

"Shh, they're coming back," Deavon warned them.

Tes pulled herself to her feet just as Raim and the mage came running into view. "What did you see?" she asked anxiously.

"Beasts," Raim managed to say between deep breaths.

"How many?" Deavon asked urgently.

"Ten, and a mage," Elddyn advised him. "There's a chasm about a mile ahead," he pointed. "About fifty feet across."

"A chasm," Tes' brow creased. "What's that?"

"A deep crack in the cave floor," Tean advised her. "Usually so deep you can't see the bottom."

"Oh," Tes said as she looked at Deavon worriedly. "How can we get across that?"

"I'll worry about that later, Tes," Deavon snapped at her. "Let them report everything they've seen first." As Tes scowled at him and looked away he turned to Raim. "Anything else?" he pressed. "Anything that might help us get past?"

"We didn't stay there long," Raim admitted. "I wanted to get back and let you know what was up ahead."

Deavon stood in thought. "So we have a chasm with a platoon of beasts on the far side," he mumbled as he looked up at Raim. "Any bridges, ledges, anywhere that we might get across."

"None that I saw," Raim shrugged.

"Aldan," Deavon called softly as he turned to the big ranger. "I want to recon the chasm; you and Naisa come with me."

They crept to the precipice of the chasm. The void opened out into a cathedral size cave. The chasm was immense, dropping into inky blackness. The mage and the beasts sat around a large fire, the flames flickered and jumped, casting glowing shadows across the cave walls. At the far end Deavon could see another passage running from the large cave, sunlight trickled through, giving the white rock an inviting luminescence. "We're almost through," he whispered while nudging Aldan and pointing to the far cave. "If only we could get past these beasts."

"Even if we could get across this chasm, we'd be hard pressed to hold off a troop of beasts," Aldan replied. "I fear we'd pay a heavy price."

"Agreed," Deavon mumbled, looking around the roof of the cathedral as he spoke. "Come on. Let's get back to the others."

Tesania limped toward Deavon. "Can we get through?" she asked anxiously.

"There doesn't appear to be a way through," he said, as the others gathered around. "We may have to backtrack to the fork we camped at yesterday and see where the other path leads."

"No," Kailyn moaned. "Not back into the caves."

"We're almost there Kailyn. I could see sunlight on the far side of the cave where the beasts are camped," Deavon assured her. "But, we can't go this way. There's no way across the chasm."

"But the other passage might lead to a dead end too," Tes frowned. "It could be a waste of time."

"It might be, Tes," Deavon sighed. "We knew before we came into the caves that we might run into dead ends or even have to abandon the caves altogether and return to Orash."

"I know," Tes whispered. "It just seems such a waste of time."

"We have no choice," Deavon assured her gently. "If we're lucky we might avoid the beasts altogether by going the other way."

"There's only ten," Giddy announced. "We could take them."

"I'm sure you could, Giddy," Deavon laughed. "We'd still have a chasm to get across, so it's back to the other passage for now."

The group reluctantly gathered their packs and headed back down the passage they had traversed during the day. They set camp once more at the fork. After a small meal and some banter between Giddy and Raim, Tes settled into her blankets and slept fitfully throughout the night.

The passage they took in the morning grew smaller as they travelled, eventually starting to rise. Tes found she had to hunch over as she labored up the steepening path, her pack catching regularly on the ceiling of the cave, wrenching her to a stop. "I hope this doesn't go on for too long," she panted back at Kailyn.

Kailyn mumbled a reply that Tes didn't understand.

"Tes," Deavon called from behind. "Is your sword humming?"

Tesania's hand shot to her sword. "No," she replied. "Why?"

"Keep your hand on it," he suggested. "I don't want to walk into a troop of beasts."

The passage shrunk further as Tes clambered up the ever increasing slope. She soon found herself crawling on her hands and knees, eventually having to remove her pack and shove it along in front of her. The light from Naisa's staff grew to almost nothing as the mages body blocked most of the passage. In the near darkness, Kailyn snatched at her foot, pulling her to a stop. "What?" Tes whispered back at the girl.

"I can't go on," Kailyn's trembling voice replied. "It's too small," she whined. "We can't possibly get through."

"What's the holdup?" Deavon called from behind them.

"Kailyn's getting scared," explained Giddy, who was next in line to the girl.

"I'm not scared," Kailyn defended. "It's just so cramped. What if we get stuck and can't get back out?" she complained, her voice cracking as if she was in tears.

"We have no choice," Tes said gently. "Naisa will tell us if it's too small to continue. We won't get stuck. I promise."

They crawled on for what seemed like hours, the cave size contracted and opened at regular intervals, even allowing Tes to stand and walk on the rare occasion. After a short break for a meal they pushed on, coming to a stop after only a few minutes as the cave walls closed to a small aperture that even Tean would not be able to crawl through. "Pass word back to Deavon that the passage is blocked," Naisa called to Tes.

The message went down the line of cramped travelers. Deavon's reply came back quickly. "Is there no way through?" Tes asked as it reached her.

Naisa shuffled forward so that her face was right near the hole. "It seems to open out after only a few inches. I could maybe blast it open with magic."

Tes waited for Deavon's reply and then said to Naisa, "He said to blast it, but quietly."

Naisa mumbled under her breath as she crawled backwards, causing Tes and the others to back up. "Quietly he says," she grumbled. "Blasting and quiet are not two words that belong together," she complained. "I'll have to do it a little at a time. Mind your eyes, Tes."

Tes looked down at the hard floor and placed her hands over her head. Naisa tried to stretch her arms as far as she could and cast a spell, a small thud echoed back along the cave as the sound of crumbling rock trickled behind it. "This may take a while," Naisa warned as she set to cast another spell. "And the dust might prove to be a problem."

Tesania kept her head down as Naisa worked, she counted the spells, coughing as the dust started to invade her throat. When she counted eleven, the mage stopped and crawled forward.

"That should do it," Naisa called back through the heavy air. "It opens out quite a bit after this."

Tes thankfully called back to Kailyn to pass the message on and then crawled after the mage, drawing a deep breath when she broke through into cleaner air. Gratefully she stood and stretched out her tired muscles, her back cracking loudly as she arched backwards. "It's so good to stand upright again," she sighed.

The others shuffled through the hole, Deavon had to pull Aldan's big frame through when he got stuck. "Is everyone ok?" he asked. When they all nodded yes, he went on. "It looks like we've cleared the cramped part of the cave, for now. Let's move on quickly," he suggested.

Elddyn took the lead from Naisa, Tes followed with Kailyn close behind. The cave grew larger as they walked, soon allowing Tes to reach out on either side without touching the walls. She wandered along behind the mage, lost in her dreams of seeing sunlight again. It was some time before she remembered to check her sword. "Oh, Elddyn! Stop!" she whispered quickly.

"What is it?" Deavon asked as he reached her side.

"The beasts, they're near."

"Ok," Deavon said to the others. "Same as before. Except this time I'll go with Raim and Elddyn to see what's ahead. The rest of you stay here."

Tes gratefully sank to the floor, pulling Kailyn down beside her. "Let's rest while we can," she suggested.

Deavon, Raim and Elddyn were gone for an interminable time. Tes was getting restless when she finally saw the mage's light glowing down the cave. She stood and nervously waited for Deavon to appear.

"About a mile," he reported in answer to Tesania's question of where the beasts were. "We've come out well above them, but still on the wrong side of the chasm."

"Any way past?" Giddy asked.

"There's a ledge that runs along the wall," Deavon said as he shook his head. "That's about it."

"So we're blocked?" Tes asked. "Do we have to go back?"

"If we do, what then?" Kailyn questioned. "Do we abandon the mission and go back to Wyvern City?"

"No!" Tes gasped. "I will not abandon it!"

"Tes, there isn't any way through," Deavon advised her.

"What about the ledge?" Tes glared at him. "Why can't we cross the chasm on that?"

"It's very narrow, Tes," Raim replied. "We'd have to walk single file, out in the open, with a mage and beasts not fifty feet below."

Tes stared at Deavon, her brow creased. "Can't you and Aldan shoot them with your bows?" she asked.

"We might get four, maybe six if we're lucky," he replied slowly. "But the rest would soon be out of our range and then they'd know that we're in here." He sighed. "It would be impossible for us to get out of the caves then."

"So you're just going to give up?" Tes accused. "You're just going to walk away because a few beasts block the path?" Shaking her head in disbelief, she scowled at him. "There may be hundreds of beasts at the Keep, were you going to run from them too?"

"Tesania! That's enough," Deavon growled as he stood and grasped her wrist. "No-one here is a coward. We all came knowing the risks." He released her arm. "I will not put everyone's lives at risk on a foolhardy plan."

"The whole plan has been foolhardy from the start," Tes scoffed. She spun around. "Nine of us against an army of beasts and mages." Slowly she turned back to him. "We came out here to rid Eldanal of Trannyth." her eyes flicked to Kailyn. "We all knew the risks involved. And.., that we may never return."

"Throwing our lives away is not going to get rid of Trannyth, Tes," Deavon insisted.

"Going back to the Wyvern City won't either," she whispered quietly. She looked at Deavon softly. "I understand what you're saying. But, I'm going on, regardless of whether you come or not."

Tes knew he was trapped, that he wouldn't abandon her and let her go on alone. She knew also that the same stood for Giddy and Kailyn and therefore Raim. Aldan would not abandon Deavon and so would continue with them. She turned to Naisa and then Tean. "You understand? Don't you?"

Naisa nodded. "I do. I will accompany you until the end."

"Tean?"

The thin monk looked to the ceiling. "I have consulted my Lord many times. It is his will that Trannyth be dispatch from the lands of mortals." His eyes snaked down the chalky walls until they met Tes'. "I am your humble servant. Where you lead I shall follow."

"It doesn't look like I get a say," Elddyn snapped. "If anyone cares. I wish to go on. Trannyth must be stopped."

Giddy stepped toward the mage. "You know," she grinned. "One day, I might get to like you."

"I won't hold my breath," Elddyn snarled as he turned and stalked into the darkness.

Deavon squatted on his haunches. "If we're going to do this we need to get past those beasts." He glanced up at Tes. "The only way I can see is along that ledge."

"What good is it?" Giddy asked. "There's no use being on the far side and still fifty feet up the wall."

"The ledge runs downward, Giddy," Deavon advised her. "At the far side it's no more than six feet from the cave floor."

"So we could jump down?" Tes asked, excitement building in her voice.

"Yes," Deavon nodded. "But first we must all creep past the beasts, who have a keen sense of smell, get off the ledge and then through the cave exit on the far side."

"If we go at night..?" Raim offered.

"Raim, dear," Giddy laughed. "We're in a cave, it's always dark."

"Yes, but the beasts are surely not expecting anybody to try and pass them. They're camped by a fifty foot chasm that's all but impassable from this side."

"Your point?" Giddy asked.

"My point," Raim growled at her, "is that they will all sleep at the same time, maybe one guard will be posted, but if they're complacent, not even that."

"It makes sense," Aldan said to Deavon. "They'd feel pretty secure here."

"So we wait till the early hours of the morning," Deavon recounted. "Sneak up to the ledge and creep along it until the far end. Jump down and walk out of the caves, the beasts never aware that we were here? Is that it?"

"Sounds like a plan," Giddy quipped.

"Sounds like suicide," Elddyn's voice drifted from the black passage.

"Didn't take you long to get back to your sour self, did it?" Giddy glared at the darkness.

"Ok," Deavon interrupted. "Let's set camp here, have something to eat and get some sleep. I'll wake you when it's time to leave."

Tes didn't sleep, she lay thinking of the night ahead and the danger she was asking her friends to walk into. "I have to," she mumbled. "For mother and father."

She shook Kailyn gently as Deavon started to wake the others. "It's time to go sleepy head."

Kailyn murmured into her blankets and rolled over. Her eyes regarding Tes in the soft glow of light. "Are you scared?" she asked quietly.

"A little," Tes answered. "But it's something I have to do."

"We could die." A tear ran down Kailyn's soft cheek.

"Yes," Tesania replied, reaching out to brush the errant tear from her friends face. "You can go back if you want. I won't hold it against you."

"I didn't say I wanted to leave," Kailyn said indignantly as she sat up.

"I know," Tes replied. "It was my idea. I want you to be safe."

"I'm coming," Kailyn whispered in a determined voice. "Don't try to stop me."

"I knew you would," Tes tried to smile but only managed a weak grin. "Stay close to me today. My sword will protect us."

Kailyn nodded as she climbed to her feet. "I will."

Tes watched her and the others as they packed their gear. *What have I gotten these people into?*

Deavon gathered them around. "It's of the utmost importance that you all stay quiet." He scanned their faces somberly. "I don't even want to hear a cough. These beasts are deadly; ten of them may be beyond what we can handle."

"Remember also," Aldan added. "If they see us we have to stand and fight, we can't afford one of them escaping to warn Trannyth of our presence."

"Let's hope it doesn't come to that," Deavon responded.

"I will pray to the Lord for guidance," Tean interrupted as he fell to his knees and started to mumble.

"Yes, thank you, Tean," Deavon sighed. "I want everyone to stay together. Tes and Kailyn, you stay at the back, I want the fighters to be first off the ledge." He looked from face to face, pausing at each to gauge their feelings. "Any questions? No? Good. Let's go."

"Tean," Tes called to the monk. "Tean!" The monk broke from his ramblings and looked up at her. "We're going, come on. You're in front of Kailyn and I."

"Did the Lord give you guidance," Giddy asked.

"Indeed," Tean answered grimly. "Indeed."

"I don't like the sound of that," Kailyn whispered to Tes.

"Don't worry about it. What will be, will be."

They walked slowly toward the entrance to the cathedral cave. Deavon stopped just at the edge of the darkness. Tes could see the flickering light from the beasts' fire illuminating the walls on the far side.

Deavon motioned to Aldan to remove his bow and make it ready for quick action, removing his own at the same time. He whispered, so lightly that Tesania only just heard him. "Move slowly, but keep up with the others. Keep quiet at all times." His eyes met Tes', for a fleeting second she saw concern, he replaced it with a small smile and turned on his heel. Her heart pounded as he disappeared around the corner.

The cathedral was well lit by the beasts' fire. The white rock allowed the light to reflect, bouncing from wall to wall until it met the ceiling. Tes peered over the edge. The beasts appeared to be asleep; she counted eight, and the mage. *Two are missing?* She wanted to warn Deavon, but was sure he had already counted. So she silently followed behind Tean, glancing back every few seconds to make sure Kailyn was right behind her.

They moved slowly, agonizingly slowly for Tes. She looked down again, they were half way across the chasm, another twenty feet and they would be there. The beasts hadn't moved, so far they had managed to evade detection. Step by step they crossed the ledge. Tes froze as a cracking sound rent the air, the ledge shook, her eyes whipped to Deavon, meeting his just as the rock collapsed under her. Her last view was him trying to get past the others to reach her.

Her stomach flew into her throat as the piece of ledge carried Kailyn and herself into the pitch darkness of the chasm. They slammed against the side, the rock from the ledge shattering around them, throwing fragments of rock into their faces. Kailyn screamed as their momentum slid them inexorably into the pits of the earth.

43 A BODY OF BEASTS

Deavon strained to get to Tesania, watching in disbelief as she disappeared into the darkness. "Tesania!" he yelled. "No!" Straining, he tried to force his way past the others.

Aldan grasped his arm, steadying him as he overbalanced on the narrow ledge. "You can't help her now," he said urgently, his eyes locked on the beasts below. "They know we're here. We need to get off this ledge."

Deavon's head flashed around. The beasts were rising from their sleeping area. The mage already had his staff raised in the air. With one quick glance at the chasm where Tesania had disappeared he snatched an arrow from its quiver, in a split second his bow was up and aiming at the mage. The air split around them, crackling as a massive spell was unleashed. Deavon watched along the arrows shaft as the mage crumpled, thrown ten feet behind where he had stood. He didn't move; his body seemingly lifeless.

Deavon's eyes flicked along the ledge. Elddyn stood with his arms raised, his face alight after unleashing the magic that had caused the demise of Trannyth's mage. The mage stared down at his target, his eyes wide, the hair on his head radiating as if blown in a wind.

"I forbid you to do that again," Naisa screamed at him. "I will not stand by while you use forbidden magic!"

Elddyn's head slowly turned toward her. "The end justifies the means," he grinned.

Deavon snapped his attention back to the beasts as Naisa renewed her verbal attack on the mage. He sighted his bow on a beast as it ran for the back of the cave, intent on finding cover behind a mountain of crumbled rocks. "No you don't," he whispered as his arrow loosed.

The beast roared in pain as the arrow pierced its back. Stumbling two paces it fell to its knees, the momentum of its charge for cover causing it to skid across the cave floor and cannon into the pile of rocks. Before the beast had crashed to a shuddering stop, Deavon's second arrow was away.

Aldan had let three arrows loose by now, all finding their targets. One struck a beast in its shoulder, punching it around as it ran. Rolling across the floor it twisted and came to its feet. Reaching behind, it snapped the arrow shaft off at its skin. Hate radiated from the beasts eyes as it glared at him, emitting a ferocious roar, its jaws wide, jagged teeth dripping saliva. Its defiance ended abruptly as Aldan's bow raised once again, the sharp tip of the arrow aimed straight at it. With a last defiant cry, the beast turned and ran for the rocks, managing to dive over just as the arrow fizzed past its ear.

"Damn," Aldan cursed. "I missed it."

"Four down," Deavon called, "four to go, and we don't know where the other two are. Let's get off this ledge."

"Wouldn't we be better to stay up here and pick them off, one by one?" Raim asked.

"No," Giddy eyes were ablaze. "Let's get down there."

"They won't come out into the open," Deavon growled, his attention on the chasm. "They'll work out a way to get at us eventually. It'll be safer to get to the cave floor and engage them. We have to keep them from getting through that cave entrance." He snatched his gaze from the chasm lip where Tesania and Kailyn had disappeared. "Let's move."

The ledge allowed them to only move at a slow pace. Deavon was mindful of the possibility of the ledge collapsing in other places and trod gingerly, feeling his way before he placed all his weight on the ancient rock, his attention split between the narrow ledge and the hiding place of the beasts. It seemed an eternity before they reached the far side of the cathedral cave and the lowest part of the ledge. Turning to the others he instructed, "They may rush us as soon as we step down. It's imperative that we all get to the floor as quickly as possible. There's no time for niceties, we have to jump."

Giddy wrung her hands around the worn leather of her sword hilt. "I'm ready," she announced, her eyes fixed on the pile of debris where the beasts had taken refuge.

"Ok," Deavon said. "Aldan, stay on the ledge and see if you can't take another one out with your bow. It might at least hold them back until we can all get down."

Aldan nodded. "But I'll be down there as soon as you engage."

"Good luck old friend," Deavon said, slapping the big ranger on the shoulder. Drawing a deep breath, he stepped toward the edge of the ledge. "Let's go." Jumping lightly into the air, his body descended to the floor where he landed and quickly moved to the right.

Giddy followed him down, Raim dropping by her side. They moved to the left. Elddyn, his hair still on end, landed heavily on the rocky ground then reached around to help Naisa down. Tean stayed with Aldan, his mumbled prayers echoing through the stillness of the cool cave air.

The beasts remained behind the rocks. Deavon motioned for Giddy and Raim to move forward. The two mages stood at the base of the ledge, staffs raised, ready to strike.

As Deavon and the two soldiers crept forward, the tension rose. The beasts refused to show their hand, remaining hidden. "We're going to have to go in after them," Deavon whispered. "Be on your guard for an attack from the top of the pile."

"I have that covered," Aldan called in a gruff voice.

Deavon nodded back at his friend then turned his attention to Giddy and Raim. His head motioned toward the beasts and he took a step closer. Slowly the dark wall behind the rock pile came into view. Deavon's brow creased. *The beasts must come out soon.* He scanned the rocks, from the base to the top. "They must be..."

Snarls rent the air as the four beasts burst from the darkness, two rushing at Deavon, two at Giddy and Raim.

"I can't get a clear shot," Aldan's voice echoed through the cave. "I'm coming down."

Deavon didn't answer; his attention fully on the flashing blades that skimmed through the air. Parrying one, he managed to sway out of the way of the other.

Giddy and Raim took the initiative, charging at the beasts before they had a chance to reach them. Giddy's sword met the oncoming beast, turning its sword aside. She flashed her own at its face, missing as the beast's head whipped back, its own sword arcing toward Giddy's thighs. Twisting, she dropped her sword hand, the clash of steel ringing through the now seemingly small cave. "Unlucky," she grinned at the beast as her boot met its shin and her sword flicked along its abdomen, blood splattered across the white rocks. The beast came on, oblivious to her blow.

Raim stumbled back under the onslaught of the beast, not having faced one in single combat he was awed by its strength and skill. Its sword came at him incessantly; it was all he could do to block the dancing weapon out.

Deavon tried vainly to hold the two beasts at bay, Naisa and Elddyn had gained a position where they could fire spells at the beasts, but the frantic movements of the battle left them little room to do anything. The odd spell that came crackling through bounced off the thick hide of the beasts, the small amount of pain hindering them only slightly as they continued their coordinated attack.

Aldan reached Deavon, deflecting a blow that would have ended Deavon's life. The heavy blade shuddered Aldan's sword in his hand, jarring his elbow. Crying out in pain, he stepped away as one of the beasts turned its attention to him.

Deavon, freed to concentrate on one beast, pressed his attack. The beast facing him was the one Aldan had caught in its shoulder with his arrow. Its left side was weakened, but its right sword hand still stung Deavon's hand with every blow. Stepping forward, he feinted. The beast swung its sword to block him, finding empty air as Deavon's sword whistled back and flicked across its throat.

The beast gurgled blood as it sank to the ground, its eyes boring into Deavon as its hand came to its throat in a vain effort to hold its life inside its severed veins.

Deavon had no time to savor his victory as a scream of pain rent the air from behind him. Spinning, he saw Aldan half crouching trying desperately to hold off the beast's attack, the fingers on his left hand severed and lying on the cave floor, curling with spasms as the nerves gave their last twitches of life.

"No!" Deavon screamed as he charged at the beast's back. "Get back Aldan," he commanded as the beast swung to face him. "You can't do any more here."

Aldan remained frozen, his face white, shock played in his eyes as he stared incredulously at the blood pumping in small fountains from his destroyed hand.

Giddy sidestepped as her beast charged at her. She tapped its sword, knocking it harmlessly away while deftly slipping her foot under its feet. The beast gave a cry of surprise as it stumbled, tried to regain its balance and crashed to the floor. Giddy danced quickly toward it; raising her sword she drove at its back. The beast rolled and caught her blow with its sword, twisting as a grin grew across its grotesque face. Giddy's sword was knocked aside, leaving her open to the beast's reply.

Raim battled ferociously with the beast. His arms grew heavier with each blow and counterblow. He drew on every training day he had ever taken part in. Parrying and thrusting, stepping and spinning, feigning and slashing in an attempt to throw the beast off its guard. He caught Giddy out of the corner of his eye, realizing instantly that she was in danger. Turning away his beast's sword he spun and darted toward her. With all his desire he reached out his sword, it rang as it contacted the beast's weapon, only inches away from impaling his friend's stomach.

Giddy took the opportunity as the beast's sword was outside the zone where it could defend itself and drove her blade deep into its chest.

Deavon gasped for breath as the beast's hand thundered into his chest. He'd parried a blow from its sword, the beast taking the opportunity to snap its fist forward and drive it into him. Stumbling, he moved backward, the beast coming at him, raining blows with its vicious weapon. A lose rock slipped from under his foot, stumbling he landed on his back. He tried to rise as the beast came at him, its sword raised with both hands on the hilt, its eyes burning with hatred as it bellowed in triumph. With a deep breath it raised the sword a few inches more, preparing to drive it into Deavon's body. Deavon held his sword out, desperate to ward off the blow. Relief flooded him as blood erupted from the beast's chest, its face registering surprise as it looked down at the sword protruding from its chest, driven into its back, tearing its way through its organs before rupturing through its thick hide.

Deavon scrambled out of the way as the beast collapsed forward, twitched and then lay motionless. He turned to Aldan who stood with his hand wrapped in his tunic, a smile spreading across his white, drawn face.

Giddy wrenched her sword free of the beast. "Watch out!" she called, reaching out to shove Raim aside. Too late, the remaining beast's sword sliced through Raim's upper right arm, blood rushed from the wound as Raim spun around in pain. Giddy drove forward. The beast's eyes widened in surprise as it saw the cold steel come from behind Raim's body. Slow to react, it screamed as Giddy's sword slipped neatly through its stomach. She stared at its face, her sweaty brow creasing as she pulled up and out with all her strength, ripping through the beast's entrails. With a low guttural moan, it collapsed to its knees. Giddy ran her razor sharp blade along its throat and lifted her leg. Placing her foot on its chest she shoved it over, its life gurgling away as it crashed to the bloodstained ground.

"Raim," Giddy spun, rushing to her friend. He sat on his knees, trying to stem the blood that gushed from his wound. "How bad is it?" she asked.

Raim's waxen face looked up at her, a dreamy smile across his lips. "It's just a scratch," he declared as he grimaced and collapsed to the ground.

Deavon smiled tiredly at his friend and then gestured to his hand. "How is it? Bad?"

"Yeah, pretty bad," Aldan replied. "I lost three fingers."

"And a lot of blood," Deavon suggested. Reaching out, he placed his hand around the ranger's shoulders. "Naisa, what can you do?" he asked as they walked toward the mages.

Naisa and Tean worked on Aldan and Raim's wounds, Deavon and Elddyn set about stoking up the fire. Finding some water that didn't seem fetid, they set it to boil in the crude pots left by the mage and his beasts.

"Get them settled," Deavon said to Naisa. "I'll be back when I've found Tesania and Kailyn."

Giddy stood, "I'm coming too."

"No," Deavon insisted. "There's two more beasts somewhere." He motioned to Raim and Aldan. "We can't leave them unprotected. I'll go alone."

"Where?" Aldan asked, wincing as Naisa washed his bloodied hand with hot water. "There's only the ledge as far as we know of." He pointed at the scar on the rock face. "And it's gone where they fell, so you won't be able to get back that way."

"There has to be a way," Deavon replied as he worriedly scanned the far side of the chasm. I can't just leave her here."

"We didn't see any other passages anyway," Elddyn offered.

"I know that!" Deavon snapped. He glared at the mage and then walked off toward the chasm. At the edge he peered into the darkness. "Tesania, Kailyn, can you hear me?"

His voice echoed down the black shaft of rocks. He waited, hoping with all his being to hear a reply. When none came, a tear quivered in the corner of his eye. "Tesania, what have I done to you?" he groaned.

44 PAINFUL DECISIONS

Deavon walked slowly back to the others, his mind in turmoil. *I failed her. She relied on me to get her safely through this, and I failed.*

"Any sign of them?" Giddy asked cautiously as she supported Raim's head in her lap.

A slight shake of his head was all that Deavon could muster. He didn't trust himself to speak. Snatching up his pack he pulled a torch from it and stuffed it angrily into the fire. He stood staring as the flame caught quickly to the oiled cloth then without looking at the others he walked toward the pile of rocks that the beasts had used as a shield.

"I'll go with him," Tean said as he stood and started to follow.

Elddyn snatched at his arm, pulling him up short. "Leave him be. He has to work through this himself."

Tean watched Deavon disappear behind the rocks, his torch throwing flickering light on the stark cave walls. "He suffers badly."

"We all know how he felt about Tesania," Giddy said. "Losing her must be devastating to him."

"What of the mission?" Raim groaned; his arm now bandaged.

"No idea," Giddy shrugged. "The sword's gone. Even if we had it still, Tes was the only one who could wield it against Trannyth."

"True enough," Raim adjusted himself on the ground, grimacing as pain shot through his nerves. "Can we achieve anything if we go on?"

Giddy glanced at the collapsed ledge. A piece, some twenty feet long, had fallen with Tesania and Kailyn. "Well, we can't go back that way." Gently she raised Raim's head and replaced her leg with a rolled up blanket. "And the Orash Pass is blocked by Trannyth." She stood and stretched her tired muscles. "I don't think we have a lot of choice." Peering across the cave, she started toward the rock pile. "I'm going after Deavon. There's two other beasts; somewhere."

~

Deavon walked along the far wall of the cathedral cave. He dragged his hand along the wall, desperate to find another entrance where he could gain the lower levels of the chasm and find Tes. He started when Giddy called to him. Turning, he waited for her to catch up. "I have to find her, Giddy. I can't leave her down there." His voice broke as he talked, tears welling in his eyes as he pointed at the blackness of the chasm.

Giddy stood silently while Deavon wiped at his tears, aware that she could say nothing to console him. After a few minutes she reached out and took the torch. "Come on. Let's see if we can find some way down there."

They covered the ground to the chasm in a few minutes. No fissures or passages presented themselves in the wall. Standing at the edge of the chasm, Giddy held the torch out. The light managed to push the blackness away for a few feet, but couldn't penetrate the darkness.

"Tesania!" Deavon called. "Kailyn!"

Giddy whistled as loudly as she could.

Silence answered them, silence and darkness.

"She's gone," Deavon whispered; his voice barely audible.

Giddy picked up a loose stone and tossed it over the edge. They waited for the stone to hit the bottom. The sound never came.

"If only I had protected you!" Deavon screamed into the darkness. "I should never have let you come on this damn mission." He looked at Giddy, his eyes wild. "What were the generals thinking, sending a defenseless girl into," he turned back to the chasm, "into this?"

"She knew the danger," Giddy answered quietly. "I don't think you could have stopped her from coming."

"And now she's dead."

Giddy placed her arm around his shoulder. "Come on, let's go back to the others."

Deavon allowed her to lead him back, lacking the will to do anything else.

"Did you find anything?" Naisa asked as Deavon sat down and stared blankly at the fire.

Giddy shook her head. "Nothing. The cave's sealed. No other passages lead off it."

"Can we climb down?" Raim asked.

Giddy grinned. "You won't be climbing anywhere, mister."

"Can you climb down then?" Raim sighed.

"No," Giddy answered seriously. "We threw a stone in, it didn't hit the bottom."

Raim looked at Deavon before asking quietly, "So they're gone?"

"It looks that way," Giddy replied somberly.

"So... What now?"

"We go on!" Deavon's eyes flickered in the firelight. "I won't let Tesania's death be in vain."

"What can we achieve now?" Elddyn enquired. "We have two cripples and the sword is gone."

"I have my sword hand; I'm no cripple," Aldan growled.

"You aren't fully fit either."

"I can do what I have to do."

"What about Raim?" Elddyn motioned. "He can't fight, not with that wound."

"It will heal," Aldan countered. "We have days, even weeks before we can even get close to Trannyth's Keep."

"How's your arm?" Deavon asked, shaking his head as he came out of his daze.

"It'll heal," The little soldier replied. "I have full feeling, so apart from a scar, it'll be fine."

"Might make you look manlier to the girls," Giddy teased.

Raim rolled his eyes. "That's all I need. I have to fight them off already."

Giddy choked on her laugh. "Fight them off?"

"And your hand?' Deavon asked Aldan.

"Three fingers gone, I'm afraid," the big man answered; his face still white. "Luckily I still have my thumb and forefinger so the hand will be of some use."

"I stitched the skin over as best I could," Naisa explained to Deavon. "As long as it's kept clean it should heal in a few weeks."

Deavon looked around the cave, the bodies of the beasts and Trannyth's mage lay scattered across the floor. "We can't stay here," he said. "The other two beasts could return at any time."

"Where do you think they are?" Aldan asked.

"I have no idea," Deavon shrugged. "They could be out getting firewood, or even have returned to the keep. Either way, we need to keep our wits about us."

"So that's it?" Elddyn asked in disgust. "You decide we continue this foolhardy mission, even though the girl is dead. And you expect us to just follow?"

"Careful," Giddy growled.

"It's ok, Giddy," Deavon said, reaching out and touched her hand. "He has a point." Standing, he walked to the mage. "What would you have us do?"

"We need to go back to Wyvern City."

"For what?"

"We can't face Trannyth as we are. Surely you can see that?" Elddyn looked at Deavon incredulously.

"Why not?" Deavon's anger grew as he stared the mage down. "You could use some of your precious forbidden magic."

"I used that in defense," Elddyn blustered. "He was going to cast a spell at us."

"That makes you as bad as Trannyth," Deavon accused. "The King has specifically outlawed its use."

"Sometimes the King doesn't know what's best!"

"You dare stand here and accuse the King of infirmness?"

"Bah, I didn't say he was stupid, I said he doesn't always see what is best. He's lead around by those imbecile advisors."

"Elddyn," Naisa interrupted. "You know full well why that type of magic is forbidden. It corrupts and leads its user down the dark path."

"I think he's just afraid," Giddy goaded. "He knows Trannyth is better and would best him in the simplest of battles."

Elddyn glared at her. "You don't know what Trannyth is capable of," he spat. "Trust me, if you did, you would be running back to Wyvern City as we speak."

"I'm not a coward," Giddy laughed. "Like you!"

Deavon held a hand up. "Enough." Turning in a circle he took in the remaining seven travelers. "We have no real choice. The way back over the mountains is blocked."

"We could find a way," Elddyn claimed.

"We go on to Trannyth's keep," Deavon announced with finality. "Who is with me?"

Giddy nodded as she grinned at Elddyn.

Raim felt his shoulder and answered, "Yes."

"Aldan?"

"Yes, I think we should go on. It may be the only chance Eldanal has."

"I too think the mission is too important to abandon," Naisa added.

"My Lord assures me that my role is at your side," Tean said. "I will go where you go."

"Well, it doesn't look like I have any choice then, does it!" Elddyn exploded.

"You can stay here and rot with these beasts for all I care," Giddy commented. "We would probably have more chance without you anyway."

"So.., what!? You're just going to waltz up to the Keep and knock on the door?" Elddyn scoffed. "Excuse me; we're here to kill Trannyth, would you be kind enough to let us in?"

"We didn't know how we were going to get in anyway," Deavon cut in. "Even when Te.., Tesania was with us."

"The mission hasn't changed," Aldan murmured. "It will just be harder now."

"You fools. You know as well as I that the sword was the only thing that could defeat Trannyth."

"Wrong!" Deavon shouted angrily. "The sword could break the orb, Trannyth is flesh and blood."

"But he..."

"Enough! We go on. Are you with us or not?" Deavon asked, glaring at the mage.

"It appears I have little choice," Elddyn responded, his voice seething.

"It's settled then," Deavon looked at the two wounded men. "Can you travel? It won't be far. I don't want to get caught in these caves if those beasts return."

"Agreed," Aldan said, grimacing as he used his good hand to rise. "This place stinks of beasts anyway."

The passage from the Owara caves was short. Deavon covered his eyes and looked away from the morning sun. "We'd better get moving. I want to be far away from these caves by nightfall."

They managed to make it off the mountain side and move a few miles inland before Deavon called a halt. Raim sank gratefully to the ground as the others set about making camp. Aldan insisted on helping, Naisa's potions having dulled the throbbing pain.

Deavon sat watch throughout the night, deciding to let the others sleep through. He couldn't bear the thought of sleep anyway. His mind went over the events in the caves. Time and again he watched Tesania disappear into the blackness. Gripping his head, he rocked back and forth, staring into the inky night.

Breakfast was basic, a gruel made by Tean over the softly glowing embers. Deavon decided to only move a few miles during the day. They moved northward, away from the mountains. Tean insisted that coming at the Keep from the north-east would help them avoid detection and be more sensible than following the line of the mountains.

Giddy supported Raim as they walked. The conversation was sparse as they all cast thoughts back to the fate of the friends they had lost. The trees of the mountain forests thinned, eventually giving way to sparse rocky plains. A small stream ran through the last stand of trees before gurgling down a crevice and disappearing into the depths of the earth. Deavon called a halt. "We'll rest here tomorrow. I'm sorry," he said turning to Raim and Aldan. "That's the best I can do. We need to move on."

"Raim's tough," Giddy quipped. "It won't be a problem."

A light cough came from behind her.

"Oh, and Aldan is too," she beamed at the ranger.

Deavon slept through the night while Giddy and the others shared the watch. The next day he walked back into the trees, sitting for most of the day against a huge old gnarled tree. Wishing he could see Tesania once more.

Naisa washed Raim and Aldan's wounds down, ensuring they were kept clean. Tean ranged out in search of food, managing to dig some bulbous roots from the compacted ground. Boiled and mashed with some of the herbs he had found, it made a bland, but enjoyable meal.

Deavon appeared from the trees at dusk. Refusing food, he sat at the far side of the camp. The sour look on his face kept the others from approaching him for some time. Giddy eventually stood and walked in his direction. "She was some kind of girl."

Deavon stared at the ground, breaking small pieces off the twig he was holding and throwing them at his feet. "Yes," was all he could manage.

"We all miss her," Giddy said soothingly. "And Kailyn."

"I know, Giddy," Deavon said softly. "I should never have let her come out here. She should be at home, with Lady Ayana, with Kailyn brushing her hair. Laughing and thinking about what to wear to the next ball." He banged his head back against the tree, looking into the night sky. "Not crawling through some god forsaken cave in the middle of nowhere."

"It was where she wanted to be," Giddy assured him, touching his arm. "With you, wherever you went."

"I should never have taken her to the King. I should have made her stay in Lyiera or Rilmir. She could have made a life for herself there."

"I can't see Tesania sitting around while the beasts still roamed Eldanal. Not while she knew she had that sword."

"I know she wouldn't, Giddy. That's one of the things I liked about her."

"You did what you could," she squeezed his hand. "You couldn't have known that ledge would collapse." She stood. "Just know that we all miss her, and we know how much she meant to you."

A weary smile crossed Deavon's face. "Thanks, Giddy."

He moved the group deeper into the wastelands the next day. They camped in the shadow of some strange rock formations, fifty feet across, shaped almost like chimneys.

Tean advised them that they would have been formed centuries, maybe thousands of years in the past when the molten centre of the earth had pushed its way through the soil. Destroying the vegetation that it encountered, leaving what they saw now; desolate rocky plains. "We can only imagine the heat," he said, shaking his head.

The night was restless for all of the travelers. Aldan was running a fever and moaned throughout the early hours. The wind swept through the valleys between the rock formations, whistling as it plucked at their blankets and clothes.

Tiredly, they set off. Turning west and heading for the Waltiln River and Trannyth's keep, some four days walk away.

45 GENERAL PERCEPTIONS

General Legana sat impatiently outside the King's stateroom. He had been summonsed earlier in the morning by a page from the King's household, delivering a short note. "Finally," he mumbled as a man informed him that the King was ready to see him.

"What news of Deavon and his party?" The King asked immediately after the General sat down.

"None, I'm afraid."

The King frowned. "When was the last you heard anything about them?"

"We know they picked Elddyn up from Carella; after that, nothing."

"If they crossed the mountains at the Draon pass," The king looked at the ceiling, calculating. "Even allowing for delays, they should have made their attack by now, surely?"

"I would think so,' the general agreed. "If they got through."

"You doubt they can get the job done?" the King asked, his eyebrow raised.

"If anyone can manage it, it would be Deavon and Aldan. But it's a big undertaking."

The King nodded. "You have your people in place?"

"Yes, three companies of rangers are camped at the foot of the Orash Pass. General Ardel has a similar number of his soldiers converging on the Draon Pass as we speak. None of Trannyth's people will get through."

"Very good. What of the beasts?"

"They appear to have retreated back over the mountains. The attacks on villages have all but stopped. The last reported one was two weeks ago."

The King pondered his words. "I wonder what Trannyth's up too?"

"Possibly gathering the beasts for a mass attack on our cities."

The King drew a quick breath. "That must not come to pass. I don't care how you do it; just make sure it never happens."

"I will do my best, as always," the general bowed as he rose. "Now that we know that the beasts are on the other side of the mountain I will dispatch the entire Ranger force to the blockade."

"Indeed," The King replied. "And pray that Deavon and the girl succeed."

46 TRANNYTH'S ARMY

"When will the last beasts arrive?" Trannyth asked his mage dryly.

"They are coming in daily, My Lord. I would expect the last ones to arrive in a few days."

Trannyth walked to the window, his long robes making it appear that he was gliding. "Very well. I want them placed under their generals as soon as they arrive."

"The Generals are waiting for the stragglers, but training has already commenced for the ones that have arrived."

"I am trusting you to make sure they are ready to leave in two weeks time," Trannyth commanded. "Do you understand?"

"Yes, My Lord." The mage bowed low, sure of what would become of him if he failed.

"It is time the King of Eldanal," Trannyth growled, "learned his place."

"My Lord."

Trannyth turned on his heel. "Have the generals summoned to a meeting in the morning. Instruct them to make plans to take Carella, Orash and Wyvern cities immediately."

"Yes, My Lord."

"From there they are to make plans to take Rilmir and the smaller towns."

"Yes, My Lord. And the people of the cities and towns; what of them?"

"Kill them!" Trannyth spun on the mage. "I should think I don't need to explain this to you."

"No, My Lord. I shall instruct them to kill all of the people of Eldanal."

"Not all, you fool," Trannyth raged. "I want to rule them, bend them to my will."

"Yes, My Lord. So don't kill them all?" the mage asked in confusion.

Trannyth's rage emanated from beneath his cowl. "Imbecile. Kill all the soldiers and rangers. Keep the women alive, we shall want them for breeding."

"Yes, My Lord," the mage backed toward the door, anxious to be away from the raging mage in front of him. "And the children?"

"Kill them, all of them," Trannyth stormed. "And make sure the King and Queen are unharmed," Trannyth ordered. "He will grovel at my feet. She will have the pleasure of being the first I bend to my will."

"I shall instruct them of this in the morning." With one last bow he turned and fled.

47 DARKNESS

Inky blackness filled every crack in the chasm. A groan echoed off the walls. Tesania dragged herself gingerly into a sitting position, her body protesting, sending shafts of pain needling their way along her nerves, demanding her brain desist from any thought of movement. "Kailyn?" she whispered into the darkness.

"What happened?" Kailyn groaned.

"The ledge collapsed. Are you alright?"

"No."

"What's wrong?" Tes asked her voice filled with concern.

"I think I've broken my arm."

Tesania managed to roll onto her knees and started crawling toward Kailyn's voice. "I'm coming over," she said, cautiously feeling her way along the rock floor. "Don't move. We don't know where we are."

"I don't think I could."

"Do you think you'll be able to walk?" Tes heard Kailyn shuffling her legs as she tested them.

"Yes," she replied. "Where are the others?"

"I have no idea," Tes answered. "I think they made it across. I hope so anyway."

"Do you think they'll come and get us?"

"They have the beasts and that mage to kill first," Tes replied as her hand bumped against Kailyn's leg. "Then they'll come looking for us."

"How far do you think we fell?"

"I lost my bearings when everything went black. It seemed like we slid forever."

"I can't see a thing," Kailyn complained.

"No," Tes agreed, looking forlornly toward the heavens. "We're a long way down the chasm. I can't even see the flames from the beasts' fire."

"Fire!" Kailyn exclaimed. "Have you still got your pack?"

"Yes," Tes replied, reaching behind her, groaning at the pain as she slung the pack off her back. "Why?"

"Get one of those torches out. I can light it." Kailyn instructed excitedly.

Tes untied her pack and pulled one of the oil soaked torches out before guiding it into Kailyn's hand.

"I can't hold it," Kailyn groaned. "My arm hurts too much."

"I'll hold it," Tes suggested. "You light it."

Kailyn reached out with her good arm, tentatively feeling for the torch in Tesania's hand. "Hold it still," she said.

Tes heard her mumbling, jumping when the torch burst to life. She immediately held it up so she could see her friend. Blood ran from multiple wounds from when the rock ledge had exploded against the sloping wall of the chasm. Yellowish blue bruising worked its way from her forehead, down the left side of her face to her chin. "You look frightful," Tes announced.

"You don't look too good yourself." Kailyn drew a sharp breath, spasms of pain racing along her broken arm causing her to cringe in agony.

"Show me your arm," Tes demanded as she crawled to the far side of the young girl and handed the torch to her. "Here, hold this."

As Kailyn reached out her good arm to take the torch. Tes dragged her pack over and quickly found what she was after, pulling an old tunic out. Rummaging deeper, she found her father's knife and cut away at the material on the back of her pack. The stitching came apart, revealing a length of wood that strengthened the back of the pack. "This might hurt a little," she warned Kailyn as she tore the tunic in two and then cut a small piece off, folding it into a small square. "Ok, bite on this."

Tes inspected Kailyn's arm. "I'm no expert," she warned. "But I don't think it is broken; sprained maybe."

"Is that good?" Kailyn asked, wincing in pain.

"It's better than broken," Tes laughed lightly. "I'll bandage this piece of wood on to keep it still."

Kailyn grimaced as Tes worked, eventually asking through clenched teeth, "How are we going to get back to the others?"

Tesania tied the last knot, not answering the question. "There. Try to keep it still." Standing she took the torch from Kailyn and walked to the edge of the ledge they had landed on. Straining, she managed to make out the far wall. Below her feet the light ended in more darkness. Leaning back, she peered into the darkness above. No movement or light showed in the blackness. "We must have fallen a long way," she said. "I can't even see the beasts' fire reflecting off the walls."

"I hope the others are ok," Kailyn said. "Maybe they killed the beasts and put the fire out."

Tes' thoughts turned for the first time to Deavon and the others and their plight against the beasts in the cave.

"They'll be alright," she half whispered, doubt clenching at her stomach as she spoke.

"They'll come and get us. Won't they?"

"If they can," Tes turned back to her, determined to drive the worrying thoughts from her mind. "Can you stand?"

"I think so." Kailyn moved her feet under herself, using her uninjured hand she reached up to Tes and pulled herself up with her friends help. "Oh," she said, closing her eyes, "I feel a little dizzy."

Tes supported her. "Take it easy, you'll be ok in a second." She looked around the bleak walls while Kailyn regained her balance. "The ledge seems to lead down that way," she gestured. "Maybe we can find a way back up there."

"I think I can walk now," Kailyn declared, pushing herself away from Tes and swaying a little. She blinked her eyes and shook her head, groaning as a headache manifested instantly. "I shouldn't have done that," she whispered miserably.

"Well, we can't just stay here," Tes said. "You stay here; I'll have a look."

"No!" Kailyn reached out, stopping her. "I want to stay together. I couldn't bear to be separated from you as well."

"Ok, come on then. Let's walk, slowly."

Together they crept along the ledge. Tes tested every footstep, mindful of the risk of this ledge collapsing from under them as well. The ash colored walls of the chasm were rough, large bulges jutted out, causing them to have to pass right on the edge of the ledge. They covered a hundred feet before a dark crack appeared in the torchlight on the wall ahead.

"What's that?" Kailyn asked.

"It looks like a passage," Tes answered hopefully. Her spirits lifting, she smiled at Kailyn. "We might be able to get back to the top."

Their pace quickened. Tes' heart beat quickly as they reached the crack. She reached forward with the torch, pushing it into the darkness. A small passage presented itself in the light. Tes looked at her friend, grinning.

"Do you think it leads back to the others?"

"Only one way to find out," Tes replied, excitement in her voice as her hopes lifted. She led the way, Kailyn following closely behind. The fire from her torch spluttered and danced, bouncing off the nearby walls. They walked on, at times having to climb over rock falls or crawl through places where the cave grew smaller. Tes slowed down to let Kailyn keep up, often turning to help her through particularly tough parts of the passage, mindful of her damaged arm.

Stopping for a brief rest after a few hours, they ate a meager amount of food from their packs. Tes insisted they move on, wanting to find the others as quickly as possible. The passage slowly inclined upward as they walked, making Kailyn's complaints come more frequently. "Can't we rest? My arm's aching and I have a headache."

"I know, Kailyn," Tes turned her head to answer. "I'm sorry. We can stop soon. I promise." She pressed on for another mile, feeling guilty for making her friend suffer. The passage widened out while they walked, eventually giving way to a cavern with a little stream crossing their path before disappearing over the edge of the floor and crashing into the depths of another crevice.

"Can we rest?" Kailyn mumbled as she sank to sit on a loose rock on the floor. "My head is throbbing," she complained. "I can't go on."

"Sorry," Tes apologized. "I know I'm pushing you. I just want to get out of here as quickly as we can."

"I do too," Kailyn assured her tiredly. "It's just my arm and my head."

"It's ok Kailyn. I understand," Tes said as she untied her water skin. "Give me your skin too. I'll fill it up."

Tes dropped her pack and unbuckled her sword, placing them on the rocky ground near the stream. Washing her hands and face, she leaned forward to take a drink. "Mm, Kailyn, this water is so cool and sweet. Come over and wash your face. You'll feel much better."

Kailyn groaned as she rose and walked slowly toward Tes.

"Here," Tes said, handing Kailyn's water skin to her, "use that. Then I'll fill it up again for you."

"Thanks," Kailyn smiled as she tipped her head back, pouring the cool water over her face. Handing the skin back, she ran her hand gingerly over her face. "That's lovely and cool." Turning, she started back for her rock, propping as a movement caught her eye. "What's that?"

"What?" Tes asked, looking up from the stream.

"I saw a light, coming down the passage. There it is again."

Tes stood and peered toward the far end of the cave. Small flickers of orange danced on the white walls. "It's the others," she exclaimed excitedly. "I told you they'd come for us."

They both walked toward the passage at the far side of the cave. The light grew more intense as the others drew closer to their cave. "Deavon, we're here," Tes, unable to control herself, called out.

The torch came into view, followed by a black sinuous arm. Tes stopped dead in her tracks, grabbing Kailyn's arm as she did so. "Beasts," she hissed.

The beast burst into the opening of the cave, drawing its sword and snarling as it swept the area with its ferocious eyes. It screamed a reverberating roar as it saw the two girls standing frozen then broke into a lumbering run; spittle flying as it came charging toward them.

"Get back!" Tes screamed as she shoved Kailyn behind her and snatched for her sword. Her hand found empty air. Desperately she looked back to her pack where the sword sat on the ground. The beast was almost upon them. "Run, Kailyn," Tes called frantically. "I have to get my sword." They ran side by side, the beast gaining, its feet slapping against the white, stone floor. "Hurry," Tes yelled, pulling at Kailyn's arm.

Tes reached her pack, sliding to a halt she snatched up her sword and wrenched it free of its sheath. The beast reached them as the blade slid clear, slapping at Tes' sword, knocking it from her grip. It clattered across the rock, balancing on the edge of the crevasse. Tes dove for it, her hand brushing against the pommel as it toppled over the side.

Kailyn sat cringing, sobbing, with her head buried in her hands.

Tes crawled toward her, her eyes never leaving the beast as it stared triumphantly at them, its chest rising and falling as it drew deep breaths. "I won't let you harm her," Tes whispered. Slowly she rose to her feet and stepped in front of the frightened girl. Raising the sword sheath that she still held in her hand, she took one of the defensive stances Giddy had taught her. "If you want her," she growled defiantly. "You will have to go through me."

The beast threw its torch on the ground and grinned at Tes, Its teeth dripping saliva, its eyes boring into her. Stepping closer, it raised its sword in the air. "You die bravely," its guttural voice said. A growl started from the pit of its stomach, building into a ferocious roar as it burst forward.

Tes braced herself as the beast came at her, ready to block its opening attack. She shook, knowing she had no way to defeat it. "I'm sorry Kailyn," she whispered, a tear running down her cheek.

The beast jerked its arm back a few more inches, Tes braced to take the blow. Not concentrating on the beast's sword, but watching the centre of its body as Giddy had instructed her. Her eyes grew wide as blood ruptured from the beast's lower chest, the point of a sword slicing into view.

The beast's eyes flew open, pain wracking its face. The sword in its body ripped downward and then withdrew.

Tesania watched incredulously, jumping aside quickly as the beast lurched forward and crashed to the ground. Her eyes whipped to the semi darkness behind where the beast had stood, her heart jerking as she saw another standing in its place. "No," she screamed, throwing her scabbard into the air once more to defend Kailyn.

The beast stumbled backward, raising its hand in placation. "No kill," it said slowly.

Tes stepped backwards, reaching down she tapped Kailyn, motioning for her to move back.

The beast reached a large boulder that sat in the middle of the floor. Tes could only see a silhouette of its body and its eyes reflecting in the firelight. Slowly, it sank to the ground and sat with its back against the boulder, laying its sword aside.

"Stand up," Tes ordered Kailyn, reaching down and pulling on her shoulder.

"What happened?" Kailyn asked. "Did that beast just kill its friend?"

"Stay where you are," Tes called out to the beast. "Don't come near us."

The beast's eyes stared back at her; it said nothing.

"What can we do?" Kailyn asked frantically. "It can kill us if it wants."

"I don't think it wants to," Tes replied, confusion playing across her face. "It killed its friend and then sat down without attacking us."

They moved into the darkness on the far side of the torch to the beast and sat down. "What should we do?" Kailyn asked.

"I have no idea," Tes answered honestly. "We can't sit here forever, so I guess we should talk to it."

"Talk to a beast?" Kailyn gasped.

"Well it just talked to us," Tes answered defensively. "So obviously it can."

"You can," Kailyn whispered. "I don't want to. It's hideous."

Tes sat in the seemingly safe darkness in thought. Eventually she called out, "Why?"

The beast didn't answer. "Maybe it didn't understand you," Kailyn suggested. "Ask it another question."

"Why did you kill your friend?" Tes tried again.

The beast's guttural voice didn't answer for some time. Tes was about to try again when it said, "Not friend."

"I don't understand."

"He controlled by man-things. Eat meat, kill. Kragh not like."

"Kragh?" Kailyn whispered to Tes.

Tes ignored her. "Kragh," she tried to pronounce the guttural name. "Is that your name?"

"Man-things say me Kragh."

"My name is Tesania, and my friend is Kailyn," Tes called out.

"Why are you telling a beast our names?" Kailyn whispered urgently.

"Shh," Tes hissed as Kragh's attempt at saying her name drifted out of the darkness. "It's ok, you can call me Tes."

"Tes," Kragh tried, the sound like gravel pouring down a washing board.

"I don't understand..., Kragh," Tes tried again. "Why did you kill the other beast?"

"Man-things make Kragh..," he paused, when he continued, sadness filled his voice. "Monster."

Tes stood and walked slowly toward the torch that lay on the floor. Gently, she asked, "What happened to you..?"

"Man-things, take Kragh, females to caves." A guttural sigh echoed in the cave. "Make, this."

Tes carefully crouched, picking up the torch. She stood and stepped closer to the beast. His face emerged from the shadows as she approached. Her mind screamed at her that this was a vicious beast, but her heart melted as she saw a tear in the corner of Kragh's eye. Setting the torch down, she sat on the far side. "And your females? Where are they now?"

Kragh shrugged, "Not know."

"You poor thing," Tesania heard herself say.

"He's a beast!" Kailyn exclaimed from behind her.

"I know," Tes turned defensively. "He didn't ask to be!"

"But, still," Kailyn insisted. "He is a beast."

"He saved our lives," Tes said angrily. "He killed another beast to save us. What more proof do you need that he's telling the truth?"

"Beasts killed your parents.., your whole village."

"Don't you think I know that?" Tes almost screamed. "I was there, remember."

"I'm just saying…"

"It doesn't matter, Kailyn," Tesania said, trying to control her emotions. "What matters is he saved us now."

"Ok," Kailyn said grumpily. "I just don't think we should trust him."

"We don't have much choice," Tes insisted. "Now come over and sit here where he can see you."

Kailyn reluctantly rose and walked toward them. She sat behind Tes, slightly to her right where she could see Kragh, quickly turning her face away when she saw his vicious, yellow tusks curling past his nose.

"I'm sorry Trannyth did this to you," Tes said gently.

Kragh stiffened. "Trannyth," he grunted twisting his hands together. "Kragh Kill."

"You want to kill Trannyth?" Kailyn's head flicked back to the beast in surprise.

Kragh nodded. "Kill Trannyth, save other from..," he raised his hand, indicating his grotesque face. "This!" he roared.

Tes stood and walked to the boulder where Kragh sat. Squatting down, she reached tentatively forward and placed her hand on his arm. "I understand," she whispered. "Trannyth is hurting my people too. We are on our way to destroy him."

"Tesania!" Kailyn gasped. "You shouldn't tell him that!"

"Why not? His friends are being used and killed, just like ours. Why shouldn't I tell him that others care as much as he does?"

"I guess," Kailyn answered sulkily. "Just be careful. We don't know him. He might betray us."

"We would already be dead if he wanted to do that."

"I know. Just be careful."

"Can you help us?" Tes asked Kragh. "Can you show us the way out of the caves?"

Kragh nodded.

Tes bent, picking up the torch. "Come on Kailyn, let's get our packs."

Kragh stood, walking to the dead beast, he cleaned his sword on its hide before sheathing it and walked to the other torch that had been discarded by his fellow beast.

Tes bent and retrieved her pack, reattaching her water skin then absentmindedly reattached her scabbard to her belt. "My sword," she gasped, the memory of it slipping over the edge of the crevasse flooding back to her. She moved to the stream, where it cascaded over the edge and held her torch out, peering down.

Kailyn approached the crevasse and knelt down. "What's that?" she asked.

Tes moved around and squinted in the direction Kailyn pointed. "I don't see anything."

"Move the torch around," Kailyn instructed. "I saw a reflection, down there, in the water."

Tes waved the torch around, pushing it forward and pulling it back. A small glint of reflection twinkled through the water and then disappeared just as quickly. "It must be my sword!" Tes said, her hopes rising.

"It must have caught on a ledge or something," Kailyn beamed, her teeth flashing in the torch light.

"But how are we going to get it?" she asked. "It's a long way down."

Kailyn shook her head. "Rope, maybe?"

"We don't have any," Tes sighed. "Giddy and Raim were carrying it."

"We could climb down."

"No," Tes said quickly. "It would be much too dangerous."

"Kragh could do it," Kailyn suggested.

The big beast arrived as she spoke and looked over the edge.

"Could you?" Tes asked him. "No," she shook her head. "I couldn't ask you to risk your life."

Kailyn looked up. The beast towered over her. "You could do it, couldn't y..?" She stopped abruptly. "I am such a ninny!" she grinned at Tes. "I could use my magic! Naisa's been teaching me how to summon things."

"Why didn't I think of that?" Tesania laughed. "Do you think you can do it?"

"I can try," Kailyn replied nervously. Closing her eyes, she drew a deep breath. "Yes, I can do it, I'm sure of it."

"Well, do it then," Tes said excitedly.

"What if I drop it?" Kailyn asked, her confidence sinking.

Tes turned to Kragh. "Do you think you could climb down there and get it?" she asked.

Kragh studied the sheer rock face, the sides slippery with moss and shook his head.

"We don't have a choice," Tes said to Kailyn. "I'm sure you can do it. You've been practicing a lot."

Kailyn touched her forefinger to her thumb and leaned over the edge. Concentrating her mind, she focused on the sword in the cascading water. Summoning it; channeling her thoughts through her clenched fingers. The sword didn't move. "I can't do it!"

"Yes you can," Tes assured her. "Remember what Naisa said. Desire it; want it with all your heart. Relax, clear your mind and try again."

Kailyn drew in a deep breath, closed her eyes and tried to relax. She focused her desire, closed her fingers and summoned it with all her being. She felt the sword move; it floated into the air then drifted slowly toward her hand. She could sense it was close, opening her eyes, she grinned; admonishing herself when the sword slipped back toward the crevasse. Quickly she regained her concentration, raising the sword the last few feet and directing it toward Tes.

Tes reached out and snatched the sword from the air. "You did it!" she exclaimed. "Kailyn, you're so wonderful."

Kailyn jumped up. "I can't believe it," she said, ignoring the pain in her arm as the two of them hugged and jumped in the air. "Naisa will be so proud."

Tes broke away from Kailyn at the mention of the mage. "We'd better get out of these caves and find them." Sheathing her sword, she picked up her pack. "Can you take us out now?" she asked Kragh.

Kragh led the way across the cavern and into the passage on the far side. Tes nudged Kailyn and nodded toward her sword. "It's not vibrating," she whispered. "I told you."

48 UNEXPECTED FRIENDSHIP

Kragh led them on for an interminable time. Tesania called him to stop as she threw her waning torch aside and held another out for Kailyn to light. "How much further?" she asked the beast.

"Far," Kragh grunted.

Kailyn groaned. Tes shrugged at her, pushing her forward. "We have to find the others."

They struggled on behind the seemingly tireless beast. A fork in the passage became evident in the flickering light, Kragh confidently veered to the left. Kailyn slowed noticeably as the march wore on. "Slow down please," Tes called to Kragh. "She's worn out." Kragh's idea of slow was not what Kailyn had in mind. Soon he disappeared ahead of them.

"Hurry up!" Tes pleaded with her friend. "I don't want to lose him." Tes peered anxiously into the gloom ahead of them, concerned that they may come to another fork. Without the beast's knowledge of the caves, they would certainly be lost again.

"I can't," Kailyn sighed, sinking to the ground and leaning against the cool rock wall.

Tes offered her water skin to the exhausted girl. "Have a drink." She looked worriedly ahead. "We can't stop long."

"He should have waited for us," Kailyn moaned defensively. "I told you we couldn't trust a beast."

"I don't think he's trying to lose us," Tes frowned.

"Not trying," Kailyn laughed nervously. "Has!"

"Come on," Tes said, dragging her to her feet. "We have to catch him."

The floor of the passage rose sharply, Kailyn stopped, grasping her arm. "I can't," she groaned. "I'm exhausted, and my arm is aching."

Tes helped her to sit. "You stay here," she suggested. "I'm going a little way ahead to see where he is."

Kailyn nodded tiredly as Tes walked away. Soon she was left in complete darkness.

Tesania struggled up the steep incline. It wasn't long before the floor flattened out; a few hundred feet more and Tes could see daylight ahead. Turning, she returned quickly to Kailyn.

Kailyn sat shivering. "Did you find him?" she asked through chattering teeth.

"Better," Tes grinned. "The cave exit isn't very far."

"How do you know?"

"I saw it, you ninny," Tes laughed. "I saw sunlight!"

"Sunlight," Kailyn sighed, a smile wandering across her face.

A short time later they stumbled into the shimmering light. Tes shielded her eyes, days of darkness making the light blinding. A few minutes later her eyes had adjusted enough to make out Kragh, standing with his back to them on the edge of a cliff.

"You could have waited for us!" Kailyn yelled at his back.

Kragh turned. "Kragh sl... slowe..." he tried to pronounce.

"Slowed down?" Tes offered.

The big beast nodded. "Man-things slo... slow."

Tes laughed. "Yes Kragh, we are slow. Please wait for us next time." She walked toward him. "How do we get down from here?" she asked, looking over the edge.

Kragh pointed toward the side of the ledge they were on. "Down."

"And where are our friends?" Tes asked.

The beast looked at her in confusion and shrugged.

"Our friends were trying to get past the..." Tes paused and looked back at Kailyn. Turning back to Kragh she continued. "My friends were trying to get past the beasts in a big cave."

Kragh pointed to the west. "Cave there. Beasts maybe kill friends."

"Don't say that," Kailyn groaned. "Deavon and Giddy would be able to kill them."

"Shh," Tes looked up at the beast. "We have to know. Can you take us there?"

Kragh nodded and started toward the path off the ledge.

"No! Not now," Tes called gently. "After we've had a rest."

"Kragh look cave," the beast suggested. "Not far. Find out."

Tes thought about it and nodded. "Ok. Please come back and let us know."

As Kragh headed off at a quick pace, Kailyn asked, "How can you trust him? He might bring all of them back here."

Tes looked at her friend forlornly. "I hope there are no beasts there. If there are I fear for the others' safety." She walked to Kailyn's side and sat down, draping her arm around her friend's shoulder. "I'm sure they're ok."

Kailyn's head shot around. "But if the others killed the beasts, and Kragh walks in, they'll kill him too!"

"You're right. We have to catch him!" Tes said urgently, pulling at Kailyn's good arm.

The two forgot their weariness as they careened down the narrow rock path that led to the foot of the mountains. Kragh was nowhere to be seen.

"This way," Tes called, setting off in the direction Kragh had pointed. Kailyn puffed along behind her, trying to keep up. "Kragh!" Tes called desperately as she saw the beast turning into some brambles in the distance. "Stop!"

Kragh turned toward them.

Tes pulled up gratefully next to the beast, bending over, a stitch clawing at her side. "If our friends are there," she breathed heavily. "They will kill you."

Kragh chortled and patted his sword. "Kragh, good fight."

"That's just it," Tesania growled at him. "I don't want you to fight them."

Understanding filled Kragh's eyes as he nodded.

"We have to go together," Kailyn announced.

"We can't," Tes said. "If the beasts are there, they'll kill us."

"But if Deavon, and the others are there," Kailyn pointed out.

"They will kill Kragh."

"Not if we tell them not to," Kailyn insisted.

Tes nodded. "True. But the fact remains that it might be the beasts up there. We can't risk it."

"Kragh, look," the beast announced.

"No," Tes said adamantly.

"Not go in," Kragh said. "Look." He crept toward a bush and peered around it to demonstrate.

"Ok," Tes replied with trepidation, a scowl crossed her face as she realized there was no other choice. "Kailyn and I will follow behind. If our friends are there they'll be certain to have a lookout posted," she told the beast. "If they see you, run back to us, we'll tell them that you saved us. Understand?"

Kragh nodded and headed straight for the brambles, disappearing quickly amongst the thick vegetation. Tes counted to twenty and then motioned Kailyn to follow behind.

The way was narrow and thick with brambles; the footing hazardous. Tes labored up the steep incline, straining as she pushed through the thick vegetation. Eventually she broke through into a small clearing. Stopping abruptly, she pushed Kailyn back into the cover of the brambles. Pulling a branch aside, she looked at the clearing. At the back was a dark crack in the rock face, a cave entrance. Kragh was nowhere to be seen.

"What is it?" Kailyn demanded from behind Tes.

"I can't see him," she replied. "He must have gone inside."

"What do we do now?" Kailyn asked, fear creeping into her voice. "He might bring the beasts after us."

"Nonsense," Tes snapped. "As I said before, if he wanted us dead, we would be. Now be quiet."

"I just think it's a little suspicious that he went straight into the cave," Kailyn sulked. "He must know the other beasts are still there."

"Shh," Tes held her hand up to quiet the girl. "Someone's coming out."

A beast came into the sunshine and walked toward them. Stopping a few feet away it waved at them to come closer. "Beasts dead," Kragh informed them as Tes and Kailyn crawled from the branches.

"What about our friends?" Tes asked, her heart racing, "Are they in there?"

Kragh shook his head. "Beasts and mage, dead."

Tes looked past him in confusion. "If the beasts are all dead, then our friends must be there."

"Kragh look. Friends no there."

Turning, Tes stared down the bushy pass they had just climbed through. "They wouldn't leave us. They must be down there," she said, pointing through the growth. "Waiting for us."

"I hope we find them soon," Kailyn groaned as she looked at the heavy vegetation. "I've had enough for today."

"I know Kailyn," Tes said, reaching out to touch her friend on the shoulder. "We have to at least go down and try to find them."

Kailyn nodded morosely. "But it's getting dark; we'll have to set camp soon anyway."

"Agreed," Tes smiled, happy to give Kailyn the thought of resting. "Let's get down there quickly," she said, setting off into the brambles once more.

The bushes opened onto grassy hills. "Deavon!" Tes called, "Giddy!" The twittering of a bird settling into its roost was the only answer she received. "They must be here somewhere," Tes said, worry contorting her face as she looked around the darkening trees.

"Maybe they moved a bit," Kailyn offered. "To get away from the cave entrance."

"Maybe," Tes conceded. "We'd better move away a little and set camp."

"Please," Kailyn begged.

"Water," Kragh pointed into the trees and lead off.

The camp was meager. With their bedding rolled out onto the grass, a small fire crackling and dancing, the two girls cooked their first hot meal in days. Kragh sat with his back against a tree, nibbling the juicy tips off the thriving bushes lining the creek bed.

Kailyn rummaged through her pack, withdrawing a bar of mildly smelling soap. Cautiously she walked toward Kragh. "Kragh," she almost whispered. "Could you wash, with this?" She held the soap out to him.

"Kailyn," Tes gasped.

"Well he stinks!" Kailyn spun on her friend. "I can't stand it, not if we're going to travel with him."

Kragh sniffed at the soap in her hand then looked up at Kailyn. "Kragh not hungry."

"No," Kailyn said quickly. "It's soap, to wash with." Walking toward the water, she moved her hand over her body.

Kragh shook his head in confusion.

Tes stepped toward Kailyn and took the soap off her. "I'm sorry Kragh," she said. "What Kailyn..," She glared back at the girl, "is trying to say; is that you're a little..," she looked into the trees, trying to think of a word. "Smelly."

"Sme-ll-y," Kragh tried to pronounce.

"Yes." Tes glared at Kailyn again. Turning back to Kragh, she pointed at him and then held her nose, screwing her face in disgust as she did.

Kragh snuffled the air, then his arm, and shrugged.

"It would help us a lot," Tes continued, "if you.., wash." she repeated the motions that Kailyn had performed earlier. "In the water..," she pointed, "with the soap." She held it out to him.

Kragh grunted and climbed to his feet. Reaching out, he took the soap and smelled it suspiciously. Looking at Kailyn he made the motions of washing.

"Yes," Kailyn said excitedly. "In the water." She pointed.

Kragh walked past her, stood at the edge of the pool and looked back at the two girls. "Wash?" he asked, stepping into the cool water as the girls nodded, yes.

Kailyn started to giggle; Tes grabbed her, dragging her away.

~

Tes woke early the next morning and started to cook breakfast. She let Kailyn sleep, aware that the girl had been driven to exhaustion the previous day. Kragh had stayed awake during the night, keeping watch over his new friends. He slept now, faint, reverberating snores issuing from his lips.

"Where are you," Tes whispered into the distance, wondering where Deavon and the others could be. "I know you wouldn't leave me to die." Shaking her head, she turned her attention back to the fire.

Kailyn dragged herself out of bed and ate sparingly as Tes packed their things and prepared to leave. Kragh woke after an hour of sleep, springing lightly to his feet. "Good morning, Kragh," Kailyn said.

Kragh grunted, walked to the creek and took a long drink.

"We need to find the others," Tes said.

"We have no idea which way they are," Kailyn turned slowly, looking in every direction. "They could be anywhere."

"I know that," Tes snapped. "Sorry," she said, abashed. "I just can't believe they didn't wait for us."

"Maybe they're looking for us?"

"They can't be Kailyn," Tes said irritably. "We fell down the chasm."

"So?"

"So," Tes sighed. "If they were looking for us, they would still be in the caves. Don't you think?" she asked, eyebrow raised.

"So they think we're dead?" Kailyn's eyes grew wide in disbelief.

"We did fall a long way down a chasm," Tes said sadly. "I suppose they would think we're dead."

"I guess," Kailyn mumbled. "What's that mean then?" she asked.

"It means we go on alone." Tes advised her. "We have to get to Trannyth."

"We can't do that alone," Kailyn gasped. "It would be suicide."

"We need to head toward the Keep. We can only hope to find the others along the way."

"What're we going to do when we get there?" Kailyn asked, still in shock that Tes would consider going on without the others.

"I don't know, Kailyn," Tes yelled angrily. "We didn't know what we were going to do, even when Deavon and the others were with us." Calming herself, she walked to the sulking girl. "I didn't mean to yell at you," she apologized. "But I'm not going to wander about here for days when the others might already be halfway to Trannyth."

"You think they're still going after Trannyth?"

"I don't think Deavon would give up, if that's what you're asking."

"But they don't have the sword..." Kailyn paused. "Or you."

"Deavon will still try to kill Trannyth." Tes shook her head. "I know he will. Even if he might die doing it."

Kailyn nodded. "He's very brave."

"Stupidly so," Tes flared. "He should have stayed in Wyvern City."

"Like that was ever going to happen!"

Tes glared at her. "Get up; let's go," she muttered, suppressing a grin. "We might be lucky and catch them."

Turning, she spoke to Kragh. "Which direction is Trannyth?"

Kragh pointed.

"Which is the quickest way?"

Kragh's arm stayed in the same direction. "Water, food, trees."

Tesania pointed north. "And that way?"

"Rocks," Kragh replied simply.

"Ok. That way it is," she nodded along the foothills of the mountains. "Kailyn, Ready?"

Kailyn sighed and pulled herself to her feet. "If I have to be."

Kragh led Tesania and Kailyn along the lower hills of the mountains. For four days they had walked steadily, even Kailyn found the going easy on the soft, grassy ground. They camped near streams and creeks whenever they could, eating small portions of their supplies.

On the fourth afternoon, as they set camp, Kragh disappeared into the hills, returning some time later with a leg of meat, skinned and ready for the fire.

"What kind of meat is it?" Kailyn asked suspiciously.

Kragh looked at her from under his heavy brows.

"Never mind, I don't want to know," Kailyn shivered.

Tesania laughed. "Ninny, does it matter what it is?" She cut pieces from the bone and fried it in her pan, adding herbs from her pack.

Kailyn's stomach growled loudly as the aroma's drifted toward her. "I haven't eaten a proper meal for so long."

"Not since the other side of the caves," Tes agreed. "It seems such a long time ago." She slid portions onto some large leaves that Kailyn had collected and offered one to Kragh. He shook his head and looked away. Confused, Tes picked up the raw bone, offering it to him. Again he refused.

"Kragh eat leaves," he informed her.

"You don't eat meat?" Tes asked in surprise.

"Man-things make beasts eat meat," he growled. "Kragh not eat meat."

"They made you eat meat?" Tes was astounded. "I'm sorry, Kragh. I assumed you would eat it."

"Because this?" he flared, pointing at himself. "Tra-nn-y-th make this. Not Kragh!"

"I didn't mean to offend you," Tes assured him quickly. "So, you like to eat leaves and roots?"

Kragh nodded. "Before, Kragh eat," he pulled a tuft of grass from the ground, letting it fall from his fingers as he spoke, "This...," he snatched up a branch, "this." picking leaves from the end, he placed them in his mouth, chewing as he regarded Tes.

"You poor thing," Kailyn offered. "They made you eat something you hated. I couldn't bear it if someone did that to me."

"How do they make all the beasts eat meat?" Tes asked. "Surely others didn't like it either."

"Trannyth, here," he said pointing at his head. "Make do."

"So Trannyth controls their minds."

Kragh stared at her uncomprehending. Shaking his head he turned his attention to his leaves.

"How disgusting," Kailyn murmured. "They take innocent animals and turn them into something they don't want to be, and then.., and then, make them eat things.., and do things that they detest."

"That's why Trannyth has to be stopped," Tes spoke softly, picking at her meal. "That's why we're here."

Tesania ate slowly. Watching the beast as he gently picked leaves off his branch and placed them in his mouth.

"Can you help us get into Trannyth's Keep?" she eventually asked.

Kragh shook his head. "Kragh never go Keep. Kragh sleep on ground."

"There has to be some way," Tes mumbled. "We have to find a way in."

"How big are the gates?" Kailyn asked.

Kragh chortled, his big chest shaking as the gravelly sound came forth.

"I take it that means big?" Kailyn asked, frustration tingeing her voice.

Silence echoed around them. Tes, in deep thought, played with the pommel of her sword. "Maybe, you could pretend you captured us and take us into the Keep."

"Tes!" Kailyn gasped. "That would be much too dangerous. They might kill us straight away."

"I don't think so. Trannyth would want to know what we're doing on this side of the mountains."

Kragh shook his head. "Kragh not go Keep. Mage take," he pointed at Tesania's hand, "sword."

"Yes," Tes sighed. "I hadn't thought of that."

"There must be a way," Kailyn said. "Otherwise, we've come all this way for nothing."

"Is there anything you can think of?" Tes asked Kragh again. "Any other way in?"

"No," Kragh answered sharply.

"Ok, ok," Tes said gently. Her mind turned back to the events of the last few days. *I wish Deavon was here. He might know what to do.* "If only we weren't separated in the caves," she grunted.

"What was that?" Kailyn asked.

Tes looked up, her face turning red. "Oh nothing. I was just wishing Deavon was here."

"No," Kailyn insisted. "The other bit."

Tes looked at her friend, confused. "I just said. If only we weren't separated in the caves."

"That's it!" Kailyn turned to Kragh. "There are caves aren't there?" Her voice filled with excitement. "On the plains; outside the Keep?"

Tes caught on. "Yes, Deavon was talking about them. It's where they make the beasts." Shaking her head she asked the young girl, "How does that help us?"

"We might be able to get into the Keep through the caves."

"What do you think, Kragh?" Tesania asked.

Kragh shrugged. "Kragh know cave, not know where go."

"Can you take us to the cave?" Kailyn asked quickly.

"Kailyn," Tes interjected. "It won't help us. There are sure to be beasts and mages everywhere outside the cave. We can't just walk up and sneak in."

Kailyn sat back dejectedly. "I was just trying to come up with an idea. You could..."

Kragh interrupted her. "Kragh see more caves."

"Where?" Kailyn asked, her eyes glittering in the firelight.

"Kragh not like meat..,"

"I know that," Kailyn sighed. "Tell us about the cave."

Kragh growled, a low rumble, then turned his head to Tesania. "Kragh eat leaves, in rocks, cave there."

"So there's a cave in the rocks behind the other cave?" Tes asked.

Kragh nodded. "Kragh eat leaves, see cave."

"Can you take us there?" Tes asked quickly. "Without anyone seeing us?"

Kragh nodded.

Tes smiled at Kailyn. "It's settled then. Tomorrow we start toward Kragh's cave."

49 WESTWARD

"How's your arm?" Deavon asked Raim as they walked along the rocky plains, heading westward toward Trannyth's Keep.

"Sore," Raim replied. "But Naisa's potions help."

"We may be in battle again," Deavon looked at him seriously. "How do you think you'll handle that?"

"I'll use my other hand."

Deavon smiled at the little soldier's tenacity. "These are beasts we're talking about."

"I know," Raim replied. "But you'll need every sword to get to Trannyth." He looked into Deavon's eyes. "I'll be there; this wound is just a hindrance."

Shaking his head and patting Raim on the shoulder, Deavon said, "You are truly Giddy's friend. But I'm glad to have you along."

Raim grinned. "I am indeed."

Four days of travelling over the rocky plains had seen them draw near the Waltiln River. The going had been easy enough, but the bland, hot, rocky plains had taken their toll on their minds and bodies. Trees grew along the river, offering the weary travelers an oasis to rest.

Deavon called them together after they had washed and drunk deeply from the fresh river water. "I believe we should hold up here for a day or two," he said. "We need the rest."

"We also need to come up with a plan," Aldan added. "We still have no idea how we're going to get into that Keep."

Deavon nodded. "We can light a fire during the day," he advised them. "Keep it small, and make sure the wood is dry to keep the smoke down. At sundown it'll need to be extinguished; on these open plains it would be seen for miles. For now; rest."

A stand of trees offered a barrier to the west. They were confident that unless an enemy came to the very banks of the river they would remain undetected. Even so, the expanse of the river would enable them to retreat before any offensive could be mounted against them. Still, Deavon maintained his guard.

Giddy, Raim and Aldan sat quietly by the fire, talking as Giddy sharpened their weapons. Naisa redressed Aldan and Raim's wounds while Elddyn walked a distance away and sat stubbornly by himself. Tean knelt in prayer, Deavon walked toward the river.

As the sun drifted lazily toward the horizon, Deavon sat with his back against a tree, staring into the distance.

Naisa approached, shuffling her feet to alert him to her presence. "We have to put the fire out soon," she advised as he turned to look at her. "Giddy's making a meal now."

Deavon nodded, then turned away. "I'll come in soon."

Naisa smiled and sank to the ground beside him. Smoothing her robes, she said, "She would do it again you know, even knowing what would happen."

"I don't want to talk about it," Deavon mumbled.

"I think you should."

"Why?" Deavon snapped. "Because you want to?"

"There is that too," Naisa replied calmly. "But, we are going into a highly dangerous situation. You need to be clear headed."

"What does it matter if I live or die? Tesania's gone!"

"It matters to me," Naisa whispered. "And I am sure it would matter to Tes, even..., even now."

"You don't know what Tes would want!" Deavon flared. "You didn't know her." He paused, staring at his feet. "Not like I did."

"I knew her well enough," Naisa replied calmly. "Enough to know that she would want you to move on and live a happy life."

"How can I be happy?" he shot at her. "I can't. Not now!"

"I know you don't want to hear this; but, life goes on. You'll meet someone else. What about the Lady Ayana that Tes kept talking about. Isn't she your friend?"

"Not like that," Deavon answered. "We're just friends; that's all it will ever be."

Naisa reached out and touched his arm. "You're a brave, wonderful man Deavon. Tes saw that, others will too. But for now, you can't afford to be reckless, not for your sake or for Giddy's or for mine for that matter." Her hand slipped off his arm. "You need to succeed. To not rid Eldanal of Trannyth will be a disaster." her eyes met his. "We are the only ones that stand in his way."

Deavon sat quietly. Eventually he looked at the mage. "You speak wisely, as always. I just miss her so." He stood, reaching down to help her stand. "Let's go. I'm sure Giddy has cooked something, err, interesting."

Naisa laughed as they walked towards the camp.

The following day, they unpacked all their gear, repaired and cleaned clothes and weapons, ready for the final onslaught on Trannyth's Keep. Deavon called them together as the sun passed its zenith and started the slow crawl to the horizon. "We need to build a makeshift raft to get across the river; big enough to carry one person and their gear."

"Shouldn't be a problem," Giddy said, looking around, "There's plenty of fallen branches, and we still have the ropes."

Deavon nodded. "You and I can work on that this afternoon, Giddy. I want to be across the river in the morning." He gazed at each of them in turn. "From the time we hit the far shore we'll be in constant danger. It's imperative that we remain undiscovered. Tonight will be our last hot meal. We won't be able to light a fire from here on in."

"Any ideas on how we're going to get into the Keep?" Naisa asked.

"None at this stage," said Deavon, shaking his head. "I want to set up camp in those rock hills we can see," he pointed. "From there we should be able to scout the area and see what possibilities arise."

"Trannyth is no fool," Elddyn snarled. "He won't leave the front door open for us."

"I'm aware of that," Deavon sighed. "We always knew that entering the keep would present a major obstacle. All we can do is scout it and see what presents itself. Agreed?" he asked the gathering.

The others nodded. "Maybe Elddyn could use his forbidden magic from the hills and destroy the Keep in one fell swoop," Giddy suggested, mischief in her eyes.

Elddyn refused to rise to the bait. "It doesn't work that way, Giddy. I can destroy a thick wall; say the wall of an inn, with a spell, not a solid stone structure."

"We won't be using forbidden magic, either way," Naisa interjected.

"We'll cross that bridge when we come to it," Deavon interrupted. "There's no use speculating about anything until we've seen what we're up against."

Giddy and Deavon worked through the afternoon lashing logs and sticks together as Tean dragged them in from underneath the surrounding trees. By twilight they had constructed a sturdy raft that could comfortably hold one.

Raim and Aldan, having refused to sit idly by, had insisted on hunting for their last hot meal. Unable to use his bow, Aldan had taken some rope and set snares. They walked proudly into camp, three cleaned and skinned carcasses held high in triumph.

"You see," Giddy nudged Deavon. "I told you they're still useful for something."

"You did," Deavon grinned. "I apologize for my inability to see that."

"None for them," Raim laughed as he threw the carcasses down on a rock beside the fire.

The evening meal was quiet. No one spoke as they all sat lost in their own thoughts of what lay ahead. "I'm turning in early," Deavon announced. "I suggest you all do the same."

Morning saw them rise early. After a small cooked breakfast Deavon doused the fire with water from the river then dispersed the stones that had formed the fire place and covered the ashes with old leaves and twigs, ensuring no one would stumble onto their camping spot and raise the alarm.

The River Waltiln ran placidly toward the north, its slow water allowing Deavon to easily swim its expanse with the raft in tow. Climbing onto the far bank, he took the rope he'd brought over and attached it to the raft. Removing his pack and clothes, he waved to Giddy to pull it back to the other side with the rope she had played out while he traversed the lazy current.

Giddy pulled, the raft slipped across the water easily. Within forty minutes all seven of the travelers stood on the Keep side of the river. Giddy untied the ropes from the raft, pushed it into the stream and watched it disappear slowly downriver. "They won't find that in a hurry," she smiled.

"Let's hope not," Deavon replied. Dressed again, he slung his pack on his back. "From here on in, we're in constant danger of being discovered," he advised them seriously. "Keep your talking to a minimum," he said, looking at Giddy.

"Me!" Giddy gasped. "I'm one of the quiet ones. Just ask..."

"That's exactly what he's talking about!" Elddyn sighed in exasperation.

Giddy grinned at him. "You bite better than any fish I've ever caught," she laughed.

"Giddy," Deavon interrupted. "He's right. You talk too much."

"It's ok," Raim smiled. "If she talks I'll kick her in the britches."

"You will not!"

Raim stood his ground, grinning whilst nodding his head.

"Giddy, you get the point," Deavon snapped. "Let's move out, eyes and ears alert."

Trannyth's Keep loomed in the distance. The turret of the tower standing proudly above the hills that the travelers approached. "Finally, we can see it," Giddy whispered.

They moved on in silence, the rocky hills rising in front of them. By mid morning they had started the climb that would eventually allow them to see the full extent of the seemingly impregnable tower that they intended to breach.

The climb started easily. Loose rocks and debris were the main obstacles that presented themselves. Soon they had to physically climb up a forty degree incline. Deavon led the way, exploring for hand and foot holds as he went. Keenly aware that Aldan and Raim would be in some stress at the climb, he chose the easiest way in preference to the fastest. The hills didn't rise far above the rocky plains, so it was only an hour or so latter that Deavon stepped onto a ledge that he could step sideways along. After helping the others up, he shuffled along to a crack in the rock face and gratefully stepped into a crevice that ran into the hill.

"It looks like this leads through," he said hopefully to the others. "Rest here awhile. Giddy and I will scout ahead."

Carefully, Deavon and the soldier crept through the crevice. Aware that guards may be placed, Deavon stopped at every bend in the narrow space, peering around before motioning Giddy forward. Half an hour later, the crevice began to widen, sunlight found its way through, bringing every angle of the ancient rock to life. A lone bird screeched in the sky as Trannyth's Keep came once more into view. Deavon motioned Giddy to crouch as they came to an open ledge. Edging forward, they eventually lay down and crawled the last few feet.

"Whoa," Giddy whispered.

Before them lay a valley which ran between the two hills on either side of them. Through this valley they could see Trannyth's Keep in its awe inspiring enormity.

A fortress, nestled between cliff faces which towered above it on three sides. Battlements protected it from any frontal attack while parapets at regular intervals allowed for mages and archers to range approaching enemies.

"How are we going to get in there?" Giddy asked, her face a mask of bemusement. "We'd have to get past the gatehouse," she said, pointing at the fortified building that protected the road up to the huge walls. "And then the gates."

"That's after we manage to walk through that," Deavon pointed.

The plains before the Keep were congested with life. Beasts sat around fires, or practiced their swordsmanship. Mages walked in between, barking orders as they wielded their whips. "There must be hundreds," Giddy moaned.

"A thousand or more, I would guess," Deavon replied. He looked at the soldier. "I never thought I'd see the day when the great Giddy wouldn't want to charge at her foe," he laughed lightly.

"I'm keen," Giddy grinned. "But even I know when the odds are against me."

"Come on," Deavon said as he slid backwards toward the safety of the crevice. "Let's get back to the others."

They found them eating a small meal when they returned. Gratefully accepting a portion, Deavon slid his back down the rock face and sat next to his friend Aldan.

"What did you see?" Naisa asked.

"You don't want to know," Giddy laughed.

"That bad?"

"It's big," Giddy mumbled around a chunk of cheese.

"Can we get in?" Raim asked.

Deavon picked up a water skin. "It's heavily fortified and guarded."

"And don't forget to tell them that there are a few beasts out the front we'll have to fight through," Giddy laughed half heartedly.

"How many," Raim asked suspiciously, knowing his friend all too well.

"A thousand I would guess," Deavon replied somberly. "At least a thousand."

"A thousand beasts!" Elddyn almost screamed. "You were mad to bring us here," he shouted, stumbling to his feet. "And you're totally insane if you expect us to even try to go through that."

"Calm down, Elddyn," Deavon motioned for him to sit. "I have no intention of walking into an army of beasts. Besides, even if we did get past them we have the small matter of a guardhouse protecting the road that leads up to the Keep." He paused to take a drink. "And then of course there is the small matter of the Keep walls to get past."

"Madness!" Elddyn snapped. "We should retreat while we're still alive. At least then we might be able to offer something. What good are we, dead?"

"Coward," Giddy mumbled.

"What?"

"I said coward," Giddy repeated as she looked at the mage.

"I'm a coward!" Elddyn blustered. "Why? Because I can see the folly in throwing our lives away in an unwinnable fight?"

"Because you won't even try!"

"He's right, Giddy," Deavon cut them off. "We can't go in the front; not straight in the front anyway."

"How then?" Elddyn asked belligerently.

"Watch your tone!" Giddy shot at him.

Deavon raised his voice. "We will know more once we've studied the Keep further. For now it's a moot conversation."

"Any signs of a way in that may be plausible?" Aldan asked.

"Not from this distance," Deavon shook his head. "We need to get closer."

"Closer!" Elddyn exclaimed. "You are insane."

"See!" Giddy pointed accusingly at the mage. "I told you all along. He doesn't want us to get to his friend." She glared at him triumphantly.

"Trannyth... Is not my friend!" Elddyn growled through clenched teeth.

"Right," Giddy replied, nodding her head knowingly. "I'll remember that. Elddyn is not Trannyth's friend."

"Giddy," Raim nudged her. "Leave it."

"Ok," Giddy grinned at Elddyn. "So we move closer, Right?"

Deavon dragged himself to his feet. "Indeed, we do."

"Madness," Elddyn muttered as the others passed him. Shaking his head, he fell in behind.

Deavon halted at the ledge where he and Giddy had observed the Keep. Two by two he allowed the others to creep forward and see for themselves what he and Giddy had witnessed earlier.

"Well," Aldan sighed as he shimmied back. "We'll have our work cut out to get in there."

Deavon nodded and pointed off into the distance. "For now we retreat into the crevice. It's too open here. Anyone in that tower could look out and see us at any time."

"You should have thought of that before you had us standing out here for all to see, shouldn't you?"

"You're right Elddyn, as always," Deavon half bowed to him. "Let's move back. At twilight I want to start along this ledge to the hill on the right there. We'll need to hole up during the day and explore by night."

50 BEASTLY CAVES

Kragh ranged out ahead of the two girls in his charge as they started toward the cave where the banmora were so painfully transformed into beasts. He had suggested in his limited words that it was safer for them if he met any oncoming beasts or mages on his own, rather than with them in tow.

"It's funny," Tes mentioned to Kailyn as they walked along the eastern banks of the Waltiln River.

"What's that?" Kailyn asked curiously.

"A few days ago," Tes started, looking toward her friend with a faint smile. "I wanted every beast dead."

"And now?"

"And now, I have one helping me," Tes laughed lightly. "You could even say he's my friend."

"He's..," Kailyn peered ahead to where the beast must be, looking for the right word, "nice," she grinned sheepishly at Tes.

Tes laughed. "Who would have ever thought we'd think a beast was nice."

"Not me!" Kailyn insisted.

Tes walked quietly for a while, thinking as she stared down at her feet. "He'll die," she whispered.

"What?" Kailyn asked quickly. "Who'll die?"

"Kragh!"

"How do you know?"

"Because, Kailyn." Tes looked at her. "Think about it."

Kailyn wandered along, her face creased in concentration. Tesania watched her. "You ninny. Kragh is a?"

"Beast," Kailyn answered.

"And when we smash the orb all the beasts are going to..?"

"Die!" Kailyn gasped. "So Kragh will die when the rest do?"

Tes nodded slowly. "Yes," she managed to answer, her throat feeling constricted at the thought of the beast, who had gone against his own kind to help her, dying because of what she had to do. "When the orb is destroyed, Kragh will die."

They walked on silently, each lost in their own thoughts. Kailyn eventually turned to Tes. "Do you think he knows?"

Tesania shook her head. "I doubt it," she answered sadly.

"Should we tell him?"

Tes thought for a long time. "I think he has a right to know."

"But he might...," Kailyn paused as she stared at Tes. "He might turn on us. I mean. He might kill us if we tell him that."

"We'll have to risk that," Tes replied resolutely. "I'm not going to let him lead us all the way to Trannyth and then watch his face as he dies. Not without telling him first. I couldn't," she sighed, a tear forming in her eye. "Not like that."

"I don't think he wants to live the way he is," Kailyn said quietly. "I know he'd do anything to save his kind from the horrible things that Trannyth's doing to them."

Tes nodded. "I think you're right."

Kailyn placed her arm around Tes' shoulders. "We'll tell him together."

"Not just yet," Tes muttered. "I want to find the right time." She looked into the distance. "Come on, we've been moving much too slowly."

They trudged on, past midday and well into the afternoon, seeing no sign of Kragh as the day wore on. As darkness approached, Kailyn spied him at the side of the river. "There he is," she pointed, "At least.., I think it's him."

"He's waving to us," Tes said. "It must be him."

Kragh stood in the shallows of the river. As they approached he turned and started into the water.

"Wait!" Tes called.

Kragh stopped and turned. "Cross river here," he grunted.

"How do we know it's safe over there," Tes pointed at the far bank.

"Kragh search," he announced. "No mage close."

"Are you sure?" Kailyn asked.

Kragh nodded, "Safe."

"Ok," Tes smiled at Kailyn. "Looks like we're going to get a little wet."

As the sun sank finally past the dark horizon, Kragh led them, wet and cold, into a crevice in the rocky plains. A rough path angled downward, leading them into a cave large enough to comfortably stand and move around in. Kragh knelt on the ground, the sharp click of stone on steel preceded bright sparks as he struck a flint and set light to a small bundle of kindling. The fire took slowly to larger pieces of wood that were arranged in a central fire place.

"What is this place?" Tes asked, turning slowly as she took in the cave. Stacks of wood ran down one wall of the cave, barrels of water stood in one corner. Chests sat at the far end of the cave. Tes approached them and saw that they contained nuts, dried fruits, dried meats, hard biscuits and bread.

"Sleep place," Kragh said.

"I can see that," Tes shook her head at him. "I mean, why is it all here, in the middle of nowhere?"

"Mages go mountain," he pointed out the dark cave entry. "Sleep."

"So.., it's like a roadhouse?" Kailyn asked.

"It looks that way," Tes replied looking around again. "Although the roadhouses I stayed in always had hot baths."

"A hot bath. I wish," Kailyn sighed.

Tes laughed. "Me too. But it's better than nothing," she said as she threw her pack down and started to untie her bedroll. A sudden thought came to her. "No one will come.., will they Kragh?"

"Night," the beast answered simply.

"I guess," Tes looked at Kailyn. "I suppose anyone travelling would have been here well before dark."

Kailyn shrugged. "I hope so," she said as she selected some dried meat and carried it to the fire. "At least we'll be able to restock," she smiled.

The meal she cooked was bland, but filling. They sat around the fire for a short time talking to Kragh. His eyes shone in the firelight as he recalled his harem and their days in the hills. Tes eventually rose and wished them a good night as she stretched and tiredly lay down on her bed.

The following day saw Kragh out ahead again as they followed along the western banks of the river. Kragh had explained that the mages and beasts coming and going from the keep would travel inland from the river and that they would be fairly safe following the line of the water. The rocky hills rose from the plains on their left as they moved farther north. Kragh came back to them as dusk took hold and the light began to fade.

"Sleep," he pointed at the ground.

"Here?" Kailyn complained. "In the open?"

"No cave."

"It's as good a place as any," Tes said as she dropped her pack. "I'm going to take a bath in the river. Coming?"

"A bath? out here?"

"Why not," Tes laughed. "It's almost dark, and I'm sure Kragh doesn't care. Besides, my hair is filthy."

Kragh stayed with them the next morning, snuffling at the wind as he led the way into the hills. By mid morning Trannyth's Keep loomed before them. "Oh my," Kailyn sighed as she saw the enormity of it.

"It is big," Tes agreed, stopping to look.

"How are we going to get in there?" Kailyn wondered out loud.

"Through the caves," Tes answered. "I hope."

"Cave," Kragh grunted, pointing along the crevasse they were traversing.

"Ok, Kragh," Tes sighed. "We're coming. We were just looking at the Keep."

"Cave," Kragh repeated, more urgently.

"Come on, Kailyn. Let's go," Tes dragged at her arm as she continued to stare at the tower of the keep.

They hurried through the rocky passage, trying to keep up with the beast. He stopped, turning; he placed his finger to his lips.

"Quiet," Tes whispered.

"We understand," Kailyn nodded at Kragh.

He moved on, his pace quickening. Tes and Kailyn started to fall behind. The big beast's gait easily outpaced them. "I hope he waits for us," Kailyn whispered between strained breaths.

"He will," Tes panted. "I wish he'd stop though." Rounding a bend, she slid to a halt. Kragh sat on the ground, tenderly running his hand over the foliage of a lone bush in the rocky surrounds. Struggling for breath, Tes stood, hands on knees. "Is this where you ate your leaves?" she labored to ask.

Kragh nodded; his attention fully on the plant.

"And where is the cave?"

Kragh pointed. Twenty or so yards away, a dark hole was visible in the rock wall.

"And that leads to the caves where they're transforming the banmoras?" she asked, eyeing the cave entrance suspiciously.

"Make Kragh, this," he answered.

Kailyn walked to the cave entrance. Peering into the darkness, she asked, "And will this lead us to the Keep?"

"Not know," Kragh growled.

"He doesn't know," Kailyn laughed nervously. Turning to Tes, she mumbled, "It might lead nowhere too."

"It might," Tesania conceded while drawing the last torch from her pack. "But we have to try."

Kragh patted his bush and scrambled to his feet. "Kragh first," he announced. Taking the torch from Tes' hand he walked to the cave entrance. Kailyn cast a spell, lighting the oiled end, coughing as the acrid smoke invaded her throat.

Kragh's eyes bored into her, his finger coming to his lips.

"I know, I know," Kailyn managed between coughs. "Quiet."

The big beast turned and squeezed into the cave mouth. "Here we go again," Tes smiled at Kailyn as she stepped in behind him.

The passage through the cave pressed in upon them. Tesania felt claustrophobic as her shoulders brushed against either wall. Unlike the rocks in the Owara Caves, these were dark and hard. Knobs and knuckles reached out and scraped at her skin, often catching her and pulling her painfully to a stop. *How is Kragh able to go through so fast?* She wondered as she tried desperately to keep up with him.

A few minutes later Kragh came to a halt. Tes stopped behind him. "What is it?" she asked.

"Big cave."

"Is there anybody there?" Tes asked, straining to see around his body.

Kragh moved forward, allowing her and Kailyn to step into the cave. A large area greeted them. Stacks of stores sat against the walls, reaching almost to the roof. Tes could see two caves leading off the one they stood in. The one opposite to where they had entered glowed with light from torches mounted in the walls. The other, to the right, stood dark. Low moans emanated from the darkness at regular intervals. "What's in there?" Tes asked Kragh.

The beast shrugged and moved toward the noise. He held the torch high as he entered. Tes pushed past him, "Oh, you poor thing!" she cried.

An ogre sat at the far side of the cave. Strong ropes bound it to the wall, its arms and legs outspread. It looked up as Tes entered the cave. "Raug, kill man-things, gnaw their bones," he roared. Hatred and malice burned out at Tes causing her to take a step backward.

"Why is he here?" she asked. When Kragh shrugged, she turned back to Raug. Slowly she walked forward. "We mean you no harm," she soothed. "Why do they have you tied up here?" she asked, softness in her voice. "How could they do this to you?"

The ogre's eyes softened a little, confusion crossing his face as he stared at the girl that came closer and closer to him. He could feel that she was different from the rest, that she meant him no harm. And yet, she was a man-thing, to be hated and reviled. Roaring once more, he strained at the ropes with his arms, trying to get to her.

"Shh," Tes held her hand out. "We're here to help you."

"Raug, kill man-things, gnaw their bones," he muttered again, his confusion causing his hatred to dim as the girl stepped closer again.

"I know," Tes whispered. "They were hurting you. Of course you want to hurt them back."

"Man-things take Raug. Raug happy in hills, gnaw bones."

"They captured you?" Tes asked softly. As the big ogre's head nodded she continued. "And they tied you up in here?"

Raug nodded again. "Point sticks at Raug, hurt."

"This must be the ogre they've been taking the life force from to make the beasts," Tes whispered back at Kailyn. "The poor thing."

"The poor thing looks like it wants to kill us. Come away from it," Kailyn whispered urgently.

"We can't leave him," Tes replied quickly.

"He can't help us."

"How do you know?" Tes asked. "Besides, it's not about him helping us."

Raug sat quietly, he didn't understand fully what the two man-things were talking about, but he could see the compassion in the close ones face. "Raug want go," he said.

"I know," Tes said as she stepped closer again. She placed her hand on her sword; it remained still under her touch. Reassured she started to draw it. "I'm going to cut the ropes." She motioned toward his arms and legs. "So you'll be free."

"Tesania!" Kailyn gasped. "It's too dangerous."

"Be quiet, Kailyn," Tes snapped. "I won't leave him here, tied up and defenseless."

"He's an ogre," Kailyn insisted.

"So was Bellowa," Tes stepped forward and started to cut at the rope holding Raug's legs to the ground. "She didn't hurt you!"

"To save herself! Not for me!"

"Still." Tes continued cutting. "It shows that they're intelligent enough to know what's happening around them."

"Tesania! Don't!" Kailyn pleaded. "It's too dangerous!"

"Nonsense," Tes shot at her. "My sword isn't vibrat..," she looked down at the hilt in her hand. Vibrations she hadn't noticed before grew as she stared. "There's something wron..."

"What is going on here?" a voice boomed from the entrance to Raug's cave. "What is the meaning of this?"

Tes spun, her sword raised. Kragh roared, his sword singing as it flew from its scabbard. Kailyn rushed to Tes' side. In the flickering light of the torch Tes could see a mage standing about eight feet away, small in stature and obviously a woman. Tes decided to stall, asking, "What right do you have, keeping this poor ogre tied up like this?"

"The ogre is not the question here," The mage countered. "The question is. Who are you? And what are you doing here?"

"We were lost," Tes answered, grimacing as she said it.

"Lost," the mage laughed. "And you found your way here? Not to the mountains and home? But to a cave outside Trannyth's Keep?"

"I'm not very good at directions," Tes shrugged, not knowing what else to say.

The mage leaned sideways, looking past Tes. "And releasing the ogre what's more. Very intriguing."

Kragh growled and moved forward. "Kragh. No!" Tes called.

"And a beast at your command? It gets more and more interesting."

"It's none of your business," Kailyn shouted.

"Keep your voice down!" the strange mage snapped. "Someone might hear you!"

"Why would you care if someone hears us?" Tes asked suspiciously. "Surely you're going to call an army of beasts down on us?"

"Why would you think that?" the mage asked.

"Cut the ogre free," Tes whispered to Kailyn. "Because you aligned yourself with Trannyth. You're one of his mages. Are you not?" she challenged the woman.

The mage sighed. "I am indeed. A decision I shall regret for the rest of my life."

The sounds of Kailyn's small knife sawing through the heavy ropes around Raug's wrists filled the small cave as Tes continued to try and delay the mage. "So you will call the beasts as soon as you... Regret?"

"Regret," the mage echoed.

"Why are you here then?"

"You don't just walk away from Trannyth," the mage explained. "Either I stay here or I'm dead. Either way, I'm not too happy."

"Help us then!"

"Tes!" Kailyn snapped. "Don't you dare tell her what we're doing."

Tes looked quickly back at her friend. "I don't think we have much choice." Her sword still vibrated, but almost imperceptibly now. "We're looking for a way into the Keep," she stated simply.

"Why?"

"To kill Trannyth!"

The mage laughed. "To kill Trannyth?"

"Why is that funny?" Tesania flared.

"Trannyth's inside his Keep, at the very top of the tower. What chance do you think you have?"

"A good one," Tes answered coldly. "Especially since we now have you to show us how."

"Me?" the mage exclaimed in surprise. "What makes you think I'll help you?"

"Won't you?" Tes asked as Raug rose behind her. A vibrating growl escaping his lips when he saw the mage. Tes held her hand out to him. "No, Raug! She's going to help us."

The little mage stood in confusion, her head whipping about when she heard a noise. "Going through these caves will get you killed," she mumbled. "Follow me."

Tes looked at Kailyn, shrugged and followed the mage out into the larger cave. The mage snatched a torch from the wall. "We have to get out of these caves," she said, leading the way along the passage from where Tes and the others had come.

Tes followed, Kailyn close behind. Kragh and Raug brought up the rear. "What's your name?" Tes called forward.

"Serran," the little mage answered. "My name is Serran."

51 REUNITED

Tesania crawled gratefully from the cave entrance where she and Kailyn had entered. Kragh walked to his bush and happily sat down, plucking two tender leaves from his faithful little tree and placed them on his tongue.

"How can we get into the Keep?" Tes asked Serran quickly.

"All in good time," the little mage answered as she stared at Kragh. "First, tell me how you came to be travelling with a beast? And a tame one at that?"

"It doesn't matter," Tes answered irritably. "What matters is stopping Trannyth."

"Did you cast some kind of spell on him?"

"No!"

"Then how?"

"I don't know." Tes turned and walked toward the big beast. "He saved us, Kailyn and I. In the Owara Caves."

"Saved you how?"

Tes spun on Serran. "What does it matter?"

"Oh, it's no matter," the mage answered. "I was just wondering is all."

"Then why are we still talking about it?"

"So he saved you in some caves? How?"

Tes sighed. "We were attacked by a beast. Kragh killed it and saved us. I have no idea why, except that he doesn't want to be a beast. He abhors it and wants Trannyth stopped."

"He told you this?"

"Yes," Tes snapped. "I just told you that."

"Funny," the little mage looked at Kragh with admiration. "I thought they were mindless." she looked at Tes. "They're supposed to only do Trannyth's bidding."

"It appears Kragh has enough intelligence to break the spell."

"Funny," Serran said again, shaking her head as she looked at Kailyn and Raug. "So this is your little band. You plan to storm the Keep and kill Trannyth with just these three?"

"Four," Tes corrected her. "You're coming too. Remember?"

"Yes, yes, quite," the mage answered.

Tes watched her, wondering if taking the mage with them was a good idea. "We hadn't planned on storming the keep," she said warily. "Maybe you know a better way in?"

"I could take you through the gates I suppose."

Tesania looked quickly at Kailyn who shook her head slightly. Slowly, she drew her hand up until it touched the pommel of her sword. No vibrations met her fingertips. "Wouldn't they be suspicious if you walk up to the gates with two girls, a beast and an ogre who's supposed to be tied up in the caves?" Tes asked, worry creasing her brow.

"The beast and I could escort you," Serran said. "We could take your weapons and pretend you're prisoners."

"No!" Tes stepped backwards. "I won't give up my sword." She flicked her eyes to Kailyn, disbelief passed between them. "And what of Raug? They won't believe he's a prisoner."

"Yes, the ogre," Serran peered at Raug. "He might be a bit hard to hide."

"A bit hard to…" Kailyn shook her head.

"Shh," Tes cut her off. "Serran, we need to find a way in that Trannyth doesn't know about. A way where he wouldn't know we were there."

Serran shook her head. "It's a fortress."

"I know that," Tes sighed. "Surely there's some way?"

The little mage stood quietly, staring at the stony ground. Eventually she looked up. "Only the caves."

"We were just in the caves!" Tes tried in vain to keep her voice down. "You said we couldn't go that way."

"Not those caves."

"Then which?"

Kragh grunted; Tesania whirled. The beast sat with his finger to his lips. "I know Kragh," Tes said quietly. Turning back to the mage, she asked, "Where are these caves?"

"This way," the mage said as she started along the crevice to the northwest.

Kailyn walked to Tes' side. "Do we trust her?" she asked as she looked along the rocks to where the mage strode along.

Tes shrugged. "Do we have a choice? Kragh, Raug, let's go."

They managed to catch up to the mage a short way along the path. Serran pointed to where she wanted to go. Kragh took the lead; Raug following behind to protect the rear. Kragh knew his way through the rocky climbs, having traversed them on training runs many times. The path remained relatively flat as they walked, rising in some places, falling in others. The afternoon sun cast shadows amongst the rocks that looked like huge monsters as they rose up the rock faces. Kragh slowed, allowing the others to catch up. "Sleep," he said simply.

"Not just yet, Kragh," Tes answered. "I'd like to find a plateau. So we can all rest comfortably."

The beast nodded, but stayed close as they continued. For another half an hour they trudged on. Tes started to wonder if they would find a suitable place for a camp or be stuck out on the exposed path. She shook her head in wonder at the predicament they were in. In the middle of Trannyth's army, with a mismatched band of companions, trying in vain to find a way to smash an orb in an impenetrable keep.

Her thoughts were ripped back to the present as a cry came from above. Kragh's sword slipped from its sheath, the hiss of metal carrying through the darkening night. A vague shape landed in front of the beast, its sword reflecting the very last light of the day.

Tes leapt forward, straining to get past Kragh. "Giddy, no!" she pleaded. "It's me, Tesania!"

"Tes?" Giddy's voice floated out of the darkness. "I'll have you free in a moment."

Tes touched Kragh's arm. "Please, Kragh, she's my friend. I promise she won't hurt me."

Kragh grunted, stepping aside to let Tes through.

"He's with me," Tes explained to the astonished soldier. "He saved our lives."

"Kailyn's alive too?" Giddy asked, her voice cracking. "We thought you were dead!"

"Well you could've waited around to find out," Kailyn accused as she stepped up beside Tes.

Giddy stepped forward, embracing them both. "I'm so glad you're safe." She eyed Kragh suspiciously. "It saved you, you say?"

Tes stepped back. "His name's Kragh. He hates being what he is."

Giddy scoffed. "He's a beast."

"Only on the outside," Tes assured her.

"If you say so, Tes," Giddy frowned. "And the others?"

"Oh, Serran. She's a mage who is helping us. And Raug, he was one of the poor ogres they were using to make the beasts."

Giddy laughed. "We leave you alone for a few days and you pick up a menagerie."

"Well if you hadn't left us alone, we wouldn't have had too!" Kailyn shot at her.

"Ok, Kailyn," Giddy said seriously. "I get your point."

"Where are the others?" Tes asked excitedly, keen to see Deavon again.

"Along the path a little ways," Giddy pointed. She looked suspiciously at Tes' new travelling partners. "Are you sure we can trust them?"

"My sword says we can," Tes replied.

"Good enough for me," Giddy nodded. "But I'll be watching them closely."

Tes laughed. "I'm sure you will." Turning she spoke to the others. "This is my friend, Giddy. She's taking us to our other friends. Ok?"

Kragh nodded. Serran stepped forward. "Just how many friends do you have in these hills?"

Tes' head flashed to Giddy, for the first time she remembered the beasts in the caves. "Did anybody get...?"

"No," Giddy assured her. "Aldan and Raim were badly injured, but everyone made it through." She looked at the mage. "There are seven of us, camped a short way ahead."

"Seven," Serran echoed. "Why didn't you tell me of this?" she asked Tes.

"I didn't know where they were," Tes said defensively. "For all I knew, they'd turned back."

"Deavon would never turn back," Giddy said, her eyes lighting with mischief. "Come on, I can't wait to see his face."

Giddy led the way along the stony path. "Wait here," she said, a grin splitting her face. "I want to warn them about the others first."

Tes watched Giddy disappear around a bend in the path. Desperate to see the others, she crept forward. Giddy's voice drifted to her.

"Deavon," she said. "I found something you might be interested in."

Tes' heart lifted as she heard Deavon's voice reply, "What's that Giddy? And couldn't it have waited until the end of your watch?"

"I don't think so," Giddy's voice was high with excitement.

"What is it then?" Deavon asked irritably.

Giddy reappeared as she said, "I'll bring it in, shall I?"

"Giddy, just get on with..," Deavon's voice stopped abruptly as Giddy pulled Tesania into the small glow of Naisa's staff. "Tesania!" he gasped. "Tesania!" he said again as he scrambled to his feet. "You're alive?" He rushed toward her. "I thought you were.., I thought you were dead," he managed to say as he took her into his arms.

The others came toward them, gathering around. Tes savored Deavon's embrace for a few short seconds and then broke free. "You could have searched for us," she accused. "You left us to die!"

Deavon staggered back, as if hit by a blow. "I never..." he started. "You fell down the chasm... We called... There was no way down... We thought you were..."

"To be fair, Tes," Naisa stepped forward and hugged her. "We're all to blame. Let us just be happy we're together again."

Tesania looked at Deavon, she could see his pain. *Why do I always have to hurt him?*

"And what of Kailyn?" Naisa pressed. "Is she..?"

Tes turned her attention back to the mage. "No, she's with me." Turning she called quietly into the darkness. "Kailyn, come on in." As Kailyn ran into the dim light and embraced Naisa, Tes turned to the others. "I'd better warn you," she said. "There is a beast, an ogre, and one of Trannyth's Mages here."

"Where?" Raim asked, stepping forward with his good hand on his sword.

"Relax," Giddy teased him. "You're so uptight sometimes."

"Around the corner," Tes advised them. "About ten feet away."

Now Deavon and Aldan came forward, Elddyn snatched up his staff, starting to prepare a spell.

"It's ok," Giddy laughed at them. "When you lot left her in the cave, Tes went off and made new friends."

"You left us too," Kailyn glared at Giddy.

"Only because..,"

"Giddy!" Deavon snapped. "Where are these others?" Deavon demanded of Tes. "Are they truly just ten feet away?"

Tes nodded.

"And you didn't warn us?" Deavon turned on Giddy. "What were you thinking?"

"Well, Tes said they were alright," Giddy defended herself.

"They're with me," Tes assured him. "They're my friends."

"How do you know that?" Deavon asked.

Tes' anger rose. "Because my sword isn't vibrating," she growled through clenched teeth. "Kragh, the beast, saved Kailyn's and my lives. I would trust him with them again."

"And the ogre? And the mage?"

"Raug was their prisoner, not their friend. They were using him to make the beasts..., had him tied up cruelly against a wall in a cave. I couldn't... I wouldn't leave him there!"

"It's ok, Tes," Deavon soothed, his own anger abating. "I just want to know who they are."

Tes drew a deep breath. "Serran is a mage. She hates Trannyth and all he stands for."

"How do you know that?" Elddyn asked.

"Because she told me," Tes flared at the horrible mage.

Elddyn scoffed. "Because she told you!"

"You can ask her yourself then," Tes scowled at him. "Serran, Kragh, Raug, come in please."

The little mage edged into the light, the huge dark body of Kragh, close behind. "I offer you no danger," she said quietly. "I want to help."

"Help us do what?" Elddyn sneered.

Serran blinked at him. "Kill Trannyth of course."

Elddyn spun on Tesania. "You told an enemy mage of our mission?"

"Well you weren't around to help me. You left me to die in the caves!"

"Enough," Deavon stepped between them. "Tes, Kailyn," he looked at them both. "I am very sorry that I left you in the caves. If I could do anything to change that now, I would." He stepped toward Tesania. "Trust me when I say, it was one of the hardest and loneliest decision I have made in my life. One I don't want to make again."

Tes' face softened as she looked into his eyes. "I thought I'd lost you too," she whispered.

Deavon smiled at her and turned toward the newcomers. "Welcome, Serran. We're pleased to have you with us. You're knowledge of Trannyth and his keep will be invaluable."

The little mage nodded and moved toward Naisa, offering her hand. Deavon moved toward Kragh. "I am indebted to you." Reaching forward, he gripped the beast's upper arm. "Thank you for bringing them back to us."

Kragh grunted as Deavon moved around him and approached the ogre. "Raug, I'm glad Tes found you and set you free. What Trannyth was doing to you was unjust and one of the reasons we're here."

Raug looked at him uncomprehendingly. "Raug kill man-things."

Deavon's hand reached for his sword. "He means Trannyth and his mages," Tes said quickly.

Deavon relaxed. "Good to have you with us," he said to the ogre. "Just make sure it's not any of us before you do the killing," he laughed.

Tes and Kailyn took turns telling the others of their journey since they fell into the chasm. Tes explained how Kragh had killed the other beast when it had attacked them in the caves. Naisa was enthralled as Kailyn told her how she lifted Tes' sword from the waterfall with her blossoming magic.

Deavon set the watch and turned in for the night, moving his bedding next to Tes, determined she wouldn't leave his sight again.

The following morning dawned overcast and dreary. Black clouds filled the skies, fog hung lazily around the Tower Keep, obscuring it from the little band of travelers view.

Tes miserably chewed a dried biscuit for her breakfast. She huddled into her cloak, shivering in the early morning cold. "Have you managed to find a way in?" she asked Giddy.

Giddy shook her head. "We were going to have a look at the Keep today. Maybe we can breach the wall."

A lilting laugh cracked the cool morning air. "The Keep's solid stone," Serran laughed. "You have no chance of breaching it."

"We haven't devised a plan," Deavon advised the mage. "Maybe you have some ideas that might help us?"

"I told the girl yesterday," Serran pointed to Tes. "The caves."

Deavon looked at Tesania. Tes shrugged. "I've no idea. She said they were this way."

"What caves?" Deavon asked the little mage.

Serran sighed. "When we first arrived here." She threw her arm out to take in the cold rocks about them "Trannyth had us build his Keep." She paused, taking a bite of her biscuit.

"And?" Deavon pressed.

"And!" Serran flashed. "We raised the Tower and the Keep from the rocks below."

"And the caves you mentioned?"

Serran stared at Deavon. "As I was saying. When we raised the Keep, we drew the rock from the ground underneath it."

"So there are caves underneath?" Tes asked.

Serran nodded. "A void was created where the stone came from." She motioned a circle with her hands. "Not only below the keep, but also around the back and sides."

"Surely Trannyth knows of these?" Deavon asked. "He wouldn't leave them unprotected?"

"We told him about it, yes," Serran replied. "Trannyth is arrogant," she added fiercely. "He thinks his Keep is safe from intruders, simply because he has the mountains blocked."

"Still, they're just caves," Aldan said. "Surely they don't just open into the Keep?"

"No," Serran replied. "There's no entrance from the Keep into the caves."

"Then it's useless!"

"No!" Serran insisted. "The caves come within a few feet of the Keep. "The walls are five, six feet thick."

"Five to six feet of solid rock," Aldan laughed. "It may as well be a mountain."

Serran stared at him. "To a mere ranger, it is a mountain," she smiled. "To three trained mages it is a simple spell."

"I will not use forbidden magic," Naisa sat bolt upright. "Do not think to speak for me, Serran," she sneered. "I will not use it, and I forbid Elddyn.., and you for that matter, from using it as well."

Deavon watched the seething mage for a few moments. Gently, he said, "I think the current mission might override the laws against forbidden magic."

"I will not see the laws of this kingdom flaunted in front of my very face," Naisa snapped. "It is the law. It's not our position to change that." She sat back. "Forbidden magic is abhorrent, that's why the laws exist!"

"Exist they might," Serran pushed. "But the fact remains that the magic is available to us." Looking at Deavon she shook her head. "It's the only way you will get inside the Keep. You have to use it!"

"We are here because of your filthy magic!" Naisa erupted. "I will not lower myself to your level," she glared at the little mage.

"Naisa," Deavon touched the angry mage on her shoulder. "No one is asking you to use it." He turned to Elddyn. "Would the two of you," he indicated Elddyn and Serran, "be able to break through that much rock by yourselves?"

Elddyn eyes gleamed with desire, his lips drawing back into a sneering grin as he looked at Naisa. "I believe we could do it," he said coldly.

"You will not!" Naisa snapped.

Deavon stood. "I don't see we have a choice, Naisa," he said to the mage. "We'll enter the Keep through the caves. Elddyn and Serran will break through the wall with their magic."

"If we use forbidden magic, we are as bad as Trannyth!" Naisa lurched to her feet. "What will stop Elddyn here from taking his place?" she glared at Deavon. "The magic eats your soul, turns you into an abomination. I won't allow it!"

Deavon held his hand out in an effort to console her. "As the leader of this mission I take full responsibility for the decision. You won't be blamed."

"Won't be blamed! You think that's why I protest against these..." She sneered at the other two mages. "...these mages using foul magic." Her voice softened as she sat again. "We will be no better than Trannyth if we do."

"There isn't any other way," Deavon sighed. "My decision is final. We go in via the caves."

Naisa looked up to Elddyn's grinning face. "You should know better," she whispered. "You've seen what it did to your friend."

The smile slipped from Elddyn's face as Naisa spoke. "He is not my friend," he growled. "I want him gone as much as you do."

"So you can replace him?" Naisa asked sadly.

"I have no int..."

"Don't worry, Naisa," Giddy snarled from where she sat listening. "I'll be there to make sure he doesn't."

"You! What could you do?" Elddyn raised himself to his full height. "A mere soldier against a mage of my ability."

"There it is," Giddy stared at Deavon. "I was wrong though," she laughed. "I've been telling you since the day we picked him up..," she turned her gaze to Elddyn, "he's with Trannyth. But now we know the truth. He wants to be Trannyth."

"Enough!" Deavon stepped between the two. "We have enough to worry about without fighting against each other. My decision is made. We move to the cave this evening, under the cover of darkness. In the morning, Elddyn and Serran will blast a hole in the rock wall and we go in." He glared around the gathering then stormed away, saying, "That's it, no more arguments."

Tesania watched him go. She decided to leave him be, other thoughts nagged at her. Touching Kailyn's arm, she whispered, "We have to talk to Kragh, and Raug. They have to know what will happen to them once the orb breaks."

"Should you tell them?" Kailyn asked. "We need their help."

"I have to," Tes shook her head. "I won't let them fight for us, only to watch their faces when they die by my hand." She stood and started toward the two big forms sitting at the far end of the campsite. "I couldn't live with myself."

Kailyn snatched at her arm. "At least take Giddy and Raim with us," she pleaded. "In case they get angry."

Tes stopped and thought for a few moments. Nodding, she walked to Giddy and Raim. "Can you come with us to talk to Kragh and Raug?" she asked quietly.

"Why?" Giddy asked, her eyebrow arching.

"You'll see," Tes answered sadly. "Just come please."

"And be ready to fight," Kailyn whispered.

Giddy's glance shot to Tes, then to Raim. Shrugging, she caught Deavon's attention and nodded toward Tes as she walked after her.

Tesania approached the ogre and beast slowly. They sat talking in their broken speech, discussing the hills and the lower mountains that they loved.

"Kragh," Tes started as she sat down beside them. "Raug."

Kragh grunted at her. Raug looked up at the approaching soldiers, turning his head when he heard Deavon coming from behind.

"I have to tell you something," Tes started. "Tomorrow, we'll be going into the Keep to kill Trannyth."

"Kragh kill Tra-n," Kragh started to say.

"I know, Kragh," Tes interrupted. "We all want him gone." She sat quietly as she thought of what to say. Looking into the beast's eyes and then to Raug, she continued. "I have to break Trannyth's Orb," she said sadly. The two looked back at her uncomprehendingly. "When I do..." finding it hard to continue, she glanced up at Deavon. He nodded to her, his eyes reflecting her own sadness at what she had to say. "When I do," she rushed. "Anything that has had their life force entwined with the orb will perish with it!"

Kragh blinked at her and shook his head, not understanding her words. Raug grunted, "Raug kill man-things; gnaw their bones."

"You don't understand!" Tes cried. "When I smash the orb," tears ran down her face. "You'll both die!"

They sat quietly as Tes' words sank in. Raug sat still, confusion still playing across his big face. Kragh leant forward, his hand reaching out to touch Tesania's cheek. "Kragh understand," he grunted as he pulled his hand away, his fingers wet with Tes' tears. "Kragh rather die.

461

Kragh not want live like this," he pointed to himself. "Kragh kill Tran-n-y-th."

"But you'll die," Tes sobbed. "I'm so sorry."

"Tes not cry," Kragh rumbled. "Kragh die when Tran-n-y-th die," he shrugged.

Tes swung her legs around and knelt before the beast. Leaning forward she closed her arms around his neck. "You're so very brave," she mumbled into the coarse hair on his neck. Drawing back, she looked at Raug. "Do you understand, Raug?"

Raug nodded slowly. "Man-things hurt Raug. Will not let hurt others."

Tes shuffled toward him. "You understand that you will die?" she asked gently. "When I smash the orb?"

Raug shrugged. "Raug kill man-things."

"Not all man-things are bad," Tes whispered, leaning forward to embrace him. "I'm so sorry you were hurt. I wish there was some other way."

Deavon stepped toward Tes, gently placing his hand under her elbow, he drew her up. Tears cascaded down her cheeks as he placed his arm around her, allowing her to bury her face in his chest as he guided her away.

The remainder of the day drifted slowly. The little group adjusted their gear and sharpened their weapons. Deavon insisted they leave any unnecessary equipment behind, wanting to travel light. As the day faded, he went to each of them, wishing them luck and reminding them of the need for strict silence. Finally, he stopped at Tesania. "And so. We are here."

Tes nodded. "Indeed."

"Take care," Deavon whispered. "I won't leave you again. I'll be with you all the way."

Tesania smiled shyly. "I know."

Deavon turned. "Right, everyone ready, let's go pay Trannyth a surprise visit."

52 THE KEEP

Darkness caused little problem to the travelers as they made their way down the slopes of the hills outside Trannyth's keep. A bright three quarter moon shone like a torch on the dark rock. Fires, seemingly hundreds, flickered and flared on the plains below them where the hordes of beasts camped. Deavon allowed Serran to lead them when they reached the plains and headed out across the flat expanse to the northern side of the rocks that encompassed the Keep. The darkness gave them a false sense of security; Deavon more than once warning Kailyn to keep her voice down.

The plains required them to wind and weave among the multitude of holes and crevices etched into the rocky surface by eons of harsh weather. The waxing moon raced toward the horizon as they neared the rocky cliffs that surrounded the Keep.

Serran paused to talk to Deavon. "The cave entrances are a little further ahead," she advised him.

"How do we know which one to take?" he asked, his face obscured in the darkness.

"We did minimal surveying of the caves," Serran answered. "But the second entrance leads almost directly to the Keep walls."

"Very well," Deavon replied. "Lead on."

"What if it's a trap?" Tes asked quietly as Serran moved off.

"I don't think so," Deavon replied. "If she wanted to betray us, she would have done it before now." He touched her arm, motioning her to move forward. "All we can do is trust her and move on."

Tes' stomach clawed with nerves as she walked behind the ranger. Months had passed since the death of her parents, months of desire for revenge. It unnerved her that Trannyth was now so close, a mere mile or two away. She steadied herself, drawing long, deep breaths as her hand played along the hilt of her sword. "Not long now, Mother," she whispered, "Give me strength, Father." Steeling herself, she hurried to catch up to Deavon.

Serran stopped beside a dark gash in the stone wall before them. "This is the one," she announced. "The keep is due south from here."

Deavon nodded, his face visible in the first rays of the morning sun searching along the barren plains. Gathering the others around, he issued final instructions. "When we hit the wall, Serran and Elddyn will use their magic to blast a hole big enough for us to pass through. Kragh and Raug," he turned to the two big creatures. "You'll be first through. Secure the gate; make sure none of those beasts on the plains can get through. Understand?" As Kragh nodded, Deavon turned to Giddy, Raim and Aldan. "You three and myself follow them up, secure the doorways to the tower, make sure no one gets near Tes."

"Will do, boss," Giddy saluted, her eyes wide and gleaming.

"Tean, Naisa, Kailyn, you stay with Tesania, make sure she gets into the tower." He stepped close to Tes. "Your mission is simple. Stay out of any fighting. Your job is to get to Trannyth." He looked at her gently. "Understand?"

Tesania stared into his eyes. "I don't want you to get hurt," she whispered, glancing at the others and feeling stupid.

"I won't," Deavon promised, smiling as he leant forward and kissed her forehead. "I'll be there every step of the way." Slowly he turned away from her, his eyes lingering on hers. "Serran. Lead the way."

Tes waited until the others had followed the mage into the darkness of the cave. Finally she and Kailyn stepped through. "I'm scared," Kailyn whispered.

"Me too," Tes replied nervously.

"Do you think we'll survive?"

"Of course we will, you ninny," Tes replied. "You still have business with the head maid. Remember?"

Kailyn cringed. "I'd forgotten about her!"

"Where would you rather be?" Tes laughed half heartedly. "Here, or there?"

Kailyn giggled. "Here, I think," she answered uncertainly.

"Hurry up and catch the others," Tes said, pushing her friend along.

Serran led them by the light of her staff for little more than an hour before stopping at a dead end. She ran her hands along the solid stone wall, mumbling as she went.

"What's she doing," Tes asked.

"A simple spell," Naisa answered. "She's looking through the rock to the other side. I imagine, seeing where we are."

Serran's mumbling stopped as she turned to Deavon. "We're at the edge of the ward," she announced. "To the left lies the wall and the gate. To the right are the tower and barracks."

"How many are we up against?" Aldan asked. "Surely it's well guarded?"

Shaking her head, the little mage answered. "Most of the mages leave at dawn for the rock plains to oversee the beasts training. Trannyth wants them ready to move on Wyvern City by the end of the moon's cycle."

"So what can we expect?" Deavon asked.

Serran shrugged. "It changes daily. I would expect no more than half a dozen mages and a few beasts."

"Only a few?" Giddy exclaimed. "I'd have the battlements full."

"I told you last night," Serran snapped. "Trannyth is arrogant. He thinks the Keep impenetrable."

"His arrogance works in our favor," Deavon grinned. "This is what we have come all this way to achieve," he said. "To get into Trannyth's keep and wipe him from the face of Eldanal." He paused. "Destroying the orb is paramount. Secondary to that, but just as important is the death of Trannyth. The best chance we have of doing either is getting Tesania and her sword to the top of the tower. Understood?" He watched for their response. "Ok then, Elddyn, Serran, go ahead," he motioned to the two mages as he ushered the others back from the wall.

Elddyn and Serran talked softly among themselves for a few minutes. Finally Elddyn nodded and stepped a few feet away. Together they raised their staffs, the air around them starting to stir as they mumbled the start of a spell. Soon it was whipping around them, throwing their robes into a fluttering frenzy. The mumbling grew to a crescendo, the air crackling as the two mages unleashed the spell at the wall.

Tes watched the rock face; nothing happened. She glanced quickly at Deavon, whipping her head back as a loud crack echoed through the cavern. The wall trembled, slowly small pieces began to crack off and fall to the floor. More cracks shot through the cave, each louder than the last as the wall disintegrated before her eyes. Dust plumed into the air, choking her airways. Coughing, she heard the guttural cries of Kragh and Raug as they scrambled over the rubble and into Trannyth's Keep.

Giddy slapped Raim on his shoulder, grinning as she let out a piercing cry and stepped nimbly up the loose rocks, Raim following close behind.

Deavon glanced at Tesania; a small smile crossing his lips as he turned to Aldan. "Let's go."

"Stay close," Naisa cautioned Tes and Kailyn. "We need to go straight for the tower."

Tes nodded and followed the mage up the slippery face, Kailyn and Tean following close behind. The dust started to clear as she reached the top. Standing transfixed, she watched the scene in front of her. Kragh hacked at a group of beasts near the gate, his sword flashing and darting. No match for him, his fellow beasts fell around his feet. Raug had a mage lifted above his head, with a scream of frustrated anger he pulled down, snapping the man-things spine in two.

"Raug! The gate!" Deavon yelled at him. "Get it shut!" Raug looked at him. Deavon pointed. "The gate!"

The big ogre nodded and turned. Rumbling toward the gate he backhanded a mage who was preparing a spell, smashing him against a wall where he crumpled limply to the ground.

Elddyn and Serran stood off to the right, between Tes and the tower, launching spells at the mages coming from the barracks into the open courtyard. Giddy and Raim twisted and stepped, engaged in battle with two beasts that had broken free of Kragh. Deavon unleashed arrows at the mages on the walls, felling two before they could flash their spells off at the attackers.

Tes' sword hummed in her hand, the vibrations shaking her arm as she looked from one battle to the next. "Kragh," she mumbled as she started down the rocks. "I have to help him."

"No!" Naisa snapped. "Your mission is Trannyth. Kragh can take care of himself."

Tes stared at the beast as Naisa dragged her off to the side toward the tower. She stumbled and fell to her knees, crying out as a shard of stone cut into her skin. Climbing to her feet, she started after Naisa, spinning as Kailyn let out a cry of anguish.

A beast sprinted toward the young girl, its sword raised. Tes lunged between them, managing to deflect the blow as it careened toward Kailyn's head. "Go!" she screamed at her friend. "Get to Naisa!"

Kailyn stumbled off, Tean supporting her as Tes stepped aside and deflected a thrust from the beast with her sword, knocking it off balance as its momentum drove it past her. The sword in her hand reacted instantly, driving forward, searching for the beast's back.

The beast spun in time to knock the blow aside. Issuing a guttural laugh, it stood before her. Tes' eyes ran quickly up its body to its grotesque face. One small eye leered at her, the other, an empty, scarred socket. "You!" Tesania exclaimed in surprise.

The beast grinned at her. "Die!" he growled as he lunged forward.

Tes deflected his blow, stepping sideways and knocking his sword downward. "You killed my parents," she spat as she flicked the sword at the beast's face, the point slicing neatly through its skin, bubbles of blood appearing along its cheek, erupting into rivulets of red.

The beast screamed; spinning about as it thrashed its hand at Tes' throat. Tes met the hand with her sword, the blade cut through the fleshy palm, splitting it down the centre, embedding into the wrist bone of the beast. It screamed in agony, ripping its hand off the sword, blood spraying across the courtyard. "This time," Tes growled through gritted teeth. "I'm not a defenseless maiden."

The beast charged, thrusting its sword at her stomach. Tes flicked her sword down, knocking the beast's weapon aside. Twisting her wrist, she flashed her blade across his chest; the wound opened immediately, a severed artery pumping blood into the battle torn air.

Jerking back, the beast ran its hand through the wound on its chest then brought it to its mouth and licked along the blood-coated fingers. His one eye glared at her as his head lifted back, a deep guttural scream issuing from his chest as he raised his sword.

Tes skipped forward, her sword coming to the beast's throat. "Know how my mother felt," she whispered as she drew the blade across its exposed skin. The beast's eye didn't leave her as it collapsed to its knees, blood staining its filthy hide as it toppled to the ground.

Deavon charged toward her and grasped her arm. "Come on," he yelled urgently. "There's no time." He dragged her toward the tower. "Get to the door."

Tes, in a daze, looked back at the dead beast. A hollow feeling spread through her. "I feel no better," she cried.

"Not now," Deavon said as he thrust her toward Naisa and turned to take a blow from an approaching beast. "Get inside!"

Tes stumbled; Kailyn caught her and managed to help her stand. "The doors are locked," she said desperately. "We can't get in."

Tes looked around the courtyard. Kragh still battled with a beast, the rest lay dead at his feet. Blood ran from deep wounds on his body. He stumbled backward under the determined attack of the last beast, found his footing and attacked again. Raug stood near the huge doors that led to the plains and the army of beasts, pinned down by a mage who was throwing spells at him. "We have to help him," Tes started into the open ward once more.

Kailyn snatched at her arm and pulled her back. "Let me," she said. Stepping forward, she searched for the mage. In a window of the barracks she could see his arms as he cast his spells. Concentrating, she closed her fingers together and focused her mind. The mage, intent on his spells, failed to see smoke rising from his robes, a few seconds later he burst into flames. Beating at his body he crashed out the door, Elddyn cast a spell that threw him off his feet. He lay still as the flames licked at his lifeless flesh.

"Raug!" Tes screamed. The big ogre looked at her. "We need you to smash this door."

Raug nodded and then started to walk before quickening his pace. By the time he hit the door it was with the shuddering force of a boulder. The door bowed, held for an instant and then shattered inward. Raug stood for a moment and stared inside. Two mages stood on the steps leading up into the tower. Their spells hit him before he could react, blasting him backward. He flew through the air, crashing to the stony ground.

"Raug!" Tes screamed.

"No Time," Naisa said as she pulled Tes from the doorway.

Serran rushed toward them, staff raised. Jumping into the doorway, she cast her spell. It ripped into the stairwell, devastating one mage as the other fled upward.

"Raug," Tes said again, pulling against Naisa's grip.

Deavon ran to the ogre, kneeling down. Sadly he looked toward Tes and shook his head.

"No!" Tes whimpered.

"He was going to die anyway," Elddyn said harshly as he ran toward them. "Let's get up these stairs before they can organize a defense."

The Keep's ward lay in ruins, blackened walls from where spells had shattered stones and bodies. Blood from the dead beasts and mages marked the scene of the battle. Kragh walked toward them, breathing heavily, blood drenched sword in hand.

Deavon arrived at Tes' side. "We have to go up," he said quickly. "Naisa, Aldan, Raim, stay here and guard our rear." Handing his bow and quiver to Aldan, he nodded. "Do your best my friend. Keep those gates closed!" He turned to the beast. "We have to go up the stairs," he pointed. "Can you lead the way?"

The beast nodded, starting into the shattered doorway. Deavon gripped his arm. "Watch out for an ambush," he warned.

Kragh looked cautiously upward and then took the first step toward Trannyth.

~

"My Lord!" a mage burst into Trannyth's rooms.

"What is the meaning of this," Trannyth snapped, rising from his chair. "How dare you barge into my quarters unannounced?"

"My Lord," the mage cowered, backing away and lowering himself to his knees. "I mean no offence."

"Then why do you disturb me?" Trannyth seethed.

"The Keep has been breached!"

Trannyth's laugh was dry; it sent shivers running down the mage's spine. "The Keep is impenetrable. There's an army of beasts protecting the gate."

"They attack as we speak."

Trannyth cocked his head, listening. "I hear nothing."

"My Lord, look down at the ward. We are under attack."

Trannyth laughed again as he strode to the windowed wall and peered downward. Bodies lay, hacked and destroyed, an ogre stood beside the barred gates. A curse rose from his chest as he watched the ogre gather speed and disappear from view. The crack of the shattering door cannoned up the stairs, echoing through the room. In a rage he spun. "How could you let this happen?" he screamed.

The groveling mage shuffled backward on his knees. "My Lord, they came through the walls."

"How could they just appear through a wall?"

"My Lord, we told you of the caves."

"Enough," Trannyth raged. "Your incompetence allowed them to breach the Keep."

"My Lor..." the mage collapsed to the floor, the deadly spell cast by Trannyth still smoking from his forehead.

~

Serran stepped cautiously, maintaining three steps between herself and Kragh as they ascended the stairs. The beast moved slowly, scanning ahead at each step before continuing forward. She marveled at the creature. So unlike any of the foul, reeking beasts she had come into contact with thus far.

Tesania climbed the stairs last, Deavon insisting she and the sword be protected. Kailyn looked back at her, worry creasing her face. Tes smiled and reached out to push her forward.

The stairs spiraled upward, following the curves of the stone walls. Cautiously Kragh approached each landing, peering over the threshold before continuing on.

"How many can we expect?" Deavon asked Serran.

"It's hard to say," Serran called lightly back to him. "Most days there are only his most trusted advisers in the tower. Six, maybe ten. And a few beasts."

"Tell Kragh to be on his guard."

Serran whispered Deavon's warning to Kragh as he approached the uppermost landing.

Two mages waited for the intruders. Staffs raised; deadly spells ready to fire at the first person to come into view. Confused looks passed between them as the head of a beast rose from the stairwell. A call came from behind the big creature. They knew the voice of their fellow mage.

"It's ok," Serran called as she motioned Deavon to wait. "We've managed to thwart the attack."

The two mages relaxed, entering the landing as Serran reached the top of the stairs. "They're all dead?" one asked.

Kragh moved toward the mage closest to him, his sword resting at his side. Serran turned to the other. "Not all dead." She whipped her staff into the air and smiled. "But soon you will be!"

Kragh's sword hissed through the air, slicing the mage before him through the neck and down into his chest.

The other mage reacted quickly, spinning on his heel as his staff flashed into the air.

Serran unleashed her spell, throwing him across the floor. A sickening crack echoed through the air as his neck snapped against the grey stone wall.

"It's ok," Serran called down the stairwell, her eyes never leaving Trannyth's door. "You can come up now."

Deavon's head appeared slowly as he looked around. "Are there any more?" he asked urgently.

"It appears not," Serran replied. "But there may be more with Trannyth."

"Where is Trannyth?"

"That door," Serran pointed.

"And the orb?"

"On a pedestal in the centre of the room, you can't miss it," she answered. "You know he won't just let you smash it. He'll be waiting for us!"

Deavon nodded. "We have to go in."

"He's very powerful," Serran warned him, her hands trembling while fear crept into her eyes. "I don't think you know what you're up against."

"It's a little late for that warning isn't it?" Giddy snapped as she stepped onto the landing.

"Either way," Deavon said. "We're here and we're going in!" Turning, he spoke to the group. "I think we can expect a barrage of spells when we go through the door." His gaze passed over them. "We don't matter. What matters is getting Tesania to that orb."

"How're we going to get past the door?" Tes asked.

"Break it down," Deavon replied.

"Smash it," Kailyn's voice drifted from the back.

"What?" Deavon asked.

"Elddyn and Serran can blast the doorway. Can't they?

Deavon nodded slowly. "You're right, Kailyn. I should have thought of that. Can you do it?" he asked the two mages as he turned to them.

Elddyn looked at Serran. "I can't see why not."

"Right," Deavon said as he started pacing. "You two blast the door. Kragh," he stopped and placed his hand on the beasts shoulder. "Can you lead us in?"

Kragh grunted, stepping toward the door.

"Giddy," Deavon continued. "You and I are in next, followed by Elddyn and Serran. Tes, I want you in last. Take advantage of the mayhem to smash the orb. Got it?"

Tesania tried to hide her fear, failing, she nodded quickly and looked away.

"Ready?" Deavon asked the mages. "Everyone stand back."

Kragh stayed near the mages as they prepared their spell. His chest rose and fell slowly, his sword twitching in his hand, his attention fully focused on the doorway that led to the man-thing responsible for destroying his happy life. As the mages cast their spell, he exploded; charging at the gaping hole in the wall, fragments of rock slicing his face as they flew from the shattered doorway. His cry reverberated around the Keep as he burst through the dust.

The blast and sudden appearance of one of his own beasts caused Trannyth to pause momentarily. Confused, he watched as Kragh's sword swung toward the mage on his left. Too late he realized the danger. Kragh's sword dug deeply into the throat of the mage as Trannyth's spell found his back. The beast arched in pain, the spell, enough to kill a lesser being instantly, took a few moments to find his heart.

Deavon threw himself to the floor and rolled as Trannyth turned and cast a spell toward him.

Elddyn stepped through the shattered doorway. "Trannyth!" he roared.

Trannyth's head snapped toward the mage. "They sent you!" he laughed. His face froze as Serran stepped to the side of Elddyn. "Traitor!" he screamed, a spell left his staff quicker than the mage could react. Elddyn tried to block it, but the spell was to his side, his counter managing to only push the deadly spell off course. Smashing into Serran's shoulder, it drove her backward and into Tean as he clambered over the rubble that was once the wall.

Groaning, Serran tried to rise. The deadly spell worked at her body. Convulsions wracked her, her back arching. Tean knelt beside her, his hands quickly coming to his chin, his prayers ringing out as Serran jerked one last time, her dead eyes staring at the ceiling.

Kailyn stopped beside him. "It's too late for prayer, Tean!" she yelled, dragging at his arm to pull him up.

Tearing his arm free, he crawled along the floor to where Kragh's body lay, mumbling incoherently.

Giddy bounded over Serran's body and charged at a beast, swinging her sword from below her hip. The beast failed to counter in time, Giddy's sword sliced into its side. Crying out in pain, it tried to counter attack. Giddy ducked under the clumsy stroke and drove her sword into its chest. Grinning, she jerked it free and turned to another beast as it rushed at Kailyn. "Oh no you don't!"

Deavon regained his feet, throwing his sword above his head as a beast slashed at him. The sword rung in his hand as it met the beast's blow. Snarling, the beast launched at him again.

Tesania's sword shivered with glee as it blocked a blow directed at Deavon's back by another beast. It spun and came at her, sword swinging.

Elddyn blocked another fizzing spell from Trannyth, casting his own in return. Trannyth knocked it aside. His laughter growing with each spell. "You always were useless," he spat.

"It is not I who was thrown from the guild," Elddyn grunted as he warded off another spell. "You disgraced yourself."

"By an old fool, who can't see the future right in front of his face!"

"What future!" Elddyn spat a spell from his staff. "You as King?"

Trannyth fumed, "I will be King! I will not be told what I can and can't do by fools. You know the power I wield. You use the same magic, even now, against me."

"To stop you!"

"To be me!" Trannyth laughed. "You want it. I know you can feel it."

"No!"

Tesania battled against her beast, it blocked every attack she made. She stepped and thrust, feinted and slashed, its sword met hers every time. The orb glowed on its pedestal behind the beast's shoulder, she attacked in an effort to drive it back. It counter attacked, driving her farther away.

Giddy edged closer to the orb, only to be driven away by her beast's fierce counterattack.

Trannyth's staff flared once more. "You can't win. Even if you manage to get out of here alive, there are a thousand beasts waiting for you on the plains."

"Once I kill you, I'll take care of the beasts!" Elddyn replied defiantly.

Trannyth's laughter echoed through the room, intermingled with the ringing of sword against sword. "Kill me," Trannyth's arms lifted, power crackling around him. "You don't begin to have the power to kill me!" Light burst from the purple stone on the end of his staff, dazzling and bright, blinding.

Tesania blinked, trying desperately to clear her sight. She stepped back to clear herself of the beast's sword. The image of Elddyn's shattered body lying on the stone floor drifted slowly into her recovering retinas.

"And now for the rest of you," Trannyth spoke quietly, as if asking one of his mages to carry a message. "What shall I do with you?" He turned, taking in the attackers. "They send a pitiful mage, a ranger, an ordinary soldier..,"

"I'm no ordinary soldier," Giddy growled as she blocked a blow from her beast. "I'll..."

"Silence!" Trannyth bellowed. "Soon you will be dead, it matters not. No one can stop me!"

Tesania skipped toward her beast, feinted right and flicked left. The beast, for the first time, failed to counter. Her sword found flesh, sinking deeply into its stomach, grazing its lower ribs as it passed. Gripping the hilt with two hands, Tes yanked it free, blood flying through the air as the sword tore out of its body. She spun, facing Trannyth. "I can stop you!" she said, her voice seething with anger. "From the day your beasts killed my parents I have vowed to stop you!"

Trannyth's laugh beat against Tesania like a drum. "A girl!" he looked down at the blood stained sword in her hand. "With a pretty sword..."

"Not just any sword!" Tes stepped forward.

Trannyth raised his staff, a spell on his lips. He lurched sideways as a spell hit him in the temple. A minor spell, not even enough to break the skin, but enough to take his attention away from Tesania.

"You dare strike me," he raged, turning his full wrath toward Kailyn, his staff spitting a spell at the young girl.

Kailyn threw herself through the shattered door as the spell ripped past her shoulder.

Tesania moved toward the orb. Trannyth stepped in front of her. "What do you mean? Not just any sword?"

"This sword was forged to kill abominations like you! And your beasts!"

Giddy stepped around her beast and moved for the orb, the beast struck at her, forcing her to re-engage. Deavon was pushed back into a corner, the beast's aggressive attack keeping him from helping Tesania.

Trannyth looked down at her sword once more. "It's just a sword."

Tes lifted the sword in an instant, driving at Trannyth's chest. He moved quickly, far quicker than Tes had anticipated, his staff knocking the sword downward, his fist exploded into her chest, knocking her back. Stumbling, she struggled to regain her balance as Trannyth raised his staff, his wild eyes glaring at her.

"Tesania!" Tean's voice cracked through the room. The orb floated from his hand where he stood by the pedestal, arcing through the air, glinting as it reflected the light.

"No!" Trannyth cried as he threw himself to his right, his arm outstretched, fingers closing around his precious orb.

Tesania lunged forward, her sword whistling through the air as it flashed out. Trannyth's fingers offered little resistance as it sliced through and ripped into the orb.

Trannyth screamed; his fingers hung in the air for a heartbeat before pattering to the floor. His eyes watched, transfixed, as the orb disintegrated in front of him. Pain gripped his spine, twisting it as his life force ripped through his eyes into the ball of energy that grew where the orb had once been.

Tesania stumbled back. The beasts fighting Deavon and Giddy began to roar in pain, their cries filling the Tower Keep as they collapsed to the floor, backs arching, writhing in pain. Light grew from their eyes, drawn to the maelstrom. Windows shattered as the power grew, the cries of a thousand beasts lifting from the plains below.

Tes rushed to Deavon. They huddled in the corner. Giddy threw herself under a table, curling into a ball. Tean dropped to his knees and prayed.

Light grew outside the room, growing stronger, then burst through the shattered glass, blinding Tesania as she looked away. The air crackled as the maelstrom drew the life force of every beast. It expanded, now half the size of the room, rotating and throbbing.

As the light streaming through the window slowed, then stopped, Tesania turned her gaze to the pulsing ball hanging in the air. She turned to Deavon. "What do we do?"

Deavon shrugged, throwing his arm around Tes' head and drawing her in as a last stream of light shot through the window. The maelstrom glowed hotly, expanded, shivered and then exploded, sending blinding light shooting through the room, bouncing off the walls before shrieking out the windows, leaving the Keep in sudden, eerie silence.

Tesania and Deavon climbed slowly to their feet and peered cautiously out of the windows. The plains below were littered with dead beasts, their bodies twisted and ruined. Trannyth's remaining mages were running, looking back fearfully as they stumbled toward the mountains.

"Is it over?" Tesania asked as Giddy climbed to her feet beside them.

"Yes Tes," Deavon replied as he drew her nearer, "Trannyth and all his beasts are dead."

Tesania clenched her father's sword in her hand, looking to the skies as she spoke to her parents. "Now you can rest in peace."

53 PEACE

Tesania fidgeted whilst Deavon stood nervously beside her. The Royal court assembled behind her, talking in hushed voices that melded into a cacophony of noise and echoed through the vaulted ceilings. Pages lined the walls, their red, embroidered garments immaculately fitted, brass buckles glinting.

Tes started as trumpets blared at the back of the hall. Without moving her head she looked at Deavon. He reached out and took her hand, calming her with his smile.

The King and Queen of Eldanal entered the room from the left, standing for a few moments as the crowd bowed and the whispers and noise slowly subsided.

Tes turned her head, looking past Giddy, Raim and the other travelers to see the Royal couple. The Queen smiled and waved her hand regally toward her. Tesania blushed and turned her attention back to the empty thrones in front of her. Unconsciously, her hand strayed to the pommel of her sword, fiddling as she waited.

With practiced ease the King made his way across the room, his left hand held out, the Queens hand resting on it as he guided her to her throne. As she took her seat, he turned, his gaze travelling along the line of adventurers in front of him, coming to rest on Tesania. A smile touched his lips as he turned and walked toward the dais in the middle of the raised throne area. Standing for a few moments, he surveyed the gathered crowd before his voice boomed forward, echoing throughout the room. "My Lords and Ladies!"

The last whispers of the crowd died as the King demanded their attention.

"Eldanal, as you know, faced a great peril." Whispers broke out amongst the gathering. The King held his hand in the air. "These people," he motioned toward Tesania and her friends, "fearlessly placed their own lives in danger to ensure our safety."

Giddy nudged Raim with her elbow, causing him to lose balance and stumble forward. Crimson red crept up his face as he hurried back into the line, the King frowning down at him as he looked up apologetically.

"The scourge that was Trannyth has been eradicated," the King continued. "No more shall the children of Eldanal be afraid. Nor shall a helpless village be annihilated by his beasts." The gathering erupted in applause, the din of voices filling the hall.

Raising his hand once more, the King called for silence. "Sadly, not all of their party survived. It would be remiss of me not to mention Elddyn of Carella City who selflessly gave his life fighting Trannyth. His name is to be remembered in eternity with honor and respect."

And a mage by the name of Serran, who misguidedly allied herself with Trannyth, but saw the folly in her ways and helped construct his downfall. To her we are grateful."

"An ogre." The crowd gasped as the king continued. "Yes, an ogre, by the name of Raug, who was cruelly used by Trannyth to make his beasts." The King paused, looking around the room. "Raug will be remembered by my wife and myself as a hero of our Realm."

The crowd buzzed. "And lastly, a beast by the name of Kragh is owed our debt." A lady, dressed in the finest linen gowns swooned and collapsed into her husband's arms. The King motioned one of his entourage to help her. "I am told that he was a gentle giant who fought against Trannyth's control, wanting only peace and his simple life as a banmora." Pausing he scanned the room. "Knowing that he would die, whatever the outcome, he still chose to fight for what he thought was right. He gave his life for us and will be remembered also as a hero."

A hush fell over the crowd as they digested the thought of holding a beast, once their vicious enemy, as a national hero. The King stepped from the dais and walked toward Naisa at the end of the line of travelers. "Naisa of Aliaga," he spoke so the gathering could hear. "The Kingdom of Eldanal is indebted to you. You are hereby granted the rank of the Eighth degree in the order of Rynem."

Naisa smiled broadly, bowing her head slightly.

"We grant you an apartment in the Royal quarter of the city. It is our hope that you shall one day hold the rank of Archmage," the King continued as he stepped along the line, stopping at Aldan. "Aldan of Rilmir City," he started, "Your deeds are well known to us. We promote you to the rank of General in the King's Rangers."

Aldan nodded, pride gleaming in his eyes as he looked toward his mother in the crowd.

"You are also granted an apartment in the Royal quarter," the King continued as he stepped away. "Tean, the Kingdom, and I'm sure, our Lord," the King said as he looked to the ceiling, "acknowledges your wisdom and courage in the face of overwhelming odds."

"The Lord provided me strength when it was required."

"I'm sure," the King smiled. "I have spoken to the Abbott; he assures me he has a lifetime of study and peace to offer you."

Tean beamed. "I would like nothing more than to study the Lord's..."

"I, however," the King interrupted, "wish to offer you something more substantial." Holding his hand up as the monk protested, he said, "We grant you an apartment in the Royal quarter."

"I don't want it!"

"Do with it what you will," the King dismissed as he stepped away. "It is yours. Perhaps you could use it as a study haven when you visit Wyvern City."

Tean bowed his head.

"Raim of Rilmir City," the King addressed the little soldier. "You come from a long line of soldiers; your father and his fathers before that. They would be proud of what you have achieved. Indeed we are proud of what you have achieved."

Raim stared at the floor, Giddy coughed, motioning for him to look at the King while he spoke.

As Raim looked up, the King continued. "You are hereby promoted to the rank of General in the King's Army." Giddy snickered, interrupting the King. "Something is funny?"

"No," Giddy grinned. "It's just that he is so short to be a general."

The King smiled. "Nonetheless, a general he now is. We also grant you an apartment."

"Could I have one in Rilmir?" Raim asked quickly, "Instead of Wyvern, I mean."

"If you so wish," the King agreed. "Giddy of Estom village," the King turned to the soldier. "We have heard many good things about you."

Giddy bowed. "I try my best."

The King laughed lightly. "Your best appears to have been enough."

"It appears so," Giddy grinned. "I had help though."

"Indeed. We wish to reward you for your part in eradicating Trannyth."

"It was nothing," Giddy dismissed with a grin.

"All the same," the King continued. "You are promoted to the rank of General in the King's Army. You are to take up the role of combat instructor in Wyvern City barracks."

"I'm not the sort to sit behind a desk," Giddy replied. "I'd rather be out in the field with my people."

The King nodded. "An admirable quality indeed. So it shall be."

"And can I have my house in Rilmir too?" Giddy asked quickly.

"A little presumptuous aren't we?"

"Well, I figured you were handing one out to the others."

"Very well, an apartment in Rilmir city it is then."

"And can I..."

"Giddy," Deavon snapped as the King moved toward Kailyn.

"I was just..."

"And the young servant," the King said. "Who ran from her employer to go on a grand adventure."

"I..," Kailyn's eyes pleaded with him.

The King held his hand in the air. "In a normal situation you would be in dire trouble. I think perhaps, under the circumstances, that we can absolve you of any punishment."

Relief flooded across the girl's face. "Really?"

"You bravery matched these trained soldiers and rangers. You stood against adversity and shone through."

"I only helped a little, collecting firewood and stuff."

"I believe you have proven quite adept at magic?"

"I can light a fire," Kailyn answered, her cheeks growing red.

"And a little more I am told."

"A little," Kailyn confessed.

The King laughed. "Kailyn of Wyvern. You are released from your duties as maid in the Lady Ayana's household. You will attend the Mages School in Carella City. Upon completion of your training you shall return to Wyvern City to study further under Naisa here." He motioned toward the mage. "We expect to see you in our court in the future." Turning, he moved toward Deavon. Pausing, he turned back. "You of course are granted an apartment in Wyvern City."

Kailyn gasped. "I couldn't possible afford its upkeep," she started to protest.

"Eldanal owes you a great debt. Do not concern yourself with matters of wealth. It will be taken care of."

Tesania leaned forward and winked at her friend, a grin spreading across her face.

"Deavon of Orash," the King approached the ranger. "Your deeds in leading this mission and ensuring its success pleases us. We sincerely believe that the mission might have failed if it was lead by any other."

Deavon bowed his head slightly then returned his gaze to the King.

"We owe you our gratitude. You are granted the title of Lord."

Deavon nodded solemnly, although his heart raced with pride.

"You are also granted lands on the Wyvern River and an apartment in Wyvern City."

"I thank you," Deavon managed to say. "It is truly more than I deserve."

"You deserve more than we can give. We only wish we could do more." The King nodded to Deavon and turned. "The sword bearer," he said to Tesania. "Who would have thought it, the brash girl who demanded her sword be returned, who stood and stated she would avenge her parents and kill Trannyth and his beasts."

Tes smiled. "He owed me a debt."

"Indeed," the King smiled back. "Truly there is nothing that we can give you that would match the magnitude of what you have achieved."

"I couldn't have achieved it without the others," Tes protested.

"All the same. We thought long and hard about what to do with you."

"You don't have to do anyth..."

"Tesania of Aryd Village," the King continued. "We grant you the title of Lady. You are welcome in our court at any time."

"Thank..."

"We further grant you all the lands and property that formally belonged to Lord Dalgliesh and his family, including his seized funds and holdings."

The gathered crowd gasped at the announcement. Tesania spun to look at Deavon, confusion in her eyes. Slowly she turned back to the King. "It's too much, I don't deserve it."

The queen stood and walked forward. "You deserve all we can give you and more, my dear. Eldanal would be lost without you."

"But, I didn't do it for reward," Tes argued. "He killed my parents."

The Queen laid her hand gently on Tesania's arm. "Lady Tesania, please accept our gifts. They are all we can do to thank you."

"But, what of Lord Dalgliesh and Lady Caitriona? It's their property. I don't understand."

"They had their captain attack a King's Ship. They have been banished from Eldanal, all their lands and belongings confiscated. These are now yours."

"Including the ship?"

"Many ships my dear, and many holdings."

Tesania shook her head. "It doesn't seem fair. To lose everything they have."

"We will not have members of our own court turning pirate against our own ships," the King interjected. "I will hear no more."

Tesania nodded and turned to Deavon, shaking her head in disbelief. He reached out and took her hand as they turned to the gathered people.

The King announced, "These people have saved our Kingdom. They will be heralded as heroes of our time, stories will be told to children in centuries to come of Lady Tesania and Lord Deavon."

The crowd cheered as Giddy nudged Raim, "And generals, Giddy and Raim."

Raim grinned. "They couldn't leave you out my love."

Giddy's eyebrow raised. "My love?"

"You heard me," Raim laughed.

The gathered people parted as Tes and Deavon lead the others toward the exit at the rear of the hall. Deavon squeezed Tes' hand and drew her closer.

Dark eyes glowered at them from under a cowled hood within the crowd. "My Lady," a voice beside the figure whispered. "We must go. You cannot be seen here."

Tesania looked sharply at Deavon.

"What is it?"

"My sword," Tesania frowned. "It's vibrating."

AUTHOR'S NOTE

Greetings.

I hope you enjoyed Tesania, Trannyth's Keep. Thanks for reading! If you enjoyed reading Tesania please tell your friends, talk about it on Facebook, your blog, Amazon or anywhere that may help Tesania's story spread. I invite you to visit www.tesania.com.au where you can get the latest news on upcoming books and www.tesania.com.au/forum where you can sign up and meet other readers who enjoyed reading the book and discuss Tesania's adventure.

Hope to see you there!

Best regards
Grant E Brazell

This book is available as an E-book online

Keep an eye out for Tesania - Tiadath Mage. Coming Soon!

My homepage: www.grantebrazell.com

Blog: www.grantebrazell.com/blog

Tesania home: www.tesania.com.au

Tesania Forums: www.tesania.com.au/forum

ABOUT THE AUTHOR

Grant E Brazell, was born in Sydney Australia in 1966 to parents of English heritage. He has been a Fantasy buff for decades and spends most of his life wide awake in dreamland. He currently lives in Rooty Hill, Australia, with his wife, one son and two cats. This is his first novel.